THE PURSUITS OF LORD KIT CAVANAUGH

There was no denying that, to her, the real Kit Cavanaugh was far more attractive than the ton version had ever been. Even though, in that ton version, for more than five years he had been her romantic ideal—her fantasy gentleman—that status had been based purely on his physical attributes; she'd never liked or approved of his character—the character she and the ton had been led to believe was his.

Although she'd reined in her senses as tightly as she could, she remained excruciatingly aware of him walking close beside her; his strength, the controlled grace investing his powerful frame, and the sheer physicality of his presence impinged on her nerves, made her lungs constrict, and set her heart to beating just a soupçon faster.

He drew her—lured her—as no other man ever had.

As she'd discovered at the wedding, when it came to him, no amount of denial—not even imagined deficits of character—made the slightest difference to that intrinsic, instinctive attraction.

STEPHANIE LAURENS

THE PURSUITS OF LORD KIT CAVANAUGH

mira

mira

ISBN-13: 978-0-7783-6989-9

The Pursuits of Lord Kit Cavanaugh

Recycling programs
for this product may
not exist in your area.

Other titles from Stephanie Laurens

Cynster Novels

Devil's Bride
A Rake's Vow
Scandal's Bride
A Rogue's Proposal
A Secret Love
All About Love
All About Passion
On a Wild Night
On a Wicked Dawn
The Perfect Lover
The Ideal Bride
The Truth About Love
What Price Love?
The Taste of Innocence
Temptation and Surrender

Cynster Sisters Trilogy

Viscount Breckenridge to the Rescue
In Pursuit of Eliza Cynster
The Capture of the Earl of Glencrae

Cynster Sisters Duo

And Then She Fell
The Taming of Ryder Cavanaugh

Cynster Specials

The Promise in a Kiss
By Winter's Light

Cynster Next Generation Novels

The Tempting of Thomas Carrick
A Match for Marcus Cynster
The Lady by His Side
An Irresistible Alliance
The Greatest Challenge of Them All
A Conquest Impossible to Resist

Lady Osbaldestone's Christmas Chronicles

Lady Osbaldestone's Christmas Goose
Lady Osbaldestone and the Missing Christmas Carols

The Casebook of Barnaby Adair Novels

Where the Heart Leads
The Peculiar Case of Lord Finsbury's Diamonds
The Masterful Mr. Montague
The Curious Case of Lady Latimer's Shoes
Loving Rose: The Redemption of Malcolm Sinclair
The Confounding Case of the Carisbrook Emeralds
The Murder at Mandeville Hall

Bastion Club Novels

Captain Jack's Woman (Prequel)
The Lady Chosen
A Gentleman's Honor
A Lady of His Own
A Fine Passion
To Distraction
Beyond Seduction
The Edge of Desire
Mastered by Love

Black Cobra Quartet

The Untamed Bride
The Elusive Bride
The Brazen Bride
The Reckless Bride

The Adventurers Quartet

The Lady's Command
A Buccaneer at Heart
The Daredevil Snared
Lord of the Privateers

The Cavanaughs

The Designs of Lord Randolph Cavanaugh

Other Novels

The Lady Risks All
The Legend of Nimway Hall—1750: Jacqueline

Medieval

Desire's Prize

Novellas

"Melting Ice"—from *Scandalous Brides*
"Rose in Bloom"—from *Scottish Brides*
"Scandalous Lord Dere"—from *Secrets of a Perfect Night*
"Lost and Found"—from *Hero, Come Back*
"The Fall of Rogue Gerrard"—from *It Happened One Night*
"The Seduction of Sebastian Trantor"—from *It Happened One Season*

Short Stories

The Wedding Planner—from the anthology *Royal Weddings*
A Return Engagement—from the anthology *Royal Bridesmaids*

UK-Style Regency Romances

Tangled Reins
Four in Hand
Impetuous Innocent
Fair Juno
The Reasons for Marriage
A Lady of Expectations
An Unwilling Conquest
A Comfortable Wife

THE PURSUITS OF
LORD KIT CAVANAUGH

One

September 18, 1843
On the Bath Road east of Bristol

"Steady, lads." Lord Christopher Cavanaugh, known to most as Kit, drew his matched bays to a stamping halt on the rough grass of the roadside lookout. The high-bred horses shifted and snorted; having recently rested in an inn's stable while Kit and his companions partook of luncheon, the pair were eager to run again.

But Kit wanted a moment to look ahead—at the roofs, towers, and spires, and the glinting silver-gray ribbon of rivers that made up the city of Bristol, displayed like a colorful patchwork in the shallow valley at the end of their road.

The day was cool but fine, with a fitful breeze meandering up the valley. Eyes narrowing, Kit surveyed the city he planned to make his home. Today would see his first true step into the future he was determined to craft and claim.

He'd been adrift all his life, with no rudder to guide him and no port to call his home. For the past decade—ever since he'd come on the town—he'd had no direction, no goal... No. Not true. His one aim—his single focused goal—had been to avoid the fate his mother, Lavinia, the late Dowager Marchioness of Raventhorne, had planned for him.

She'd been a schemer of near-unimaginable degree, intent on controlling and exploiting the lives of her four children for her own gain. In Kit's case—as for his older and younger brothers—

she'd expected to barter the position of their wives for wealth or, at the very least, valuable influence. Kit had reacted by painting himself as an indolent rake of the sort no sane parent would want anywhere near their daughter. His reputation in the ton had become a solid shield, one that had enabled him to walk society's halls without fear of being trapped in order to help his younger sister, Stacie, avoid a similar fate.

Lavinia had been a demon in human guise. They—her four children—had been beyond shocked when they'd finally learned the full gamut of her evil schemes. She'd tried to kill her stepson, Ryder, Kit's older half brother, whom Kit and his siblings adored, in order to replace Ryder, then the marquess, with her eldest son, Kit's older brother Rand; only Ryder's remarkable strength, physical and mental, and the support of his wife, Mary, then the marchioness, had allowed them both to survive. Subsequently captured, Lavinia had lost her life in a vain attempt to flee justice.

Even now, the thought of her and her doings chilled Kit's heart.

His mother had died in the summer of 1837, bringing to an abrupt end a chapter in his and his siblings' lives that they all had thought would never end. Nevertheless, it had taken years for the effects of her version of mothering to start to fade—for Rand, Kit, Stacie, and their youngest brother, Godfrey, to shed the invisible chains and adjust their now-instinctive, habitual reactions toward others as well as themselves.

Or, Kit temporized, at least shake loose enough of those chains to take up the challenge of shaping their own lives and make a start.

For Rand—arguably the most impacted by their mother's schemes, but also the oldest of the four siblings and possessing a quiet inner strength similar to Ryder's implacable will—that had meant becoming a leading light in investor circles, specializing in supporting promising inventions. Less than a month ago, Rand had taken what Kit saw as the final step in emerging from their shared past by marrying Felicia Throgmorton, the daughter of one of the inventors Rand had backed.

Kit had seen Rand and Felicia two days ago, when they'd driven over from their new house to visit with Ryder and Mary at Raventhorne Abbey, the family's ancestral pile, where, since the wedding, Kit had been staying. Contentment had settled about Rand like a cloak, and a species of happiness had infused his eyes and his expression whenever he'd looked at Felicia, leaving Kit to surmise that Rand and Felicia were well on the way to finding the same sense of settled peace and relaxed joy in life that Ryder had found with Mary.

The atmosphere of happy family life that now pervaded the Abbey was something Kit had never experienced over the decades he'd called the Abbey home. He envied his nephews and niece—Ryder and Mary's children—the warmth and unqualified acceptance in which they were growing up. The unstated yet all-embracing love and support of their parents.

Having watched Rand steadily making his own way—his own name—in society and beyond, Kit had decided it was time he did the same—that it was time he made a start on assembling the various elements of the life he wanted for his own.

He wanted to build ocean-going yachts. More—he aspired to be the pre-eminent force in the evolving field. In the same way that dealing with investments played to Rand's strengths and interests, Kit felt that yacht-building would make the most of his longtime obsession with all things sailing and his ability to lead men and act as manager, facilitator, and negotiator.

He was good with his hands, and he was good with his head. He always had been.

When Rand had announced his engagement, Kit had been on his way to Bermuda, chasing down Wayland Cobworth. Wayland was an old friend of Kit's from Eton days who shared his passion for superbly designed sailing vessels; coming from a significantly less wealthy family than the Cavanaughs, instead of going to university, Wayland had apprenticed to an expert draftsman and ship-designer and was now one of the up-and-coming designers of yachts.

Wayland knew the quality of Kit's determination—that when he set his sights on achieving some goal, that goal would be achieved; convincing Wayland of Kit's vision for Cavanaugh Yachts and of the desirability of Wayland's potential position in the company hadn't been all that hard.

Kit had had to take ship back to England almost immediately in order not to miss Rand's wedding; he'd made it, but with only minutes to spare. Wayland had had to finish a design for the company he'd been working for before heading back to England, sailing directly to Bristol.

"It's bigger than I'd thought," Smiggs, Kit's groom-cum-stableman, observed, breaking through Kit's introspection.

Smiggs was perched behind Kit. Kit had co-opted Smiggs, several years older than he, from the Abbey stables when he'd first gone on the town. Smiggs had eagerly thrown in his lot with Kit, and subsequently, they'd shared many an adventure. Kit considered Smiggs a confidant of sorts and knew he could rely on the wiry man's support in any situation.

"This is one of the few decent views of the city sprawl," Kit said, "and last time, we didn't stop to look."

"Last time" being two weeks before, when he and Smiggs had driven over for a few days to allow Kit to make the necessary arrangements for taking up residence in the city. Among other things, he'd finalized the purchase of a decent-sized house in a good neighborhood and had discussed leasing a warehouse on the Floating Harbor with the Bristol Dock Company.

"So, Mr. Cobworth should have arrived a few days ago," Smiggs said.

Kit nodded. "He wrote that his ship would dock on the sixteenth." Kit grinned expectantly. "I imagine that, after having two days to reconnoiter, Wayland will be eager to forge on."

"When's your meeting with the Dock Company?" Smiggs asked.

Kit shifted to draw out his fob watch. "Not until half past three." He checked the time, then tucked the watch back. "It's just after two o'clock. We'd better get moving."

"Will Mr. Cobworth be staying with us?"

Turning his head, Kit glanced at the younger man standing behind the rail alongside Smiggs and smiled. "No, Gordon." Until recently, Gordon had been a footman at the Abbey, but Mary had allowed Kit to lure him away to fill the role of Kit's majordomo. "Mr. Cobworth likes his own space, for which we should all be thankful—as he tends to lose himself in his work and often works very odd hours, he's not a comfortable house-guest."

"Oh." Gordon's eyes had widened. He was of similar age to Kit, but had led a much more sheltered life.

Reminded of the tasks he had to complete before he joined Wayland at the scheduled meeting—during which Kit hoped they would be able to sign the lease on the warehouse he intended to convert to their yacht-building workshop—he faced forward and lifted the reins. "We'll drive straight to the solicitor's office and pick up the house keys, then go and take possession." Of the first house he'd ever owned. Releasing the brake, he continued, "I'll leave you two to get settled and organized. The solicitor will have the direction of a household staff employment agency. Gordon—you'll know the sort of people we need."

"Yes, my lord," Gordon promptly replied. "You may leave all that to me."

Kit smiled at the eager pride in Gordon's voice; he had no doubt Gordon would take to his duties with the keen fervor of one out to make his mark. Thinking further, Kit said, "I left a note at the shipping office to be given to Mr. Cobworth when he landed. I imagine he'll be waiting impatiently outside the door of the Bristol Dock Company at half past three." Champing at the bit to get on.

As were Kit's horses. He steered them out of the lookout and back onto the road.

Then, smile deepening and with a sense of expectation—and, yes, eagerness—welling, Kit flicked the reins and set the bays trotting.

He might have lived for twenty-nine years, yet to his mind, today was the first day of his adult life.

★ ★ ★

Across a long, highly polished table, Kit, with Wayland beside him, faced five members of the board of the Bristol Dock Company.

"So"—the chairman, a Mr. Hemmings, exchanged a swift glance with his fellow directors before returning his gaze to Kit—"are we correct in thinking that you anticipate hiring local men to build your ships?"

Kit nodded. "To build and, ultimately, to service our yachts. Once we've established Cavanaugh Yachts as a going concern, we intend to look into sailmaking as well, either to invest in an established business or commence one of our own."

He was unsurprised by the direction of the chairman's probing; he'd done his homework and knew the Dock Company was under increasing pressure from the local council over the loss of jobs on the docks. With the advent of steamships and the changes in materials and practices building such vessels entailed, many men who had previously had steady employment in the shipyards were now out of work. Restless, unhappy, and at a loose end—prime targets for those sowing social discord.

"I understand," Kit continued, "that we should be able to find workers with the expertise we require reasonably easily."

"Oh, indeed—indeed," huffed another of the directors.

"Good to know that the old ways of sail aren't going to completely disappear, what?"

Just two months earlier, Brunel, who had launched his first ocean-going iron ship, the SS *Great Western*, five years before, had launched his latest wonder, the SS *Great Britain*, the first propeller-driven, ocean-going iron ship—both ships built in the Bristol yards.

Steam power had changed the face of ship building, tossing many shipyard workers on the scrap heap.

Cavanaugh Yachts held out the prospect of giving some of those workers a new lease on working life.

Kit smiled. "Just so. And from my earlier visit, I gathered that, what with the difficulties the Floating Harbor poses to larger-draft ships and the consequent drift of shipyards and warehousing to Avonmouth, there are quite a few opportunities to secure space of the sort we need on the docks here."

At that, the company men exchanged another meaning-laden glance, then Hemmings clasped his hands before him, leaned forward, and met Kit's gaze. "As you say, my lord, we'll be happy to see Cavanaugh Yachts take up residence on our docks."

The company secretary, a Mr. Finch, a desiccated man in sober black, cleared his throat and looked down as he shuffled several papers. "We understand you're interested in the warehouse off the Grove."

Kit nodded. "That seemed the most suitable. We require ready access to the harbor, and in size and location, that seemed the best of the properties you showed me earlier."

Wayland shifted; several inches taller than Kit, he was long and lanky and exuded the air of a man who possessed little patience for the minutiae of life. Wayland fixed the secretary with his dark gaze. "Do you have any other properties similar in size and location to that one?"

Finch blinked at Wayland, then looked down. "No—that's

really the only warehouse in that stretch that's immediately available."

As if suddenly reminded of something, the chairman glanced at Kit. "You propose to commence work soon?" An "I hope" hovered in the air.

Kit exchanged a swift look with Wayland, then replied, "If we can come to an agreement today, then we are prepared to start hiring immediately."

"Ah…" Finch caught Hemmings's eye. "As to that…when I said the warehouse was *immediately* available, I was referring to the fact that it's not formally leased. However, there's a charity group that has been using the space free of charge—I expect they will need a few days to vacate."

"How long?" Wayland's tone suggested the point might influence his and Kit's thinking.

"Oh—just a few days." Hemmings sent the secretary a sharp look.

One of the other directors leaned forward to suggest, "Shall we say by the end of the week?"

The other company men, including Hemmings and Finch, nodded and, faintly anxious, looked at Kit.

Kit glanced at Wayland, hesitated for effect, then said, "I suppose we could use the next few days to hire workers and organize supplies." In truth, a few days was no skin off their noses, but given they'd yet to discuss the details of the lease, keeping the directors off balance seemed wise.

Wayland replied with a somewhat sulky shrug.

Kit looked back at Hemmings and Finch. "Perhaps, gentlemen, we should get down to brass tacks."

The directors were very ready to do so, but neither Kit nor Wayland were new to the art of negotiating deals. Both Ryder and Rand had taken ten percent stakes in Cavanaugh Yachts, and Kit used their names and backing to further strengthen his and Wayland's hand. The discussion went back and forth, re-visiting this point before agreeing on that.

Finally, the directors agreed to a price and conditions that Kit and Wayland were prepared to accept, including a stipulation they had pressed for—an indefinite option to purchase the warehouse outright after a period of two years.

While Wayland had a thirty percent stake in the company, Kit remained the majority owner. Consequently, when Finch prepared and presented the lease, it was Kit who signed first, then he passed the document and pen to Wayland while doing his best to conceal the elation that filled him.

They'd made their first major commitment and had secured the space they needed to forge on.

Wayland, also battling a grin, signed with a flourish, and the secretary and chairman quickly countersigned.

Finch duly presented Kit with their copy of the lease.

"Thank you." Kit glanced at the document, then folded it. As he tucked it into his coat pocket, he looked at the directors and smiled. "Thank you, gentlemen. It's been a pleasure doing business with you."

"I must insist that the pleasure is all ours, your lordship." Hemmings rose and, beaming genially, waved toward a nearby sideboard. "Can I offer you a small libation to celebrate our deal?"

Kit and Wayland accepted glasses of brandy and stood and chatted about the city—extracting as much useful information as they could. After the other three directors made their excuses and left, Kit turned to Finch. "Although our tenancy doesn't commence until the beginning of next week, Mr. Cobworth and I would like to take a quick look at the inside of the warehouse. While I've been inside before, Mr. Cobworth hasn't, and to ensure we order the correct timbers for the initial fitting out, he needs to note the placement of the beams."

"If we could gain access for half an hour today, that would be ideal," Wayland put in.

Finch and Hemmings exchanged a long glance—long enough for Kit to wonder what unvoiced thoughts passed between them. Then, lips primming, Finch nodded. "If you can indulge us regarding the time—will five-thirty this evening suit?"

Kit looked at Wayland and arched his brows.

"It'll be close to dark by then." Wayland's faint frown suggested he was thinking rapidly. "But I can pick up a few lanterns." Expression clearing, he met Finch's gaze. "Yes—that will do."

"Excellent." Hemmings clapped his palms together. "We'll meet you outside the warehouse at five-thirty, then."

Wondering why they couldn't go now, Kit asked, "Is there any difficulty with us taking a look around the outside earlier? Now, for instance."

Again, Hemmings's and Finch's gazes met, then Finch cleared his throat and explained, "We haven't yet broken the news to the charity that's been using the space, and we won't be able to do so until tomorrow, when their manager is in their office. It would be…awkward if those at the warehouse were to learn of the situation prior to the manager being informed."

"Ah—I see." At least as far as them going to the warehouse now. Kit inclined his head to both men. "In that case, we'll hie off to find some lanterns and will see you gentlemen outside the soon-to-be Cavanaugh Yachts workshop in…just over an hour."

Finch's and Hemmings's faces lit with what Kit saw as pleasure tinged with relief. With a return to their celebratory mood, the pair farewelled Kit and Wayland, vowing to meet them shortly.

Kit was inwardly shaking his head as, with Wayland beside him, he stepped onto the pavement outside the Dock Company building.

For his part, Wayland was actually shaking his head.

Kit halted and eyed his friend. "What?"

Wayland shrugged. "Nervy lot." He looked around. "I think the nearest hardware store is that way." He pointed down the quay.

Sliding his hands into his pockets, Kit fell in beside Wayland as he led the way.

★ ★ ★

When, an hour later, Kit and Wayland rounded the end of Princes Street and walked onto the stretch of waterfront known as the Grove, it was to see Finch and Hemmings waiting farther along, outside the door of the third warehouse from the corner.

Evening had fallen and was edging toward night, and the slap of wavelets against the pilings was increasingly audible as other workaday noises faded. The row of warehouses fronted directly onto the Grove, with a narrow, cobbled lane separating their façades from the rough grass beneath the line of trees that gave the area its name. Beyond the trees, lamps were spaced along the river's edge, but the warehouses lay far enough back that only faint light reached their doors.

Wayland huffed. "Just as well we got these lanterns."

They'd bought four hurricane lanterns, reasoning that they would surely need them as the days grew shorter.

As they approached the warehouse, Kit nodded in greeting. "Hemmings. Finch."

Hemmings smiled and half bowed.

"My lord. Mr. Cobworth." Having already unlocked the padlock that secured the doors, Finch lifted the latch and drew one of the double doors back.

Kit caught the edge of the second door and hauled it wide.

Wayland walked inside, then halted and, through the dimness, looked around. After several seconds, he bent and set down the two lanterns he'd carried and crouched to light them.

Kit stopped a pace away. He put the two lanterns he'd carried beside Wayland's two. When light flared and Wayland replaced the glass surround on the first lantern, then turned to light the next, Kit picked up the first lantern, raised it, and played the beam around the gloomy space.

Although his hands remained busy lighting the lanterns, Wayland looked up, too. After a moment, he said, "The floor's good—nice and even and the planks are well-laid and the surface smooth. As for layout...offices to the right, along the side wall. Receptionist and foreman in one closer to the door, then the rest of that space is mine."

By which Wayland meant that his design studio would take up the space behind the front office. Kit grunted in agreement; as Wayland gave his attention to the lanterns, Kit turned and swept the lantern's beam over the other side of the warehouse.

The doors were off center, closer to the right, leaving the bulk of the warehouse to the left. The space was surprisingly uncluttered; there was no detritus—no ropes, broken struts, hessian, or any of the usual accumulated rubbish one tended to find in the corners of such buildings.

Wayland rose, a lantern in his hand; standing beside Kit, he directed the lantern upward, splashing light across the beams overhead. After a moment of studying them, Wayland murmured, "Good call choosing this place. Those are solid." With the lantern, he traced one of the three main beams across to the wall, playing light over the upright support there, then he turned and examined the support on the other side. Then he flashed Kit a grin. "We'll be able to set our pulleys up there and lift our hulls with no problem at all."

"Excellent." Kit peered deeper into the shadows to the left and spotted a row of raised desks lined up along the side wall. They looked like a conglomeration of clerk's desks and draftsman's desks with sloping tops. A goodly number of tall stools stood clustered at one end of the line.

"Presumably from the charity," Wayland said. "The desks look to be in too-good condition to be discards."

Surveying the desks, Kit murmured, "It must be some sort of

charity for the indigent. I assume they'll take them away." Kit turned back to survey the area they'd elected to make into offices. "Where do you want to start measuring?"

Wayland waved. "Let's start by the door."

Wayland always carried an extendible metal measuring rod, along with notebook, pencil, and chalk. Between them, they marked and measured the dimensions of the offices, with Wayland noting everything down so he could draw up a plan and work out what timbers were required for the construction.

Once they'd finished measuring the offices, ignoring the pair at the door, who shifted restlessly as darkness encroached and a chill rose off the river, Kit helped Wayland make a series of measurements relating to the pulley gantry Wayland had in mind to allow them to work on multiple hulls at the same time with only one overhead hoist.

Finally, still busily jotting in his notebook, Wayland declared, "That's all I need for now. I'll draw up the plans and check in with you tomorrow. Once you sign off, I'll get the timbers ordered. We'll also need steel for the gantry." He paused to glance around the shadowy space. "Depending on the caliber of the men we hire, it'll take a few days to construct the offices and the gantry. By then, I'll have the hull design ready, and we can move the men on to the frame for that."

He met Kit's eyes. "That'll be a good start."

Kit nodded. "An excellent start, even if we do have to wait until Monday to commence."

Looking around one last time, Wayland muttered, "We'll have to see what level of carpenters we can find."

Kit waved toward the door; Hemmings and Finch were still waiting there. As he and Wayland crossed toward them, Kit called, "Thank you for arranging this, gentlemen."

"Our pleasure, your lordship." Rubbing his hands together, Hemmings stepped back as Kit and Wayland, having collected and doused the lanterns, emerged from the warehouse. "I take it all is satisfactory?"

"Entirely," Kit returned with a reassuring smile.

Wayland handed his lanterns to Kit and helped Finch close the warehouse doors.

Kit watched Finch secure the latch with the padlock. Recalling the desks they'd seen and with Wayland's words rolling around in his head, when Finch turned, Kit caught his eye. "Might some of the men attending the charity"—Kit tipped his head toward the warehouse—"be suitable for employment in our yacht-building enterprise?"

Finch blinked, then cut another of those weighted glances at Hemmings. After a second, Finch returned his gaze to Kit and shook his head. "That's highly unlikely, my lord. But there's an excellent labor exchange just around the corner on the quay." Finch pointed in that direction. "For carpenters and the like, that's where I'd ask—it's the most likely place to find workmen of the sort I believe you'll need."

Keeping his expression relaxed and uninformative, Kit studied Finch for a heartbeat; something about the charity made Finch and Hemmings nervous, but Kit couldn't imagine what it might be. "Thank you." Kit inclined his head to Finch. "Either myself or Mr. Cobworth will call there tomorrow."

He and Wayland parted from the two Dock Company men with handshakes, renewed thanks, and cordiality all around, then, on Hemmings's recommendation, Kit and Wayland headed for the Dragon's Head public house for dinner.

★ ★ ★

Sylvia Buckleberry sat at the small desk in her cramped office in the shadow of Christ Church and, head bent, carefully tallied her ledgers, penny by penny accounting for the expenditures of the previous month.

Outside the small window at her back, the morning was fine, the sky a soft autumnal blue with a gentle breeze skating fluffy white clouds across the heavens. The cooing of the doves that nested around the church tower provided a pleasant background drone, punctuated by the skittering of ravens on nearby roofs.

Sylvia did her best to blot out the distractions of the pleasant day. Arithmetic had never been her strong suit, but given she was spending the parish's funds, she made sure the bills added up to the last halfpenny.

She'd almost reached the end of the last column when a sharp rap fell on her closed door. Suppressing a most unladylike hiss, she grabbed a scrap of paper and scribbled a note of her total, then set aside her pencil and, closing the ledger, looked up and called, "Come in."

The door opened, and three gentlemen filed in—or tried to; they had to leave the door open to have room enough to stand.

Sylvia's heart sank as she recognized her callers. It had been over two years since she'd last seen the three together; all were figures in the local community and served on the Bristol Dock Company's board—Mr. Forsythe, the mayor, Mr. Hoskins, one of the aldermen, and, lastly, Mr. Finch, secretary to the board.

Oh, no. The sight of Finch, in particular, did not bode well.

She forced a bright smile to her lips and adopted an expression she hoped appeared guileless. "Mr. Forsythe, Mr. Hoskins, and Mr. Finch." She inclined her head to each. "Good morning, gentlemen. To what do I owe this pleasure?"

The three exchanged glances, then the mayor shuffled forward to take the single small chair that sat before the desk. The chair creaked faintly as his weight settled upon it, then he leaned forward and earnestly said, "My dear Miss Buckleberry, I'm sure you recall the terms of our agreement regarding your school using the premises on the Grove."

Sylvia recalled the stipulations attached to the use of the old warehouse very well. However, she simply stared blankly at the mayor while her mind scrambled...

Surely not. The dockyards were in decline. Who on earth would want the old warehouse?

When the mayor seemed as disinclined to speak as she, she ventured, "I'm not sure I understand…" Always better to have them think her a dim-witted female; she was more likely to gain concessions that way.

Mr. Hoskins cleared his throat, then offered, "Our allowing the school to use the warehouse was, if you recall, on the condition that no business required the space—that is, no business that would pay to lease the place and create jobs for the local men."

Sylvia had transferred her gaze to Hoskins; his words sent a chill lancing through her.

Finch shifted impatiently. "The truth, Miss Buckleberry, is that a new business has taken a lease on the warehouse, commencing from the beginning of next week. The school will need to vacate the premises by week's end."

Trust Finch to put it bluntly; his words were the blow Sylvia had suspected was coming the instant she'd seen his face. He'd always been a reluctant supporter, but whether it was her he didn't approve of or the notion behind the school, she'd never determined.

"As we're all well aware," the mayor hurried to say, "the city is facing some difficulty regarding ongoing work for our many ship workers and dockworkers. It's not a crisis, per se, but…well, we can't afford to turn any such business away."

Sylvia blinked. "Surely there are other warehouses?"

"Not of the sort this company needs. Not on our docks," Mr. Hoskins informed her. "And while we realize this must come as an unwelcome surprise, we're sure you'll agree that it's critically important to accommodate the sort of businesses who can hire the men otherwise unemployed—men like the parents of your pupils."

"Sad though I am to say it, Miss Buckleberry," the mayor

went on, "jobs for the fathers must take precedence over teaching the sons."

Sylvia knew the situation in the city, especially on the docks. In the circumstances, she couldn't argue.

"Besides," Finch said, "as I understand it, the end purpose of teaching the boys is to enable them to get jobs, but if there are no jobs, then what is the point of schools such as yours?"

It was on the tip of her tongue to retort that the school wasn't "hers," yet it didn't really matter; Finch was correct.

Reluctantly, she inclined her head, accepting if not exactly agreeing. She focused on the mayor. "You say we must be out of the warehouse by Friday. I'm left facing the question of where the school is to go." She arched her brows and, with her gaze, included all three men. "Do you have any suggestions, gentlemen?"

Even Finch had the grace to look sheepish—or at least as sheepish as he could.

"Sadly, I don't." The mayor shifted on the chair, eliciting a protesting creak.

"If I hear of any possible location," Mr. Hoskins said, "I will immediately let you know."

"There is no other suitable property on the company's books," Finch stated.

The mayor hauled out his fob watch and looked at it. "Good gracious! Is that the time?" Tucking the watch back into his waistcoat pocket, he rose and essayed a commiserating smile. "The Dock Company regrets the impact on the school, my dear, but we cannot be other than pleased to welcome a new business to our docks."

She was forced to murmur appropriate phrases as the men took their leave.

As the door closed behind them, she slumped back in her chair.

Of all the potential disasters...

After two years at the warehouse and given the draining of work from the docks, she'd assumed the school's use of the premises was secure.

What am I going to do?

The sounds of a busy morning reached her through the thin glass at her back; horses crisply clopping down the streets, the sound of hurrying footsteps on the pavements, the occasional hailing of a hackney—people rushing about their business. Yet inside her office, her brain seemed to have slowed.

Finch hadn't been entirely in error—the school was effectively hers. Her dream, her creation—her purpose in life.

After having shared a London Season with her distant cousin and close friend, Felicia Throgmorton, during which neither of them had taken, Sylvia and Felicia both had seen enough of ton life to be quite certain that their futures lay outside that gilded circle.

For Felicia, her "what else?" had been obvious; she'd had an inventor father and inventor brother to keep house for, to corral, steer, and anchor. Admittedly, Felicia had recently married—to a member of the nobility, no less—but she'd met Randolph Cavanaugh at her home, and as Sylvia understood it, neither had any great ambition to waltz in the ton; their interests lay elsewhere, namely in inventions and investing, and Sylvia had to admit that a life at Rand's side would suit Felicia to the ground.

Sylvia, however, hadn't been needed at home. Her widowed father, Reverend Buckleberry, held a comfortable living at Saltford, between Bristol and Bath, and had a highly efficient housekeeper to keep him in line and see to all his needs. Her father was a hearty, active soul, deeply engaged with his parish; he hadn't needed Sylvia to stand by his side.

After returning from London, Sylvia had spent a wasted year at the vicarage, trying to find a purpose to devote herself to. No gentleman had ever tempted her to consider marriage, and somewhere along the way, she'd set aside all dreams of a home and family of her own. She felt perfectly certain that particular option was never going to come her way.

But with marriage off her table, she'd needed some other occupation—something to which to devote her mind, heart, and considerable organizational talents. But with no formal training in anything beyond the usual subjects deemed suitable for young ladies and no fervent obsession to guide her, she'd all but despaired of finding any project with which to occupy her days.

She'd been close to falling into a dejected funk when her father's close friend the Bishop of Bath and Wells had called at Saltford to spend a few days discussing parish matters with her father, and she'd overheard the bishop bewailing the fact that, despite pressure from the upper levels of both church and state, in Bristol, as yet no progress had been made on establishing a school for the underclass—specifically, for boys whose fathers worked on the docks and in the associated shipyards.

That had been her call to arms—her epiphany when a light had shone from above and illuminated the right path forward.

With the bishop's and her father's support, she'd enlisted the aid of the Dean of Christ Church in Bristol—another of her father's old friends—and, by sheer force of will and personality, had convinced the Christ Church Parish Council to back the establishment of such a school. The parish had agreed to fund the salary for two teachers and an assistant as well as paying for all sundry items such as books, chalks, and slates.

But the council's one stipulation had been that they couldn't afford to pay the rent for premises; they had made their offer of funds conditional on a suitable venue being donated free of charge.

Sylvia suspected the elders on the council had thought that stipulation would prove an insurmountable hurdle, but having noticed the empty warehouse facing the Grove and understanding that dockside business was ebbing from the city, she'd petitioned the Dock Company board to grant the school the right to use the warehouse free of charge.

Of course, first, she'd made a point of meeting each of the wives of the gentlemen on the board—at morning teas, at the city library, and at the salon of the city's most-favored modiste. By dint of casting the school as a socially desirable charity—one the city should support in order to bolster its credentials as a civilized place—she'd enlisted the support of sufficient ladies so that when she'd gone before the board and made her case, she'd been fairly certain of success.

But now that she—the school—had lost the use of the warehouse, and the Dock Company didn't have another building the school might use...

Without premises donated by some similar entity, the school would not survive.

The thought of the school closing curdled her stomach. She might have started the school as a way to occupy herself, but it had become the obsession she hadn't previously had. Bad enough that she couldn't imagine how she would fill her days without it, but now there was far more at stake than that; under her guidance, the teachers and pupils—all seventeen currently attending—had grown into a remarkably engaged group. The pupils attended because they wanted to—because they'd developed a thirst for knowledge and had taken to heart her oft-repeated litany that education was the pathway to their future.

The pupils were committed, the teachers even more so. University-trained, both were devoted educators, as was their less-qualified but equally dedicated assistant.

Sylvia had worked for two and more years to get the school to where it was, and it now delivered something vital for the pupils, the teachers, and, indeed, the city itself—just as she'd told the board members' wives all those months ago.

She'd succeeded, and all had been running so smoothly...

She stared at the door, then set her chin. "I am not going to allow the school to close."

That was the first decision—the one from which all else would stem.

"I need to find new premises that someone will donate—I did that once, and I can do it again." It would be up to her to pull the school's irons out of the fire. Although the school operated under the aegis of the Dean, from the start, their understanding had been that the school was hers to manage. It was her challenge; there was no one else to act as the school's champion. That was her role—the role she'd fought for.

"Just as I'm going to fight through this." Lips thinning, eyes narrowing, she considered her options. Staring at the door, she muttered, "So...what can I do?"

Two

There was one thing Sylvia wasn't prepared to do, and that was give up. The following morning, she strode briskly along King Street, her goal the Dock Company offices on Broad Quay.

The previous day, after the Dock Company directors had dropped their bombshell and shattered her peace of mind, she'd gathered herself and her thoughts and had sought an urgent meeting with the Dean, he under whose auspices her school for dockyard boys had been created. Although the Dean had been, as ever, sympathetic and supportive, he hadn't had any suggestions to make as to who she might approach to secure new premises for the school.

That meeting had been followed hours later by another with the parish council, the previous evening being the night of the council's regular weekly conference. The outcome had been less than satisfactory—indeed, close to horrifying—which had only hardened her resolve.

Depressingly, between informing the Dean and, later, the parish council of the unexpected change in the school's circumstances, she'd felt compelled to visit the school and inform the staff and students that, due to unforeseen events, it was possible that the school might have to close for a week or so after the end of the week. Unsurprisingly, her announcement had caused dismay and consternation, but better they heard it from her than via the dockside rumor mill. She'd done her best to allay everyone's concerns, reassuring them all that if it came to a closure, it would only last until new premises were secured, yet the expressions haunting so many of the students—the anxiety etched on their young faces—had clutched at her heart.

They weren't her children, and she didn't think of them as such, but she knew each and every one now, knew their stories, their families, and, in most cases, their hopes and dreams, and felt an almost-parental responsibility for each boy.

Most had had to fight and win battles of their own to be allowed to attend regularly rather than find whatever work they could; each of the seventeen regular pupils had had to gain the support of their family, and given the current lack of prosperity on the Bristol docks, that had been a feat in itself.

She was determined not to let them—and the teachers and assistant—down. She would find a place—would find someone willing to donate either a venue or the rent for one.

She had to—and quickly—or the parish council would redirect the school's funds to some other worthy cause.

While none of the council members had had any advice to offer regarding where she might find new premises for the school, they had made it clear, albeit gently, that as the council could not afford to rent such premises itself, if appropriate donated space was not forthcoming, the council would have to withdraw all funding. As the chairman had explained, there simply wasn't sufficient money in the parish coffers to support a nonfunctioning school; in the current climate, the parish had too many other calls on its funds.

She'd left that meeting with a hideous sinking feeling in the pit of her stomach. But after a night of tossing and turning and, in between bouts of sleep, evaluating increasingly fanciful options, she'd woken with a start—and a rather bold, certainly desperate, but possible way forward clear in her mind.

Hence her impending visit to the Dock Company offices.

On reaching the end of King Street, she turned right into Broad Quay. The Dock Company offices faced the Frome and were quite grand, with a semicircular set of steps leading up to a pair of glossy, green-painted doors with glass panels bearing the company's name and logo inset into each. Sylvia pushed on the brass handle and walked briskly into the tiled foyer. Having been to the building before, she didn't pause but continued to the stairs at the end of the foyer and went up to the first floor.

There, she rapped peremptorily on the door facing the stairs. On hearing a somewhat testy "Come," she opened the door and walked inside.

She fixed the black-suited figure behind the desk with an uncompromising gaze. "Good morning, Mr. Finch."

Finch didn't look pleased but, nevertheless, got to his feet, returning her greeting with a curt nod. "Miss Buckleberry. I do hope you aren't here to tell me that there will be any difficulty over the school vacating the warehouse."

Sylvia allowed her gaze to rest heavily on Finch until he grew restless and started fingering the buttons on his coat. Then she simply said, "No. I'm here to inquire as to the name of the new tenant and where I may find him."

Slowly, Finch blinked. "Ah...why do you need such information?"

Sylvia smiled as innocently as she could. "I merely wish to ask if he—presumably having recently surveyed the available warehouses around the docks—has any information on empty premises the school might be able to lease." That would be her opening question, but she doubted Finch would approve of what else she intended asking the new tenant, much less the manner in which she intended to ask.

"Ah. I see." Finch appeared to be considering telling her, but then he refocused on her face, and his expression grew stern. "I'm afraid, Miss Buckleberry, that without the gentleman's permission, I am unable to share such information—it might be seen as a breach of trust."

Sylvia fought to keep exasperation from her face and, instead, heaved a put-upon sigh. "Mr. Finch, surely you can see that in order to ensure the school removes as required—"

His face turning to granite, Finch held up a hand. "Miss Buckleberry, I do hope you aren't thinking to sway me by suggesting the school might not be out of the warehouse by Friday afternoon at the latest."

Sylvia managed not to glare, but it was a near-run thing. Lips firming, she replied, "Of course not. I'm merely attempting to do the best for the school and locate new premises—"

"As I am endeavoring to do what's best for the Dock Company." Finch held her gaze. "I'm glad we understand each other, Miss Buckleberry."

Sylvia stared at the annoying man and inwardly conceded; he'd dug in his heels and she would get nothing from him. That decided, she favored him with a brief nod, turned, and walked to the still-open door. With her hand on the knob, she glanced back and said, "Normally, I would thank you for your help, sir, but sadly, you've been no help at all."

She walked out and shut the door with a definite click.

She swept down the stairs, through the front doors, down the steps, and halted on the quay. "Men!"

The muffled exclamation and her exasperated expression drew a few looks from passersby. She ignored them and focused on her goal.

How was she to learn the identity of the new tenant?

Finch had said gentleman, singular; that was the only piece of helpful information he'd dropped. She hadn't yet decided how, precisely, she would approach the new tenant—whether she would opt for engagement and appeal to his better social nature or if she would play on his guilt over ousting the school. She would make that decision when she faced him, as she was determined to do. One way or another, she intended to beard the new tenant, explain matters in simple terms, and see if she could extract some degree of help from that quarter.

Having tapped all those with whom she was familiar, those who knew enough to appreciate her cause, and got nowhere, she was willing to approach the one player in the drama she didn't know—the newcomer to the docks.

The irony in that hadn't escaped her; in lieu of gaining help from any locals for a project to further local good, she was seeking assistance from a stranger.

How can I find him?

No inspiration struck. Frowning, she turned south, slowly walking back along Broad Quay. She'd taken only a few paces when, glancing ahead, she saw men gathered in groups in front of a labor exchange.

She halted. The exchanges were how men out of work learned of new jobs on the docks and elsewhere. Several such exchanges were scattered around the city, but the one before her, on the corner of Currant Lane and the narrower quay that ran along the eastern bank of the Frome, was the closest to the warehouse.

If the new tenant needed to hire workers, then the Currant Lane exchange was where he would post his notices.

Slowly, Sylvia smiled, then she stepped out more confidently, heading for the door of the labor exchange.

★ ★ ★

"How can I help you, miss?" The young clerk behind the counter looked at Sylvia uncertainly; she wasn't the usual sort of client who appeared in front of him.

She smiled. "You're Elroy's brother, aren't you?"

The clerk blinked, then his eyes widened. "Oh—you're the school lady." The clerk relaxed. "Sorry, miss, I didn't recognize you at first. Have you come to list a job?"

"No, sadly, but I wondered if you might be able to help me."

"If I can, I will." The clerk puffed out his thin chest. "What is it you need help with?"

"I'm trying to learn the name of the businessman who's taken the lease on the warehouse the school's been using. It's a new business coming to town, so I'm sure he'll have listed at least a few positions with this office."

"Oh." Now the clerk looked wary. His eyes shifted to the older man serving others farther along the counter. Then the clerk leaned closer and lowered his voice. "I don't know as how I can, miss. That sort of information is only given to those who need to know—we don't even tell the men we send who they'll be speaking to, who listed the position. We only give out the details of the position and where to apply."

Sylvia frowned. "Surely you give out the name of the business?"

"Oh. Yes—we do that. The gentleman I think you're after posted several positions for Cavanaugh Yachts."

For an instant, Sylvia thought bells were ringing, distorting her hearing. "*Cavanaugh* Yachts?"

The clerk looked at her anxiously. "Are you all right, miss?"

She waved aside his concern. There were three Cavanaugh brothers—four if you counted the marquess, but this man couldn't be he. And it was unlikely to be Rand, either, and Godfrey was surely too young...

She licked her suddenly dry lips. "Tell me," she said, not truly seeing the clerk anymore but a tall man in a morning suit. "Was this gentleman on the tallish side, with wide shoulders and brown hair..." She cast about for words to describe the aura that hung about her nemesis. "And looked to be the sort of gentleman who would laugh in the devil's face?"

Refocusing on the clerk, she saw he was frowning.

"Actually," Elroy's brother said, "now I think of it, there were two of them. Two gentlemen who came in at different times, but hiring for the same business. The first was tall and thin, lanky-like, and he had dark brown hair, but the other gent— the one who listed a position for a secretary this morning—he was like you said." The clerk nodded earnestly. "Had just such an air about him, you know?"

Sylvia knew all about the airs affected by Lord Kit Cavana-ugh. Her wits were reeling, but she seized the straw the clerk had just offered her. "If I wanted to apply for the position of secretary to Cavanaugh Yachts, where would I go?"

The answer was a recently completed building in King Street. Sylvia thanked the clerk, then left the exchange and, gaze leveled and purpose in her stride, walked briskly toward King Street, an explosive mix of determination and rising anger simmering in her veins.

★ ★ ★

Kit stood in his inner office and studied the plans spread on the desk before him. Wayland must have been up half the night drawing the detailed sketches, but he'd been bright-eyed and eager when he'd dropped off the plans ten minutes ago with strict instructions that he expected Kit to have checked and ap-proved them by the time Wayland called back in the early af-ternoon.

"I want to order the timber today," Wayland had said. "It'll take at least a day, maybe more, to fill such an order, and I don't want to find that we're still waiting on Monday."

Kit had agreed. While Wayland went off to check at the labor exchange to see who had replied to their various listings, Kit had settled to peruse the plans.

The silence about him impinged; it was not what he was used to. The building was newly completed and, thus far, only par-tially let; the offices to either side lay empty. In addition, the builders had used thicker glass in the windows, which muted the sounds of the traffic along King Street to a distant rumble.

He glanced up—through the doorway to the outer office; he'd left the door between open so he could see the corridor door. He needed to find a secretary; he'd put up a listing that morning, but doubted anything would come of it for at least a few days. The clerk at the labor exchange had said he would circulate the listing to the exchanges in those parts of the city more likely to harbor a suitable female.

Until he hired someone, he was on his own, yet to his mind, getting the Cavanaugh Yachts workshop functional as soon as possible had to remain his pre-eminent goal.

While approving Wayland's design was easy enough, checking his figures required concentration; marshaling his, Kit started on the dimensions of the office closer to the warehouse door, matching them with Wayland's suggested timber frame.

Someone hammered on the outer door.

Startled, Kit looked up—in time to see the door flung open and a neatly dressed lady storm in.

She halted, saw him, and skewered him with a scorching glare.

Tall, with a willowy figure and svelte curves, garbed in a violet-blue walking dress over a white silk blouse, her wheat-blond hair drawn back from an arresting face carved from alabaster—

Recognition slammed into him and scrambled his brain.

Sylvia Buckleberry?

At his stupefied reaction, her eyes narrowed even further. She whirled and shut the door, then, with a furious swishing of skirts, marched through the outer office.

She stepped into his inner sanctum and let fly. *"I might have known!"* Her tone dripped acid; her bosom swelled as she drew breath. "Of all the cities in England, you had to choose this one, and, of course, you think nothing of trampling over whomever and whatever stands in your way." She locked her eyes on his as she halted on the other side of the desk, then dramatically flung her arms wide. "I can just imagine the reactions of the Dock Company directors. 'Yes, my lord. No, my lord. Three bags full, my lord.'" Indigo sparks flared in the periwinkle-blue of her eyes. Her lush lips set in a thin line, she glared at him accusingly. "I'm quite sure that's how it went."

She railed on, but while Kit's brain registered her words, he wasn't really listening.

Instead, he could only stare, grappling to make sense of the transformation of Sylvia Buckleberry that had manifested before him.

The first and last time he'd seen her—just weeks ago at Rand's wedding, where, courtesy of Sylvia being one of Felicia's bridesmaids and Kit being one of Rand's groomsmen, Kit had been Sylvia's partner—she'd treated him to a very effective cold shoulder. More, she'd given every indication of being a rigidly buttoned-down, haughtily dismissive, and chillingly distant sort of lady.

The lady before him was anything but.

This Sylvia Buckleberry was all fire and passion and life.

Blatantly driven by determination and willpower, she was a force of nature done up in a very attractive package.

On an intellectual level, he was aware that he'd noticed her physical attributes before, but at the time, their impact had been negated by her attitude. Now, however, this Sylvia Buckleberry was fixing his attention in a much more avid way.

She had, quite literally, transfixed his senses and scattered his wits.

And his lack of response to her tirade was making her seethe.

The glare she leveled at him was all hellfire and brimstone. "I'm well aware that London rakes cannot be expected to care in the slightest over a dockyard school, but why couldn't you remain in London? Why did you have to come here and spoil *everything*? Do you have any notion of how much damage you're likely to do to the fabric of local society?"

Those words finally penetrated the haze fogging his brain. He blinked, then frowned. "What the devil are you accusing me of?"

The look she bent on him was all dismissive scorn. "As if you don't know."

His own temper rising, he narrowed his eyes back. "I have absolutely no idea—" He broke off as several facts coalesced in his brain, and he realized what the Dock Company men hadn't told him. "Wait." He held up a hand as he rapidly replayed various exchanges, and suspicion hardened to fact. He refocused on her. "The charity using the warehouse is a school?"

"Yes!" Fists clenched, Sylvia wanted to rage on, but the look on his face—the open chagrin—took the wind from her sails.

It was patently obvious that he hadn't known his leasing of the warehouse meant the eviction of a school. He could be acting, but she didn't think he was—that he would bother. She frowned. "The Dock Company didn't tell you?"

"No. They didn't." The words were clipped and boded ill for whomever had omitted to mention the fact. "Indeed, they took great care to avoid doing so."

She wanted to cling to her anger, to the strength of the fury that anger had converted to during the short walk to his office, but if he hadn't known about the school…

Aside from all else, it seemed that, instead of being the indolent, care-for-naught hedonist she'd labeled him, he was actually trying to establish a business that would bring jobs to the struggling docklands.

While such an action was the last thing she would have expected of him, the evidence was too definite to doubt.

Her anger drained in a rush, taking her righteousness with it. Her shoulders fell; dejection loomed.

She was vaguely aware of his sharp gaze on her face, then he waved her to one of the chairs angled before the desk.

"Please—sit down. I need to know more about this school."

Kit waited until she'd subsided onto the chair, then drew up the admiral's chair he'd earlier pushed back and sat. Her expression had shuttered, her attention seemingly turned inward—to him, her retreat felt like the withdrawing of a source of warmth. But having once laid eyes on the real Sylvia Buckleberry, he wasn't about to let her hide away behind a wall of chilly disdain. He caught her eyes. "Tell me all—all about this school."

Frowning faintly, she hesitated, but then complied, describing the establishment of the school under the auspices of the Dean of Christ Church and the funding she'd secured from the parish council on condition that the premises for the school were found free of cost. "Two years ago, the only vacant building that was suitable was the old warehouse on the Grove—our requirements are rather specific in that the location of the school must be within walking distance of the boys' homes. Given the boys are from dockworking and shipyard families, that means somewhere along the docks or close by, but other than on the docks themselves, the alternatives are the inner city, which is generally unsuitable, or more well-to-do areas, which are unaffordable." She paused to draw breath, then went on, "With the help of their wives, I managed to convince the Dock Company board to allow the school to use the old warehouse. The secretary, Finch, was never in favor, but I managed to arrange sufficient votes to carry the day.

"So we set up with two teachers and an assistant and have gathered seventeen long-term pupils. We usually get a handful of new pupils each year, and once we've trained the boys, they should be able to get jobs in the various offices in the city."

She met his gaze. "It's taken time to overcome the suspicions of the dockyard families especially—they don't like to think that their boys might need different training from their fathers. Or that, if schooled, the sons might well earn more than their fathers. These past few months have been more settled, and we all thought things were rolling along well...and now this." She waved a hand in a helpless gesture and looked away. "We have no grounds on which to protest our eviction—and, indeed, all will welcome a new business that promises more jobs for ship workers." She paused, her frowning gaze fixed past his shoulder, then said, "It's not us leaving the warehouse that's the crux of the problem—the finding and securing of new premises is."

She straightened on the chair, her expressive face attesting to a gathering of inner strength. "I've already asked the Dean and the parish council, and the representatives of the Dock Company, too, but no one could suggest any other group or company who have a suitable space that they might possibly allow the school to use."

When she fell silent, he hesitated, but he needed to know all of it. "And if you don't find new premises immediately?"

She sighed. "If I haven't found new premises by the end of the week, I'll have to close the school—at least temporarily. But the parish council has informed me that they will not be able to continue funding if the school isn't functioning."

She was facing the eradication of all she'd accomplished over the past two years.

She looked down at her hands, clasped in her lap. "The worst part of that is how it will affect the boys. The seventeen who attend have grown so much in confidence, but this will set them back. If I'm forced to close the school, even if only for a week, I suspect we'll lose at least some of them. Longer than a week, and we might lose them all and have to start all over again, winning them and their families over to the idea that an education is the best way to secure their future."

Her belief in that concept, her commitment to that ideal, and her devotion to the dockyard brats for whom she'd fought to get schooling was evident in her tone, her expression, her anxiety, and her imminent despondency.

Kit knew about personal obsession; he could relate.

He stirred, rapidly reviewing an idea that had taken shape as she'd spoken; one of his business strengths lay in recognizing opportunity when it came his way and seizing it. Of course, his first impulse had been to offer to help her, purely for her sake, but he knew how prickly she could become, and he wanted to avoid giving her any excuse to revert to her previous behavior with him—to poker up and make everything harder. Painting his interest as entirely self-serving would play into her preconceived notions of his character, avoiding the simple truth that he enjoyed helping people and would have helped her regardless.

"As it happens," he said, and somewhat surprised, she raised her head and looked at him, "I believe that I—or rather, Cavanaugh Yachts—might be able to assist." He hesitated for only a second, then leaned his forearms on the desk and fixed his gaze on her eyes. "I'll be absolutely frank. I'm new to the city, and with a business to get off the ground, I need to establish my bona fides, to establish Cavanaugh Yachts as a trustworthy employer and, moreover, one seeking to put down roots and involve itself in the community—to signal that we're here for the long haul. It sounds as if the boys attending your school come from precisely the subset of families from which my business will be seeking to attract workers. To my way of thinking, if I fund the rent for not just another venue but a better venue for the school, that will go a substantial way toward establishing the Cavanaugh name among the dockworkers and shipyard families."

She blinked at him. "You're prepared to do that?"

"Yes." To drive his excuse home, he added, "Your pupils will have fathers, older brothers, uncles, and cousins, some of whom will be the sort of men I and my partner need to hire. Funding your school is an excellent way to forge a link with such craftsmen."

She looked much struck. "I hadn't thought of that—of that angle."

He smiled, all teeth. "Well, you've already found a sponsor, so you won't need to make the argument to anyone else. My one stipulation—and I'm sure you'll agree that, in the circumstances, it's reasonable—is that I view and approve the new venue. Indeed, I'll be happy to assist with negotiating the lease, and I'm prepared to stand as guarantor if required."

Of course, such a stipulation would also ensure that he got to spend more time with this new, much improved, and utterly fascinating Miss Buckleberry.

Sylvia stared at him and tried not to gape. His gaze remained steady, and his lips were slightly curved. He looked quite pleased with himself, which gave her pause—but only for a second. He'd just offered her all—and more than—she'd hoped to gain from the owner of the business taking over the warehouse. And wonder of wonders, he seemed inclined to take an active interest, and regardless of her view of him and his lordly status, that would unquestionably help the school's standing with the Dean and the parish council—let alone the mayor.

Yet as he sat behind his desk—at a distance of a yard or more—and patiently waited for her to accept his offer, her unwanted reactions to him, initially overridden by her fury, inexorably rose with every breath, until she could almost feel physical awareness crawling over her skin. Significantly taller than she, broad shouldered and vigorous, with ruffled hair of a rich mid-brown, warm, light brown eyes, an austere and uncompromisingly patrician cast to his features, and sensual lips, from the first instant she'd set eyes on him, he'd been the visual embodiment of her fantasy gentleman. Just the sight of him affected her as no other man ever had. That said, she'd dealt with her silly sensitivity throughout the full day of Felicia's wedding, had successfully suppressed and concealed it. Surely she could do the same again?

Yet now, his impact on her senses and her involuntary response seemed heightened—more intense. Possibly because she was dealing with the real man—one significantly more real than the rake who haunted her dreams—and without the predictable framework of a wedding and reception to act as a formal structure, directing and defining their interactions.

Here, now, they were interacting freely, adult to adult, with no screens, no masks. No façades.

Letting the silence stretch, she eyed him assessingly. She would dearly love to retreat to the chilly reserve she'd previously maintained with him—infinitely safer, without a shadow of a doubt—

but the intent look in his caramel eyes and that faint suggestion of a smile about his lips gave warning that she would be unwise to attempt it; barging into his office in full and furious flight had shattered the mask she'd worn before, and no amount of acting was going to patch it back together.

So. Her response to his proposition ultimately hinged on the question of how much she was willing to give—to risk—to ensure the continuation of the school.

No question, when all was said and done.

He'd shown not the slightest sign of being discomfited by her prolonged scrutiny. Still holding his gaze, she tipped her chin higher. "How do you suggest we proceed?"

A tacit acceptance, one, it appeared, he was perfectly willing to seize. He glanced at the plans scattered over the desk. "We want to begin fitting out the warehouse on Monday—so as we would prefer not to have to close the school, even for a few days, we should move quickly to secure new premises." He tipped his head at the plans. "I have to finish checking these and authorize them by early afternoon. Also, I don't know the city well."

He met her gaze and faintly arched his brows. "Might I suggest you make inquiries as to available and suitable buildings to lease—preferably in a better part of town than the warehouse, yet still within easy reach for the boys? Then you and I can meet here—shall we say at three?—and together, we can go and view the possibilities and make our choice."

She had a sneaking suspicion that, somewhere in all this, she was being…not manipulated but steered. Yet she had no reason to even quibble with anything he'd suggested. Mentally throwing her hands in the air—she was about to willingly make a deal with her personal devil—she inclined her head with what grace she could muster. "Thank you. I'll assemble a list of suitable premises for lease and return here at three o'clock."

Gripping her reticule, she rose, bringing him to his feet—

which made her stupid senses leap. Hurriedly, she waved him back to his chair. "I know the way out. I'll see you later."

With that, she turned and—metaphorically, at least—fled.

Kit watched her go. Only after she'd closed the outer door did he allow a smile of equal parts satisfaction and anticipation to curve his lips.

Three

At three o'clock that afternoon, Sylvia found Kit Cavanaugh waiting on the steps of the building housing his office. He smiled as she approached, and her pulse fluttered.

Studiously ignoring that and the inexorable tightening about her lungs, she briskly nodded as she halted beside him. She made a production of consulting the list she held in one hand, then announced, "Our first possibility lies in Puddle Avenue." She swiveled and pointed to the south. "It's that way—off Queen Square."

With a graceful gesture, he waved her forward. "Lead on."

She started walking, and he fell in beside her, adjusting his long strides to her slightly shorter ones. While in the company of other women and, indeed, most men, she felt on the tallish side, with him, her head barely cleared his chin, leaving her feeling…more feminine than usual. She was glad he made no attempt to take her arm; she wasn't sure what she would do if he tried. Just walking beside him was entirely close enough; her senses were skittering as it was.

She drew in a breath—one rather too restricted—and reminded herself that she would need to keep her wits about her, especially now she'd been forced to drop her previous haughty mask.

They crossed to the south side of King Street and took to the eastern pavement of Princes Street. In an attempt to keep her mind from wandering his way, she glanced down at the list she'd prepared for this excursion. On leaving their earlier meeting, she'd visited several leasing companies. Through them, she'd identified a total of eight presently untenanted buildings that lay within the area the boys could reach and that sounded large enough to house the school.

She'd listed the buildings in order of desirability based on her general knowledge of location, but as she had no way by which to gauge Cavanaugh's commitment—how much he was truly willing to commit—she'd decided to start at the bottom of the list.

They reached the corner of Puddle Avenue and paused. She looked up, searching for numbers on the nearer buildings. "It's number fifteen."

She glanced at his face; his expression was impassive, but she sensed he wasn't impressed with Puddle Avenue.

Nevertheless, he gestured her onward and kept pace beside her as she walked slowly along the street.

Number 15 Puddle Avenue proved to be a run-down building wedged between two warehouses; the flanking buildings appeared to be holding Number 15 up. What paint still clung to its timber facing was peeling away in curls, and there were visible cracks in the stone foundations.

She cleared her throat. "Obviously, I shouldn't have relied on the property manager's description."

Cavanaugh grunted. "Obviously not." His features were hard as his gaze swept the exterior of the building. Then he turned his head and met her gaze. "Where's the next place?"

★ ★ ★

The hall off Bell Lane was only marginally better than the Puddle Avenue building.

Regardless, Kit felt compelled to look inside before passing judgment, and the feisty Miss Buckleberry agreed—although she hung back as, after pushing through the slightly warped door, he walked into the musty space.

He stopped two paces in, looked around, then turned and walked back to where she stood on the threshold.

Jaw firming, he met her eyes. "Next?"

★ ★ ★

The third place she took him to was, he supposed, a possible venue for the school. At a stretch. But the hall was dark, over-shadowed by taller buildings on either side and on the other side of the narrow street, and a telltale odor of mildew and mold rose from the ancient lining boards, leaving him in little doubt that the timbers behind were rotting.

The notion of setting young boys to work through their days in such surroundings...he simply couldn't see it.

He glanced at Sylvia. She'd been watching him—his face—but had glanced down at her list of potential properties.

On impulse, Kit reached out and, with a quick tug, filched the list from her gloved fingers.

She sucked in a breath, but then pressed her lips tightly together and clasped her hands before her.

Kit focused on the list. "There has to be somewhere better."

He ran his gaze down the entries and, despite his lack of knowledge of Bristol, realized there definitely was. From the addresses, it appeared that the inestimable Miss Buckleberry had started at the bottom of her list of possible places...

He could guess why—she wasn't sure he would sponsor the school properly.

For a second, he considered being annoyed about that, but then decided that, with a female like Sylvia Buckleberry, see-ing would be believing.

His expression impassive, he held out the list. "Let's look at the place in Trinity Street."

If she was surprised, she hid it well. Taking back the list, she said, "I have to warn you that the Trinity Street property is the most expensive option. It's owned by St. Augustine's Abbey, and the rent is…well, in keeping with that and the location, which is on a street between the Abbey and the Frome."

Kit gave a noncommittal shrug. "As I'm sure you've guessed, I can afford it, and such a location—and landlord—sounds much more like the sort of accommodation I'd want a school I was sponsoring to have."

Facing her, he waved imperiously to the door. "I suggest we go directly there."

Although her gaze stated she was still uncertain, she allowed him to usher her outside.

★ ★ ★

It was close to five o'clock when they reached Trinity Street, but the instant they halted outside the old hall, Kit felt certain they'd found the right place. Judging by the expression on Sylvia's face as she stood beside him and scanned the front façade, she thought the same.

In keeping with the Augustinian creed, the building had few ornate features. Built of stone and weathered oak, it was solid and functional—the sort of place that would easily withstand the rigors of hosting a school. Although he'd gone to Eton, Kit doubted that boys whose fathers worked on the docks would be any less vigorous than scions of the nobility.

A small tiled porch protected the oak door. Without thinking, Kit touched his palm to the back of Sylvia's waist, urging her toward the porch steps. She froze for a fraction of a second, but then, with a rather tense inclination of her head, walked forward and climbed the three steps to the porch.

After fishing in her reticule for the key, she unlocked the door and led the way inside.

Kit followed her into a comfortable space, well-lit despite the time of day, with the last rays of the westering sun pouring through high, clerestory windows. The floor was well-worn oak, smooth and clean. Kit glanced around. "No drafts."

Sylvia had halted in the middle of the good-sized hall. "That will make a huge difference in winter."

Kit nodded at the three small fireplaces built into the side walls. "And there's those, too."

Sinking his hands into the pockets of his greatcoat, he started on a circuit of the hall—following Sylvia as she did the same. They poked their heads into the small kitchen at the rear of the hall.

"This will be an added boon," Sylvia said, and he could hear the building excitement in her voice.

He hid a smile and ambled at her heels as she proceeded to open the back door. He looked out over her head at the decent-looking privy standing in the small, cobbled rear yard.

Everything was neat and clean—and solid and enduring.

Sylvia shut and locked the back door, then turned and faced him; he had to wonder if she knew her hopes were shining in her eyes. "This will do admirably," she said.

He almost looked to see if she'd crossed her fingers.

He contented himself with an easy smile and an acquiescing nod. "How much is the rent?"

Sylvia held her breath; now she'd seen inside the hall, it was even more perfect than the outside had promised. It would be a huge improvement over their current quarters. She could so easily see the boys and the school prospering here, she was almost reluctant to tell him how much it would cost for fear of hearing him say it was too expensive.

But...she cleared her throat, forced herself to meet his eyes, and stated the price the Abbey's prior, sympathetic to her and the school's plight, had named.

Then she hurriedly added, "Unfortunately, that's the lowest price the Abbey can accept, and it's still significantly more than the second place on my list."

She looked down at the list, still clutched in her hand—only to see Cavanaugh's hand come into view. He closed his fingers—broad-tipped, strong fingers—about the edge of the paper and gently tugged. She watched the list slide from her grasp and wondered what he was thinking—what decision he'd made.

"I don't believe we need to look at any other places."

Hope leaping in her chest, she looked up and saw him tucking the list, now folded, into his pocket.

He glanced around. "This place is ideal, and the rent seems reasonable and fair."

He brought his gaze back to her face and lightly arched his brows. "So who do we see about the lease?"

★ ★ ★

The following morning, Sylvia set out for the school, light of heart and eager to tell the teachers and students of their good fortune.

She was especially glad to be able to lift the pall of doubt and uncertainty that had descended on both staff and pupils when she'd told them of having to quit the warehouse. Indeed, she felt like skipping at the prospect.

The meeting with the prior, with Kit Cavanaugh by her side, had gone extremely well. Not only was the Abbey happy to have the hall put to such use, but the prior had gone so far as to suggest that if the school ever needed medical assistance, they could call on the Abbey's infirmarian.

She was worldly enough to know that she and the school had Cavanaugh—Kit—to thank for that. He'd stood like a rock— a distinctly noble rock—at her back throughout the process of leasing the hall.

She hurried across the end of Bell Lane, then cut between buildings to reach the Grove. Looking ahead, she spied a tall, greatcoated figure leaning against the bole of a tree opposite the warehouse the school presently occupied.

She blinked and looked again, confirming that the figure was indeed Kit. He saw her, pushed away from the tree, and ambled to intercept her.

Was she surprised? She wasn't sure she was. After all, at the end of their successful foray yesterday, in return for his help in getting the prior to commence the lease on the Trinity Street hall immediately, she'd agreed that the school would move premises today, allowing Kit and his men access to the warehouse tomorrow, a day earlier than they'd hoped.

He'd said he would notify the Dock Company, and she had no doubt he had—or would. He was efficient and effective—she would give him that.

He'd halted, waiting for her, and as she neared, she discovered an entirely spontaneous smile of greeting had taken up residence on her face. "Good morning. Have you come to help me break the news?"

Kit drank in that smile—the first sincere smile she'd ever bestowed on him. He returned it with an easy smile of his own, nothing to get her bristling. "Good morning to you—and no." He glanced at the warehouse. "You can do the honors. I've come to lend a hand with moving the school."

She blinked in surprise, and he couldn't stop his smile from deepening. To hide it, he glanced vaguely around. "Do you know of any men we can hire to help?"

"Hire?"

From her tone, the notion hadn't entered her head—probably because she wasn't accustomed to having the wherewithal to pay for such help.

But after several seconds, she said, "The boys will help, of course. And some of them will have older brothers out of work and possibly fathers as well..."

He nodded. "We can ask." He waved her on. "Let's go in, and you can break the good news."

Kit followed her through the door. He halted just inside. In his mind, he could already see the transformation of the space that he and Wayland had planned. While Wayland busied himself checking on his orders and interviewing men for the key role of foreman as well as hiring a small team of carpenters to make a start on their necessary alterations, Kit had elected to devote himself to ensuring that the school's vacating of the warehouse went smoothly.

Ahead of him, Sylvia came to a halt before the two rows of desks that were now lined up across the warehouse floor. Two gentlemen—Kit judged them to be much of an age with himself—both neatly and conservatively dressed, had been standing before the desks, one to either side, addressing the boys before them; having heard Sylvia's heels on the boards, they, along with their pupils, had turned their attention to her.

She tipped her head to each man. "Mr. Jellicoe. Mr. Cross. If I could have a moment of everyone's time, I have an announcement to make."

Her expression gave away her news—or at least, it's nature; the looks on the boys' faces as they stared at her could only be described as ones of rising hope.

Assured of everyone's attention, her hands clasped before her, she stated, "Yesterday evening, courtesy of Lord Cavanaugh"—she glanced back at Kit, still standing just inside the door, gracefully waved in his direction, then turned back to her audience—"the lease on a hall in Trinity Street was secured for the school. We have new premises, and they are a great deal better than this warehouse."

The cheer that erupted from the boys and staff matched the joy and relief that suffused their faces.

Several of the older boys thumped on their desks, and the others took up the drumbeat.

The teachers glanced at Kit, and he inclined his head to them, and they nodded politely in return. Then at a smiling word from Sylvia, both teachers turned back to their charges and waved them to silence.

Somewhat to Kit's surprise, silence returned quite quickly.

Into it, Sylvia said, "Lord Cavanaugh is the owner of the business that has leased this warehouse, and once he learned of the school, he kindly agreed to fund the lease for our new school hall. In return, I agreed that we would move to our new hall today. I'm therefore declaring today a holiday—at least from your studies. However, I expect every one of you to assist us—me, Mr. Jellicoe, Mr. Cross, and Miss Meggs, too, once she comes in, and Lord Cavanaugh, who has come to help as well—to move all the school's furniture, books, boards, slates, supplies, and all to our new hall."

Wily Sylvia. Kit had already noted the curiosity that had flared in every boy's face at the revelation that he was a lord; for such boys, nobles were a rarely encountered species. By mentioning that he would be helping with the move, Sylvia had ensured that every single boy would remain to do their part.

Eager agreement abounded, and when Sylvia asked if any of the boys had older male relatives who might be free to help for a price, five hands shot into the air.

Kit raised his voice. "You can tell anyone who agrees to help that the rate will be three shillings for the day." That was the current rate for laborers on the docks.

The boys who'd raised their hands leapt to their feet.

Sylvia gave them leave to run home and ask and return to the warehouse promptly with anyone willing to help. The other boys she directed to start gathering their books and slates.

Kit walked forward, allowing the boys leaving free access to the door. They grinned at him as they passed, and some bobbed their heads and murmured, "Your lordship."

Kit grinned back at them, which sent their grins even wider, then they were gone.

Jellicoe and Cross approached as Kit halted. He had no difficulty in pegging both as younger sons of the gentry who'd had to make their own way; from their families, they would have received a sound education, but little else.

Jellicoe held out his hand. "Thank you, my lord. We were

fearing that the school would close, and that would have been the end for these boys' educations."

"Indeed." Cross waited until Kit released Jellicoe's hand to offer his own. "You might not realize it, but this is a very good deed you've done, my lord."

Kit shifted, uncomfortable with the praise. "Don't credit me with too much altruism, gentlemen—I wanted the warehouse as soon as possible and finding the school new premises seemed the easiest way to that goal."

Neither Jellicoe nor Cross looked as if they believed him, and in truth, gaining the use of the warehouse early had never been Kit's primary objective. Acknowledging that, he added, "However, I do support the notion of education for the masses, so I was happy to help in this way." And seeing the transformation in the faces of the boys and the teachers had already been sufficient reward.

That, both teachers accepted. As Sylvia came to join them, they looked at her with an eagerness to rival their pupils'.

"How should we do this?" Cross asked.

Kit listened as Sylvia outlined a plan to move the heavier items first—the desks and the two blackboards; Kit assumed the latter had been brought in by the teachers—they hadn't been there when he and Wayland had viewed the space.

"Once we have those arranged in the new hall," Sylvia went on, "we can return here and ferry everything else across." She paused, then added, "I don't want the boys struggling with anything they might drop while they're crossing the Frome."

"No, indeed." Jellicoe looked at the boys who had remained in the warehouse; they were busily emptying the desks and stacking books, slates, chalks, and papers on the tops. "We'll need at least two trips for the smaller stuff, and depending on how many men turn up, at least two for the desks and boards. Even emptied, those desks are too unwieldy for any one man to manage on his own—even a dockyard navvy."

Just then, a thin, faded older lady, gray hair pulled back in a tight bun, walked into the warehouse.

"Miss Meggs." Sylvia went forward to greet her. "I'm relieved to say that we've had some excellent news."

While Sylvia explained about the new school hall, bringing a relieved expression to Miss Meggs's face, Jellicoe murmured, "Our assistant. She's a good soul and handles the boys surprisingly well."

Cross softly huffed. "I think the boys see her as a vague but doting aunt they need to take care of—which is not a bad thing."

Jellicoe laughed softly. "I think she plays up to that—when it comes to organizing our lessons, she's as sharp as a tack."

Kit watched Sylvia animatedly explaining the school's change in circumstances to the older woman. Their meeting with the prior the previous evening had gone much as he'd anticipated, with one major difference; the prior, Sylvia, and Kit had discussed various payment options, and, in the end, in order to avoid any future onus falling on Sylvia regarding the rent, they had agreed—Kit reluctantly—to put the lease in his name, with him making payments directly to the Abbey, rather than having Sylvia's name on the lease, with him standing as formal guarantor, and the payments routed through her. While she'd been perfectly content with the arrangement, Kit had to wonder if she realized just how much at his mercy that left the school. Of course, he would never do anything untoward, like renege on payments or cancel the lease, but she didn't know that. He'd ended with the distinct impression that Miss Sylvia Buckleberry, clergyman's daughter, trusted too easily for her own good.

Except, of course, when it came to him, but he was working on that.

One of the boys who'd gone to fetch family members returned, towing his older brother by the sleeve. The pair were quickly followed by the other four boys with their willing elders in tow. Most weren't fathers but older brothers and cousins, hale and strong from working on the docks. When all were assembled, they had twelve men, in addition to Jellicoe, Cross, and Kit himself.

Kit glanced at Sylvia, and she stepped forward. In a clear voice, she thanked the men for coming and outlined the proposed sequence of ferrying items to Trinity Street. "I'll go ahead and open up the hall there. Please, before you leave the warehouse with anything, notify Miss Meggs"—Sylvia waved to the school assistant, who now stood by the warehouse door, board and pencil in hand—"so she can ensure that we successfully get everything to its new home."

The men nodded readily.

One said, "We're pleased to help, miss. But about our money...?"

Kit stepped forward. "Come to me at the end of the day for payment—at that time, I'll be at the Trinity Street hall." Kit ran his gaze over the boys and men alike. "And the end of our day is as soon as we clear this building and ferry everything to the new hall."

The boys cheered, and the men looked eager to start lifting and carrying.

Kit waved them forward with the stipulation "Two to a desk. We don't want any dropped and broken."

The move got under way, with everyone in high good spirits. The men could easily handle a desk between two, and the boys loaded their arms with books and slates.

As Kit had suspected, Jellicoe and Cross folded the stands of the two big blackboards, then carefully set the boards into straplike slings and set off, each carrying one of the boards slung on his back and the folded stand in his hands.

There was no spare man with whom Kit could partner. He looked around, amid the chaos of boys arguing over who should take what, trying to assess what item would be most useful for him to cart.

Sylvia had paused to speak with Miss Meggs and ensure that everyone was having their loads noted. Kit lifted a pile of slates, which was surprisingly heavy; wrapping his arms about the stack, he hoisted it and joined Sylvia as—apparently realizing how many men and desks had already passed out of the warehouse on their way to Trinity Street—she somewhat distractedly fare-welled Miss Meggs. Seeing Kit with the slates, she waved him on and bent to lift a smaller box of chalks. Miss Meggs made a note and smiled and nodded to them both to proceed. Kit stepped out, pleased to find Sylvia falling in beside him.

"We'll have to hurry." She was, indeed, bustling along pur-posefully. "There's no sense in the men reaching the hall before us. They won't know where to leave the desks."

Smiling, Kit inclined his head and, lengthening his stride, easily kept pace.

They strode quickly up Princes Street, electing to avoid the busy quay for as long as they could. She glanced sidelong at him several times, then said, "I didn't expect you to carry things yourself. Your coat is likely to get chalk dust on it."

He bent a faintly teasing smile on her. "My man will tut, but I really don't care. A coat is a coat, after all."

When she continued to look as if him carting things was something of a social solecism, he sighed. "Think of this as me ensuring that the warehouse is completely cleared by day's end."

At that, she looked openly disbelieving. "You didn't have to help carry things to ensure that—you've already done more than I expected."

He held her gaze for an instant, then quietly said, "Is it so hard to believe that I honestly like helping people?"

The way she blinked at him before she faced forward sug-gested it had been, despite her "Of course not. I just…hadn't expected it."

He hoped she was readjusting her image of him—one of his less-obvious motives.

Their procession had to cross the drawbridge over the Frome, and as the bridge was presently raised, they caught up with their eager helpers there, in the shadow of Viell's Tower. The instant the ship had passed and the bridge was lowered, everyone set off again. Less encumbered than the other adults, Sylvia and Kit drew ahead.

When they got to the hall, he reached across and lifted the box of chalks from her arms. When she looked about to protest—*the chalk!*—he grinned. "I might as well be hung for a sheep as a lamb."

She humphed, but consented to dive into her reticule and drag out the key. She unlocked the door and set it wide.

Kit followed her inside. "Where do you want these sorts of things?"

She pointed to the far-right corner. "Over there. Once we have the desks set up again, the boys will put what they each should have back into their desks."

While he crossed to the designated spot and set down his burdens, she stood by the door and welcomed the men and boys who'd been following them.

He returned to her side and stood behind her as she directed the men as to where she wished them to place the desks, then Jellicoe and Cross arrived with their unwieldy burdens.

The teachers set the blackboards down along the front of the room.

"Well!" Jellicoe turned and, eyes lighting appreciatively, surveyed the hall. "This is certainly a step up."

"And it's going to be much closer for us," Cross said. To Kit, he explained, "Our digs are on this side of the river—along St. Augustine's Back."

Jellicoe nodded. "Just a few minutes away, and we won't have to wait for the drawbridge ever again."

Sylvia came up. "Can you two remain here for the moment and oversee the boys?" She handed Jellicoe the key. "Once they're all on their way back, you can lock up and bring the key back to the warehouse. I want to check on Miss Meggs, but by the time you get back, I'll be ready to head over here again."

Jellicoe took the key, and Cross tipped her a salute. "Given there are twenty desks, we'll have to pitch in and muscle over a couple between us. We'll see you back at the warehouse."

"Thank you." With a relieved smile, Sylvia turned away. She collected Kit with a glance. "Coming?"

As was becoming his habit, he grinned and waved her to the door. "Lead on."

They went back and forth; on reaching the hall a second time, Kit left Sylvia chatting with the teachers and boys and slipped out to the tavern he'd spotted just around the corner. Emerging five minutes later, he fell in with several of the hired men hauling desks between them. He smiled. "Pass the word, if you would—sandwiches and cider for all who've helped with the move at the new hall at noon."

The men's eyes lit, and they hoisted their burdens with renewed purpose. "Thank ye, m'lord," several called, while others tipped their heads to him.

Kit strode ahead, meeting Sylvia as she reappeared on the hall's porch. "There are more desks just turning into the street. And I ordered food—sandwiches and cider—for everyone. The tavern keeper's wife said she and her girls will deliver the food here at noon."

Sylvia stared at him. "Thank you. I hadn't thought…"

He grinned. "I'm used to working with men. We get hungry. And I could hardly eat all by myself."

She sent him a look that seemed to say that she'd adjusted her preconceived notions of him already, then she looked into the hall. "Cross—did you hear?"

"Aye, and very welcome the sustenance will be," Cross called.

Together with Sylvia, Kit set out for the warehouse again. Once they'd crossed the bridge and reached the top of King

Street, he halted and turned to her. "You go ahead—I have to deal with something, but I'll join you in ten minutes or so."

She looked faintly surprised, but nodded. "All right. I'll meet you at the warehouse."

He saw her across the street, then turned and strode for his bank. He needed a small mound of shillings.

When he reached the warehouse fifteen minutes later, he was vaguely aware he was clinking with every step. Ignoring that, he halted beside Sylvia near the door and scanned the almost-empty space.

She looked up with a pleased smile. "The last of the desks has gone on its way. We're almost finished. Just a few more packages of books." With her head, she indicated a small pile of packages trussed up with twine. "I have to admit I had no idea the boys had borrowed so many books from the lending library. Cross and Miss Meggs take the boys to exchange and borrow new books every week."

"Has it proved useful—the lending library?"

"Immensely. An adventure book is just the thing to help the boys learn to read."

Six of the older boys appeared, returning for their next loads.

"We're the last, Miss Buckleberry," one of the boys reported. "Mr. Jellicoe and Mr. Cross kept the others back to start unpacking and putting everything away."

"Excellent." Sylvia waved the group toward the pile of books. "Take one or two packages each—whatever you can safely carry. I sent Miss Meggs on, so please report to me as you go out."

"Yes, miss!" came the enthusiastic reply.

With Kit, Sylvia did a quick circuit of the warehouse while the boys picked over the book pile.

"There's nothing left but the books," Sylvia stated with satisfaction. "I wouldn't have believed we could move everything so quickly. Well," she temporized, "we wouldn't have if we'd had to move the desks without help." She caught Kit's eye. "Again, thank you."

You can thank me by not tarring me with an undeserved brush. Kit held the words back; he had no idea why her opinion of him should matter so much. All he knew was that it did. Smiling easily, he waved at the empty space. "This is my reward."

She smiled back, then crossed to the door.

As the boys, each laden with packages, trudged up to the door, Sylvia blinked at the leading pair; the two oldest lads were carrying three packages each, their arms wrapped awkwardly about the bundles. "Boys, are you sure you can manage those?"

"Yes, miss," the pair chorused. "We'll manage."

She hesitated, clearly unsure.

Standing behind her shoulder, Kit ducked his head and spoke softly, for her ears alone. "Let them go—they're trying to do what they think they should in clearing the place completely. We'll be following close behind, after all."

Sylvia nodded at the pair. "Just take care. If you get into difficulties, please wait, and we'll be along shortly."

Kit could have told her that was a futile instruction; the last thing the lads would want was for him to see them fail in their self-appointed task.

As the oldest lads departed, the other four trailed up to the door.

One boy fixed Kit with an eager look. "Is it true, then, your lordship, that there'll be food and cider for us all?"

Kit smiled. "Yes—for everyone who helped move the school, and that definitely includes all you boys."

The lad beamed, then turned to the boy behind him. "Told you. His lordship's no pinchpenny."

With a confident smile for Kit, the first boy led the way out, those behind him looking grateful and eager as well.

"You've made friends there," Sylvia commented.

Kit glanced at her and arched a brow. "Boys are easy to bribe—food almost always works."

She chuckled, then looked at the book pile; only two packages remained. "We can take those, and then, I believe, you will have your wish—the warehouse properly and thoroughly vacated and ready for your men to move in."

Kit crossed to the packages and hoisted both up, tucking them under one arm. "I didn't imagine we'd be this efficient, either, so we'll have to wait until morning for the delivery of the timbers we'll need, but come morning, we'll be here."

His heart lifted at the thought.

He followed Sylvia out of the open doors and helped her tug them shut. She secured the simple latch with the padlock, turned the key, then offered it to him. "I believe this is now yours."

Kit accepted the key and dropped it into his pocket. "Thank you."

In companionable mood, they set out to catch up with the boys.

Sylvia found herself inwardly marveling. Not just at the fact they'd managed to move the school, lock, stock, and barrel, in just one morning, but also that the transfer had run so smoothly.

A boon she was well aware she owed to the man striding so easily beside her.

She glanced sidelong at him—just a quick glance, enough to take in his relaxed, confident, and assured expression. Just long enough to sense again the tug on her senses. That hadn't abated with exposure, much as she'd hoped it would; he remained a lodestone for her senses, for her attention. Indeed, if anything, the result of spending more time in his company had only increased the intensity of what, in her view, remained a dangerous attraction.

For as long as she'd been aware of it—from the first month of her London Season—Kit Cavanaugh's reputation had painted him as a charming, dangerously flirtatious nobleman, one who was wealthy but indolent, who meant nothing by anything he said, and who was very much a care-for-naught—the sort of gentleman all sane young ladies and all careful parents avoided like the plague.

Yet the man by her side was none of that.

He definitely wasn't the gentleman she'd met at Felicia's wedding…or perhaps he was the same, but she'd assumed he was quite different.

The Kit Cavanaugh she'd seen over the past days was a gentleman of a very different stripe.

The sort of gentleman who could be good company, but who had a serious side. A practical side. On top of that, he seemed to know how to deal with people, especially those not of his class.

She'd met enough aristocrats to know that wasn't a widely held talent.

Quite what she thought of the Kit Cavanaugh who was walking beside her, she wasn't entirely sure.

Was what he was now showing her of him real? Or was this the façade?

Four

"Careful." Kit gripped Sylvia's elbow to steer her safely across the cobbles of King Street.

His touch sent thrills lancing up her arm; her breath caught, but he gave no sign of noticing, and once they'd reached the wider expanse of Broad Quay, he released her and resumed his steady pacing alongside her.

She decided she was not going to look his way; instead, she surveyed the pedestrians before them. "I haven't yet caught sight of the boys—they must have rushed ahead."

It was close to noon, and the crowds on the quay limited how far she could see.

Head raised, Kit was scanning the throng. "A couple of the boys are approaching the bridge."

As she and Kit neared the drawbridge over the Frome, she got a clear view of the two oldest lads; more heavily burdened, the pair were trudging doggedly along. The other boys with their lighter loads must have gone ahead; there was no sign of them. As by Kit's side, she wove through the crowd, making for the steps leading up to the drawbridge, she saw the two lads struggle up the stone steps, heave their loads higher in their arms, and tramp out onto the wooden span.

She and Kit were almost at the steps when she heard a loud hail.

Looking up at the bridge, she saw the two school lads being bailed up by a gang of older youths. The four youths pushed and taunted the two schoolboys; it was blatantly apparent that

the gang thought to enliven their day by making the younger
lads drop their precious packages over the bridge's railing into
the churning waters below.

"Oh, no!" Sylvia tensed to run forward, but Kit thrust the
packages he'd been carrying at her feet, all but tripping her.

"Wait here and watch those."

She had little choice as he strode to the rescue, taking the steps
up to the bridge in two strides, then descending on the pack of
louts like an avenging angel.

The gang saw him coming and paused, instantly recognizing a predator of much higher status than they. But they didn't
back away from the schoolboys. Instead, the youths waited, as-
suming Kit—who, whatever he wore or wherever he was, carried his status like a mantle—would stride disinterestedly past
and leave their victims to them.

Kit assessed the situation with a keen eye, then veered to halt
behind the two schoolboys. He dropped a hand on each lad's
shoulder. "Is there some problem here?"

He directed the question to the lout he judged to be the leader
of the gang, a gangling youth of perhaps seventeen years.

Kit allowed his gaze to dwell, coldly, on the youth's pasty
face and waited with icy calm.

Beneath his hands, he felt the two school lads straighten, confidence returning. One of them said, "Don't rightly know what
this lot want with us."

"Indeed?" Kit arched a brow at the gang leader. "Perhaps
you'd like to enlighten us."

The other members of the gang started to edge away. The
leader glanced around, then swung back to face Kit and swallowed. "Ah…no. No problem." The youth licked his lips and
added, "We was just asking if they perhaps needed a hand with
them packages, is all, sir."

Kit allowed a shark-like smile to curve his lips. "It's not 'sir'—
it's 'my lord.' And how kind of you to volunteer to help."

The youth's eyes flew wide. "Wot?"

But Kit was already speaking to the schoolboys. "We have six packages and, all together, I see six lads before me." He patted the schoolboys' shoulders encouragingly. "Let's pass the packages around to these helpful lads, and we'll be at the school that much faster. Here—let me help."

Kit plucked a package out of the arms of one of the schoolboys and pushed it into the chest of the gang leader.

Instinctively, the youth grabbed the package.

Before his mates could flee, Kit pointed at them and beckoned. "Come along—don't be shy."

In less than a minute, each of the gang members was clutching one of the packages.

"Let's get moving, then." Kit waved the six toward the other end of the bridge. "Boys"—he caught the eyes of the two school lads—"why don't you lead the way?"

Leaving him to pace behind the gang members.

Now carrying only one package each, the schoolboys happily took off, and reluctantly, with an almost disbelieving air, the gang fell in behind them.

Kit watched for an instant, then turned to fetch Sylvia and the packages he'd been carrying—only to discover her a yard away with the packages at her feet.

She met his eyes, and the amused smile on her face was something to see—a sight he hadn't seen before but wanted to see more often. He frowned, wondering where that thought had come from. "You shouldn't have struggled with those."

"They weren't that heavy, just unwieldy." Sylvia nodded to where the four youths were lagging and casting glances over their shoulders. "And you'll need to keep up with that lot if we want those books to reach the school."

He grunted. Settling the two packages under his arm again, he fixed his gaze on the gang members, who immediately faced forward and picked up their pace. "Come on."

Sylvia fell in beside him.

As they descended the steps at the other end of the bridge, she glanced at his face. "They'll never forget that, you know." She meant not just the gang members but also the two lads from the school—the dockyard brats who'd had a lord stand up for them.

"That's a good thing, isn't it?" He sounded as if he wasn't entirely sure, then added, "I hope they'll also remember that bullying others can have unforeseen consequences."

"Indeed." She looked at the now-subdued youths walking ahead of them.

Her mind scrolled through several vignettes from the morning—of Kit helping some of the younger boys load up, of him answering questions from the avidly curious lads. After a moment, she ventured, "You deal well with children."

He lightly shrugged. "I was a boy once, too."

"Be that as it may, you seem to have retained the ability to interact with them, which not all adults do."

"Ah—that's the influence of Ryder and Mary's brood. I spent the last weeks with them, playing at being Uncle Kit." Briefly, he met her eyes, an amused smile in his. "Trust me when I say that my brother's children are a very much more difficult proposition to manage than your school lads and their ilk. Aside from all else, my niece and nephews aren't impressed by, much less cowed by, my rank."

She chuckled. "I hadn't thought of that—as the children of a marquess, they share the same rank as you."

"And they already have the confidence that goes with that."

They'd reached Trinity Street, and she looked ahead to see the four youths milling uncertainly on the pavement in front of the hall, the packages they'd carried still in their arms.

Kit had seen them, too. He touched a light hand to Sylvia's back. "Go inside and let me handle this."

The lads he'd rescued must have already been inside, and judging from the many boys who, their faces alight with smiles and wonder, came to the door to peek out at the gang, the tale of the school lads' rescue and the gang members' resulting discomfiture was already doing the rounds.

"Perhaps just have them stack the packages on the porch," Sylvia murmured.

Kit nodded and halted, facing the now-surly gang. Sylvia walked on and went up the steps and into the hall, gathering the younger boys who had been hanging about the door and shooing them deeper into the hall.

As soon as she'd passed inside, Kit tipped his head toward the porch. "Stack the packages there, and then I'd like a word."

Warily, the youths complied, then re-formed in a close knot on the pavement before Kit, who had set his packages at his feet.

"Right, then." He studied the four, who shifted and shuffled. He waited until they were completely still, then said, "The moral of this story is don't pick on others smaller or younger than yourselves. It's an easy rule to remember, and I trust you will, indeed, remember it from now on. I've taken up residence in the city, and should I hear of any of you being involved in a similar incident or anything worse, I'll make a point of taking it up with the local authorities. In a nutshell, whenever you're tempted to do something wrong, remember that there's always a chance that someone—like me—will be watching. Do you understand?"

They shuffled some more, but managed to mumble, "Yes, m'lord."

Kit wasn't entirely satisfied, but there was only so much he could do. "Very well. I believe you have somewhere else to be."

It took them a second to comprehend that they were being dismissed, then—still wary—they bobbed their heads and skirted around him, giving him a wide berth before, increasingly rapidly, walking back toward the river.

Kit watched them go, then inwardly shook his head. He'd been tempted to see if any of the four needed a job, but the likelihood was that all of them did, and he couldn't saddle Wayland and whoever he hired as foreman with all four.

Bending, Kit scooped up the packages he'd carried and carted them into the hall.

The scene inside was one of furious activity, with the hired men shifting desks into position and boys running this way and that, ferrying stools, unpacked books, slates, chalks, and all manner of educational impedimenta hither and yon. Jellicoe, Cross, and Miss Meggs were directing the scurrying ant-like flow.

Sylvia stood to one side, watching it all with a smile on her face.

Kit set down the last two packages on a desk. Miss Meggs sent him a distracted smile, then directed two boys to untie the strings.

Kit sauntered over to Sylvia. She glanced at him, and he was again struck by the immense difference between the woman now before him and the chilly, reserved lady he'd encountered at his brother's wedding. "I take it all is going well?" he asked.

"Astonishingly well." After a further moment of surveying the action, she said, "Once they get everything tidied away, I believe they'll have earned the rest of the day off."

"They have worked diligently."

A shadow darkened the door, and he and Sylvia turned to see the tavern keeper's wife bearing a huge tray laden with sandwiches.

Miss Meggs hurried forward. She waved the woman to a long trestle table set up along the front wall of the hall. "If you'll set everything down there…?"

With a grin at the boys and the men—who had all stopped to watch—the tavern wife came in and set down her burden. She was followed by three younger women carting pottery jars of cider and a basket of tin mugs. At the rear of the procession came a burly youth bearing another huge platter of sandwiches.

"There you go, your lordship." The tavern wife, having set

down her burden, turned to Kit with a huge smile. "Been a pleasure doing business, and if you need anything else, just send, and we'll deliver."

Kit smiled. "Thank you. This should be sufficient, but"—he tipped his head toward the boys, now gathering in an expectant pack and eyeing the sandwiches as if they were gold—"with a lot like this, one never knows."

"Aye, you have that right." The tavern wife beamed at the children, then looked shrewdly around. "A good idea, this— keeps them off the streets and teaches them their letters and hopefully"—she mock-glared at the boys—"some manners as well."

The entire platoon of boys adopted angelic expressions.

"Huh." The tavern wife turned from the boys and looked at Sylvia. "If you'd like, miss, me and Bertha can stay and take the platters and things away later. And we'll make sure there's no ruckus over the serving."

"Thank you. That would be a help." Sylvia motioned to Miss Meggs. "We'll get the boys in order and send them to you."

Kit found a stool against the wall, perched on it, and watched Sylvia and Miss Meggs, assisted by Jellicoe and Cross, marshal the boys into a queue in order of youngest to oldest.

Next came the men he'd hired, all good-naturedly grinning and chatting with each other and, occasionally, with the two teachers.

Once the boys and men had helped themselves, Sylvia waved Jellicoe, Cross, and Miss Meggs to the table, then looked at Kit.

He rose and ambled across to join her as she trailed at the end of the queue.

The platters of sandwiches had held up under the onslaught; there were still more than enough left to satisfy even Kit. Not that he was all that hungry; he'd enjoyed a substantial breakfast courtesy of Dalgetty, the male cook Gordon had hired, who had proved to have an excellent grasp of what men like Kit preferred to eat.

After helping himself to one of the substantial sandwiches and a mug of the sharp cider, he perched on a stool beside Sylvia and the teachers and Miss Meggs and ate.

Cross gestured at Kit with his sandwich. "Thank you, my lord. This sets the icing on our day."

"Indeed." Jellicoe tipped his head Kit's way. "I have to own to being amazed. I would never have imagined we could shift the entire school in less than a day. And with no fuss, much less major dramas." Jellicoe gestured widely with his mug. "This took teamwork—and is an excellent lesson for the boys in what can be accomplished when we all pull together."

The others, Kit included, nodded.

From the corner of his eye, he watched Sylvia nibble delicately on a sandwich…

He shifted on the stool and told himself to focus on something else.

Such as Cavanaugh Yachts and what more he could do to move things along.

The answer was: not a great deal at this moment in time.

Strangely, he felt comfortably resigned to that.

He'd been facing a day of frustrating inactivity as far as getting the workshop under way, but thanks to Sylvia and the school and all who had crossed his path that day, he was feeling content in the sense of having achieved something worthwhile.

He glanced around the hall—at the boys happily sitting cross-legged on the floor, at the men…

An earlier idea resurfaced in his mind.

He turned to Sylvia and the others. When they looked at him inquiringly, he tipped his head toward the men, gathered in a circle beyond the boys. "Do any of you know if any of those who've assisted us today are carpenters? Or for that matter, whether any of the boys' fathers or relatives are shipwrights or carpenters?"

Jellicoe replied, "I would say almost certainly, but we tend not to make a point of their fathers' occupations."

"That said," Miss Meggs put in, "I do know that several of the boys are only at the school because it's free, and their fathers aren't here now because they're out looking for work, as they are every day. Other men, sadly, have simply given up. What with the new iron ships and what I understand are changes in construction, a lot of the older shipwrights and carpenters have been out of work for years."

Kit nodded. "Those are the sort of experienced craftsmen my partner and I are seeking to hire." He transferred his gaze to Sylvia. "Would it be all right if I asked the boys to take home word of Cavanaugh Yachts and that we're hiring shipwrights and carpenters?"

"I can't see why not." Sylvia looked at Jellicoe, Cross, and Miss Meggs, who all looked as unperturbed by Kit's suggestion as she. She turned back to him. "By all means. The more boys with fathers employed, the better."

Kit grinned and polished off his sandwich. He drained his mug, then returned it to the trestle and continued deeper into the hall. After passing the boys with a general smile, he stopped by the men, seated on the floor; when they started to gather themselves to rise, he waved them back.

"First, to your wages." He drew the pouch of shillings from his pocket, crouched, counted out the coins, and paid each man.

All grinned and thanked him, genial and relaxed.

"Now, to further business." Kit returned the depleted pouch to his pocket. "My partner and I are starting up a yacht-building business in the old warehouse—that's why we had to move the school here. We're looking to hire shipwrights and carpenters—those skilled in assembling wooden hulls." He now had the men's avid attention—and that of the boys, their ears wagging as well;

he included the latter group with a glance. "If you know of any craftsmen with experience in those fields, then my partner—Mr. Wayland Cobworth—would be happy to see them at the warehouse from tomorrow. We'll be starting work then, fitting out the warehouse as our workshop."

The men exchanged glances, then one of them said, "We'll pass the word around. Some may be interested."

Kit nodded and rose. "Thank you." He looked at the tavern wife and her nearly empty table. "By all means take any food left over—we wouldn't want it to go to waste."

The men grinned and scrambled to their feet. "Aye, m'lord." One saluted him. "We'll head off now, if all's done?"

Kit consulted Sylvia, then they stood together on the porch and waved the men away.

At a call for a moment's assistance from Miss Meggs, Kit ducked back inside.

The tavern wife and her daughter, carrying the empty platters and jugs and the basket of mugs, appeared in the doorway.

Sylvia stepped aside to allow them to pass. "Thank you for that feast."

"Our pleasure, miss," the tavern wife replied. "If you've ever the need for the like again, just stop in—we're only around the corner on the Butts."

Sylvia assured the woman that she would remember, then stood and watched the pair walk off up the street. She was about to turn inside when her attention snagged on an older lady, garbed head to toe in black bombazine, who was standing poker straight behind the gate of a house farther up the street. The woman was staring fixedly at the school. There was something in the concerted focus of the woman's stare that left Sylvia with the impression it was more of a glare.

After a moment, she mentally shrugged, turned, and went into the hall.

"I can't believe we're almost done!" Miss Meggs appeared and

showed Sylvia the long list of activities the assistant had com-
piled, each now struck through. Miss Meggs looked to where Kit
was assisting Cross and Jellicoe in placing the big blackboards,
which, given that the hall was properly leased, they could now
leave in situ. Miss Meggs lowered her voice. "I have to say I was
surprised to see his lordship…well, get his hands dirty, as it were.
One would have thought he would hold himself above carting
books and slates and fiddling with blackboards."

One would. Sylvia studied Kit. "He enjoys it, I think." He'd
certainly seemed to, and the readiness with which he'd helped
had earned him an acceptance among all at the school—and with
the hired men, too—he wouldn't otherwise have had.

Finally, the blackboards were positioned and every last book,
slate, and piece of chalk had been put in its proper place. Jellicoe
and Cross declared themselves satisfied that all was in readiness
to commence lessons the next day.

The boys cheered.

Then Sylvia called them to attention and announced that, in
light of their sterling efforts, given all was as it needed to be for
the school to carry on, she believed the boys could be excused
for the day.

The cheer her words elicited rattled the rafters.

"Very well, boys," Jellicoe said. "You've heard Miss Buckleberry. Off you go, and make sure you're here on time tomorrow morning."

With whoops and more cheers, the boys headed for the door
and streamed out and away.

Kit waited while Sylvia consulted with Jellicoe and Cross,
then farewelled Miss Meggs. He followed the teachers and Sylvia out of the door.

She locked up and held out the key to Jellicoe. "I'll call some-
time tomorrow to see if anything has cropped up."

"I can't see what will." Jellicoe accepted the key, then glanced
at Kit and smiled. "We now have a stable place to call home,

and Cross and I, and Meggs, too, are determined to make the most of it."

Kit returned the smile and lightly touched Sylvia's back, urging her down the steps before him. He'd had other motives—ulterior motives—beyond helping the school, yet that ambition had grown during the day to be significantly more important than it had been that morning.

Miss Meggs had already hurried up the street toward the Abbey. After noting her dwindling figure, the rest of them turned toward the river.

They ambled along in the westering light, a sense of contentment—of achievement—wrapping about the four of them. They turned left into the street that followed the river—the Butts, as it was called. A little farther on, they passed the churchyard of St. Augustine's Church and continued into the section of street known as St. Augustine's Back. Kit and Sylvia parted from Jellicoe and Cross just before the drawbridge. The teachers entered a tall lodging house, while Kit and Sylvia continued to the steps and climbed onto the bridge.

They paused by the railing to watch a ship steaming down the Frome, then walked on.

"When you were talking to the men," Sylvia said, "you mentioned a partner—a Mr. Cobworth."

Kit nodded. "Wayland Cobworth. He's an old school friend from Eton days and has become a designer of yachts. He and I share a passion for ocean-going yachts and have for more than a decade, so when I decided building yachts was what I wanted to do, finding Wayland and convincing him to become my partner was the obvious next step." He caught her eyes and smiled. "You can't build yachts without a designer, and Wayland is world-class."

She lightly frowned. "Was he the man you were chasing in the West Indies when Rand and Felicia announced their engagement?"

"Yes—I was in Bermuda when the letter telling me of their impending nuptials reached me. I had to leap on the next ship to make it back in time, but luckily, by then, I'd persuaded Wayland to throw in his lot with mine." Kit glanced in the direction of the warehouse. "He had to remain for several more weeks, but he followed and arrived last week. He's been spending the day interviewing men for the business."

She looked at him curiously. "You're not involved?"

His lips twitched into a grin. "Wayland and I make a good team—we have complementary skills. He's a superb designer and knows to a T what sort of craftsmen we need and which particular supplies, tools, and timbers. As a designer, a creator, he's exacting and precise, but he's hopeless at organizing beyond that sphere—dealing with suppliers, bankers, invoices and wages, investors, and all that sort of thing. He's too impatient—he just wants to build yachts."

She nodded. "All the day-to-day decisions and actions." She glanced at his face. "That's not so very different to my role with the school."

He inclined his head. "Indeed, it's very much the same. You organize, and Jellicoe and Cross teach. I organize, and Wayland designs and builds."

"And when it comes to selling what you build?"

"That will be mostly up to me, with Wayland enthusing in the background." His fond smile fading, he glanced at her. "I can't tell you how thrilled Wayland was at the prospect of getting into the warehouse a day early. He's champing at the bit to start transforming the space into our workshop, so that when the bulk of the men he's hiring turn up on Monday, he'll have everything ready to start laying our first keel."

They'd reached the front of the building that housed Kit's office. He halted and looked at her. "Which way are you headed?"

"Home." She waved farther along King Street. "I live not far away, and with the school ready but shut, there's nothing more I need to do today."

He waved her on. "I'll see you home."

Sylvia hesitated for only a second, then inclined her head in acceptance. "Thank you." Were this London, any gentleman of his class would make the same offer, and any lady with her head on her shoulders would acquiesce. Viewed in that light, him escorting her home didn't mean anything beyond simple courtesy, something she suspected that, in him, was ingrained.

Side by side, they strolled on along King Street, the soft sunshine of the afternoon laying gently across their shoulders.

He'd slipped his hands into his greatcoat pockets and was looking down at the pavement before them. "I also want to thank you—and the school—for the chance to reach out to the sort of craftsmen Wayland and I most need to contact. That was a bonus."

Smiling at his earnestness, she looked ahead. "I think all associated with the school would say that you've earned any advantage the school community can hand you."

He shrugged. "It wasn't that much—it was easy for me to do." He glanced briefly at her. "It was you who showed me the way—who opened my door and laid the opportunity at my feet. I just picked it up."

She suppressed a snort, but there was no real way to counter that argument.

She wasn't even sure she wanted to. It was close enough to the truth, yet...

She was starting to realize he had a habit of self-deprecation, of making light of what he did—often, it seemed, because he was wealthy and matters were easy for him to arrange. Because his assistance cost him nothing beyond money he could readily afford.

But was it correct to discount his contribution purely because it was easy for him to make?

She suspected her father would say not and, instead, maintain that the actions of men possessed the same intrinsic value regardless of wealth.

They reached the corner of King Street and Back Street, and she waved to their left. "It's this way."

As they strolled on, she asked, "Have you seen Rand and Felicia recently?"

He nodded. "After the wedding, I stayed at Raventhorne Abbey, and they visited several times—their last visit was just before I left to come here." He glanced at her face. "They're both well." After a moment, he asked, "Does Felicia know you live here—in Bristol?"

She blinked, then, considering the question, frowned. "I honestly don't know. I've mentioned the school—she knows all about that and my association with it—but I'm not sure I've actually told her I've removed to Bristol myself." She glanced briefly his way and met his caramel eyes. "I do know she sent news of her wedding to my home in the country—my father sent it on."

"And where is your home in the country?"

"Saltford. It's a small town on the Bath Road between Bristol and Bath. My father has the living there." She glanced at him. "Do you have a house in the country you call home?"

He looked ahead. "Not as such. The Abbey is now Ryder and Mary's home and purely a place to visit."

"No house in London?" She imagined a London rakehell of his wealth would definitely have a house in town.

"I used to share lodgings with Rand, but now... If I want to stay in town, I'll just use my room in Raventhorne House in Mount Street." His lips twisted wryly. "Truth to tell, I avoid London as much as I can."

"You do?" That surprised her. "Why?"

He looked at her, meeting her gaze. "The more pertinent question would be: Why wouldn't I?" When, at a loss, she blinked at him, he elaborated, "There's nothing that attracts me in London, much less holds my interest. No yacht-building. No sailing of that sort." He shrugged and looked at the pavement again. "Nothing I fancy."

Nothing he fancied? Sylvia might have thought he was pulling her leg, but he looked and sounded utterly sincere and combined with what she'd seen of him and learned of him that day...

She was starting to suspect her earlier opinion of Kit Cavanaugh had been not just inaccurate but comprehensively in error.

Which raised the tantalizing prospect of who the man beside her truly was—what manner of man he actually was.

Pondering that, she gestured to the left. "My lodging house is this way, on the far side of the park."

He turned with her, then asked, "Tell me what you know of the Dock Company."

That didn't take long, but his subsequent questions about the city, about the atmosphere now that, with the advent of larger, heavier ships, the dock work was shifting downriver, displayed an inherent grasp of what made communities tick and prosper.

"So," he said, "the mayor and the city council are stable and entrenched, but are floundering regarding the adjustments necessary to meet the challenges confronting the city."

She tipped her head. "That's a reasonable summation. As yet, there's been no major public protests, but from time to time, the mood turns rather ugly—or should I say dejected?"

He nodded in understanding. "The latter sounds nearer the mark."

"This is it." Sylvia paused outside the gate of the terrace house in which she lodged and turned to face the man she had for years regarded as her romantic nemesis; thankfully, he would never know. She put out her hand. "Thank you for your escort."

He looked down at her hand—and for an instant, she was sure a hint of the wolf she'd seen in London peeked through—but then he grasped her fingers, engulfing them in his much larger hand, and gently shook. He caught her eyes and smiled—

a charming, Lord Kit Cavanaugh smile. "The pleasure of your company was thanks enough." He released her hand and stepped back, faultlessly executing a graceful bow that consigned every other man in Bristol to the shade. "A good afternoon to you, Miss Buckleberry. No doubt we'll meet again soon."

With a lingering smile and a nod, he turned and walked away.

Sylvia watched him go, amazed by the fact that, against odds she'd thought insurmountable, she and the man behind Kit Cavanaugh's handsome face had reached a comfortable, even companionable, accord.

★ ★ ★

Kit reached the warehouse before eight o'clock the next morning, eager to meet the men Wayland had hired to commence work on transforming the building into the Cavanaugh Yachts workshop—their next step in creating the yacht-building enterprise they wanted their company to be.

Wayland was already there, waiting outside and as eager as Kit to welcome their new employees; Wayland leaned against the door as Kit unlocked it. "I concentrated on finding the best possible foreman, and I think I succeeded in that. Mulligan has experience from clipper days and has even worked on several yachts. He understood everything I spoke of, which you must admit is encouraging."

Kit grinned as he hauled the doors open. Most men found Wayland's descriptions and directions difficult to interpret, rendered in specialized jargon as they were.

Together, he and Wayland propped the doors wide, then returned to stand shoulder to shoulder on the threshold, looking out.

"And *then*," Wayland said, rocking on his heels, "I asked Mulligan to help me select four carpenters to make up a senior team to work under him." Wayland's grin grew wider. "Best decision I've made in years. We had the right men in a trice. All were out of work thanks to the switch to iron ships, and they're as eager to leap into yacht-building as we are."

"Excellent!" Kit saw five large men rolling along the lane toward them. "What wages did you offer?"

Wayland named a sum for the carpenters and a larger figure for Mulligan.

"Fair, indeed generous, but not outrageous." Kit tipped his head in approval. "Good work."

Wayland shrugged. "If all goes well, these men will be the core of our workforce, and given their experience, it seemed wise to make them feel valued."

Kit nodded as the five men reached them.

Wayland bade the five welcome, shook their hands, then introduced Kit as "Kit Cavanaugh, the majority partner in the business."

Kit offered his hand as well. To Kit, his title was neither here nor there, and better the men got to know him before they learned of it; in his experience—and Wayland's—people held a lot of preconceived notions about the nobility that he would be happy to avoid if he could. He echoed Wayland's welcome and added his hopes that, through developing Cavanaugh Yachts into a thriving business, they would all prosper.

"That's certainly our hope, sir," Mulligan rumbled. The largest of the group, he was a heavily built man of indeterminate age with a virtually bald pate circled by a narrow tonsure of graying brown hair. His features were florid—as were those of all the men—but not in the way of men who overindulged in drink. Rather, their ruddy complexions had come courtesy of wind whipping off water and working outdoors.

The other men were Shaw, Hodgkins, Miller, and Boots. Once the introductions and welcomes were behind them, Kit said, "I'll pay you this afternoon for your work today, at our agreed rates. I'm hoping that by next Friday, we'll have a secretary in place, and she'll disburse all wages every Friday afternoon."

The men nodded, and Mulligan said, "Thank ye, sir—that's good to know."

All five men looked eagerly, almost longingly, into the warehouse.

Smiling, Wayland turned, spread his arms wide, and walked inside. "Right, then. This is to be a modern workshop expressly tooled to build ocean-going yachts. To that end—"

Kit stood back and watched and listened as Wayland described his vision of the workshop, with words and gestures bringing offices and hull-frames and a gantry of pulleys to life. Mulligan asked a sensible question, which caused Wayland to pause and explain. Emboldened by the easy way Wayland responded, several of the others posed further questions. Kit grinned. It was clear Wayland had, indeed, gathered a group of men who would form a tight-knit crew and work with him and Kit in transforming their dream into a reality.

At the end of his exposition, Wayland showed the men the new tools he'd assembled and arranged on the floor along the far side of the warehouse, then pointed out the stacks of timbers he'd begged and pleaded and managed to have delivered late yesterday—solid beams for the gantries, and pieces of various sizes for supports, frames, and struts.

The men pored over the tools like children on Christmas Day.

Wayland whipped out his notebook and asked what else they would need.

Several requests came for certain types of wood files, and two smaller saws and more vises. Wayland jotted it all down.

Then Mulligan, who, with the others, had been crouching and examining the tools, rose and, planting his massive hands on his hips, turned to Wayland. "Seems like the very first things we need to build are racks to hold all these tools. Can't keep them on the floor like this—they'll end damaged."

"Ah." Wayland hesitated. Kit knew his partner had assumed they would immediately start on framing the offices, but then Wayland nodded. "I hadn't thought of that, but you're right. So—tool racks first. Then"—he looked at Mulligan—"I thought we could rough-in the frames for the offices before starting work on the gantry. Once we have that up, two men could continue working on the offices while the rest of us make a start on the frame for our first keel."

Mulligan mulled, then nodded. "That should work." He looked at the others. "Right, lads. Let's get to it."

Wayland had already draped his coat over a pile of wood closer to the door.

Kit shrugged out of his coat, laid it with Wayland's, and started rolling up his sleeves.

"So," Wayland said, also rolling up his sleeves, "you have six men to put to work."

Mulligan was bent over, sorting timber. At that, he looked up. "Six?" Then he saw Wayland's and Kit's preparations, and his brows rose. "You two want to work in with us?"

"If you'll have us," Kit replied. "We each have two hands, and both of us have some small experience in carpentry."

Along with the other men, Mulligan stared at them for a moment, then Mulligan snorted. "I won't say no—we've a lot to do, and you two are the bosses, after all. But"—his eyes twinkled—"p'rhaps you'd better leave the hammering to us. I suspect you'll need your thumbs."

Once the chuckles from the men and the resigned looks from Kit and Wayland had faded, they got to work on two racks for the tools.

Within half an hour, Mulligan and the team had forgotten about Kit and Wayland being the bosses and were treating them like apprentices, which made Wayland and Kit grin.

Every now and then, some hopeful carpenter would turn up at the open door, and Wayland and Mulligan would go and chat to them and decide whether or not they were of the right caliber to join the workforce of Cavanaugh Yachts. Mulligan had suggested and Kit and Wayland had agreed that any employees they hired that day would start on Monday.

"Too many cooks, otherwise," Mulligan had said.

After two hours' hard work, Wayland paused, then looked at Mulligan. "Why not put these racks on wheels? Then we can move them around the hulls. I'd hope to have at least two hulls in progress at any given time, and it's likely we'll have another being polished off." Wayland waved around them. "We've space enough for three."

Mulligan slowly nodded. "That's not a bad idea."

They worked out the logistics, then Kit and Wayland left to purchase two sets of large iron wheels, four wheels for each rack.

As they rolled the heavy wheels, lashed together, back to the warehouse, Wayland said, "I can barely believe we've actually made a start—that we've managed to get this far this fast and all relatively smoothly."

"Don't jinx us," Kit replied. "But yes—it's..." He realized he was lost for words to describe the effervescent enthusiasm coursing his veins.

"Uplifting," Wayland supplied. "I feel positively giddy."

Kit laughed. They reached the cobbled lane along the Grove and had to slow, wrestling the wheels along.

While laughing with Wayland at their efforts to keep the wheels heading more or less in the right direction, Kit was struck by how simply happy he was.

Their enterprise was progressing step by steady step, and everything was, thus far, going well. There'd been nothing about the day that he would choose to change.

His mind slid sideways to whether Sylvia and the school were also having a good day—their first in their new premises.

Her intention in storming into his office on Wednesday morning hadn't been to assist him in getting to where he now was, yet in reality, her tempestuous arrival had been a critical juncture in the evolution of Cavanaugh Yachts.

Wayland and Mulligan had been enthused by the quality of men turning up at the workshop door, largely sent their way by connections associated with the school.

"I hadn't realized we had so many men who'd worked on the old ships still here," Mulligan had said. "I'd thought a lot had moved on, but seems they've just been waiting and hoping."

They were close to having a full roster of men—all experienced hands.

Kit couldn't help but think that, despite her former prickliness and regardless of her intentions in storming into his office, Sylvia Buckleberry had contributed significantly to easing the path for Cavanaugh Yachts.

Five

At noon on Friday, Sylvia set out to call at the school, ostensibly to check on the state of supplies, but in reality, to see how everything was going and to reassure herself that everyone was settling into their new home.

She felt a happy thrill on setting eyes on the hall—solid and respectable, a much better place for the school, for teaching the boys that, with education and application, they, too, could aspire to inhabit such an area.

She opened the door and stepped inside to find lunchtime in progress—the boys seated cross-legged on the floor, munching whatever they'd brought from home and on the apples the school, through the good offices of Miss Meggs, provided. The boys were listening to Cross, who was perched on a stool and reading aloud from a boys' adventure novel.

All heads turned her way, and happy smiles spread across every face.

Closing the door behind her, Sylvia smiled back. It was transparently clear that the members of her small school community were reveling in their new surrounds.

She crossed to where Miss Meggs sat behind one of the unused desks. Sylvia caught the assistant's eye. "All in order?"

"Indeed, Miss Buckleberry." Miss Meggs's smile said it all. "We're all so much more comfortable here." She nodded toward the boys, who had returned their attention to Cross. "They've settled right in and have been behaving themselves and, I would say, paying even greater attention to their lessons. Mr. Jellicoe,

Mr. Cross, and I were saying just before that the change of venue seems to have convinced them that what they learn could truly make a difference."

Sylvia nodded. "One of those intangible effects, but all to the good."

"Indeed."

The door at the rear of the hall opened, and Jellicoe came in. He saw Sylvia, nodded and smiled in greeting, then strolled around the hall to join her.

Sylvia turned to Miss Meggs. "Do you need any further supplies?"

"Actually, yes." The assistant started hunting through the papers on her desk. "I've been making a list... Ah, here it is." She handed Sylvia a note with several items listed. "Just some chalks and more ink."

Sylvia took the list, scanned it, then tucked it into her reticule. "I'll probably call in on Monday—I'll bring them then."

Jellicoe halted beside her, his expression conveying his satisfaction. "Next time you see Lord Cavanaugh, do pass on our profound thanks for our change of scenery." He grinned. "It's reawakened our enthusiasm—and not just ours, but theirs, too." He tipped his head toward their pupils, then drew out his watch, consulted it, and tucked the timepiece back into his waistcoat pocket. "Time to get back to our lessons."

A sharp rap on the front door had him pausing. "Hello," he said, as the door opened to reveal a somewhat rotund gentleman. "Who's this?"

The gentleman paused on the threshold. He carried a cane and wore a short top hat, and his striped waistcoat strained to remain decently anchored over his stomach. After several seconds of surveying the scene—Cross had stopped reading and, along with the boys, was silently staring at the stranger—the gentleman harrumphed and, in a manner that screamed self-importance, walked in.

Sylvia moved to intercept him. "Can I help you, sir?"

The gentleman's gaze, which had fixed on Jellicoe, shifted to her. A slight frown drew the man's brows down. "And you are?"

Sylvia did not like his tone, but kept an assured smile on her face. "Miss Buckleberry. I'm the school's administrator."

"Are you, indeed?" The man looked faintly surprised, then his earlier, somewhat peevish expression returned. "In that case, Miss Buckleberry, it is, indeed, you to whom I wish to address my most strident protest over this school being moved into this area."

Planting his cane between the toes of his boots and leaning on it, the gentleman glowered—at Sylvia, then at all those behind her, the boys especially. Sylvia could almost see the horrid man's lip curl.

She drew herself up. "And you are, sir?" Her tone had turned decidedly frosty.

"I, Miss Buckleberry, am Councilor Peabody." The man returned his gaze to her face and, as if the words gave him license to crush all there, triumphantly added, "Councilor for this ward." He rolled on, "And I am here to tell you that siting a school such as this in this neighborhood is entirely unacceptable. My constituents don't want dockside brats running amok around their houses. All well and good to bring education to the poor, but institutions such as this should remain in their proper place—in this case, by the docks."

Sylvia had encountered men like Peabody before. With icy calm, she met his gaze and arched her brows. "Indeed? Tell me, does the Abbey fall within your ward?"

Peabody nodded with smug satisfaction. "It does, indeed. The Abbey and all the surrounding streets."

"In that case, sir, I'm surprised you haven't realized that this hall belongs to the Abbey. The school couldn't be here had the Abbey not agreed to lease us the hall."

Peabody blinked. After a silent second, he blustered, "Clearly, the prior had no notion of what manner of school he was accommodating." Peabody's gaze returned accusingly to Sylvia. "You may be sure that I will bring the matter to his attention immediately, and then you and this school will be out on your collective ear."

Sylvia walked forward, forcing Peabody to turn to keep her in sight—to turn toward the door. "If you wish, sir, by all means, do speak with Prior Robert, but I assure you he knows precisely what manner of school this is. He even went so far as to offer the services of the Abbey infirmarian, should we ever require medical assistance." She continued walking slowly toward the door, drawing the obnoxious Peabody with her. "I have to say that I myself would be reluctant to suggest that Prior Robert had leased us the building without convincing himself of our bona fides."

That gave Peabody pause. His expression grew faintly concerned. "I… Ah, yes. I take your point." But then he rallied and straightened. "Be that as it may, secularly speaking, having a school such as this bringing dockside brats into this neighborhood cannot be borne. The residents won't stand for it—and I certainly won't."

He'd worked himself into a lather of righteous indignation again. Sylvia hesitated for only a second before saying, "As to that, sir, we will have to disagree, but before you think to mount any major push against the school, you might like to know that the school exists under the auspices of the Dean of Christ Church and has the financial backing of Lord Christopher Cavanaugh, who has recently taken up residence in the city. As a member of the nobility, Lord Cavanaugh follows the lead given by Prince Albert and our Queen regarding the education of those less fortunate in order to ensure the prosperity of the nation as a whole."

Peabody had been trailing beside her toward the door. Now, he halted on the threshold, his eyes widening. "Lord Cavanaugh?"

"Yes." Sylvia saw no reason not to gild the school's lily. "His brother is the Marquess of Raventhorne. I understand the marquess and his wife are known to Prince Albert and the Queen, and one of the marquess's other brothers is also associated with the Prince via their shared interest in inventions. Lord Christopher Cavanaugh's interest lies in building yachts, and he's in the throes of establishing a new workshop on the docks—indeed, his workshop has taken over the school's previous premises off the Grove, and through that, Lord Cavanaugh elected to become the school's sponsor."

Peabody grunted. After a moment, he scowled and harrumphed. "Regardless of what his lordship thinks he's doing, I'm sure that, once I see him and recast the matter in its true light, he'll agree that this school should not be here." He flung a disparaging glance back at the boys, still sitting on the floor, silent and listening. Then he narrowed his eyes at Sylvia. "Off the Grove, you said?"

Eager to have him gone, she nodded. "The third warehouse from the corner of Princes Street. He'll either be there or at his office in that new building on King Street."

"Good. I will hunt him down and speak with him directly. We'll soon see this settled." Peabody faced forward and stepped onto the porch. "Mark my words, Miss Buckleberry"—he emphasized his declaration with a jab of his cane—"you will have to move your school from this neighborhood. It doesn't belong here."

With that parting shot, Peabody descended the steps, then, affecting his self-important swagger, strode toward the river and the docks beyond.

Sylvia was about to turn inside—to do what she could to repair the damage Peabody's words had doubtless wrought—when she noticed the severe-looking lady in black standing once more at her gate. As before, the lady was staring—it seemed malevolently—at the school, then she turned and, leaning heavily on her cane, stumped along the short path and up the steps to her front door and disappeared inside.

Inwardly shaking her head, Sylvia turned back into the hall to hear Jellicoe telling the boys, "You heard Miss Buckleberry tell the councilor where to find his lordship. After he spent all day yesterday helping us move here, what do you think his lordship is going to say to a suggestion the school ought to move somewhere else?"

The boys all grinned, and one called out, "His lordship will laugh and say no."

"Exactly." Cross had shut the book from which he'd been reading. He waved the boys up from the floor. "And now it's time we did right by his lordship and got back to our lessons."

The boys rose with alacrity and returned to their desks.

Sylvia watched Cross and Jellicoe, and even more the boys, settle back into their lessons with no hint of lingering anxiety; evidently, they all had unshakeable faith that Lord Cavanaugh would see off any threat from Peabody and his ilk.

She, too, had instinctively—without a single thought—assumed Kit would do just that and every bit as effectively as the boys might imagine. Not the slightest whisper of doubt over his support had risen in her mind; her trust had been instant and absolute.

Evidently, her recent experience of him had overwritten her previous assumptions and the distrust those had generated.

Like the boys and the teachers, her confidence in him and his support was rock-solid; she would own herself flabbergasted if Peabody made the slightest headway against Kit Cavanaugh.

Crossing to Miss Meggs, who was working on drawing up next week's timetable, Sylvia said, "I'll be on my way. I won't forget the chalk and ink, and I'll see you all on Monday." She caught Jellicoe's and Cross's eyes and nodded a farewell, then raised her voice and called, "Goodbye, boys. Enjoy your days off, and I'll see you all here on Monday."

"Yes, Miss Buckleberry!" they enthusiastically chorused.

With that happy sound ringing in her ears, Sylvia went out of the door, tugged it closed, and headed for her office.

★ ★ ★

After a break for lunch, Kit, along with Wayland, Mulligan, and the other four carpenters, started constructing Wayland's pulley gantry. They'd already trimmed the beams and struts to the correct sizes. Using ropes and smaller pulleys, they hauled one end of the first of the heavier beams up, then with four men anchoring the ropes, keeping the huge beam upright, Kit and Mulligan heaved and swore and shoved the base of the beam into place. The instant they had it correctly positioned, Wayland set a ladder against it and, with Kit and Mulligan steadying the beam, climbed up and quickly attached iron braces, locking the beam in place against one of the massive timber ribs of the old warehouse.

Wayland came down the ladder, moved it away, attached another set of braces at knee height, then stepped back and motioned for the men to release the ropes, which they slowly did.

Catching their breath, they all stared at the beam, standing straight and solid.

Wayland smiled widely. "Excellent!"

Mulligan and the carpenters grinned, as did Kit.

Wayland swung to face them. "As soon as you're ready, we can start on the second one."

The men mock-groaned, but they were soon wrestling the second beam into place, equally successfully.

There were six beams to be positioned, spaced in pairs down the workshop, three beams on each longer side. They'd got all six up and were discussing the logistics of hauling up and securing the crossbeams when a tap on the frame of the open doors drew their attention.

A small, round woman with gray hair pulled back in a tight bun stood peering into the workshop's gloom. "Lord Cavanaugh?"

Kit grabbed his coat and shrugged into it as Mulligan and the carpenters turned to stare at him. "Lord?" Mulligan asked.

Kit flashed them a grin. "For my sins." Settling his coat sleeves, he crossed to the woman. "Miss Petty—come in."

The previous afternoon, when he'd returned to his office after seeing Sylvia home, he'd found Miss Petty waiting. She'd been sent around by the labor exchange. He'd let her into the office and, after a quick discussion of her past experience—with a recently defunct ship-building firm—and the duties he would like her to fulfill, he'd hired her and considered himself blessed.

This morning, despite his early start, she'd been into the office before him; he'd left her organizing and ordering supplies and had told her to call at the workshop in the early afternoon to meet Mulligan and the senior carpenters and to see where she would be spending some of her hours each week.

She advanced, not tentatively but rather with a certain curiosity, her eyes sharp behind a pair of brass-rimmed spectacles as she looked up, taking in what they were working on. "A gantry, is it?"

"Indeed." Kit paused to glance back at the work in progress and noticed the struck look on Mulligan's and the other men's faces. Knowing Miss Petty's background, her comment hadn't struck Kit as odd, but meeting a woman with a lick of ship-building understanding had clearly surprised the others.

Grinning, Kit waved the men forward. "This is the company's new secretary, Miss Petty." Wayland smiled and came up, keen to make Miss Petty's acquaintance; the others followed, somewhat more bashfully, in his wake.

Kit made the introductions, then announced, "Miss Petty will be spending roughly half her time here." Kit gestured at the rough framework for the offices they'd already set in place. "She'll be sharing the front office with Mulligan. Miss Petty will be responsible for disbursing wages and paying any bills that get presented here, rather than to our office in King Street."

Miss Petty acknowledged Mulligan's and the others' bobbed heads with a serene smile and gentle nods, then said, "It will be a pleasure to work with a ship-building concern again. I was born in the city, and my father was a shipwright." She paused, then went on, "I should perhaps add that while I will not tolerate any disrespectful language being directed toward me, I am extremely good at not hearing things that are none of my business." She ended with a cheery smile that, together with her words, got the men relaxing again, and their chorus of "Pleased to meet you, miss" rang sincere.

"If you don't mind, your lordship, I'll just take some measurements in the office." Miss Petty gestured to the area in question. "Perhaps, Mr. Mulligan, you might show me what you have planned for the space, and once I have the measurements, I'll order whatever's necessary."

Mulligan looked strangely uncertain, but nodded. "Aye. We could do that."

He and Miss Petty moved toward the office.

With Wayland and the others, Kit started walking back to where the gantry struts lay spread on the floor.

A tentative rap on the warehouse door frame had Kit and Wayland glancing that way, then pausing.

A thin boy of about thirteen or fourteen stood in the open doorway, nervously shifting his weight from foot to foot. He cleared his throat and said, "Sir, can you tell me who to see about a job?"

The boy's piping tenor carried easily through the empty building. Mulligan and Miss Petty halted and turned to study the lad. The other men halted, too, and looked curiously his way.

The lad was tow-headed, and his clothes had seen better days, but he'd clearly made an effort to appear neat and as presentable as he could. Under the combined scrutiny, he stood with his chin up, but Kit noticed he was mangling a threadbare cap between his hands.

That hint of vulnerability made Kit walk across with an easy gait. "I'm one of the owners." His first impulse had been to tell the boy he should head to the school, but as he got closer, he glimpsed desperation and a hint of despair in the lad's face. "What sort of work were you looking for?"

The lad swallowed and, after a second, found his voice. "Anything, really. I can fetch and carry, and run messages and such." His gaze went past Kit to the racks of new tools now standing against the rear wall. The boy's eyes lit. "And I'm a dab hand at keeping tools in good nick. My da was a carpenter." The last was said with aching pride.

Kit didn't miss the past tense the boy had used.

Kit felt a tug on his sleeve and turned his head to find Mulligan beside him.

Raising his gaze from the boy, Mulligan jerked his head to the side. "If I could have a word, your lordship?"

Kit turned back to the boy to see his eyes flare wide—that *lordship* thing again. Kit nodded to the lad and said, "Wait here." With that, Kit followed Mulligan deeper into the warehouse. Kit felt fairly confident that while there was an outside chance of a job, the boy would remain, and Kit was reasonably certain there would be a story behind the boy's request and Mulligan was about to tell him of it.

Sure enough, Mulligan halted and, facing away from the door, caught Kit's eyes as Kit stopped beside him. "His name is Jack Deaver—Jack the Lad, we all call him. His father was a master carpenter, but he died a year or so ago in a fall from a ship in dry dock. Since then, Jack's been the only breadwinner in the family—he's the eldest of five, and his mother is near witless trying to make ends meet. Jack gets what work he can, but he and his mother both are too proud to take charity." Mulligan paused, then went on, "I heard that you'd funded the school that used to be here to move to a better hall. I'm guessing that means you're all for young'uns like Jack learning his letters and such.

But if you turn him away, he won't be going to that school—he can't. He has to do what he can to earn coin...and I'm thinking"—Mulligan looked intently at Kit—"that there's more than one sort of learning."

Mulligan nodded at the other men—all four of whom had ambled closer, watching and waiting. "Jack does have a feeling for working with wood—got that from his da, no doubt. Me and the others would be happy to take Jack under our wing. If he turns out to be even half the carpenter his old man was, he'll soon be worth his weight to us."

Kit tipped his head, his gaze holding Mulligan's as Kit narrowed his eyes in thought. Then he glanced at the other men and beckoned them nearer. Once they were close enough to hear, Kit quietly asked, "What about an apprenticeship? A formal one? Jack the Lad working under you, Mulligan, and you others, to learn the trade."

Mulligan blinked. Then he nodded, and the other men did, too. "That'd do nicely," Mulligan said. "He'll work hard for that—he's a good lad, and you won't find any man more determined and loyal."

Kit grinned and clapped Mulligan on the shoulder. "Right, then—let's tell him the good news."

On the way to the door, Kit paused beside Wayland to mention the notion of them taking on their first apprentice. Wayland had no objections; Kit hadn't imagined he would. Joining Mulligan at the door, Kit looked at Jack, who had, as instructed, remained precisely on the same spot.

Kit couldn't help smiling as he said, "You're in luck. Mulligan and the others need an apprentice to train under them. You're the first to come and ask, and the men have said they're willing to give you a chance."

Jack's eyes grew round. He glanced at Mulligan, then looked back at Kit. "But I'll get paid?"

"Aye, lad." Mulligan lightly cuffed Jack, then looked at Kit. "The same rates as any apprentice—right, my lord?"

Kit nodded. "Exactly." He waited for a moment, drinking in the dawning wonder in Jack's face, then asked, "So what do you say? Are you the lad we need as our apprentice?"

Jack's eyes lit. "Cor—too right I am, sir—your lordship!" Jack bobbed multiple times.

Kit laughed and set a hand on his shoulder. "In that case, welcome aboard." He glanced at Miss Petty. "Why don't you and Mulligan give Miss Petty your full name and let her sign you on to the payroll and work out your wages so you'll get them next Friday with the other men?" Kit nodded at the gantry struts that the others had gone back to assembling. "Then you can join us in putting the gantry together."

Leaving Mulligan to steer a dazed Jack to where Miss Petty stood waiting, Kit shrugged out of his coat, set it aside, and returned to assist Wayland and the other men.

Mulligan soon returned, with Jack the Lad in tow. As they worked, first Wayland, then Mulligan and the other men took to sending Jack to fetch and return tools. When Wayland asked Jack for an angle, Jack returned with a selection as Wayland hadn't specified.

Miss Petty seemed to be the only employee who viewed Jack as if she was as yet unconvinced of the wisdom of taking him on; Kit was aware of her hovering at the edge of the action, writing notes on what she needed to order for her and Mulligan's office as well as the larger office Wayland would make his design studio, yet also keeping a sharp eye on proceedings and on Jack especially.

Eventually, they reached the point of driving in the final large nails to lock the main section of the moveable gantry together. The four carpenters, together with Wayland and Kit, had to exert themselves to hold various struts tensioned and steady while the honors of driving in the nails fell to Mulligan.

"Better get the nails in quick," Wayland warned. "We can't hold everything in place for long without something shifting."

Mulligan nodded and hefted a hammer—one of middling weight.

Shaw saw and snorted. "Even you'll need something heavier. You'll want to drive through the struts in just one or two blows."

Mulligan looked at the hammer as if surprised it was the wrong one and grunted—then Jack was by his side, offering the heaviest hammer and reaching for the lighter one...

The lad had anticipated the need and had fetched the weightier tool.

Mulligan flicked a glance at Kit as he accepted the heavy hammer, then with well-placed blows, he efficiently drove the nails down, locking the gantry into its final rigid shape.

As soon as the last nail went in, Wayland released the strut he'd been holding and reached for a right-angle, and again, Jack was there, holding out the correct tool. Wayland nodded his thanks as he took it and quickly went over the corners of the gantry, then he sat back on his heels with a smile and a relieved sigh. "Perfect. Now we can get on."

After a while, Kit saw Miss Petty waiting and went over to speak with her. She had, he noticed, stopped watching Jack.

She held up her notebook as Kit approached. "I believe I have all the information I need, my lord. I'll get the necessary orders in first thing in the morning."

Kit nodded. "Good. If at all possible, push for delivery on Monday. We want to get this space fully transformed and functioning as soon as may be."

"I understand you expect more men to commence on Monday?"

"Yes. It would be helpful, perhaps, were you to spend at least half the day here, taking down details. Mulligan or Mr. Cobworth can help you with rates—not my forte, I fear."

"Of course, my lord. I'll pop into the office on Monday

morning and deal with anything urgent, then I'll make my way here."

A burst of general laughter had Kit glancing to where the men were working at attaching various anchors for wheels and pulleys to the gantry prior to hoisting it into position above their heads. The men were still chuckling, and from the direction of their gazes, it was clear the source of merriment was Jack. But the men weren't laughing at him but with him, and from the pleased smile on Jack's face, he knew it.

Kit surmised Jack had made some comment that had elicited the laughter. In an environment in which activity could sometimes become intense, that wasn't a bad talent to have.

Beside him, Miss Petty cleared her throat. "I have to say that although I harbored reservations, Jack seems a worthwhile addition to the crew."

"He does, indeed." Kit noticed a gentleman sporting a cane— one more for show than use—walking briskly toward the workshop door. "Who's this, I wonder?"

Miss Petty looked, then swept around. "I will ask, my lord. One moment."

Bemused, Kit watched as Miss Petty sailed up as the gentleman, seeing her coming, halted just outside the open doors. Straining his ears over the steady din of hammering, Kit heard Miss Petty inquire, "Can I help you, sir?"

The gentleman looked rather peeved to have been forestalled, but he offered, "Councilor Peabody to see Lord Cavanaugh. It's about the school."

"Please wait here, and I will inquire as to whether his lordship is available." Miss Petty swung around and walked toward Kit, her eyes widening in question.

Realizing that his remarkable secretary was giving him a chance to avoid the man, Kit sent her a nod of thanks and moved forward, passing her on his way to the door.

Fetching up before the shorter man, Kit arched his brows. "Lord Cavanaugh. What did you wish to say about the school?"

"My name is Peabody, my lord—Councilor Peabody." Peabody sketched a bow, then straightened and fixed Kit with a man-to-man look. "I have the honor of being the councilor for Abbey Ward, into which neighborhood the school that previously occupied this warehouse has moved. I spoke with the school administrator this morning, and she directed me to you— she claimed you have agreed to stand as sponsor to the school?"

Kit inclined his head. "I have."

Peabody looked ingratiating. "I understand that you have underwritten the transfer of the school to its new premises and that Prior Robert—a godly man with scant experience of secular matters—at your petition, agreed to the school moving into the Abbey's hall. However, I suspect no one in the city has yet made known to you the…ah, community expectations that apply in various areas. For instance"—Peabody gestured widely—"this area, around the docks and harbor, plays host to homes that house dockside and shipyard workers, as is sensible. In contrast, the area around the Abbey is inhabited by citizens of rather higher social standing. To relocate a school for dockyard brats to such an area risks disrupting the social norms."

Despite having taken a deep dislike to the man, Kit kept his expression unreadable and arched his brows. "Is that so? Pray tell, which of society's norms do you consider to be at risk?"

Peabody blinked. The silence stretched as he patently tried to find acceptable words in which to cloak his complaint.

Kit made no move to help him out and simply waited.

Peabody's color rose, then he harrumphed and said, "Social norms such as in which areas the various classes live."

"I wasn't aware the city imposes restrictions on where people of various classes reside." Kit kept his tone mild. "But regardless, the boys are only visiting, as it were. They're not taking up residence in Trinity Street."

"Be that as it may," Peabody huffed, "those who do live in Trinity Street are complaining!"

"Indeed?" Kit looked thoughtful. "The school relocated yesterday—today was the first day of classes. How many people have complained?"

Peabody looked frustrated. He glowered. "When even one of my constituents complain, it is incumbent on me to act."

"Indeed." Kit smiled, the epitome of helpfulness. "You've acted and brought the complaint to my notice. Sadly for whoever complained, I'm less than impressed."

Peabody started to gobble, but Kit rolled on, ruthlessly charming. "You see, I happen to adhere to the doctrine espoused by Prince Albert and the Queen regarding the education of the poor." He continued, smoothly explaining the belief that education could alleviate poverty. "And you must admit that in a city suffering under the difficulties currently afflicting Bristol, then it is—to use your phrase—incumbent on every gentleman to do his part. Why, my brother the marquess and his wife have established several schools in their area, and at the moment, it's a rather more prosperous one than Bristol."

Enough of Kit's words penetrated Peabody's brain that, judging by his expression, his belief in the righteousness of his complaint started to falter.

Kit continued, enumerating the various local bodies who, in addition to himself, supported the school—namely the Abbey, the Dean, and the Christ Church Parish Council. "Naturally, I also have contacts on the Dock Company board, including the mayor and several aldermen." Kit was willing to wager a significant sum that Peabody would not contemplate opposing any institution with such wide-ranging support. "I believe you—and your complainant—will discover that the general tide of civic responsibility is firmly behind the school."

And if necessary, Kit would ensure that was so.

Peabody was clever enough to sense the concealed threat.

After a moment of weighing his options, he drew in a long breath, then gravely inclined his head. "Clearly, my lord, I had little notion of the true situation regarding the school. In the circumstances, I will endeavor to convey to the complainant the...er..."

Kit smiled. "The futility of attempting to oust the school?"

Peabody's lips primmed, but again, he inclined his head. "Just so, my lord." After a second's pause, Peabody reached into his pocket, extracted a card, and offered it. "My card, my lord. If there is any way in which I can assist you in your...civic endeavors, please don't hesitate to call on me."

Kit smiled a perfectly genuine smile. "Thank you, councilor. We will hope the school and all its works prosper."

That was a trifle rich for Peabody, but all he returned was "Indeed." With a brief bow and a "my lord," Peabody beat a strategic retreat.

Grinning, Kit watched him stride off across the cobbles, then turned inside to discover Miss Petty, Jack, and all the men—with the exception of Wayland—regarding him quizzically.

Kit arched his brows. "What?"

The men shook their heads, but Jack blurted, "You told him to pull in his head."

Kit considered Jack, then mildly said, "Not, you will note, in those words."

The men chortled. Miss Petty looked prim, but pleased.

Kit threw an arm around Jack's bony shoulders and steered him back to the gantry. "Now, where were we?"

They worked like navvies, and by the end of the day, they'd hoisted the gantry, now a moveable frame suspended from the massive braced beams and running along the attached struts, above the workshop floor.

Miss Petty had left by then, but Kit, Wayland, Mulligan, and the carpenters—and Jack—stood looking up at their creation with, at least on Kit's part, immense satisfaction.

He was in an excellent mood, not solely because of how much they'd managed to accomplish in the workshop, but because Sylvia had sent Peabody his way. Kit realized that, in his mind, he already saw himself as the principal champion of the school—and the fact Sylvia apparently viewed him in a similar light set warmth unfurling inside him.

That curious and richly satisfying glow filled his chest. He liked to feel needed, liked to make things happen—good things like bringing a yacht-building workshop into existence in a city starved of the jobs such an enterprise created. Like helping a threatened school to carry on and protecting it from those wishing it ill.

Helping Sylvia, helping the teachers, the boys, and all at the school, helping Wayland manifest his dreams, helping Mulligan and his crew and Jack the Lad…and, ultimately, helping himself.

For him, helping others in one guise or another was how he'd always found his greatest satisfaction, his deepest content.

He paid the men—and Jack—for the day, adding a little extra to each man's wage and a little bit more again to Jack's in appreciation of their sterling efforts.

His mood remained buoyant as he farewelled the men and Jack, then helped Wayland lock up the warehouse.

After parting from Wayland, Kit turned his footsteps toward his new home.

His heart felt remarkably light. He was in what Wayland had termed an uplifted mood, and he owed much of that to Sylvia and her willingness to accept his protection for her school.

Six

The following day was Saturday, a half day for most workers. Kit and Wayland joined Mulligan and the others in finishing off the gantry and the partitions for the offices.

After the men left at midday, Kit and Wayland continued lining the offices with oak planks.

At one point, Wayland stood, stretched, then shifted to stare out at their evolving workshop. "I can't quite believe we're not only here, but have got this far so quickly."

Crouched by one wall with nails held between his teeth, Kit merely nodded. Once he'd used the nails to secure the next plank, he replied, "It is hard to take in. Everything's fallen into place, and how often does that happen?" He rose, stretched his back, then joined Wayland at what would soon be the door to Wayland's design office. "The offices won't be ready on Monday, but the workshop is." Kit couldn't keep the enthusiasm from his voice. "We'll be ready to welcome our workforce and plunge into the first project."

Wayland nodded, his eagerness apparent. "I think we should set one team to finish the offices—perhaps under Shaw. He has a fine eye for detail. I'll need the space soon, and I suspect Miss Petty will be glad to take possession of her office here, too."

"No doubt. She's another unexpected boon—who would have thought we'd find a secretary with actual experience of this sort of business?"

"Definitely an unlooked-for blessing." Wayland went on, "I'll set the second team of carpenters under Mulligan to make up the frame for our first hull."

Kit shook his head in something approaching wonder. "Our first hull—at last!"

"So soon," Wayland countered. "That's what's so remarkable."

"It feels as if, in bringing our hopes and dreams here, now, at this moment in time, that we've fallen into a slot that was just waiting for someone like us to fill it."

Wayland nodded. After several seconds more of drinking in the sight of their workshop ready for action, he moved back and picked up another board, then glanced at Kit as he did the same. "Actually, there's something I wanted to suggest."

Hefting up a board, Kit arched his brows, and Wayland went on, "Now we're up and running, I think it's time for a sign." Balancing his board against one hip, he spread his hands in the air. "'Cavanaugh Yachts. Home to quality ocean-going yachts.'"

Kit laughed. "You've been thinking."

"Indeed. And I think it's time we started advertising. Our first four hulls might be already spoken for, but we want to keep the work ticking over, and building an ocean-going yacht on spec is where this business gets risky."

Kit nodded; that was indisputable, and consequently, they needed to open their order book. He envisioned the sign in his mind, thought of how it would look on the front of the building. After a second, he glanced around; they'd fixed the lining boards for half the larger office. He glanced at Wayland, hammering another board into place. "We've done enough for today—the men can finish in here on Monday. Why don't you design the sign, and I'll look into the best place to have it made?"

"Excellent idea!" Wayland straightened and set down his hammer on a nearby trestle. "I'll get the sign designed tonight. For my money, the sooner we get the name of Cavanaugh Yachts associated with this place, the better."

Kit agreed. He and Wayland locked up, then parted. Wayland headed off quite jauntily, enthused at the prospect of designing something new. Kit grinned and set off to visit the two sign makers' shops he remembered passing on his meanderings through the city.

Both shops were closed, but in the window of each were displayed a range of different signs. From examining those, Kit decided the second shop was the one he would use; he knew the style of Wayland's work, and the second sign maker looked to have the higher level of skill required to do justice to Wayland's designs.

With that decided, Kit paused. The impulse to tell Sylvia of his encounter with Peabody had been hovering in his mind ever since Peabody had walked away. Now, that impulse pressed even more insistently; he really should reassure her of the outcome.

He'd resisted until now because he hadn't been sure how to present his part in Peabody's conversion. The school was so very much Sylvia's creation, he hadn't wanted to have her think that he had in any way stepped on her toes, even if she hadn't been there and had, in fact, sent Peabody to him.

But he needed to tell her that Peabody had climbed down; she might view him not doing so in an even worse light.

He turned his steps toward her lodgings. It was after three-thirty; she should be there.

His attitude to Sylvia—his uncertainty in dealing with her and what drove that—was odd, curious, and a touch unnerving. Had she been a different sort of lady—a London sort of lady—after glimpsing her passion when she'd burst into his office and ranted at him over the school, he would have pursued her openly and directly. But she was a country clergyman's daughter, and although he hadn't met her before Rand's wedding, in London or anywhere else—he felt sure he would remember her if he had—her opinion of him as displayed during the wedding, presumably based solely on his ton reputation, had been anything but flattering. He'd created that reputation as a shield to protect himself from the importunities of young ladies and their match-making mamas, and in that regard, it had served him well for over a decade. Now, however, that defensive shield had turned into a hurdle.

Not an insurmountable one, but a hurdle nonetheless.

The unrelenting determination that welled from somewhere deep inside him to successfully overcome that stumbling block was the aspect that most unnerved him.

He hauled his mind from dwelling on it further and, instead, thought of the sign and of Peabody, too...

The idea that sparked had him blinking, then thinking, weighing up whether the notion was sound and something to be pursued or if Sylvia would see it as an unwarranted encroachment.

Before he could decide, he fetched up on the pavement before her lodging house. He opened the gate, walked up the short path, and climbed the steps to the front porch. He paused to straighten his jacket, then lifted the brass knocker and beat a polite tattoo.

After a minute of silence, footsteps—not Sylvia's—approached the door. It opened to reveal an older woman of perhaps fifty summers, with graying brown hair drawn back in a bun and a knitted shawl draped about her shoulders. Her faded brown eyes passed over Kit in a careful perusal, then she inquired, "Yes, sir?"

Kit smiled his most charming smile. "Good afternoon. I wonder if I might have a word with Miss Buckleberry."

The woman, presumably Sylvia's landlady, regarded him shrewdly for several seconds, then asked, "And who shall I say is calling?"

Kit kept his smile in place; on one level, it was comforting to know that Sylvia had a dragon, however mild, guarding her door. "Lord Kit Cavanaugh."

The woman eyed him with increased interest. Then something in her stance changed, and Kit realized she'd decided to approve of him. As if to confirm that, she nodded, more to herself than to him, then she bobbed and said, "Miss Sylvia hasn't come home yet, my lord. She'll be in her office for a good hour more. Dedicated to that school, she is. She has a very good heart."

The last was said as if to impress the fact on him. Kit smiled more genuinely. "I know. And it's about the school that I wish to speak with her." Sylvia hadn't mentioned an office. "Can you direct me to her office?"

The woman considered him again, but must have seen enough in his face to trust him. "It's in the building beside Christ Church, up along Broad Street. Her office is on the second floor, at the back overlooking the rear of the church."

"Thank you." Kit smiled. "And your name?"

She bobbed again. "Mrs. Macintyre, your lordship."

Kit inclined his head. "Again, thank you, Mrs. Macintyre. My best wishes for a pleasant evening."

"And to you, your lordship."

Kit tipped her a salute, turned, and went down the path. He closed the gate behind him, paused to consider his way, then strode for Christ Church and the building beside it.

The latter proved to be as old as the church. The door was unlocked. Kit went in and looked around the small foyer. From the list of tenants' names displayed on a board on the wall inside the door, he surmised that the building was owned by the church and used primarily for church-linked organizations. Although it was quiet, the hum of distant conversations and the occasional footstep testified to the presence of others in the various offices.

Kit climbed the narrow stone stairs, continuing past the first floor to the second. He stepped off the stairs onto a worn runner and followed it toward the back of the building. There he found a row of small offices, most with their doors shut. He approached the door that stood wide open, shedding the last of the afternoon's light into the dimly lit corridor.

He walked slowly—silently—into the doorway and saw Sylvia, head bent, seated behind an ancient desk. She was scribbling in an open ledger. He raised a hand and rapped lightly on the frame.

She looked up and blinked in surprise.

Lips curving, Kit inclined his head. "Good afternoon. Can I disturb you?"

She blinked again, then waved him in. "Of course." Then she fixed him with widening eyes. "Is there a problem?"

Kit thought she looked delightful, with wisps of golden hair escaping from her usually neat bun. "No," he assured her with a smile. "Nothing's wrong."

He moved forward to take the chair she'd indicated, the one before the desk. The office felt close, pokey and cramped, yet she'd made it her own with journals and books on education practices lined up along the top of a small bureau and an incongruously bright silk scarf looped over the hat stand in the corner.

Kit subsided into the chair and smiled into her eyes. "I just wanted to let you know that Councilor Peabody called on me yesterday, and we discussed his views on the school's new location. I believe I convinced him to rethink his opposition, but I understand he called at the school first."

Her expression grew stern, and she clasped her hands before her. "Indeed, and in a quite vexing way. It was our first day there, and everything had been going swimmingly, then Peabody walked in and declared his hateful stance." She hesitated, then went on, "Of course, the boys heard him—he made it quite clear that he didn't want dockside brats, as he labeled them, in that neighborhood." Censure rang in her tone. "After that, I felt it was necessary for the boys to hear my defense of them."

Kit wished he'd witnessed it.

She raised her gaze and met his eyes. "I made sure to mention—for the boys' ears as well as Peabody's—all the support the school has received from respectable and powerful quarters. Your name, especially, gave Peabody pause, enough that he wanted to check with you before pushing further. I hope it was all right to send him your way."

"Yes." Kit nodded decisively. "That was precisely the right thing to do—and if, in the future, the school is visited by others of Peabody's ilk, I hope you will refer them to me. I stand ready and willing to put them straight regarding the school and its value to the community."

Her smile was reward and more. "Thank you. That's…something of a relief. I'll make sure Jellicoe and Cross know to"—her smile deepened, and the blue of her eyes darkened—"wield your title like a shield."

His gaze locked with hers, Kit chuckled. "Indeed." Then he sobered. "Actually…"

Now it came to it, he was reluctant to share his most recent idea with her—just in case she took umbrage—yet it would be so easy to do, and the incident with Peabody was the perfect illustration of what they could hope to avoid.

Looking into her pretty blue eyes, he forced himself to explain, "I'm about to order a sign for our workshop—Cavanaugh Yachts. And after this business with Peabody, I wondered if you would consider it appropriate for the school to have a sign, too. Say 'Cavanaugh's School' or something similar. Some label that declares my interest in the school, thus deflecting further attacks from the likes of Peabody." He paused, then added, "Of course, such a sign would also advertise my name and help establish it within the wider community, which, from a business perspective, is something I need to do. As I mentioned earlier, I intend to put down roots here, and making the Cavanaugh name visible is an important part of that."

He'd decided to couch his suggestion as something that benefited him as much as, if not more than, the school to reduce the chance of her feeling the school, and therefore she, would be even more beholden to him than was already the case.

Apparently, he needn't have bothered; she stared at him as if much struck, and although he looked closely, he couldn't detect any hint of disapproval in her face or her eyes.

When she didn't immediately speak, he added, somewhat diffidently, "If you approve, I thought I could order the sign for the school together with the one for the workshop."

Sylvia let the full implication of his suggestion sink in. The benefits would be *enormous*; what was surprising was that she hadn't thought of it herself. "That," she breathed, looking into a far more stable future, "would be marvelous."

She refocused on Kit in time to see his quick, slightly lopsided, and, she now knew, entirely genuine smile flash into being. Eagerly, she went on, "The boys, the staff, and all associated with the school will be delighted." To be attending a school publicly acknowledged as supported by Lord Cavanaugh would be a huge boost to the boys' confidence and that of the staff as well. Simply having his name attached to the school would ensure ongoing funding from the parish council and the continued support of the Abbey. And it would give people like the disapproving old lady in Trinity Street reason to rethink their views.

She realized she was beaming and directed her smile at him. "That truly is a wonderful offer. On behalf of the school, I can't thank you enough." If he'd been less of a danger to her senses, she would have leapt up, rounded the desk, and given him an appreciative hug.

Just the thought made her feel warm, and she thrust it down and focused on the practical. "Of course, as the school exists under the Dean's auspices, we'll need to get his approval, but he's a sensible man, and I can't see him disagreeing."

"If you could check with him," Kit said, "I'll speak to the prior. As the Abbey owns the hall, we should get their permission to put up a sign. That said, I expect they will welcome the suggestion—the sign will subtly link my name with the Abbey as well."

"Yes, that's true." Enthusiasm bubbled through her. "I'll speak with the Dean after the service tomorrow and send you word."

"Excellent. I'll visit the Abbey tomorrow as well, and with luck, I'll be able to order the signs on Monday."

Sylvia was still beaming. She met Kit's eyes, and it seemed they shared a moment of perfect understanding and achievement.

"So tell me," Kit said, pleased by the depth of their connection yet slightly unnerved by it as well, "how are the boys and the staff taking to their new digs?"

"They are close to ecstatic. When I called around yesterday to see how they were doing, the boys—"

Kit listened as she described the scene and what the teachers had said and Miss Meggs's evident pleasure. Even more, he watched her face, marveling at the animation that infused her features when she spoke of the school—her passion. It was the same with him and yachts; he fully understood the intense satisfaction when things went right.

"And," Sylvia continued, forearms resting on her ledgers, which she'd plainly forgotten all about, "it's doubly fortunate that Jellicoe and Cross share lodgings just around the corner. It makes opening and locking up the school each day so much easier."

When she focused on his eyes, he smiled back, letting her see that, in truth, he was just as pleased as she—that he shared her commitment to the school. Again, the moment held—a shimmering, intangible connection flowing between them.

The thunder of footsteps racing along the corridor tore them from their momentary fixation and had them both shifting to look at the open doorway.

A boy skidded into view, gasping, his eyes wild.

Sylvia pushed to her feet. "Eddie! What's the matter?"

The boy made a valiant attempt to catch his breath. Grabbing hold of the door frame, he blurted, "It's the school, miss. It's on fire!"

Already on his feet, Kit bit back an oath. He met Sylvia's shocked gaze, then waved her to the door. "Come on." He caught Eddie's shoulder, steadying the boy. He eased Eddie back into the corridor as Sylvia rushed around her desk, swiped up her reticule from the top of the bureau, and hurried after them.

Kit briefly met her eyes, then strode with Eddie toward the stairs. "Don't try to speak yet," Kit told the boy. "You can tell us all once we're in a hackney."

He heard Sylvia shut and lock her office door, then she came rushing along behind them.

They went down the stairs at a run. Emerging onto the pavement, Kit put his fingers to his lips and blew a shrill note. A hackney driver farther up the street heard and quickly steered his horse their way.

The instant the carriage halted, Kit lifted Eddie up. "In you go." He turned and handed Sylvia up, then paused with his boot on the step and looked at the driver. "Trinity Street. It's an emergency. There's a guinea in it for you if you get us there fast."

The driver straightened and saluted. "Right, guv."

Kit flung himself onto the seat beside Sylvia, and the driver swung the carriage into a tight turn, then sent his horse racing for the Frome Bridge.

Given it was Saturday afternoon, the traffic was light, and the driver took Kit's challenge to heart. The hackney racketed along the cobbles at a punishing pace.

"Oh!" Sylvia tried to catch her balance as the jarvey turned onto the bridge at speed.

Kit laid his arm along the back of the seat, closed his hand about her right shoulder, and braced her against his chest. He sensed the jolt that shot through her at his touch, but she didn't shake free of his protective hold.

Good, his inner self said.

Once the hackney had turned off the bridge, he leaned forward and, across Sylvia, caught Eddie's still-wide eyes. "Now—tell us what happened."

"I'd brought me mum and the nippers to see the new hall—just from the outside." Eddie gulped in air, the moment apparently etched in his young mind. "We were on the pavement in front of the school when Mr. Cross came charging up that little alley that runs beside the hall—the one that leads to the backyard. Mr. Cross was coughing something fearful, but he saw me and caught my arm and told me someone had set fire to the hall and that I had to go and fetch help. He said he had to get back to Mr. Jellicoe, and he went." Eddie paused, eyes round. "I didn't know where to go—who I was supposed to tell—and neither did me mum. We'd come to your office when I first joined the school, so I thought I should look for you there."

Kit nodded reassuringly. "Well done." Eddie would have done better to run to the firehouse, but Kit didn't know where that was and doubted Eddie or his mum did, either.

Sylvia patted Eddie's hand. "You did very well."

The hackney rocketed along St. Augustine's Back and on along the Butts and finally swung into Trinity Street.

The first thing they saw was a thick pall of smoke roiling and billowing upward from the rear of the new school hall.

Seven

The jarvey halted his horse upwind of the smoke. "Close as I can get, guv'nor, if that's where you're headed."

"Thank you. It is." Grim-faced, Kit got down, tossed the jarvey a guinea, then helped Sylvia, who was scrambling to the pavement.

Her hand clutching his, she straightened and stared at the smoke pouring up and out from the school's rear yard. "Dear God!"

"Don't panic." Kit had noticed that there was surprisingly little activity in the street—just a woman and three young children waiting by the hall's steps. "From the look of that smoke, they've already put out the blaze."

"Oh, thank heavens!" Relief swamped Sylvia's features.

Keeping hold of her hand—holding her back from rushing down the alley toward the fire—Kit nodded to Eddie as the boy leapt down from the hackney. "You did well to fetch us, but now go with your mother."

"Yes, sir—my lord." Big-eyed, Eddie scampered toward his family.

Gripping Sylvia's hand more firmly, Kit led the way down the narrow alley that ran along the side of the hall.

The smoke was thinning as they stepped onto the cobbles of the rear yard.

Sylvia held her breath and swiftly scanned the scene. A deeper wave of relief swept through her at the sight of Jellicoe and Cross, soot-streaked and mopping tears from their eyes, but otherwise apparently unharmed.

A bevy of neighbors was hanging over the rear fence and both side fences; from the buckets dangling from several hands, the neighbors had helped ferry water to put out the flames. Evidently, not everyone wished the school gone.

Kit released her hand and nodded to Jellicoe and Cross.

Sylvia hurried to where they were slumped against the side of the privy. "Are you all right?" When both nodded, she asked, "What happened?"

Jellicoe waved a hand before his face, batting away the lingering smoke. "We came to take a look at our notes for Monday's lessons, smelt smoke, tried to get out of the back door and couldn't, then we raced around and found that." He pointed to a pile of wood stacked against the hall's back door. "It was well alight—or so we thought—with flames leaping up against the door. I sent Cross to get help while I tried to beat out the flames with a sack. Then the sack caught fire as well."

Cross took up the tale. "I found Eddie out front—sheer luck—and sent him for help." Cross squinted up at her through watering eyes. "I take it he thought I meant you."

Sylvia smiled gently. "He did."

Cross humphed. "Luckily, the neighbors smelt the smoke, too, and came to help." He waved at the watching men. "Thank you all."

The men nodded and smiled, and one called, "Put all of us at risk, the blighters did—fires spread quickly in streets like ours. Any idea who it was?"

A dark murmur of agreement rippled through the onlookers.

Kit, who had been studying the smoldering wood, replied, "Not yet."

Words and tone held a promise of retribution that seemed to satisfy the watching men.

Then Kit flicked out a handkerchief, anchored it over his

nose, and walked to the still-smoking pile. He stared for a moment, then bent, picked up a broken branch, and prodded and scraped at what looked like remnants of rags hanging off the logs. After a moment, he said, "These rags were soaked in some sort of liquid fuel—that's why your sack caught fire. But the rags were placed on top of the wood, so although the rags burned merrily, most of the wood didn't catch, then when you tried to force the back door, the pile shifted, and the rags fell over the front of the logs."

Slowly, Kit rose, frowning down at the detritus. Then he raised his gaze and scanned the hall's rear wall.

Sylvia followed his gaze, taking in the blistered paintwork on the door and the soot streaks on the solid stone walls.

Glancing around, she saw that the neighbors were watching Kit with interest. She doubted he realized just how definite was the aura of not just status and wealth but also command that hung from his shoulders, an invisible mantle a large portion of the populace instinctively recognized.

She watched as he stepped back from the now-damp stack of wood and walked over to join her before Cross and Jellicoe, who were still slumped against the privy.

Kit extended his hand to Jellicoe.

Jellicoe looked faintly startled, but then took the proffered hand and let Kit haul him to his feet.

"Good work, you two." Kit lightly thumped Jellicoe's shoulder, then reached down and helped Cross up as well.

As soon as he was on his feet, Cross, now frowning, went to stare at the smoking pile. After a moment, he grunted. "Now I can see how this was laid, I'm having trouble believing there was ever much of a threat."

Jellicoe coughed and went to look, too, then nodded. "I see what you mean. Whoever set this had no idea what they were doing."

His hands sunk in his greatcoat pockets, Kit joined the teachers.

Sylvia followed and halted on Cross's other side. "What do you mean?" she asked.

Kit pointed at the rags. "If you wanted that pile to burn, any sensible person would have put the rags beneath the wood—at least in the center of the pile."

Jellicoe snorted. "And why try to set fire to a thick oak door set in a stone wall anyway? Even if the door had caught"—he directed his gaze up, above the door—"the wall is so high, the rafters would almost certainly be out of reach of any flames."

"The hall wouldn't have burned," Kit concluded. "Which leaves us with the question of whether whoever set the fire intended it merely as a warning, or if they truly were so inept that they had no notion of how to set an effective blaze. Regardless, I believe we can be certain that no expert arsonist was involved."

Jellicoe snorted a laugh and ended up coughing.

Cross thumped him on the back. "Wait until your lungs clear before you try that again."

Sylvia saw Kit glance at their still-watching audience. Then he turned back to Cross and Jellicoe and, in a voice slightly raised to reach the onlookers, said, "Incidentally, I'm having a sign made for the front of the hall. 'Lord Cavanaugh's School.' Seeing you're here, you could help me take the measurements."

Both Jellicoe and Cross looked thoroughly pleased.

From the corner of her eye, Sylvia saw the neighbors exchange duly impressed looks. None of them would protest about the school now. Indeed, more than likely they would brag about the fire and seeing a real lord and having his school next door.

"Right-ho." His usual ebullient manner re-emerging, Cross waved down the alley. "Let's leave this mess to finish smoldering. We'll get it cleared away tomorrow."

The three men stood back to allow Sylvia to go first. She

emerged onto the pavement before the school steps. Eddie and his mother and siblings had gone.

Sylvia stood back and watched as the three men worked out the optimal dimensions for a sign to fit above the hall door.

She'd noted that Kit had added his title to his proposed name for the school and was grateful he'd done so. His name would help, but when combined with his title, the result was a far stronger shield. Being labeled "Lord Cavanaugh's School" would protect the school as nothing short of a royal warrant could.

Listening to Cross, Jellicoe, and Kit discuss the positioning of the sign, she felt the last of her fire-induced tension drain away. Most of the onlookers had retreated into their homes, doubtless to share what they'd seen and heard.

The day was slowly sliding toward evening.

With the placement and size of the sign decided, Cross and Jellicoe, both now understandably weary, took their leave. Sylvia thanked them effusively, then let them go. She watched them walk slowly up the street—and noticed the disapproving lady in black standing, once more, at her gate, glaring in Sylvia's direction, then, as before, the woman turned and stumped back into her house. Considering the sight, Sylvia asked, "Who do you think did it?"

She felt certain Kit would at least have a theory.

Kit halted beside Sylvia, his gaze resting on the hackney, still loitering farther up the street. He waved to the driver, who acknowledged the hail with a salute. Kit gently grasped Sylvia's elbow and steered her toward the carriage; this time, she didn't seem to react to his touch. "I don't know," he replied, "but I believe I need to pay Councilor Peabody a visit."

Startled, she glanced at him. "You think Peabody was involved?"

Kit considered that, then shook his head. "No. But it occurs to me that the good councilor arrived, breathing fire, on the school's doorstep within hours of it opening its doors." Briefly, he met her gaze. "How did he know?"

He watched her face as she worked it out.

Then her eyes widened, and she looked up at him. "Someone complained."

Jaw firming, he nodded. "And I suspect whoever did will have more of an idea of who set the fire than Peabody."

He ushered her on.

When they reached the carriage's side, she swung to face him. "I'm coming with you." Dogged determination flared in her eyes, violet deepening the periwinkle-blue.

He'd anticipated her resolve and inclined his head. "If you wish." He'd long ago learned that, when dealing with ladies, it paid to give way on the smaller issues, and visiting Peabody in Kit's company held no danger at all. "I expect we'll find him at his home. Do you know where he lives— No, wait. He gave me his card." He hunted in his jacket pocket and found the card.

As Sylvia turned and climbed into the carriage, Kit looked at the driver. "Park Street. No need for any heroics this time."

The driver grinned and saluted with his whip. "Right, guv'nor. Climb aboard."

Kit did. He sat beside Sylvia, the driver flicked the reins, and they rattled off.

★ ★ ★

On presenting themselves at Councilor Peabody's door, Kit gave his name, and they were immediately shown into the councilor's drawing room.

Peabody didn't keep them waiting, but arrived on his butler's heels in what appeared to be a distinctly conciliatory mood. He bowed to them both, then waved them to the chaise. Taking in their serious expressions, he took the armchair opposite and, faintly trepidatiously, asked, "What brings you here?"

Succinctly, Kit outlined the facts of the fire.

As he'd expected, Peabody looked genuinely shocked. "Dear me—how appalling! Why, the entire neighborhood might have gone up."

"A point made by one of the neighbors who helped douse the flames," Sylvia said. "They were not at all impressed that some miscreant had tried to set alight what is to be known as Lord Cavanaugh's School."

Peabody blinked. "Indeed..." His gaze flicked from Sylvia to Kit and back again, then Peabody straightened. "I assure you I had absolutely nothing to do with this fire—or with the miscreant who laid it."

"We hadn't imagined you did," Kit stated. His matter-of-fact tone calmed Peabody. "However, the fact remains that someone attempted to set fire to the school, thereby threatening the entire neighborhood. Whoever it was demonstrably had no thought or care for the neighbors, either."

Peabody nodded. "I agree. Although nothing terrible happened, the intention and the risk were there."

"Quite," Kit said. "Which is why we feel we need to get to the bottom of this, even though no lasting damage was done. To that end, we wondered which of your constituents had complained about the school—it's possible they may have some idea of who was responsible for setting the fire."

Peabody frowned.

Kit caught Sylvia's gaze and willed her to patience; he was rather surprised she'd left so much of the talking to him.

Eventually, Peabody conceded, "I take your point, but I can't see how it could be so." He met their gazes. "The complaint— and yes, it was only one—came from Mrs. Stenshaw, a widow of more than middle years who lives on Trinity Street."

The image of the lady in black sprang to Sylvia's mind. "A lady of average height who always dresses in black and lives in a house on the opposite side of the street to the school, several doors closer to the river?"

Peabody nodded. "That's Mrs. Stenshaw, and if you've seen her, you'll realize why I seriously doubt she could have had anything to do with the fire."

"But it was she who complained?" Kit asked.

"Yes—vociferously. She was deeply put out over the school moving into her street and, as she put it, lowering the tone of the neighborhood. Well, you can imagine the sort of things she said, but that's really all her complaint boiled down to."

"Have you informed her that you won't be taking the matter further?" Kit asked.

Peabody met his gaze, then slowly nodded. "Yes. I called on her later on Friday afternoon. I thought it best to get that unhappy task over with sooner rather than later."

"And how did she take the news?"

Peabody wrinkled his nose. "She was furious. She accused me of… Well, again, I'm sure you can guess the sort of tirade she indulged in. She's a most…difficult woman."

Sylvia had no trouble believing him; she was actually starting to feel sympathy for the councilor.

Kit was still pondering. "A widow, so no husband, but what about some other male relative—a brother or a cousin, someone she might turn to?"

But Peabody was already shaking his head, then he stopped and frowned. "There's no one of her generation, but she does have two layabout sons." He paused, then more slowly added, "I've heard…less than edifying tales of her sons, yet I understand Mrs. Stenshaw believes they're angels and springs like a lioness to their defense."

Peabody met Kit's gaze and arched a brow.

Kit held the councilor's gaze for a moment, then nodded. "The sons are a possibility. If we learn anything definite, we'll let you know."

"Thank you." Peabody rose as they did and solicitously ushered them out. On the doorstep, he met Kit's gaze. "As I said before, if there's anything I can do to ease your path, my lord, please feel free to call."

Kit inclined his head, and they parted in significantly better accord than before.

★ ★ ★

Although the light had faded and evening was drawing in, Sylvia insisted on returning to Trinity Street with Kit.

When they arrived, he tried to convince her to take the hackney to her lodgings or at least remain in the carriage while he questioned the difficult Mrs. Stenshaw on the grounds the woman might turn nasty, but Sylvia was having none of it. Her blood was up, and she was determined to learn who had been responsible for such a thoughtless and cowardly act and, at the very least, give them a piece of her mind.

After she said as much in a distinctly incensed tone, Kit raised his hands in defeat, stepped back from the hackney, then offered his hand to assist her down.

Lips set, she gripped his fingers and descended. Courtesy of the unavoidable instances of contact the dramas of the day had forced on her, her senses were growing more accustomed to the riot his touch invariably caused.

Apparently, familiarity could breed acceptance instead of contempt.

Once on the pavement, she shook her skirts straight, then allowed Kit to usher her through Mrs. Stenshaw's gate and up the short path to the porch. Head high, she stood beside him as he lifted the knocker and rapped.

Light footsteps rapidly approached the door, and it opened to reveal a harassed-looking maid. Her eyes widened as she took them in. "Yes, sir? Ma'am?"

Kit handed over one of his cards. "We're here to see Mrs. Stenshaw."

The maid took the thick ivory card. Her eyes widened as she

read the words inscribed upon it, then she looked up, bobbed, and said, "If you'll wait here, sir—my lord—I'll see if the mistress is receiving."

With that, the maid stepped back and closed the door.

Kit arched a cynical brow at Sylvia.

She met his eyes, then her gaze shifted past his shoulder. He followed it, turning his head in time to catch the lace curtain in the front room's bow window settling back into place.

Then the maid was back. She bobbed twice and said, "I'm sorry, my lord, but Mrs. Stenshaw is indisposed."

Kit smiled reassuringly at the maid. Raising his voice, he said, "Please inform your mistress that Miss Buckleberry and I are investigating the fire that was deliberately set at the rear of the hall on the other side of the street, and if Mrs. Stenshaw prefers, I'm perfectly willing to place the matter in the hands of the local constabulary and return with them later—"

Something moved in the dimness of the hall. The maid swung around, then stepped back, and Mrs. Stenshaw, gloomy and forbidding in black bombazine, stumped forward, planted her cane on the threshold, and, her expression carved from stone, faced them.

Before Kit could part his lips, Mrs. Stenshaw declared, "I know nothing about any fire. But as I warned Councilor Peabody, such disruptive occurrences are guaranteed to happen now that a school for dockside brats has moved into our street." She snorted inelegantly and brought her dark gaze to bear on Sylvia. "Bringing such uncouth elements into our peaceful streets— what did you expect would happen? It was doubtless some of those ungrateful brats unhappy about being sent to school."

Sylvia drew in a sharp breath.

Kit felt his expression harden. "Having met each and every one of the school's pupils, I've seen nothing of any such negative feelings about the school." He caught Mrs. Stenshaw's gaze. "But perhaps you know more about the boys than we do?"

Mrs. Stenshaw looked horrified—much as if he'd accused her of dealing with the devil. "I know nothing of those boys—or any dockside brats. The very idea!"

Appeared to have almost given her palpitations.

"I see," Kit said. "So you have no knowledge or evidence to link any of the students to the fire, and furthermore, your opposition to the school and your opinion of the students are based solely on prejudice and nothing more."

Mrs. Stenshaw's expression remained truculent.

Sylvia, by the sound of her voice barely containing her ire, sternly said, "It might interest you to know that the fire was set against the rear door of the school. If the teachers hadn't arrived unexpectedly and, assisted by neighbors, acted quickly to put out the flames, it's possible the entire neighborhood might have burned."

Mrs. Stenshaw paled, but snapped back, "That's precisely the sort of danger I warned those boys would bring to this neighborhood!"

"Yet neither the boys nor anyone else associated with the school had any reason to set the fire. Indeed, all involved worked extremely hard to relocate the school. On the other hand"— Kit trapped Mrs. Stenshaw's gaze—"we've been informed that you—and only you—have taken against the school to the extent of lodging an immediate protest with your councilor." Kit paused, his gaze on Mrs. Stenshaw's dark eyes. His tone unrelenting, he added, "I'm sure you can see how that looks."

Mrs. Stenshaw's complexion turned an even more ghastly shade, but she trenchantly declared, "Yes, I lodged a protest—a strong protest—with Councilor Peabody, and I am well within my rights to do so. But I had absolutely nothing to do with that fire, and you won't prove otherwise."

There was something in her attitude—her certainty—that

convinced Kit she was telling the truth. He exchanged a quick glance with Sylvia; she'd come to the same conclusion. Then he looked again at Mrs. Stenshaw. "Perhaps we might speak with your sons. Are they at home?"

Fleetingly, Mrs. Stenshaw's eyes widened, then her expression snapped into a stony mask. Yet by the way her eyes flicked back and forth, Kit's words had suggested a possibility she didn't like. After too many seconds had passed, she replied, "They aren't here. They went out after luncheon."

"Indeed?" Sylvia said. "So they could have set the fire."

"Don't be ridiculous!" Mrs. Stenshaw attempted to look down her nose at Sylvia—difficult as Sylvia was several inches taller. "My sons wouldn't have had anything to do with that. I'm sure that, as usual, they went straight into the city."

"Where in the city might we find them?" Kit asked.

Mrs. Stenshaw bridled. "I'm sure I don't know." Then she drew in a breath and said, "I daresay they went to the museum or the library or some similar, civilized place."

Kit's smile was edged. "So for all any of us know, influenced by your stance, your sons might have set the fire that could have threatened the entire neighborhood—perhaps because they share your views or perhaps to ingratiate themselves with you."

It was the latter Mrs. Stenshaw feared; Kit saw it in her eyes.

But inevitably, she drew herself up and glared—first at him, then at Sylvia. "How dare you come to my door and accuse my sons—who are well on the way to becoming staunch, upright citizens just like their late father—of acting in such a manner! It's outrageous!" As if, in her panic, her mind had searched for and found a solid defense, she swung her glare fully on Kit and all but spat, "You said I had no proof that the students set the fire. Well, do you have any proof that my sons were involved?" When Kit didn't reply, the intensity of her glare increased. "Well?"

Kit inclined his head. "As yet, we've nothing beyond your attitude and their opportunity—"

"There you are, then!" Mrs. Stenshaw flung out a dismissive hand. "You have no grounds on which to persecute me and my sons over that fire." She waved curtly at the gate. "Now kindly take yourselves off."

Kit reached for Sylvia's arm, but before he stepped back, he met Mrs. Stenshaw's eyes. "As you will shortly see from the sign that will go up over the front door of the hall, the school is now operating under my aegis, as well as that of the Dean of Christ Church, with the full support of the Abbey."

Mrs. Stenshaw made a scoffing sound and, her glare still in place, waved them off her porch.

With pointed politeness, Kit nodded. "Good day."

Setting Sylvia's hand on his arm, he turned and steered her down the steps and on toward the gate. He could feel her vibrating with barely suppressed anger.

Behind them, he heard Mrs. Stenshaw shuffle back and the door close.

He halted on the pavement.

Sylvia drew her hand from his sleeve and swung to face him. "You saw her expression—she's worried her sons were responsible for the fire and hopes that we'll go away."

He grimaced. "We'll have to hope that when her sons come in, she reads them the riot act, and that they'll leave the school alone from now on."

Sylvia snorted softly. "Youths like that are rarely the sort who pay attention to their mother's prohibitions." She crossed her arms, gripping her elbows. "Worse, having set the fire, been suspected, yet not being brought to face any sort of justice will only strengthen the belief her sons likely already hold that they are immune—that they can act like that and get away with it." She shook her head. "It will be only a matter of time before they try something else—try to damage the school in some other, more drastic way."

The hackney they'd taken to Peabody's and back had halted

by the curb a little closer to the river. Kit gently grasped Sylvia's arm and urged her toward it; as she fell in beside him, her gaze on the pavement, he murmured, "Short of finding more damning evidence, I can't see what else we can do."

She sighed, raised her head, and rather glumly admitted, "I know. I just wish we could be sure there won't be another incident—"

"Psst!"

The sound had them both halting and looking to their left— to where a boy of about ten stood just inside the runnel that ran along the side of the Stenshaw house. The pale oval of his face peered out at them from the shadows. He was dressed neatly enough, suggesting he was a servant at one of the nearby houses.

Seeing he'd caught their attention, the boy beckoned them closer.

Curious, they approached.

The boy cast a swift glance behind him, then, when they reached him, whispered, "I saw them two do it—set the fire behind the school."

"Saw who?" Kit asked. "Which two?"

Impatiently, the boy tipped his head at the Stenshaw house. "Her two—Cedric and James. No others around here as nasty as they are."

Kit glanced at the front of the house, but they were out of sight of the bow window. Looking back at the boy, Kit crouched and mildly asked, "What's your name? And how was it you saw them?"

"I'm Oliver, but everyone calls me Ollie." Ollie looked up at Sylvia. "You're the lady from the school—I've seen you over there." He returned his open gaze to Kit's face. "I knew Cedric and James were up to no good when they told me to fetch the lamp oil—the whole jar. It's not as if they'd ever stir themselves to fill any lamps. When I gave them the jar, they took it, and they was whispering to each other and laughing as they went out of the back door. I saw they'd stuffed rags in their pockets, so I followed them. I snuck down this alley after them and across to the school. I crept along the alley down the side of the school, and I peeked around the corner. They was stacking wood from the hall's woodpile against the back door. Then they pulled out the rags from their pockets and got them all wet with the lamp oil—they used it all up—then they stacked the rags on top of the pile in a ball."

Ollie paused, then said, "Could've told them that wasn't going to work, but I didn't want the hall to burn down, so I kept mum. Then Cedric got out his tinderbox and lit the rags—they went up with a *whoosh*! That was when I scarpered."

He looked up at Sylvia. "I didn't dare yell out or anything— they would've found me and beaten me bloody." He drew in a breath and said, "So I got back to the kitchen, and they came in a few minutes later, laughing and clapping each other on the back."

Ollie wrung his hands. "I knew it was all wrong, what they'd done. I've heard the missus ranting and raving about the school coming to the street, but at least schools like that give boys like me a chance, and it's wrong of the Stenshaws to try to get rid of it just on account of they don't like it." Ollie looked miserable. "But I didn't dare tell anyone what I'd seen."

Kit laid a hand on Ollie's shoulder. "You've been brave to come and tell us."

"But if they"—Ollie tipped his head toward the house—"hear I've spoken up, I'll lose me place and be out on me ear quicker'n you can blink. And me ma's dead, and so's me da, and I've nowhere else to go."

Lightly gripping Ollie's thin shoulder—in case the boy's courage gave out and he bolted—Kit met Sylvia's eyes, then looked back at Ollie. "Do you like working for Mrs. Stenshaw?"

Ollie looked at him as if he was insane. "Lord no! She's mean to everyone. Folks only work here until they can find some-where better."

"Well, then." Kit eased his grip. Rising, he patted Ollie's shoulder. "Would you like to leave Mrs. Stenshaw's employ and come and work for me at my house? I'm new to the city, and I could use a bright bootboy and messenger who I and the rest of my staff can rely on to run errands and the like. If you'd like to do that, you can tell the truth about Cedric and James and what you saw them do, then thumb your nose at Mrs. Stenshaw and leave with us."

"And," Sylvia put in, "in between running errands and clean-ing his lordship's boots, you can come to the school and learn your letters with the other boys."

Ollie's eyes had widened at the mention of Kit's title, and his gaze had swung to Kit, but at the word "school," his eyes grew huge, and his gaze shot back to Sylvia. He stared at her as if she'd offered him the moon. "Cor...you mean it?"

She nodded. "Indeed. Lord Cavanaugh"—with one hand, she indicated Kit—"is the sponsor and patron of the school, so yes." She raised her gaze to Kit's face. "Attending school is part of his offer."

Kit hid a smile and looked inquiringly at Ollie.

The boy's expression said he wanted to seize the offer with both hands, but fear held him back. After a moment, he swal-lowed and asked, "Will I have to say what I saw to her face?"

In light of the trepidation he could see in Ollie's eyes, Kit shook his head. "No. You can leave speaking with Mrs. Sten-shaw to us—and we won't mention your name to her."

Ollie's fear fell away. His eyes shining like stars, he straight-ened to attention and looked up at Kit. "Then yes, please, your lordship! I'd like to come and work for you and go to school, too."

Kit smiled. "Then you shall." He glanced down the runnel. "Why don't you go inside and get your things? Tell anyone who asks that you've had a better offer, and you're leaving without notice. Then meet us back here." He glanced at Sylvia. "We're just going to have another word or two with Mrs. Stenshaw, then we'll come back and fetch you, and"—Kit pointed to the hackney—"we'll leave in that hackney."

Ollie was transformed, his face alight. "Yes, sir, your lordship!" Then he turned and ran down the runnel.

"Well." Beside Kit, Sylvia watched Ollie go. "That was a stroke of luck—and the act of a good heart."

Kit nodded. "It took courage to lie in wait and tell us. If we leave him in the household, most likely the sons will work out who spoke against them and beat him as badly as he fears before throwing him out. They sound the vindictive sort."

"Indeed. But now, thanks to Ollie, we have the evidence to put the fear of gaol into the Stenshaw boys—at least as far as attacking the school goes."

The look Kit sent her was keenly anticipatory. With a graceful gesture, he waved her back to Mrs. Stenshaw's door.

After Kit informed the maid that her mistress would not appreciate what they had to say being bruited about in the street, their second interview with the old besom was conducted in her drawing room.

Courtesy of Ollie's information, this interview went very much more satisfactorily than the one before. Sylvia listened appreciatively as Kit informed Mrs. Stenshaw that a credible eyewitness had come forward and was prepared to swear that he'd seen her sons, Cedric and James, lay the fire at the rear of the school and set it alight.

Kit went on, "The witness's description matches what was found at the scene, verifying his information. The witness's testimony is more than sufficient to see your sons taken up for trespass and arson."

Seated poker straight in an armchair, Mrs. Stenshaw's expression had shifted from belligerent resistance and recalcitrance to one of dawning horror. Weakly, she said, "No—I can't believe it."

"If you wish to verify our witness's information, I suggest you ask to see your household's lamp oil jar." Kit's tone held no hint of softness. "If you ask, you'll discover it was emptied this afternoon, but not by any of your staff. Indeed, the jar might not even be back in the house."

As if finally accepting the seriousness of what her sons now faced, Mrs. Stenshaw's granite-like façade cracked, and she reached out a hand. "You would take my sons from me?"

Sylvia watched as Kit held Mrs. Stenshaw's gaze, then without giving the slightest sign of weakening his stance, he stated, "In light of the school being new to the area, we are hesitant to press charges."

Sylvia blinked, but she trusted him enough to make no protest.

He glanced swiftly at her, read her acquiescence—at least for the moment—then looked back at Mrs. Stenshaw and, his tone hardening, continued, "However, should there be any further trouble visited on the school—of any sort whatsoever—we will assume that you and your sons have failed to learn the lessons of this current incident and are, once again, to blame." He straightened, his features as coldly forbidding as Mrs. Stenshaw's had ever been. "In such circumstances, we will have no hesitation in laying the evidence now in our hands before the magistrates and pursuing the matter to the point of seeing both your sons behind bars."

Sylvia pressed her palms together to refrain from applauding.

Kit capped his performance with a direct demand. "Is that clear?"

Mrs. Stenshaw looked like she'd sucked three lemons, but she swallowed and croaked, "Yes, my lord."

"Excellent." Kit stood and held out his hand to Sylvia. As she grasped it and rose, he nodded curtly to Mrs. Stenshaw. "Good day, madam. We'll see ourselves out."

He escorted Sylvia from the room, and the maid—who from her expression had been listening at the door and had found the exchange heartening—smiled and bobbed them from the house.

Sylvia paused on the porch, and Kit halted beside her. When the door shut behind them, she drew in a huge breath, then met his eyes and smiled widely. "That was…" She couldn't find the words.

He grinned. "Immensely satisfying."

"Yes!" She started down the steps, and he fell in beside her.

He held the gate for her, then followed her through. "I predict the school will have no further trouble."

"Not from that quarter, at any rate. Or for that matter, from the rest of the street." Feeling jaunty and carefree, Sylvia walked toward the mouth of the runnel.

Sliding his hands into his pockets, Kit ambled beside her. "If one were so inclined, you could view that—the intangible ongoing protection the school has gained—as the silver lining to today's cloud."

Sylvia slanted him a bright smile. "Indeed, one could." She paused and beamed at Ollie, waiting inside the entrance to the runnel with a bundle at his feet. "Along with this young man. Well, Ollie, are you ready to start your new life?"

Ollie grinned up at her. "Yes, please, miss."

"In that case"—Kit waved him to the hackney—"lead the way."

As Ollie scampered ahead of them, Kit looked at Sylvia, drank in the bubblingly happy smile that lit her face, then he offered her his arm. "Shall we?"

She slipped her arm through his. "Let's shall."

They strode for the hackney beside which Ollie was now waiting.

Kit helped Sylvia up, then nodded for Ollie to get in and followed. After he and Sylvia had settled Ollie between them, Kit called to the driver to take them to Sylvia's lodgings.

Thoroughly satisfied with his day, he sat back as the carriage rocked toward the city. And he still had seeing Sylvia to her door to look forward to, before taking himself and his new bootboy-cum-message-runner home.

Eight

Sylvia couldn't resist calling at the school on Sunday afternoon. She told herself she needed to check on stationery supplies and see how much ink they actually required, but in reality, her motivation owed more to a simple wish to reassure herself that no further attack had occurred.

To convince herself that Mrs. Stenshaw had been successful in impressing on her wayward sons the magnitude of the risk they now courted in even thinking of harming the school.

But all was well at the hall. She checked the rear yard, and it was clear Jellicoe and Cross had been back; the woodpile had been reassembled against the rear fence, the cobbles had been swept, and there was little to show for the previous day's drama—just a few blackened and blistering streaks on the paint of the back door.

Making a mental note to have a workman in to strip and re-paint the door, Sylvia relocked it, then returned to the hall to do a quick stocktake of the stationery supplies.

As she sorted and made notes, her mind circled through the events of the previous day. Reviewing her feelings and the way she'd reacted, not just to the happenings but also to Kit and his role in them.

He'd been…more than supportive. He'd been a rock, unwavering in his commitment to what, in her heart, was her school. Her creation.

She snorted softly—at herself. When he'd offered to put his name on the school, she'd instantly seen the benefits, but had wondered about what drawbacks might also accrue. Such as him taking over.

After all, his role in his yacht-building enterprise was very much the mirror of hers at the school. He organized and made things happen.

She'd been alert to the possibility that he might decide to organize her and the school as well.

But he hadn't.

All through yesterday, he'd referred to her—sometimes with just a glance, yet invariably, he'd checked that he'd had her approval before taking action regarding the school. Indeed, throughout the various incidents and interviews, they'd made an effective team.

Perhaps through filling a similar role in his own business, he was more sensitive to how she saw her role with the school.

Regardless, his assistance had been an unalloyed boon; the downside she'd feared hadn't eventuated in even the slightest degree.

Of course, he had tried to shield her from the nastiness of Mrs. Stenshaw, but from all she'd learned from Felicia and, even more, from Felicia's sister-in-law, Mary, that was only to be expected of men of his family—men of his background; apparently, they were bred to be protective to a fault.

After checking the shelves of the small cabinet Miss Meggs used to store the stationery, Sylvia scanned her notes, then closed her notebook and slipped it into her reticule. She tugged the reticule's strings tight as she cast a last glance around the hall.

All appeared in prefect order for Monday's lessons.

Satisfied—still feeling the buoying effect of their previous evening's triumph—she walked to the front door and let herself out. After locking the door, she went down the steps and set out along the pavement, heading toward the river. She glanced across the street at the Stenshaw house, but saw no movement, not even of the curtains.

Smiling to herself, she walked on.

She'd just turned into the Butts, the street that ran along the west bank of the Frome, when the sensation of being watched raised the hairs on her nape.

Keeping her expression relaxed, she walked on for some yards, but the sensation persisted—indeed, it grew stronger.

She halted and pretended to search for something in her reticule, shifting so that she could surreptitiously look back the way she'd come.

The street was far from deserted; it was a popular place for strolling on a Sunday afternoon. A dozen or so couples were indulging in the last of the afternoon's sunshine and steadfastly ignoring the three touts, who wore placards front and back and were exhorting all and sundry to attend one or other chapel.

Such touts were a common sight throughout the city. Being a major center in Methodist country, Bristol played host to literally dozens of chapels, some more sincerely God-fearing than others. Sylvia had heard that some chapels were little more than venues in which charlatans preached fire and brimstone in order to fleece those gullible enough to flock through their doors.

Lowering her reticule, she straightened and openly surveyed the street and the houses fronting it, but could see no sign of anyone who might have been staring at her. Indeed, the sensation had ceased as soon as she'd swung around.

Lips primming, she raised her chin, turned, and continued on her way.

It had to be the Stenshaw boys, watching her from some alleyway.

"Nasty people," she muttered and made for the bridge.

★ ★ ★

As Monday waned and the end of the working day approached, Kit used a rag to wipe his hands, then shrugged on his coat and walked to where Wayland stood studying the bilge board currently taking shape in the framework they'd erected to support their first hull.

Kit halted beside his friend and surveyed the sight with appreciation and not a little satisfaction. One team of carpenters, working under Mulligan, was shaping the board that would become the central base plank of the keel, while another team under Shaw's direction was hammering away in the offices, which were nearly ready for occupation.

Glancing that way, Kit noticed Miss Petty keeping a watchful eye on the finishing touches Shaw himself was installing. She'd arrived not long ago to check the progress on what would be her space—hers and Mulligan's—in the workshop. Her arrival had instantly put Mulligan—and the men and even Jack—on their best behavior, a change that both Kit and Wayland viewed with considerable amusement.

All was settling so very smoothly into place, Kit was almost starting to feel nervous.

Almost, but not quite; after all, he'd worked hard to ensure everything did come together, men, building, and tools included.

After several seconds more of looking around and finding nothing remotely amiss, Kit glanced at Wayland.

Before Kit could speak, Wayland waved at the new keel. "If I wasn't seeing this with my own eyes, I wouldn't believe we've got so far so quickly." He met Kit's eyes and grinned. "For the record, I'm damned glad I threw in my lot with you and your mad idea of Cavanaugh Yachts."

Kit grinned back. "Nothing mad about it—as my brothers will tell you, this is a finely crafted venture."

"Hah!" Wayland looked back at the keel. "As your designer-builder, I can hardly disagree."

Kit shifted, then said, "As everything is going well here, I think I'll call in at the school."

Instantly, Wayland—who Kit had told about the fire—sobered. He met Kit's eyes and nodded. "Yes. Go. If those blighters are watching, then seeing you checking in might underscore that they need to keep a good distance."

Kit nodded. "Indeed."

Wayland waved. "Go. I'll lock up here." He started toward the men, flinging over his shoulder, "We've all in hand."

Kit smiled. He turned toward the open doors, then remembered and diverted to the office to tell Miss Petty he was off to the school.

She looked at him with approval. "Very good, my lord. Should anyone inquire for you at this late hour, I will take their details and suggest they try again tomorrow."

"Thank you, Miss Petty." Kit grinned at Shaw, who was having to work under her eagle eye. "I'll leave you to your supervising."

Unseen by Miss Petty, Shaw rolled his eyes, but by the time she turned back, he was hammering again.

Kit stepped out of the workshop into the rather gloomy day. It had been overcast from morning, and a chill wind was whipping off the choppy waters of the Floating Harbor. Sliding his hands into his pockets, he started off along the cobbles toward Princes Street. As he drew level with the mouth of an alley, he sensed movement, turned his head, and saw a man striding away up the alley.

He watched the man for a second, but the fellow continued on, then Kit was past the alley and turned his eyes and mind toward the school.

★ ★ ★

Kit wasn't surprised to find Sylvia at the school; in many respects, they seemed to think along similar lines.

He halted just inside the open door. As it was past four o'clock, the boys were long gone, and judging by their scarves and coats, Jellicoe, Cross, and Miss Meggs were on the point of leaving.

Jellicoe and Cross nodded genially Kit's way, and Miss Meggs bobbed a curtsy.

Sylvia, tidying something away in a cupboard, turned and welcomed him with a smile.

Kit smiled back, then nodded to the other three. "All well here?"

"Better than well," Cross replied, winding his scarf about his neck. "The excitement of the fire has proved a seven-day wonder with the boys, and Jellicoe and I have been elevated to the status of heroes."

"As for you," Jellicoe said, "now the news of you adding your name to the school and putting up a sign to prove it has broken, you occupy an even higher level in the boys' estimation."

Miss Meggs, a trifle pink, murmured, "Your claiming of them, as it were, has made a very real impression on the boys."

With nods of farewell to him and to Sylvia, Jellicoe and Cross escorted Miss Meggs out of the door.

Sylvia, her reticule now in hand and her coat on, walked up. She paused beside Kit and, with her gaze on the departing trio, said, "All three of them stressed how deeply you attaching your name to the school and arranging a sign that will make that public has affected the boys. It seems they've all taken it to heart—their behavior has improved, along with their application." She briefly met his eyes, the approval in hers very real. "I know you thought to protect the school by having your name and title so openly stamped upon it, yet in truth, the rise in the boys' confidence—in their belief in their own self-worth— might well be the most valuable benefit to come from the sign."

He lightly shrugged. "I'll be delighted if that's so." He waved her on. As he followed her through the door, he realized he'd spoken truly; he did feel a certain pleasure—one of unlooked-for achievement—at the thought.

He waited while she locked the door. When she turned and arched her brows at him, he asked, "Wither away?"

She looked along the street toward the city. "To my office. There are a few invoices and orders I need to clear away."

He understood the impulse to clear one's desk at the end of the day. "I'll escort you there."

Sylvia accepted his offer with an inclination of her head and started down the steps.

They strolled side by side through the gathering dusk. The scents of autumn were riding the rising breeze, adding an earthy tang to the air.

They drew level with the Stenshaw house, and Sylvia glanced that way, but again, saw no sign of activity. She hadn't seen Mrs. Stenshaw since they'd left her in her drawing room on Saturday.

Kit had noticed her look. "Any further trouble from that quarter?"

His tone suggested he would react if there had been; she debated mentioning her odd sense of being watched the previous afternoon, but... "No." She shook her head. "Mrs. Stenshaw seems to have given up all active opposition to the school. She doesn't even come out to glower at us."

"Good."

They walked around the corner onto the Butts.

She glanced at his face; as usual, it told her little. "How are things going at the warehouse?"

A quick grin flashed into being, and he met her eyes. "I'm amazed. Wayland's amazed. We've actually laid the bilge board of our first keel."

She smiled. "I take it that's a remarkable achievement."

"In just a few days? It most certainly is, especially as we had to do a great deal of preparation work to convert the warehouse to a functioning yacht-building workshop."

"What sort of preparation?"

He grew animated as he told her, strong hands waving to indicate size and position.

She hadn't seen him like this before—in full flight, given over to his passion.

"Actually," he said as they neared the drawbridge and he took her elbow to steady her up the steps, "I have to thank you anew for the chance to use your pupils as messengers. Several of the men we've hired came to us because the boys spread the word—we wouldn't have found them otherwise."

She nodded in understanding. "Many of the older craftsmen have given up and are no longer even looking for work."

"Exactly—and some of those are the very craftsmen we need to build our yachts to the quality we're determined to achieve."

And he was off again, describing the features they hoped to incorporate into their yachts. She found his enthusiasm very like that of the boys—infectious and engaging.

They were descending the steps on the east bank of the Frome when she again sensed that disturbing—unnerving—tickle of primitive reaction slithering across her nape. Stepping down to the pavement, she glanced swiftly around.

Kit noticed. Instantly alert, he raised his head and looked around, too—and the sensation vanished.

"What is it?" Kit demanded. Every protective instinct he possessed had leapt to the fore the instant she'd abruptly paused and glanced around, and the way she'd looked around had only escalated his concern. He returned his gaze to her face to see her frowning into the distance.

Then she grimaced. Her chin firming, she shook her head. "It's…annoying more than anything else." She glanced at him and briefly met his eyes before starting to walk again, more purposefully now.

He fell in beside her. When he simply waited, his gaze on her profile, she sighed and said, "Yesterday, I stopped by the school to check supplies, to check in general, and when I was walking home, I got that feeling one gets when someone is watching you."

Kit glanced back, thinking of the route they'd covered. "Was it in the same place that you sensed the watcher? Around the bridge on this side?"

"No. Yesterday, it happened while I was on the Butts. I looked around then, too, but…" She gestured. "All I saw was the same thing I saw today—that you saw as well. Lots of ordinary people going about their business. No one skulking. Especially no suspicious youths."

"You think it's the Stenshaw lads?"

"It's possible, isn't it? But"—she shrugged—"who knows?"

She kept walking, and he paced alongside her, more bothered than he let show.

After several yards, she murmured, "Perhaps I'm just jumpy after the fire."

He seriously doubted that was the case; from all he'd seen of her, she had a backbone of iron and nerves of steel.

They continued along Clare Street into Corn Street. He could see the tower of Christ Church looming ahead.

In his mind, he assessed every possible angle—every direction from which a threat might come. He remembered the man he'd seen walking away from the warehouse. He hadn't been in the city long enough to have acquired any enemies here. After a moment, he asked, "Do you know of any enemies—people who might wish you ill?"

The look she bent on him suggested he'd taken leave of his senses. "No. Of course not. I have no enemies."

He grimaced and let the matter drop, but he wasn't going to forget it. He'd long ago learned to trust intuition regarding such nebulous threats—and not only his intuition. No matter how she tried to downplay it, she'd been disturbed by the watcher's attention. That alone meant something, and it wasn't anything good.

Surreptitiously, he glanced around again, but no one seemed to be paying any attention to them.

Looking at her, he studied what little he could see of her face, then ventured, "You would be entertained if you could be a fly on the wall and see the change in our men—and in Jack the Lad—whenever Miss Petty darkens the workshop door."

Sylvia smiled and met his eyes. "Miss Petty and Jack the Lad?"

"Haven't I mentioned them?" Kit put his experience at being a charming companion to good use and soon had Sylvia smiling and laughing again.

But as he followed her through the door of the building beside the church, he decided that, instead of leaving her at her office door, he would dally and walk her all the way home.

Nine

The following morning, Kit reached the workshop to find Wayland staring aghast at the wreckage of their first keel.

Kit was struck speechless. Then he looked at Wayland. "What happened?"

Wayland gestured helplessly at the broken timbers. "I don't know. I just arrived, found the latch on the door broken, and walked in to discover"—he waved—"*this*!" With both hands, he snatched at his hair. "Aargh! I knew it was too good to be true."

Kit felt the same way. They'd been rolling along without so much as a glitch and, now, this.

But this wasn't any accident.

"Who?" Wayland said. "That's what I want to know."

Grimly, Kit nodded. An image of the man he'd glimpsed walking away up the alley the day before swam into his mind. During working hours, the doors of the workshop were always propped open. If the man had been skulking in the Grove, he would have been able to see what was being built inside. "When I left yesterday, I saw a man in the alley two buildings away. I didn't see his face. When I saw him, he was walking away, but I got the impression he was leaving…that I'd disturbed him and sent him off."

Wayland studied Kit's face. "You think he'd been watching us?"

Thinking back over the moment, Kit nodded. "I suspect so. We're the only active enterprise along this stretch—all the other buildings are stores or offices."

And then there was whoever had been watching Sylvia. Were the two "watchers" one and the same?

Was Sylvia being watched because she was connected with him? Anyone who had been following him over the past days would have seen him with her.

A large shape loomed in the doorway, then Mulligan pulled up short. "What on earth?"

His features grim, Wayland nodded. "Exactly. Apparently, someone doesn't want us to succeed."

Mulligan's face set. "We'll see about that." The burly foreman walked in and paced around the frame supporting the keel. Then he halted and snorted. "Luckily, it's not as bad as it looks. The center part of the frame is intact. The outer sections will have to be replaced, but there's no damage I can see to the bilge board. That would have set us back."

"Hmm." Wayland joined Mulligan in examining the damage more critically. "We've plenty of timber—how long do you think it will take to strip out the damaged pieces and replace them?"

Mulligan glanced at the offices, which were nearly complete. "If we pull Shaw and his team off the offices today and use them alongside my group on the frame and keel, we should be back to where we were by early afternoon. Then we can push on. And Shaw will only need one man for a single day to polish off everything in the offices, so pulling him and his team off today won't set things back too much."

Wayland nodded. "Let's do that." He looked at Kit, brows rising.

"Yes," Kit said, in reply to that look. "I'm sure that, in the circumstances, Miss Petty won't be at all perturbed over having to wait another day to get into her new office."

Mulligan grunted, and then the other men started streaming in, giving rise to more exclamations and subsequent explanations.

Briefly, Kit addressed the assembled men, admitting that he and Wayland had no idea who might have broken in and tried to wreck the build. "However, I do know that the best way forward after incidents like this is to put it behind us and get on—to repair, redo, and forge ahead."

Although angry and dismayed, the men determinedly nodded at that. Kit waved Mulligan forward, and the foreman took over, assigning the day's tasks.

Kit worked with Wayland and Mulligan to get the men settled and focused again, with rectifying the damage as their top priority.

Once everyone was busy and the repairs under way, Kit stepped back beside one of the moveable tool racks. With his gaze on the men climbing about the frame as they pulled out damaged timbers, he pummeled his brain for who might be responsible—for any rhyme or reason behind the sabotage.

Wayland slouched up and halted beside him, his gaze on the men as well. After a moment, he said, "I keep coming back to the question of who would do something like this." He raked his fingers through his hair in a vain attempt to smooth down the tufts he'd created.

Kit shook his head. "I can't imagine. I've been wracking my brains trying to think of any enemies I have, or even might have, who would stoop to this, but I can't think of anyone."

"Especially anyone who might be here—in Bristol." After a second, Wayland said, "I haven't come up with any potential suspects, either."

They watched Jack scurry back and forth, fetching tools for the men as they called for them—and sometimes when they didn't.

After a long moment of pondering, Kit said, "Over the last few days, Sylvia Buckleberry has been disturbed by the sensation of someone watching her. Ever since the fire. She hasn't spotted anyone but, given the location of the incidents, wondered if it was the Stenshaw lads—those two who set the fire at the school."

Wayland nodded his understanding, and Kit continued, "It occurs to me that if those two were vicious enough to try to unnerve her by stalking her, then perhaps they thought to strike at me as well. In reality, they'd have more reason to come after me, and therefore this workshop, than her."

Wayland tipped his head. "I suppose that's possible. And we don't have all that many possibilities."

"None except for that man I saw yesterday, but he could simply have been an interested bystander—no malicious intentions at all."

"True."

"Jack!" Shaw bellowed. "Where's that screwdriver?"

"Coming!" Jack darted out from the other side of the tool rack and raced across to hand Shaw the tool.

Wayland looked toward the doors. "We'll need to do something to secure this place rather better."

"Leave that to Mulligan and me. I'll talk to him when he can spare a minute." Kit glanced at Wayland, then looked toward the larger office, which was almost ready for occupation. "Aren't you impatient to get back to your designing?"

Wayland grinned. "I am, actually." He glanced at the men. "Once they reach the point of moving on to new construction, I plan to slip away and start sorting out the space."

Kit grinned, then, seeing Mulligan step back from the fray about the keel, ambled over to consult the foreman about what they could do to ensure there wasn't another break-in.

After discussing all the options and deciding on the simplest and likely most efficient way of securing the workshop—namely heavy door handles plus a heavy-gauge chain and padlock—Kit quit the workshop and made his way into the city.

His first stop was the ironmonger Mulligan had recommended

for the chain and handles, then he called in at a hardware store for the padlock—the largest and heaviest they had.

Weighed down with his purchases, he headed for his office. Having gained approval from both the Dean and the Abbey by Sunday afternoon, he'd ordered the signs for the workshop and school on Monday; the sign maker had promised to have both signs ready by the end of the week.

Miss Petty was seated at a new desk in his outer office, which now looked like an efficient office and not a deserted space. He told her about the damage at the warehouse, then held up the packages he carried as proof that they were taking steps to improve the workshop's security.

She pursed her lips, then shook her head. "The maliciousness of certain people never fails to surprise me. I'm no expert on carpentry, but that keel was shaping up to be a thing of beauty."

Kit agreed. "Luckily, the damage proved to be relatively minor." He paused, then said, "It really wasn't that bad. I think that because everything's been going along so well, the attack was a bigger shock than, perhaps, the actual damage warranted."

With a nod, he continued into his office, turning that observation over and around in his mind. The damage hadn't been that bad. Given the many tools ready to hand, why had the perpetrator limited himself to inflicting only minor—relatively easily rectified—damage? He could have wrecked the very expensive bilge board. That would have caused Kit, Wayland, and their crew considerable grief. Instead...

Had the attacker intended to cause serious harm, but not known enough to do so? Or had he been interrupted by something, and he'd fled before he could do serious damage?

The first scenario would fit the Stenshaw lads. The second... some unknown someone else.

Kit realized he'd come to a halt before his desk. He set down the packages and rounded the desk to sink into his admiral's chair. Several letters had been laid neatly on his blotter, and there were several others he needed to write, as well as the reports he'd promised his brothers.

Pushing the question of who had broken into the workshop to the back of his mind, he picked up his letter opener and got to work.

In midafternoon, he walked with Miss Petty to the workshop.

The only evidence of the break-in that remained was a pile of broken struts in one corner and the broken latch dangling uselessly on one door.

Shaw and one of his team were once again busy in the offices, Shaw plainly doing his best to finish off Miss Petty's space. He waved a nail at the secretary, who was eyeing him straitly. "Be done by knock-off time today—promise."

Kit saw Miss Petty's lips twitch, but she subdued them and regally inclined her head. "Good. Because I will need to move my files in before I can sort out your wages."

His eyes widening, Shaw waved. "Done by this evening— you have my word." He set the nail in place and drove it home.

Kit handed his purchases to Mulligan, who immediately started attaching the handles to the main doors.

Wayland came up, frowning over one of his sketches. Kit spent the next half hour discussing curves and drag and the best timbers for decking.

Once Wayland went off, grumbling beneath his breath, Kit lent a hand with the work on the keel, keeping himself busy for the rest of the day and ignoring the insistent prick and prod of his instincts.

He wanted to see Sylvia—purely to assure himself that she was all right. Given he really wasn't sure what might be evolving between them, he shouldn't be over-attentive. He shouldn't hover. Much as he wished to.

She'd lived in Bristol for two years without his protection; this was her city more than his.

Yet...

By dint of a significant exercise of will, he forced himself to concentrate on what should be uppermost in his mind—namely, the business of Cavanaugh Yachts.

Regardless of who had broken in, that person or persons had intended harm. They'd damaged the business, albeit in a relatively minor way, but there was no reason to believe they would stop there.

By the end of the day, when Kit watched Wayland and Mulligan lock the workshop up tight, heavy chain, padlock, and all, then parted from them and headed for Queen Square and a hackney to ferry him home, he'd come to the conclusion that it was time he met the Stenshaw lads.

★ ★ ★

As midnight approached, Kit and Smiggs stood hunched into their coats in the alley that ran down the side of the Cockle and Crake, a seedy dockside watering hole. They were waiting for the Stenshaw lads to decide it was time to stagger home.

Having learned from Ollie that Cedric and James Stenshaw frequently slipped out of their mother's house late at night— when she thought them safely tucked up in their beds—to visit some tavern, Kit and Smiggs had been lurking in the shadows of Trinity Street when the Stenshaws had slipped out of the house.

They'd tracked the pair here—no respectable tavern but a gathering place for the dregs of the docks. Smiggs had stuck his head through the door and confirmed the pair were there, sitting in a shadowy booth and downing pints of, in Smiggs's words, "whatever piss this place is serving as ale."

That had been nearly an hour ago, and the cold had long ago seeped through Kit's coat. Rather than his usual greatcoat, for the occasion he'd had Gordon find an older, more threadbare jacket, a caution he was now regretting.

He blew on his hands.

Then the door to the Cockle and Crake swung open, and on a gust of warmer air, two slight figures stumbled into the street.

The Stenshaw lads were well away.

Kit smiled wolfishly, then glanced at Smiggs, who nodded. Together, they stepped out of the alley and followed silently in the Stenshaw boys' weaving wake.

The youths were so drunk, they didn't notice the larger men trailing them.

As he'd arranged with Smiggs, Kit waited until the boys reached the runnel that ran down the side of their mother's house.

Then he and Smiggs pounced. They each caught one boy by the collar, hauling him up and back and slapping a gloved hand over his mouth to muffle any cry.

Once he and Smiggs had the boys subdued—simply by twisting their collars until they were in danger of choking—Kit lowered his head and murmured, loud enough for both boys to hear, "You don't want to rouse the household and have your mother see you like this."

Both boys froze.

In the dimness, Kit smiled. "Good. Now, if you remain quiet and answer my questions truthfully, my friend and I might let you go without any further damage. Do you understand?"

Above the gloves covering half their faces, both boys' eyes showed white, and they quickly nodded.

"Right, then." Kit eased his hand from the face of the boy he held, and the youth sucked in a quick breath. But he made no sound beyond a faint, frightened whimper.

"First," Kit said, "you can tell me about the fire you set behind the school on Saturday."

He didn't have to press; both boys immediately started gabbling about how it had been only a lark, and that they'd just thought to make their mother happy by getting the school to move, and much more in that vein. At no point did either boy think to deny they'd set and lit the fire.

Once they ran down—by which time both were sniveling—

Kit said, "Very well. Now, what about the break-in at the work-shop on the Grove?"

The boy facing him blinked at him uncomprehendingly, while the boy Kit held before him turned his head to frown in puzzlement at Kit. "What?"

They weren't that good actors; they weren't acting at all.

"We don't know about any workshop," came from the boy Smiggs held, while the boy Kit restrained blurted, "We haven't been anywhere near the Grove."

Both boys' eyes were wide; Kit could sense their welling panic, no doubt occasioned by his sudden switch to events un-known to them.

Kit met Smiggs's gaze, saw his longtime henchman fraction-ally shake his head, and inwardly sighed. He thought for a mo-ment, then lightly shook the boy whose collar he held. "Have you been following the lady from the school, thinking to un-nerve her?"

All he received were puzzled blinks.

Lips tightening, he persisted, "Someone has been following her. Was it you?"

"No," they chorused.

The pair exchanged a look, then the one in Smiggs's grip said, "We never thought of that."

"Don't," Kit advised, his tone promising instant and terrible retribution. He caught first one, then the other boy's eyes. "In fact," he went on, in that same chilling tone, "I would strongly recommend that you both give everything and everybody as-sociated with the school a very wide berth. That includes the teachers, the pupils, and anyone who visits. Should I find you've approached or interfered in any way—caused any problem at all, even from a distance—I'll be back, and next time, I'll bring the constable with me." He'd kept his voice low throughout. He paused, then demanded, "Is that clear?"

The boys swallowed, bobbed their heads, and chorused, "Yes, sir. Quite clear."

It seemed neither boy had realized who, exactly, had bailed them up. Kit wasn't about to enlighten them. He released his hold on the collar of the youth he'd held, and Smiggs did the same with his brother.

"I suggest you get inside," Kit murmured, and both boys fled down the runnel.

Kit met Smiggs's gaze and tipped his head toward the street. He followed Smiggs out of the confined space, and they started walking toward the river.

Eventually, Smiggs offered, "It wasn't them—not at your workshop and not following the lady."

"No." Kit had really hoped that the Stenshaws were responsible, that the reasons behind the sudden rash of problems would be that obvious and easy to deal with. Now...

They reached the Butts and found a hackney forlornly idling. Smiggs hailed it, and they climbed up and slumped on the seat as the carriage rattled slowly north and west toward Kit's house on Queen's Parade.

He stared unseeing at the passing streetscapes. If not the Stenshaw lads, then who?

Who for the warehouse? Who for stalking Sylvia?

Two separate people? Or were the two actions parts of one man's plan?

Kit turned those questions over in his mind, but could discern no route via which to learn the answers.

Stymied, he shifted to considering why—what reason could anyone have for either action?

No answer to that shone in his mind, either, but the realization that, as far as he knew, he was the only link between the workshop and Sylvia left him with a sinking feeling in the pit of his stomach.

The thought that he might be the reason she was being stalked chilled him. Yet he couldn't for the life of him think of anyone who wished him ill—not to the extent of damaging a build and stalking an innocent lady simply because he'd been seen with her.

When it came to it, he didn't have business competitors, not in Bristol and not even in England, not for the type of yachts he and Wayland were building. If they'd been in France, it would be a different matter, but this was Bristol, not Le Havre or Marseilles.

As the hackney rattled on through the night, Kit found himself facing the single fact that most contributed to his welling uneasiness. Regarding the break-in at the warehouse and Sylvia being stalked, he didn't know what to think—and, therefore, had no clue how to act.

For someone of his temperament, that was worse than wearing a hair shirt.

★ ★ ★

The next morning, Kit forced himself not to hunt down Sylvia— he had no reason to; what excuse could he give?—and, instead, turned up at the workshop, hoping to lose himself in helping with the work, enough, at least, to get his mind off the futile track it had been treading for the better part of the night.

The men were already busy adding the ribs of the hull to the solid structure that now surrounded the bilge board. Before Kit could join them, Wayland hailed him and beckoned him to join him in the new design office.

Kit found his friend ears deep in sketches.

For the next several hours, he worked alongside Wayland in selecting those design elements they felt would best serve to set the yachts they built apart from all others.

"As our aim is to make ocean-going yachts people will beat a path to our door to purchase, we need to make them special," Wayland said, repeating the mantra they'd decided on when he'd agreed to come back to England and become a partner in Cavanaugh Yachts.

Wayland proceeded to present his next amazing idea—which Kit pointed out would surely make the ship too heavy and unbalanced as well.

"Ah." Wayland stared at his diagram for several silent moments, then set it aside and picked up the next.

They'd always worked like this, with Wayland spouting ideas left and right, and Kit picking those that might work and cutting and trimming them to fit.

Hours passed. It was late morning when Mulligan propped his bulk in the doorway of the design office. When Kit and Wayland looked up, directing inquiring looks Mulligan's way, he nodded at Kit. "Man here to see you."

Kit straightened. "Any idea who?"

Mulligan hesitated.

Kit's instincts pricked. "What?"

Mulligan shifted farther into the office, then said, "His name's Bill Johnson. He says he's not here about a job, and I believe him because the daft beggar is too proud to ask." Mulligan crossed his beefy arms across his chest. "I didn't know he was still in Bristol, or I'd have suggested you hire him earlier, when we were taking on men. Like I said, he's too proud for his own good, but he's a right handy man to have in a workshop, even though he has no skills. He's a lifter, see? He's good at moving and positioning things, then holding them in place while we work around him. Lots of bits in ship work are long and clumsy—Bill can easily handle them all. Us older men all know him and trust him to do things right. It really helps move things along to have a man like him working alongside us."

Kit nodded. "You've made a good case. I take it you and the others wouldn't be averse if I offered this Johnson a position here."

Mulligan flashed him a grin. "You've got the gist of it." He tipped his head toward the workshop doors. "But I've no idea what he wants with you."

With a glance at Wayland, Kit tossed the sketch he'd been studying on the table. "In that case, best I come and see."

Mulligan returned to the men about the hull that was taking shape in the first bay of the three they'd set up in the workshop.

Kit walked to where a large, hefty, obviously very strong man stood waiting to one side of the open doors, incongruously twisting his cloth cap between his massive hands. Kit halted in the doorway and nodded. "I understand you wish to speak with me."

Johnson bobbed his huge head. "Yes, sir, your lordship." He moistened his lips, then blurted, "I've seen you at the school, and I've come to ask if you'll use your influence to get them at the school to stop teaching my nipper."

Kit blinked several times as he took that in. Of all the things he might have imagined being asked, that wasn't even on the list. "You want me to ask the school to stop teaching your boy…" He focused on Johnson. "What's the lad's name?"

"Ned. He's Ned." Johnson continued to wring his cap. His earnest, almost-desperate expression left Kit in no doubt that whatever his reasoning, Johnson's request was sincere.

Puzzled and curious—and faintly concerned, for this was the first he'd heard of any parent being unhappy over their son attending the school—Kit turned and glanced into Miss Petty's office to discover that two desks and chairs had appeared that morning. He looked back at Johnson and waved to the office. "You'd better come in and tell me what the problem is."

The big man was reluctant, but Kit gave him little choice, ushering him in and closing the door behind them. Then he waved Johnson to one of the chairs and drew the other to him and sat.

He waited while Johnson gingerly lowered his massive frame onto the rather small chair. Once he had, Kit fixed him with a commanding but unthreatening gaze. "Right, then. Tell me why you want the school to stop teaching Ned." As he said the words, Kit realized their oddity. Why couldn't Johnson simply stop his boy from attending?

It took more than half an hour of carefully probing questions and considerable patience to tease the full tale from Johnson, but finally, Kit felt he had it straight.

The problem centered on Johnson's fear that, once educated, Ned wouldn't want anything to do with his father. That fear was compounded by the fact that, at the present time, Ned wasn't living with Johnson but with Johnson's sister-in-law.

Johnson finally relaxed enough to explain, "I lost my Myra shortly after Ned was born, see, and then I lost my job when the big shipyards moved down to Avonmouth. I couldn't pay the rent after that, and so I had to move to one of the working men's hostels. That was no place for Ned—and that's when Cora, Myra's sister, took Ned in." Johnson swiped his cap across his mouth and, almost in a whisper, went on, "I might get work if I move to Avonmouth, but I don't want to leave Ned behind." The big man met Kit's gaze, his own full of quiet anguish. "He's all I have left."

Kit nodded. "I understand." And he did; Johnson's devotion to his son was written all over his homely face.

"It's not that I've anything against the school itself, mind," Johnson conceded, his mind plainly following a track much trodden. "All of the people there seem nice, not that I've spoken to them, but you can tell—the kids all like them and are happy at the school. But in my case—in Ned's case—that's not the problem." Johnson raised his gaze to Kit's face. "Once Ned learns a trade, he won't want anything more to do with me—I'll just be his out-of-work, layabout father. Cora's already hinted that I shouldn't come around to her house too often, that Ned would be better off being left to make his own way..."

Johnson choked and looked down. After a moment, in a remarkably small voice for such a mountain of a man, he whispered, "But he's all I have."

Kit was suddenly beyond certain that he wanted to help—that he would help Johnson and his Ned.

After a second of rapid thought, he said, "Buck up, Johnson. I think I can see a way around this."

Blinking, Johnson looked up. "You can?" As yet, there was no sign of hope in his eyes.

Slowly, Kit nodded. "I can." Reminded of Mulligan's warning about Johnson's pride, Kit said, "I'm willing to make a deal with you, one I believe will solve all your troubles and get you back to where you want to be—by which I mean living in your own place with Ned. Am I right in thinking that's what you want?"

Now hope flared in Johnson's eyes, but was swiftly reined back by native shrewdness. "Yes. But how?" He swallowed and asked, "What deal?"

"I'll explain in a moment, but first, I want you to clarify something for me." Kit hadn't missed the reference to the people at the school. "Have you been watching the school?"

Johnson's expression turned wary, but he nodded. "At times. I just wanted to see Ned, but I didn't want to go up to him while he was with his friends, so I just looked from out there"—he tipped his head, indicating outside the workshop—"and now the school's moved, from the Abbey gardens at the end of the street or from down on the Butts."

"Have you ever seen Miss Buckleberry—the lady who runs the school?"

Johnson nodded. "Nice-looking lady—what does she want with running a school?"

Kit hid a wry grin and said, "She's a clergyman's daughter."

As he'd expected, that made perfect sense to Johnson, who mouthed an "Oh," and nodded.

"On the days you saw Miss Buckleberry," Kit said, "did you ever follow her?"

Johnson looked sheepish as he met Kit's eyes. "I did once or twice. Well, several times. I was trying to get up the courage to speak to her about Ned, but…well, I couldn't. I don't rightly know how to speak with ladies."

Satisfied—and significantly relieved at the thought that it had most likely been Johnson, who was no threat to anyone, who Sylvia had sensed watching her—Kit nodded and swung his thoughts to how best to manage the big man; he had no wish to see a good man, a good worker and potentially good father, lost. "So now, here's my deal. First, how old is Ned?"

"Eleven," Johnson said.

That would work. "I want Ned to remain at school, and after you hear me out, I think you will, too. What I propose is this—I'll take you on here as a general hand to help the carpenters. Mulligan recommended you, and as he pointed out, we need a strong back and an experienced pair of hands in this work, and as yet, we haven't hired anyone in that role." Kit paused, his gaze on Johnson's face, then went on, "My one condition is that you allow Ned to continue with his schooling. If you agree to that, then after your first two weeks on the job, I'm prepared to stand guarantor for you to rent a suitable home—one you and Ned can live in together. No charity—it'll be some place you can afford to rent, but after being out of work, you'll need someone to guarantee that your position is ongoing."

Johnson looked stunned. "You'd do that? For me?"

"For you and Ned," Kit replied. "And there's one more thing—I think it would be a good idea if, after school each day, Ned came here, to the workshop, to see where you work and what goes on here, then he can walk home with you. That's not only a suggestion to help Ned understand the work you do. We have another lad working here—Jack Deaver."

Johnson blinked. "Jack the Lad?"

"Yes, that's him. I want to get Jack thinking about going to school eventually—he's bright and will do well, and will end up being able to earn substantially more. My first step's been to make Jack an apprentice under Mulligan. Perhaps, if Ned comes here and likes what he sees of the work, in time, he might join Jack as an apprentice, and Jack might join Ned at the school."

When Kit fell silent and looked at Johnson, inviting his response, Johnson, who had been staring as if mesmerized, swallowed and said, "That sounds too good to be true."

Kit flashed him a smile. "Sometimes, in order to seize the good things in life, you just have to have faith and make a start." He paused, his eyes on Johnson's face as, clutching his cap tight, the big man blinked and looked back at him. Then Kit asked, "So what do you say? Come and work here and let's see what we can manage—for Ned as well as yourself."

Kit knew he hadn't entirely assuaged Johnson's deepest fear and added, "At the end of the day, you know you're not the sort of father who will stand in the way of his son's future."

That set Johnson thinking, then he straightened in the chair, met Kit's eyes, and nodded. "You're right. I wasn't thinking straight." He drew breath and, raising his chin, said, "I'd be right pleased to come and work here. I know Mulligan and some of the others—I'd fit right in."

Kit smiled and rose, bringing Johnson to his feet. "So they tell me." He clapped Johnson on the shoulder, opened the office door, and steered the big man through. "Welcome to the crew of Cavanaugh Yachts."

Mulligan, together with the other older men, looked across at the sound of footsteps.

Kit grinned and waved at Johnson. "We have a new recruit." He halted with Johnson as Mulligan came up, dusting off his hands. "I'll leave you with Mulligan. My secretary, Miss Petty, will be in later this afternoon—Mulligan will help you sign on with her, and then you'll be one of this motley crew."

The other men grinned, waved, or nodded in greeting, then continued with their work.

Mulligan nodded to Kit, then said to Johnson, "Come along, Bill. Caps and coats over here." Mulligan led Johnson off to the rack of pegs the men had fixed along the workshop's wall.

"And then we could use your brawn right now—we've a lot of ribs to fix."

Kit retreated to Wayland's office, a satisfied glow warming his chest. He'd done something good, something worthwhile—he felt sure Sylvia would agree when he told her of it.

Ten

In the afternoon, armed with the excuse of needing to tell Sylvia about Bill Johnson having watched her over recent days as well as the news that Ned would definitely be continuing at the school, Kit left the workshop and headed to Sylvia's office. On finding the door shut, he turned his steps toward the school.

He found Sylvia there, overseeing the end of the school day.

"Wednesday is Miss Meggs's day off," Sylvia explained, even though he hadn't asked, "so I always come over to help Jellicoe and Cross with getting the tribe away." Illustrating the need, she raised her voice. "Johnny, you've forgotten your scarf."

One young urchin skidded to a halt in his mad dash for the door and, swinging around, flashed her a grin. "Thank you, miss." Then he raced back to his desk, grabbed the scarf from the seat where it had languished, and raced to catch up with his friends.

"It's like a stampede," Kit said, smiling at the thunder of feet and jostling bodies.

"They're boys," Sylvia countered. "They always move like that."

The last of the herd vanished through the door, leaving Jellicoe and Cross catching their breaths. They waved up the hall at Kit, then retreated to their desks along the side wall, presumably to neaten their lesson sheets and get ready for the next day.

After returning their salutes, Kit swung to face Sylvia. "Speaking of boys, did you know one of those attending here—Ned Johnson—is living with his aunt while his father looks for work?"

Sylvia nodded. "It's a rather sad case. Ned's been quieter since he had to go and stay with his aunt—I think he misses his father."

Kit realized he hadn't thought of Ned feeling any other way; he blew out a short breath. "Well, that's a relief, because I spent an hour this afternoon engineering a way for his father—Bill Johnson—to be able to rent a home in a few weeks and so have Ned live with him again."

"You have?" Delight filled Sylvia's eyes, her reaction even more of a fillip to his soul than Kit had hoped it would be.

Drinking in her expression, he slid his hands into his pockets and nodded. "Johnson came to ask me to intercede with you to get the school to stop teaching Ned." As Cross and Jellicoe, alerted by Sylvia's reaction, drew closer and settled to listen, Kit explained Bill Johnson's fear that education would lead to Ned disowning him. "It seemed the situation with Ned living with his sister-in-law had exacerbated Johnson's understandable anxiety. He has no book learning of any sort himself."

Cross nodded sagely. "We run into that attitude more often than you might think." He tipped his head at Sylvia. "Sylvia usually prevails, but we've lost a few along the way."

"Sadly, that's true," Sylvia confirmed. "Mr. Johnson's belief isn't uncommon."

"So how did you convince Johnson to leave Ned at school?" Jellicoe asked. "Whatever you did, we can only applaud—Ned is one of those pupils we would least like to lose."

With Cross and Sylvia nodding in agreement, Kit felt even more vindicated in his meddling. "The long and the short of it is that I made a deal with Johnson—he's already started working for Cavanaugh Yachts, and in return for him allowing Ned to continue at the school, in two weeks' time, I'll stand guarantor for Johnson's income so he can rent a place of his own. He's currently living in a hostel, which is why Ned's with his aunt."

"And then Ned can go back to living with his father?" Sylvia confirmed.

Kit nodded. "That will ease one issue, but I went a few steps further." And he wasn't sure, now, how they would react to his scheme. "I suggested that, after school each day, Ned should come to the workshop—to see the work his father does and appreciate what he helps to create."

Cross and Jellicoe arched their brows, but as both thought, they slowly nodded.

"A sound idea," Jellicoe said.

Relieved, Kit went on to explain about Jack the Lad and Kit's notion of blending school attendance and apprenticeship, and was relieved anew to find the idea enthusiastically received.

"That's a real step forward," Sylvia said, her expression alight. "And now you've inspired me to approach other businesses and see if they might be interested in similar apprentice-school partnerships."

Kit felt the glow he'd experienced earlier swell. "You can use my name and title, if that will help."

Sylvia laughed and lightly touched his arm. "Oh, it'll help. Thank you."

Something in Kit froze; that was the first time she'd spontaneously touched him.

Cross and Jellicoe, now talking excitedly, had already donned their coats. With farewell waves, they headed for the door.

"I said I'd lock up," Sylvia said. "Just let me get my things."

Kit prowled in her wake and held her coat for her, then he waited while, reticule swinging, she crossed to the back door and locked it, then came walking up the hall to where he stood by the front door.

He watched her approach, her gaze shifting to either side as she checked this and that. Helping Bill Johnson and his Ned had left him feeling... He decided the word he was seeking was the one Wayland had earlier suggested: "uplifted." He couldn't recall setting out to deliberately help someone—a total stranger, someone he didn't know—before. He suspected that was Sylvia's influence rubbing off on him.

The buoyant feeling was rather addictive.

As she neared, he waved her through the door and followed, tugging the door shut behind him. He waited beside her while she locked the door and returned the key to her reticule, then— because impulse prodded and he hoped she would see the gesture as appropriate—he offered her his arm.

She paused for only a second, then flashed him a gentle smile and set her hand on his sleeve.

Pleased—a touch relieved—he guided her down the steps, then started them pacing in relaxed fashion along the pavement. Although they'd walked together through the city several times, this was the first time since Rand's wedding he'd walked with her properly on his arm. The effect of having her just that bit closer feathered across his senses; her long legs set a stride that was easy for him to match, and her unconscious gracefulness captivated the more predatory part of his mind.

With some effort, he drew his thoughts from such simple pleasures and focused on the here and now. "Are you heading to your office or your lodgings?"

"Lodgings," she replied, her gaze on the flagstones ahead of them. "I've finished all I need to do today."

He saw her glance across the street at the Stenshaw residence. As she looked ahead again, he said, "Incidentally, have you been troubled by that sensation of being watched today?"

A slight frown tangled her brows; she was tall enough that he didn't have to bend his head to see her face. "Now that you mention it, no." She met his eyes. "Not this morning when I walked to the office, and not when I walked over here, either."

"Johnson admitted he'd been watching the school—trying to catch glimpses of Ned without Ned or anyone else seeing him.

He also said he'd watched you over recent days, trying to get up the courage to speak to you."

"Oh." Her face cleared. "That must have been what I sensed."

Kit tipped his head. "Possibly. But now that Johnson is working at Cavanaugh Yachts, you shouldn't feel that odd sensation again."

Sylvia smiled a touch self-deprecatingly. "It's a relief to know it was something so innocent. It must have been the aftermath of the fire that made me think there was something…malevolent in the gaze."

The word "malevolent" disturbed Kit; he couldn't imagine that Johnson's anguished but innocent staring would have triggered such a feeling, fire or not.

They reached the Butts and turned toward the bridge. Sylvia lightly gripped his arm, refocusing his attention. "You know how things at the school are going. So tell me about your progress at the workshop." She turned bright eyes on him. "How is work on your first boat going?"

"Ship," he corrected, all but instinctively. Then he tipped his head. "But more accurately, yacht."

The look she sent him was playfully long-suffering. "Your first yacht, then."

He paused to help her onto the drawbridge. As they fell into step again, he said, "Unfortunately, we suffered an unexpected setback." He met her questioning, incipiently concerned gaze. "On Monday night or early Tuesday morning, someone broke in and sabotaged the work we'd done on our first keel."

"Good Lord." She gripped his arm more tightly. Her gaze searched his face. "Was anyone hurt?"

He shook his head. "No. The damage was all to the new work." Hearing his own words gave him pause. He frowned.

"Did whoever it was steal much?" Sylvia asked.

"No." He blinked. "Nothing at all. And yes, that strikes me as strange."

They stepped down off the drawbridge and, wending through knots of people, made their way into Clare Street. Once they were pacing steadily again, Kit went on, "That said, we've already put the incident behind us and forged on. Our carpenters have started setting in the ribs of the hull."

Sylvia listened as he described the current state of the hull, struggling to mute her smile as enthusiasm flowed through his tone and lit his face. He sounded so much like the students— very much a case of "boys will be boys."

When they crossed into Corn Street and he reached the end of his description with a "That's how it stands as of today," she remarked, "I admit I'm having trouble imagining the old warehouse being such a hive of activity—it always seemed such a cavernous space."

"Oh, we've changed things—altered it to suit our needs." He described the new offices, the gantry, and the huge tool racks.

She stared in unfeigned amazement. "You and your men have certainly been busy."

He grinned at her. "We have."

There was a wealth of sincere satisfaction in his expression; she studied it in something close to wonder. Had anyone told her— even a month ago—that Lord Kit Cavanaugh would find this degree of pleasure and joy in such work, she would have scoffed.

Yet hadn't she already accepted that the man she'd believed him to be didn't exist? That the man on whose arm she was entirely contentedly strolling was someone else entirely?

She looked ahead. It was nearly five o'clock, and the pavements were increasingly crowded with people heading home. They reached the intersection of Small and Corn Streets and were about to turn right when someone behind them stumbled, and the resulting jostling shoved her forward.

Kit caught her, steadied her, then, drawing her closer and linking her arm with his, using his larger frame to shield her, he quickly steered her around the corner.

Within a few paces, the press of bodies eased. She drew in a tight breath. "Thank you."

He flashed her a smile—a genuine one, not the charming gesture she'd seen him deploy in ballrooms. "My pleasure."

She knew he meant the words, too. He honestly liked protecting people, ladies especially. She now understood that had nothing to do with his rakish reputation but was simply an expression of the sort of man he was.

The man he truly was—the real man she was coming to know.

She looked ahead as they continued strolling, still close with her arm linked with his, their clothes lightly brushing with each stride as they progressed down the street.

The Lord Kit Cavanaugh she was coming to know was so unlike the man his reputation and her own observations-from-a-distance had led her to think he was—had convinced her he was—that it was almost as if he was a completely different, unrelated man.

The sort of lord she'd thought he was would never have devoted himself to a project such as Cavanaugh Yachts, would certainly never have bethought himself to aid the school in finding a new venue—and the thought of that imagined lordling bestirring himself over the plight of Johnson and Ned was simply laughable.

Yet the real Kit Cavanaugh, the man walking by her side, had done all those things, freely and willingly.

They—his actions—were the true measure of the man he was.

There was no denying that, to her, the real Kit Cavanaugh was far more attractive than the ton version had ever been. Even though, in that ton version, for more than five years he had been her romantic ideal—her fantasy gentleman—that status had been based purely on his physical attributes; she'd never liked or approved of his character—the character she and the ton had been led to believe was his.

Although she'd reined in her senses as tightly as she could, she remained excruciatingly aware of him walking close beside her; his strength, the controlled grace investing his powerful frame, and the sheer physicality of his presence impinged on her nerves, made her lungs constrict, and set her heart to beating just a soupçon faster.

He drew her—lured her—as no other man ever had.

As she'd discovered at the wedding, when it came to him, no amount of denial—not even imagined deficits of character—made the slightest difference to that intrinsic, instinctive attraction.

In an effort to stop dwelling on her reaction to him—at least not while he was so close—she searched for distraction… "This other boy—the one you call Jack the Lad. How old is he?"

"Thirteen, I believe." He met her eyes. "I gather he's known up and down the docks by that moniker." Without her having to further prompt, he told her of Jack's story and of how he came to be an apprentice at Cavanaugh Yachts.

Watching his face as he related what she realized were merely the bald facts, Sylvia felt her heart soften even further. He was a good man, although she doubted he thought of himself in such terms. He was focused on marching toward his goal, and, she suspected, he viewed his acts of kindness and generosity as very much incidental—in one way or another supporting his efforts to reach said goal. He could help, so he did, and in his eyes, that simply made his path easier.

Yet the fact was he saw and cared when things were wrong and acted to set matters right—or as right as he could make them.

She was aware that some of the ancient noble families still lived by the creed of noblesse oblige. Having met Kit's older half brother, the marquess, she suspected that the House of Raventhorne was one such family.

With such desirable characteristics combining with his undeniable physical attractiveness, it was no wonder at all that he, the real Kit Cavanaugh, lured her in so very many ways, engaging her mind as well as her senses.

They reached Baldwin Street and crossed the cobbles to Back Street. Her lodgings were less than ten minutes away.

Kit sensed his time with Sylvia drawing to a close; he wanted to prolong it, but aside from the fact he couldn't imagine how, caution raised its head. Better he used the time to learn more than to do anything that might make her skittish.

Tipping his head, he caught her eyes. "Other than your work for the school, how do you fill your time?" When she blinked at him, he elaborated, "What entertainments does the city offer that draw you?"

She smiled a trifle self-consciously. "I expect I lead a very circumscribed life, at least by London standards."

He swallowed a grunt. "We're not in London."

"No. So…" She looked ahead. "I enjoy music of all sorts—in summer, there's often concerts in the parks, and in winter, there's the theater as well as the occasional recital. And, of course, I sing in the choir at Christ Church"—the glance she slanted him was playfully self-deprecatory—"like any good clergyman's daughter."

He smiled. "Your father's vicarage is near, isn't it?"

"Yes, and I visit fairly regularly. Papa has always been interested in the school. He'll be delighted to hear of your involvement and our new premises." She paused, her brow lightly furrowing, then looked ahead. "I should visit him soon and see what advice he has to offer about establishing a scheme such as you suggested—one linking school and apprenticeships."

"Would he know about that sort of thing?"

She smiled fondly. "Papa is a font of wisdom on many matters, but in this instance, I'm hoping he'll have some insights into how best to present the idea to the Dean and the parish council."

"Ah." Kit smiled. "I have to admit that any form of politics, at any level, is not my forte." Briefly, he met her eyes. "I'm more a 'do what needs to be done and worry about getting permission later' sort of person."

She laughed, and the sound slid beneath his skin and teased. In his opinion, she didn't laugh enough.

When she looked ahead, he allowed his gaze to dwell—just for a few seconds—on her profile. Then smoothly, he faced forward. He'd sensed every tiny reaction that his being so close beside her had evoked and had noted every response to his touch that she'd worked so hard to suppress.

At the wedding, he'd realized he affected her in what, to a gentleman of his experience, was a distinctly telltale manner. He knew what such reactions—those instinctive, impossible-to-prevent leaps of the senses—portended, what they were symptoms of.

Yet at the wedding, the almost-desperate way she'd scrambled to suppress those revealing reactions had left him unsure.

Even now, he didn't know if she recognized the implication of such reactions, much less whether she would welcome exploring them further.

While he was increasingly sure of what he wanted vis-à-vis her, he had no idea what she wished for when it came to him.

That wasn't a quandary he'd ever faced with any other woman.

They turned into her street. Her lodgings lay at the far end, where the street curved around the leafy park. He guided her along the pavement that ran beside the grass.

He knew what he wanted to do next, what he wanted to ask of her, but an uncharacteristic hesitancy laid hold of his tongue.

A whisper of uncertainty threaded through his mind and warned him that before he made his next move—*any* further move—he needed to be absolutely sure of his direction. And he needed to know more. He should evaluate his options first...

They reached the corner and crossed the cobbles to Mrs. Macintyre's house.

Feeling nearly suffocated by his wretched uncertainty—so unlike the bold self-confidence with which he normally faced the world—he fought to draw in a deeper breath.

Sylvia halted on the pavement before the gate, and he halted beside her. She gently disengaged and drew her arm from his; he had to battle an urge to snatch her hand back and only just won.

Smiling, she turned to him. "I haven't asked where you're living." She immediately looked conscious for having voiced such a question.

Before she could blush, he shoved his hands into his pockets—to ensure he didn't reach for her—and replied, "I bought a house in Queen's Parade, facing up Brandon Hill."

"Ah." Her smile returned. "That's a pretty area."

He shrugged lightly. "I wanted a house that was big enough, but not too big."

"I saw Ollie at school. How's he settling in with your people?"

Her assumption that he would have "people" made him smile. Holding her gaze, he said, "There's only my majordomo, Gordon, my groom, Smiggs, and our cook, Dalgetty, so Ollie is far from overwhelmed. In fact, he might even be underwhelmed by my paucity of servitors, but I've heard him chatting freely with the others, and they're the sort who'll take a lad under their wings."

"I see." Her smile remained, but her eyes studied his, and as the moment stretched, her smile slowly faded…

Then she sucked in a tight breath and flashed him another smile—one much less certain—and turned to the gate. "I should go in."

Why?

But he reached over the gate, lifted the latch, swung the gate open, and held it for her to pass through.

This time, he didn't follow. That damned uncertainty anchored his boots to the pavement.

She paused on the path and looked back at him. For a moment, her eyes searched his features, then she met his gaze. Her smile was soft, but real and more assured. "Thank you for escorting me home."

He let his lips curve and inclined his head. "As always in your company, the pleasure was mine."

Her smile deepened a touch before, with a dip of her head, she turned and walked on.

He watched her climb the steps, open the door, and go inside. He stared at the door as it closed and the lock clicked into place.

After a second more of mindless staring, he forced his feet to move.

Striding back along the park, he kept his eyes peeled for an available hackney; several were trotting along the cobbles, ferrying people home as twilight descended. He found one disgorging its passenger—a businessman with top hat and cane. The instant the hackney was free, Kit climbed aboard and gave the jarvey his address.

Kit sprawled on the seat. After turning the carriage, the driver whipped up his horse. Kit stared unseeing at the streetscapes flashing past as he headed home—to his all-male household and his lonely bed.

If he wanted to alter either of those facts, one thing had just become crystal clear.

Before he next met Sylvia Buckleberry, he needed to devise a plan of campaign.

A campaign unlike any he'd ever waged.

Because he'd never felt so wretchedly unsure of himself with any woman before.

Eleven

The following afternoon, Kit tracked Sylvia to the school. He'd spent half the night plotting and planning and had settled on a strategy and a course of action. After spending most of the day at the workshop, mentally rehearsing his approach while working alongside Wayland and the men, he'd set off for Sylvia's office, girded his loins, and knocked on the door, only to discover she wasn't there.

As he climbed the school steps, he heard her voice, and a curious mix of trepidation and anticipation slid through him. He couldn't recall feeling the like for more than a decade, not since he'd been a wet-behind-the-ears youth who'd just come on the town.

And even then...

Then, the outcome hadn't really mattered.

Now, it did.

He stood back to allow two boys to barrel through the door, then ducked inside before the next group clogged the entry.

To one side, Sylvia and Miss Meggs were discussing something in some book.

When they looked up, smiles lighting both their faces, he quashed his instinctive impulse to cross to them—to Sylvia—and, instead, raised a hand in a salute and continued down the hall to where Cross and Jellicoe had just dismissed the older lads and now stood comparing notes.

The teachers saw Kit coming and turned to greet him.

He had his excuses for calling polished and ready; he halted before the pair and, after exchanging nods, said, "I came to see how Ned was today—whether he'd heard his father's good news and, if so, how he was taking it."

Both Cross's and Jellicoe's faces creased with smiles.

"He's a different lad," Cross said. "It's as if a spark that should have been glowing inside him all this time has ignited again."

Jellicoe nodded. "That's not a bad description. From what I overheard him telling the other lads at lunchtime, his father called at his aunt's house last night and told Ned of his new job and that you'd offered to stand guarantor for him renting another place to live, and that once that was done, Ned could live with him again."

"A transformation is the only way to describe it," Cross averred. "We'd put Ned down as naturally quiet, but it seems that's not the case at all."

Jellicoe's lips twitched. "No, indeed, but along with his sudden liveliness has come a renewed determination to succeed with his lessons. Whether his father actually said so or if Ned is reading between the lines, it seems he's realized that his father might end quite proud of him for his learning."

"And your suggestion of Ned going to the workshop after school was inspired," Cross said. "He used to be one of the dawdlers, but today, he was out of here like a shot the instant we ended the last lesson."

Jellicoe chuckled. "The one drawback I foresee to your plan is that you might well find you have a small platoon of boys hovering about your workshop door and goggling at your men."

Kit grinned. "I'm sure the men will take that in stride. And if they don't, I can rely on my secretary, Miss Petty, to sort the boys out." Kit tipped his head. "Who knows? As the boys grow older, we might end with more school-apprentice arrangements. Speaking of which, how is Ollie faring? He's also in something of a school-apprenticeship situation, although in his case, he's training for domestic service. My majordomo reports that Ollie's bright and quick-witted. Gordon thinks that, depending on how Ollie grows, he might be able to go as a footman or even aspire to becoming a butler."

"I wouldn't disagree with that assessment." Jellicoe exchanged a look with Cross. "We've been putting Ollie through his paces to see what level of schooling he needs." Jellicoe met Kit's eyes. "We've also noticed his quick thinking, and in light of what you've just said, I rather think we'll work with Ollie to move him along rather faster."

Cross returned from fetching his coat and Jellicoe's. Handing Jellicoe's over, Cross humphed. "Ollie's an excellent example of the waste of good intellect that occurs when children are forced into service too young." Shrugging on his coat, Cross grinned at Kit. "Thankfully, we have our hooks in him now, and with luck, he'll reach his full potential."

His questions about Ned and Ollie had been intended to account for his appearance at the school, but nevertheless, Kit felt gratified. That warm glow opened up inside him again and spread through his chest.

He sauntered beside Cross and Jellicoe as the pair walked to the door. Miss Meggs had departed, and Sylvia was waiting, a smile for them all on her face.

Cross and Jellicoe said their farewells and departed, leaving Sylvia smiling at Kit. "I heard you asking about Ned and Ollie. Did Cross and Jellicoe fill you in?"

He nodded and waved her to precede him through the door. "They did, indeed." Following her into the weak sunshine, he added, "I'm glad both boys are, it seems, applying themselves with enthusiasm."

"Oh, they definitely are." Sylvia turned to lock the door. "Miss Meggs said Ned was bouncing with happiness, and Ollie seems to have settled in quickly."

When, after stuffing the heavy key into her reticule, she swung back to the pavement, Kit offered his arm. She stared at it for a second, then, instead of setting her hand upon it—keeping him at a greater distance—she stepped nearer and tucked her gloved hand in the crook of his elbow.

His confidence regarding her and his strategy leapt and surged. He guided her down the steps and, strolling like any other couple, they set course for the Frome and the city beyond.

He'd planned on waiting to take the next step in his carefully considered campaign until they were closer to her lodgings—so if she declined and things grew awkward, they wouldn't have far to go in each other's company—but now, he realized there would be much more noise and a lot of other distractions the farther they went.

It was more peaceful here, on the west bank of the Frome, and his natural impulsiveness was pushing and prodding him to take advantage of the moment and ask her *now*.

Surreptitiously, he cleared his throat, then, in an even tone, ventured, "There's to be a classical music concert at the Council House hall this Friday evening. I wondered if, enjoying music as you do, you would like to accompany me to the event."

She turned her head and looked at him. For several seconds, she simply stared, and he was unable to read anything at all in her face.

Trepidation welled, and his gut chilled. "I thought," he offered, having to restrain himself from babbling, "that with the entire outing in public, as it were, it would be entirely above board, and you wouldn't require a chaperon." He'd intended explaining that before actually asking her.

She blinked up at him.

For the first time in his life, he understood what being on tenterhooks felt like.

Then her eyes focused on his, and a smile curved her lips. "Thank you." She dipped her head and faced forward. "I would enjoy that."

He felt ridiculously pleased—as if he'd succeeded in securing far more than her agreement to attend a concert.

Given her previous view of him, perhaps he had.

He could hope that her acceptance meant she'd laid aside all previous judgments of him and had, at least to some degree, reassessed.

As he steered her through the crowd on the Butts and on toward the steps to the drawbridge, he told himself it was only a small victory—a public concert, for heaven's sake!

He still felt thrilled that she'd agreed to go with him.

They covered the distance to her office with both of them smiling—in her case, with her habitual serenity, in his, rather inanely.

He escorted her to her office and, propping his shoulder against the door frame, watched as she tidied papers and files away.

Sylvia hoped she was putting things away in the right places. She was operating entirely by rote, her mind scrambling to adjust to a reality that, despite their recent equable interactions, she hadn't allowed herself to contemplate.

Going to a public concert with Lord Kit Cavanaugh. Walking into the Council House hall on his arm, beneath the interested eyes of the cream of local society...

Did he realize that was what it would be like? Did he have any inkling how local society would interpret such a sighting?

She ducked her head, swallowing the scoffing sound she'd nearly given vent to. Of course, he realized. He might not be the rakehell she'd imagined him, but he'd been raised within the ton. He understood the nuances of social behavior very likely better than she did.

Almost certainly better than she did...

Him asking her to accompany him did mean what she thought it meant, didn't it?

For a second, uncertainty rose and shook her, then she realized she was merely giddy.

Hardly surprising when a situation she'd fantasized about—admittedly with a very different imaginary man—was on the cusp of coming true. And with a gentleman who was much more to her taste than her imaginary lord had ever been.

Placing a stack of papers in her bottom drawer, she glanced at her desktop and found it cleared. She drew in a deep breath and straightened. She had to get a grip on her wayward senses before she did something truly foolish—like smile at him with stars in her eyes.

She looked at him and smiled—and fought to ensure it was an appropriate expression rather than one too revealing. "There's nothing more I need to do here." She picked up her reticule and walked toward the door.

He watched her approach, then stepped back and waved her into the corridor. "In that case, I'll escort you wherever you intend to go."

She had intended to pick up some laundry, but that seemed far too mundane an activity to do with him by her side.

They stepped onto the pavement of Broad Street, and he offered her his arm. She took it, feeling steel beneath her fingertips, then hesitated.

He glanced at her face. "Your lodgings?"

She nodded. "But that's in the opposite direction to your house." She lowered her lids and watched his face through her lashes. "You don't have to escort me all the way there, you know." She'd been walking the streets of Bristol for the past two years without incident; she had very little fear of the areas she had to traverse.

He started them strolling toward the nearby intersection with Wine Street. His expression was unperturbed as he replied, "I do, as it happens—both know that and yet have to escort you to your door."

Her lips curved more deeply, and she looked ahead. After a moment, she murmured, "Ah—I see."

He steered her across the busy intersection, and they continued down High Street.

Somewhat sternly, she told herself not to read too much into what he very likely saw as common courtesy. Or at least the sort of gentlemanly attention he would bestow on any lady he knew were she to set out to cross a city the likes of Bristol.

Still, it was impossible not to feel a fillip of happiness that he was willing to go so far out of his way to see her safely home.

Her pleasant mood made the icy chill that slithered across her nape all the more noticeable. She tensed, then quickly looked around.

"What is it?" Kit halted, every instinct on high alert. He scanned the crowds behind them—a bustling throng jostling along the pavements of Corn Street to the left and Wine Street to the right, with people dodging and weaving through the equally strong flow of pedestrians going up and down Broad and High Streets. "The watcher?"

"Yes." Sylvia's tone was quietly furious. "And whoever he is, he's a coward—as soon as I look, he stops."

Kit drew her to the side of the pavement, putting their backs to the building while he searched the scurrying sea of humanity.

Beside him, Sylvia, doing the same, huffed disgruntledly. "There's so many people, yet not one of them looks out of place."

He had to agree. There were businessmen of all stripes as well as hawkers of this and that, a chestnut vendor, and the ubiquitous men carrying placards advertising one or other chapel. There were messenger boys darting in and out, weaving their way through the throng, and older women as well as girls trudging home after working as shop assistants or the like.

After a moment more of fruitless searching, Kit closed his hand over Sylvia's, now gripping his arm. "Come. Let's walk on."

She nodded tersely and settled into step beside him. "Maybe

he'll follow us, and we'll get a better sighting in the less-populated streets."

He glanced at her. "Tell me the instant you sense him, but don't stop or look around."

Briefly, she met his eyes and nodded.

They remained on high alert all the way to Mrs. Macintyre's house. As they approached the gate, in response to Kit's inquiring look, her lips tight, Sylvia shook her head. "Nothing. He didn't follow."

Kit escorted her up the steps to the porch and waited while she hunted in her reticule and found her latchkey. She inserted it into the lock, then paused and looked up at him. "Thank you. It was less…bothersome because you were with me."

She couldn't have said anything better designed to soothe his flaring instincts.

He searched her eyes, then stated, "Obviously, your watcher isn't Bill Johnson."

"No."

"And I doubt it was the Stenshaw lads, either." He paused, then admitted, "My groom, Smiggs, and I caught up with the Stenshaws on Tuesday night. I wanted to make sure they hadn't been behind the sabotage at the warehouse. But I seriously doubt they had any involvement in that incident, nor had they been watching you."

She sighed, her gaze going past him to the street. "I wonder who it is—and even more importantly, why? A clergyman's daughter already on the shelf is hardly an attractive target for abduction and ransom."

He nearly disputed her description of herself, but decided how he saw her wasn't germane to the discussion.

He debated doing something to appease his clawing instincts—such as demanding she allow him to escort her everywhere—but that, he felt sure, would put her back up. He was forced to settle for capturing her gaze and saying, "Please promise me you'll take care when out walking and that you won't venture out at night alone or anything similar."

The look she bent on him was the same long-suffering, "don't be foolish" look he'd seen Mary bestow on Ryder times beyond counting.

"Of course, I won't do anything senseless. Besides," she said, finally turning the key, "I have no nighttime excursions planned other than Friday's concert with you."

The reminder of that event improved his mood considerably. Enough for him to share a last smile with her and bow gracefully in farewell. He waited on the step until she was inside and had closed the door, then swung around and strode quickly down the path and along the pavement to where he'd seen a hackney idling.

After hailing it, he climbed up and dropped onto the seat. As the jarvey turned his horse toward Queen's Parade, Kit frowned into the softly gathering twilight.

Could the person who was watching Sylvia with malignant intent be somehow connected to the break-in at the workshop? No matter how he twisted the facts, he couldn't dismiss the possibility.

As the hackney rattled on, Kit found himself facing the disturbing prospect that the reason behind Sylvia being watched might have more to do with him than her.

★ ★ ★

After eating a solitary dinner in a dining room that, courtesy of Gordon's efforts, was starting to look like a dining room and no longer part of an empty house, Kit adjourned to his study.

Along with his bedroom, the study had been one of the first rooms to be completely furnished. Kit crossed to the tantalus, poured himself a good inch of French brandy, then sank into one of the comfortable wing chairs angled before the hearth.

Every now and then—usually every month or so—past experience prodded him to stop and take stock. To retreat to an appropriate mental distance and review what he'd accomplished and what he planned to do next, the better to keep his feet firmly on the most direct path to his ultimate goal.

The activity had become habit in the years during which circumstances had forced him to live under his mother's thumb, subject to her manipulative whims. Of Lavinia's four children, he'd been the least susceptible to her ploys; he'd quickly learned to plot and plan so she had as little chance as possible to dictate his actions. The other three—Rand, Stacie, and Godfrey—had been aware of Lavinia's machinations and her interference in their lives, but although Rand, too, had resisted, the other two had had a harder time of it, Stacie especially.

Kit sipped and felt the fiery amber liquid slide smoothly down his throat. He hadn't sat down intending to become mired in the past, yet...

Since Lavinia's death six years ago, he'd been drifting, both physically and emotionally. Flitting here, then there, not settling anywhere.

Until now.

He considered that reality—the past from which he'd come— then took another larger sip of brandy and firmly turned his mind to his present.

To Cavanaugh Yachts and the progress made over the past two weeks.

When he'd driven into Bristol, Cavanaugh Yachts had been nothing more than a name and a concept—and a lot of hopes. Eleven days on, and Cavanaugh Yachts was a going concern, with suitable premises, a workforce more able than he and Wayland could have hoped to assemble so quickly, and despite the attempted sabotage, they had a first hull taking shape.

There was nothing in that with which to quibble. Satisfaction welled. They'd done well, laid a solid foundation, and could go forward from there.

Their next step? Orders. With luck, their sign would be up within the week. Once it was, he would start spreading word of their existence, yet realistically, until they had their first yacht completed and on the water, wise buyers would hang back.

He and Wayland had agreed that their first hull should remain the property of the company, a showpiece on which to take prospective buyers out on the waves. He would buy the second yacht they built, Wayland would take the third, and Ryder and Rand were going to go in together to purchase the fourth. That would give the company enough work to see them well into the new year. After that was when having a steady stream of orders would become essential.

There was little he could do in terms of securing further orders at present. Better he spent his time working with Wayland and the men to ensure their first yacht was as perfect as they could make it.

With that settled, he shifted his focus to the other side of his life—to home and hearth. His house was his, and his small household was taking shape nicely. The staff worked efficiently and had knitted into a comfortable core of mutual support; he deemed no adjustments to be necessary. However, Gordon and Smiggs had started dropping hints that they needed to hire a housekeeper, yet that was one selection neither felt capable of making—and Kit boggled at doing so himself.

Hiring housekeepers, maids, and the like was the province of the lady of the house—a position that, in this house, was currently vacant.

He shifted in the chair and sipped again. He hadn't consciously considered marrying for a very long time. Not since his mother and her machinations had turned him off the entire concept, tarnishing the ideal to such an extent that he and all in him had revolted and rebelled.

But Lavinia was six years dead, and her effect on him had faded along with his memories of her interference.

Ryder had married, yet he'd never truly been under Lavinia's influence so hadn't had the same hurdles to overcome. But now

Rand had found love, too. From all Kit had seen of them and their wives, Ryder and Rand were both now living the ideal he'd thought would be forever denied all Lavinia's children.

Clearly, his assumption had proved false.

So what about him?

He eyed the amber liquid in his glass, then swirled it and sipped—and admitted to himself that he was definitely considering marrying now. Not only did it seem to be time, but he'd discovered a lady who attracted him as no other ever had—on multiple planes and in multiple ways.

Inviting Sylvia to attend the concert with him hadn't been any rashly impulsive act. He'd hunted for the right place to take her—one that would advance his cause by making it clear that he was courting her.

That he was intent on wooing and winning her.

He had no recollection of when he'd made that decision, if he'd made it at all.

He'd been attracted to her from the first moment he'd seen her at Rand and Felicia's wedding, but her off-putting behavior had all but immediately soured his mood. At the end of the day, he'd turned his back and driven away and hadn't expected to meet her again.

In truth, he hadn't. The Sylvia who had stormed into his office just over a week ago was a completely different lady.

A completely different prospect.

They'd been in and out of each other's company ever since. They'd worked together to achieve minor goals that advanced her, his, and oft-times both their current aims.

They'd formed an effective alliance in dealing with threats and steadily advancing their now-mutual goals to the extent that he now longed for her company, and she didn't seem at all averse to his.

He wanted to bring that alliance home and establish it here— at the center of his private life.

Leaning his head back against the chair, he stared unseeing at the ceiling.

Even without closing his eyes, he could imagine her sitting in the chair across from him, perhaps working on some list or reading a novel.

She would fit into his household effortlessly. She understood people with much the same facility he did.

In his estimation, she was the perfect candidate to fill his vacant position.

His lips curved self-deprecatingly, and he raised the glass and sipped. A clergyman's daughter—who would have thought it?

Certainly not the racy matrons of the ton—those ladies who would invite him to their beds while doing their utmost to direct their daughters' eyes elsewhere.

He grinned at the thought of how those ladies would react were he successful in winning Sylvia's hand.

Mentally, he pulled himself up short. He *was* going to win her—there was no question about that.

Again, he sipped, leaving only dregs. He wasn't normally afflicted with self-doubt; that ran all but counter to his character. He was usually utterly confident in moving forward, assured that, even if something along the way went wrong, he would ultimately triumph.

With Sylvia…uncertainty dogged him; he constantly felt as if he was feeling his way with her, never sure how she would react. With her, he felt like a green youth and not the experienced nobleman-about-town he most definitely was.

His difficulty, he suspected, stemmed from two sources. Her attitude to him at the wedding had flummoxed him and still did; he had no idea why she'd treated him so dismissively and disdainfully. His reputation couldn't have been the sole cause; she might have disapproved of him for that, but her aversion— the intensity of her antipathy—had to have sprung from some deeper motivation.

Indeed, even after the revelations of that meeting in his office, if she hadn't needed his help with the school, he doubted he would have got closer to her; she would have held him at a distance, as she had at the wedding.

The somewhat unnerving thought that she might, at any time, revert to viewing him as she previously had left him understandably wary.

On top of that, he'd never interacted with a lady of her ilk before, not with any amorous intent. She was a very different proposition from ladies reared within the bosom of the ton. As their acquaintance deepened, that, more than any other factor, was what was undermining his native confidence and making him second-guess himself over every little step he thought to take.

In short, the seduction of Sylvia Buckleberry would be a very different dance set to a very different beat than any seduction he'd undertaken before. When it came to capturing the affections of a clergyman's daughter in Bristol, he had no experience to fall back on at all.

She'd only just consented to take his arm and walk more definitely by his side.

Somewhat grimly dwelling on that, he drained the last drops of brandy from his glass, then set it aside and pushed to his feet.

In the matter of securing Sylvia Buckleberry as his wife, he had a long way to go.

He was determined that their excursion on Friday night would significantly advance his cause.

Turning down the lamp, he headed for the door—and his empty bed, which he fervently hoped would not remain empty for much longer.

★ ★ ★

The next morning, Kit walked into the workshop to see Wayland scowling at a heavy chain, examining the links he was passing between his hands.

Kit focused on the chain and felt his hackles rise. It was the chain they'd used to secure the workshop doors. He halted beside Wayland. "Problem?"

Grimly, Wayland said, "Some blighter tried to cut this. See?" He held up a thick iron link and pointed to the telltale scratches. "He failed. But..."

Now equally grim, Kit nodded. "He tried. Therefore, he'll return better equipped and try again."

Wayland sighed, lowered the chain, and met Kit's gaze. "Whoever he is, he's intent on causing us harm." His brow furrowed. "I still can't imagine who he could be."

Kit shook his head, then paused.

Wayland read his expression. "What?"

Lips compressed, Kit thought, then said, "Yesterday, after I left here in the afternoon and was walking with Sylvia along High Street, she felt the eyes of the watcher again."

Wayland glanced to where their teams of carpenters were hard at work on the new hull; the incessant hammering would drown out his and Kit's conversation. Puzzled, Wayland said, "I thought it was Johnson watching her, wanting to speak with her." The big man was holding one of the huge ribs in place while two of the others hammered nails into its base.

"That's what I'd put the sensation down to, but yesterday, Johnson would have been here with Ned. It couldn't have been him." Kit slid his hands into his pockets. "I'd already started wondering if the watcher's real target all along was me. Me and this place. And unlike Sylvia, I'm oblivious to his surveillance."

Wayland's eyes widened. "You think he started watching Sylvia after seeing her with you?"

Kit nodded. "The timing fits. She first started sensing him after we'd been walking together around town for several days."

"Hmm." Wayland looked as troubled as Kit felt. After a moment, Wayland glanced at the men, then tipped his head toward his office.

Kit followed his partner into the relative quiet and shut the door.

Wayland put the chain on his drafting table and turned to Kit. "We've got to put a stop to this. I don't like the fact he—whoever he is—is stalking your Miss Buckleberry any more than I imagine you do."

"Indeed." Kit's tone was terse. "We have to catch the bastard—preferably red-handed."

"What about the authorities?" Wayland asked. "Should we report this?"

Kit considered, then shook his head. "What can we tell them? That someone broke in here on Monday night and caused minor damage. That earlier on Monday, I glimpsed a man who might have been watching the workshop walking away down an alley I was passing. And that on several occasions, Sylvia has sensed someone watching her, but when she looks, he stops, and she and I have searched but failed to spot anyone paying her undue attention."

Wayland grimaced. "Put like that, I agree—there's no sense in involving the magistrates." He paused, then said, "Whoever he is, he's tested our security." Wayland waved at the chain. "That was what last night's visit accomplished. He'll be back, and I imagine that, next time, he'll bring the right tools to pry open the padlock."

Kit nodded. "There's no other way into the workshop other than through those doors—and there's no lock that's impossible for a determined man to pick."

"Precisely." Wayland stared at the chain. "But he won't know we know he's been back—that he's still trying to break in and wreak havoc. I only found the evidence because Jack, with his sharp eyes, spotted the scratches. I doubt anyone else would have."

"All right. We agree he's going to come back," Kit said. "When?"

Grimly, Wayland said, "Either tonight, Saturday night, or Sunday night. Why wait? The sooner he can hit us again, the more damage he'll do to our business."

Kit nodded. "Which night will probably depend on how urgent he feels his need to attack us is."

Wayland met Kit's eyes. "We need to set up a watch."

Kit stared at his friend while he thought, then said, "Given we don't know who this blackguard is—what his past association with us is or why he's targeted Cavanaugh Yachts—then I suggest we don't involve the men." He refocused on Wayland's eyes. "Not until we know what this is all about."

Wayland nodded. "I agree. *Especially* as neither you nor I have a clue what the man's motive is."

"Also, judging by the damage he did last time, it seems he's acting alone, so the two of us should be sufficient to the task."

Wayland grinned. "Quite like old times." Then he sobered. "You don't think he'll hire others to help him?"

Kit thought, then shook his head. "What he's doing is illegal, and the damage he alone can do will be sufficient to cause us major problems. Why invite witnesses?"

Wayland conceded with a tip of his head. He started gathering up the chain. "So we'll start our watch tonight."

Kit hadn't forgotten the concert. "There's an event I have to attend this evening, but I'll return here after that. I doubt I'll be much later than ten o'clock." More was the pity, but he'd accepted that, with Sylvia, there was a definite limit to how far he might advance that night.

Wayland had placed the chain on the floor and was looking at a diagram. Distractedly, he said, "I can't imagine our blighter will make a move before that."

"Indeed." Kit bent and picked up the chain. "I'll take this out to the door, then come back. I want to go over the deck plan again."

Without taking his eyes from his sketch, Wayland gave vent to a chuff of frustrated agreement.

Kit hefted the chain and turned to the door. Tonight looked set to be a long night—he hoped it also proved eventful, one way or the other or both.

Twelve

Sylvia stared at the cheval glass in her bedroom. She was holding her two favorite evening gowns against her—first one, then the other—trying to decide which made her look more the sort of lady people would expect to see gracing Lord Kit Cavanaugh's arm.

"Mauve?" she muttered, holding up the first gown. "Or pale green?" She swung the second gown into place, then, undecided, repeated the exercise yet again.

The realization that she would be going to the concert with a bona fide scion of the nobility had dawned on her as she'd hurried home that afternoon. Kit Cavanaugh was a lord born and bred, something she'd largely forgotten over the past weeks of working alongside him, grappling with school affairs and hearing of his business successes. Over that time, the man she'd seen was so very different from the image of Lord Kit Cavanaugh that she'd carried in her head for years that she'd fallen into the habit of thinking of the here-and-now man as someone quite separate—as a gentleman far more worthy of her attention.

He was still Lord Kit Cavanaugh.

And tonight, at least half of Bristol society would see her on his arm.

"Oh, God." She wasn't given to taking the Lord's name in vain, but the situation seemed to warrant it. She stared at her reflection and almost wailed, "Which one?"

A tap sounded on the door. She whirled as it opened, revealing Mrs. Macintyre, who she'd asked to come up and help with her laces.

Seeing her hovering in indecision, Mrs. Macintyre tsked. "Still not ready?" Then she raked her gaze over the two gowns and declared, "It's obvious—the green one with that pretty lace. That shade makes your skin look as if it's glowing and your hair appear more golden."

Sylvia blew out a breath and laid aside the mauve gown. "All right." She felt breathless and strangely giddy, and her nerves were all but twanging. She couldn't recall feeling this way during her London Season, much less at any other time. She shrugged out of her robe and started climbing into the apple-green silk gown with its fullish skirt and lightly embroidered bodice and overskirt.

"Wait." Mrs. Macintyre stepped behind her, flicked loose her corset strings, then wrenched them a great deal tighter.

Sylvia gasped at the sudden constriction that locked about her ribs and waist. "I need to breathe!"

"Not that much, you don't. And you want to make the most of the assets God gave you." Ruthlessly, Mrs. Macintyre tied off the strings, then peered over Sylvia's shoulder.

Sylvia followed her landlady's gaze to the mirror to see her breasts mounding above the corset's bodice, while her waist was nipped to the point a man's hands could span it and the curve of her hips was an attractive line.

"There!" Mrs. Macintyre beamed. "That's better."

Sylvia wasn't so sure, but then she thought of what Kit might think…

There wasn't enough time to fuss with her corset. Mrs. Macintyre eased her fully into the gown, then helped settle the skirts. Fussing with the hem at the rear, Mrs. Macintyre said, "It's good to see you walking out with such a suitable gentleman. A lord, no less, so you'll become a ladyship once you're wed."

What little breath Sylvia had managed to draw in left her.

Her eyes widening, she blurted, "He... I..." Desperate, she got out, "It's not like that at all."

Straightening behind her, Mrs. Macintyre met her gaze in the mirror, her own expression one of deep skepticism. "Is that so? Seems awfully like it to me. Why ever would a lord like him ask you to this concert if he wasn't keen on you?"

Sylvia blinked. That was an excellent question. Her mind skittering this way and that, the only answer she could come up with—other than the obvious conclusion Mrs. Macintyre had leapt to, which Sylvia didn't think she was yet ready to even contemplate—was that Kit, as he'd mentioned, was new to the city. He wouldn't know who was whom and knew she would be able to guide him.

The thought acted on her giddiness like a dash of cold water.

Her unacknowledged hope abruptly deflated, leaving her feeling hollow inside.

Of course, that had to be it.

Subdued, she sat and let Mrs. Macintyre arrange her hair. Her landlady was always a help and a support; Sylvia was grateful for her ministrations, but she could have wished that, in this instance, Mrs. Macintyre had kept her mouth shut and not jarred her to earth quite so soon.

She wouldn't have minded feeling like Cinderella going to the ball for just a little longer...

She blinked at her reflection, then frowned. What was she thinking?

Had her long-ago infatuation with Lord Kit Cavanaugh resurfaced while she wasn't paying attention?

The thought horrified her, but then she had to don her jewelry—her mother's pearls and earbobs—and check her evening reticule, pull on her gloves, and allow Mrs. Macintyre to brush her velvet cloak.

Then the knocker on the front door beat an imperious tattoo, and it was too late to panic. She sucked in a breath and looked at Mrs. Macintyre.

Her landlady beamed. "You look lovely, dear. I'll just go and get the door—you wait a moment before you follow."

Sylvia forced in several deep breaths and sternly told herself to stop questioning and simply enjoy the evening. Whatever Kit's reasons for inviting her to accompany him, she'd learn them soon enough.

Remembering to glide, she started along the corridor. She'd attended dinners, musical soirées, and the like at the houses of various of the city's hostesses, but given she avoided the morning teas and at-homes, she was considered something of an eccentric. Not quite a bluestocking, but close to it.

She reached the stairs and started down, her mind on who they might meet, then she felt Kit's gaze and raised her own to see him standing in the front hall, looking up at her.

Her breath tangled in her throat; her lungs seized, and she stopped breathing.

He looked… "Magnificent" didn't come close to doing him justice.

Oh, my!

His often unruly hair sat in neat, tamed waves about his well-shaped head. His clean-shaven features appeared chiseled, aristocratically severe, while his superbly cut coat emphasized the width of his quite remarkable chest. His attire was impeccable, from ivory silk cravat, striped waistcoat in varying shades of gray, and trousers that clung to his powerful thighs before falling to brush the tops of highly polished boots.

Although from on the stairs, his height was less obvious, she knew he towered a full head taller than she—he would be taller than the majority of men at the concert.

More, the aura of dominance that hung about him wasn't purely a matter of physical attributes. Dressed like this, he looked exactly what he was—a nobleman of understated power.

Then he smiled a slow, deeply appreciative smile—one she didn't even need to see his eyes to read—and what wits she'd retained scattered like autumn leaves in a gale.

Savoring the moment, Kit waited for her to come to him. His mouth had dried; the instant he'd seen her starting down the stairs, a sylph in truth, slender as a reed in her pale green gown, his attention had locked on her, and he'd forgotten the rest of the world.

For these few minutes, she demanded and captured his mind, and he was more than happy to devote his senses to her.

To drinking in her feminine delights, such as the delectable curve of her swan-like neck, exposed above the raised collar of her gown. From high at her nape, that embroidered collar, edged with fine Belgian lace, swept down and around, showcasing the luscious mounds of her breasts. He hadn't previously seen those; the gowns she normally wore covered her from the neck down, and her bridesmaid's gown had also possessed a modest neckline.

She'd been hiding herself away—just as she'd concealed the fiery, passionate nature that had sent her barging into his office over a week ago.

On reaching the last stair, she stepped down to the tiles, and he managed at last to fill his lungs and realized his smile revealed rather more than he wished it to—at least at this point—but she merely smiled serenely back; she didn't seem unnerved by his appreciation.

Relaxing somewhat—reminding himself that even if this felt like the first time, he'd done this sort of thing countless times before—he held out his hand. When, coloring faintly, she glided the last feet to him and laid her fingers in his, he swept her an elegant bow. Straightening, he met her eyes—and saw something of her usual dry wit appear, as if she'd recognized the gesture for the extravagance it was. "Good evening, my dear Sylvia. You look…utterly divine." He reached out and took the cloak of midnight velvet her landlady offered and held it up for Sylvia to don.

She sent him a faintly warning look and swiveled to give him her back.

He gently draped the cloak in place, then lightly rested his palms on her shoulders. Tipping his head, he met her eyes. "If you're ready, our carriage awaits."

Throughout the next minutes, Sylvia felt like some magical princess floating on air. Kit swept her out of the door, down the steps, and into a carriage so new she could still smell the faint scent of varnish. Inside, the carriage was the epitome of luxurious comfort, with well-padded leather-covered seats and paneling of golden oak accented with brass fittings.

Kit sat beside her and the carriage moved off. As the equipage turned into Back Street and rolled smoothly north toward the Council House, it seemed that the latest in modern engineering had eliminated a great deal of the usual rocking.

Even through the dimness, she could feel Kit's gaze on her—mostly on her face, her profile—yet even though she was swathed in her cloak, occasionally, that heated gaze slipped lower before he raised it again.

After a second's silence in which she didn't think he or she breathed, he softly said, "You really are a stunning sight. You've taken my breath away—literally—and it might take a while for me to get it back."

Surprised, she glanced at him.

Through the fluctuating darkness, he met her eyes, and she saw his lips curve in what she thought was a self-deprecatory smile. "And yes, I really mean that." His eyes searched hers, then he said, "I won't say more on that head and disturb you... I just wanted you to know."

She blinked, her mind and wits tumbling anew.

His smile deepened, and he gracefully waved. "You must tell

me what you think of this carriage. I've hired it from the maker for tonight—I'm thinking of ordering one similar."

She recognized a diversion when she heard one. She grabbed it with both hands. "It's exceedingly comfortable. I appreciate how well-sprung it is."

"It's a new type of spring. Rand has a share in the company that makes them, but thus far, only a few carriage makers are using them. I was lucky to find one here."

"How are Rand and Felicia getting on—have you heard from them since you arrived?"

He shook his head. "Rand isn't a great letter-writer, but then, neither am I."

She chuckled. "However bad you and Rand are, I can assure you Felicia is worse. Once, I hadn't heard from her for so long, I felt moved to visit—simply to reassure myself that she was still alive."

He grinned—a flash of white teeth in the dimness. "In that case, I'll have to rely on Mary—she believes in keeping abreast of all developments in the family and letting everyone know. The counterside to that is that woe betide you if you do not respond to one of her chatty and informative letters with information of your own."

From the affectionate amusement that colored his tone, she could tell he was fond of his senior sister-in-law. Looking out at the streetscapes, she mentally arched her brows. That Mary, Marchioness of Raventhorne, corresponded with Kit—ergo, approved of him—told a tale of its own. Sylvia had met Mary only once, but it had been obvious the marchioness was no one's fool.

Indeed, given Mary dealt with Kit's half brother, Ryder, on a daily basis, that she was as shrewd as she could hold together went without saying.

And she approved of Kit.

Before Sylvia could dwell further on that, or on the fact that she, too, approved of Kit—this Kit, the man she'd recently come to know—the carriage slowed to a plod, then drew up directly before the steps leading up to the Council House doors.

She blinked in surprise, then the carriage door swung open. Kit descended, turned, and offered her his hand.

She took it, aware of his firm clasp and how safe his touch made her feel. Nonsensical, really; if there was any threat to her here, it lay with him.

Then she was on the pavement. After smoothing down her skirts, she looked around—and saw, as she'd expected, a long line of carriages waiting to disgorge their occupants before the steps.

Eyes widening, she looked at Kit. "How...?"

His rakish grin flashed. "Livery is still good for something."

She glanced at the groom holding her door—and was stunned again. "Ollie?"

Manfully restraining his usual big smile, Ollie executed a neat bow. "Miss."

He looked utterly different in perfect livery; now she'd looked, she recognized the Raventhorne colors. She glanced briefly at the coachman on the box—also resplendent in livery—then felt Kit take her arm. All she could think to say to Ollie was "Don't get cold."

At that, his grin broke through. "I won't, miss. We've blankets and a flask of cocoa and seed cake."

Everything a boy would need. Surrendering to Kit's gentle insistence, she allowed him to lead her up the steps. On reaching the top, she glanced back and saw the carriage rumble off into the night—no doubt to draw up and wait on one of the less-crowded side streets.

"Don't worry." Kit's breath brushed the curls floating about her ear, sending a delicious shiver slithering down her spine. "Smiggs will keep a close eye on Ollie. He's made quite a hit with my staff."

Turning to the doors, she murmured, "I thought Ollie was training to be a footman."

"He is. Tonight is part of that training."

"Oh." Of course. Not a groom, a footman.

Kit steered Sylvia through the main doors and into the wide foyer. As they halted under the glare of the chandeliers high above, he felt her stiffen beside him.

Then an attendant was bowing before them. "Might I take madam's cloak?"

Kit stepped behind Sylvia and lifted the heavy silk-lined velvet from her. He sensed her hesitation—almost as if she wanted to clutch the cloak to her, whirl, and flee—but her head rose, and she waited, outwardly serenely patient, as he handed the cloak to the attendant and received a ticket in return.

This, Kit thought, might be more difficult than he'd foreseen. Sylvia's guardedness reached him—but what she was guarding against, he didn't know. She'd weathered a London Season, so it couldn't be the event or the crowd that was unnerving her. He sincerely hoped she wasn't regretting agreeing to this evening with him—agreeing to be seen in public by his side.

Sylvia waited to see what Kit would do—what tack he would take. Whether he intended to request her assistance in navigating the cream of Bristol society's upper crust that was steadily streaming into the foyer. The crowd rapidly filled the space with a fabulous palette of colorful gowns that contrasted with the gentlemen's evening black. Conversations swirled, and the cacophony built, voices rising to the ornate ceiling high above along with a miasma of heady perfumes.

However, other than taking her gloved hand and tucking it firmly in the crook of his elbow, Kit merely waited, his large frame protecting her from the buffeting flow of other patrons. After a moment, he dipped his head and asked, "Do you know how long before the doors open, and we can escape to our box?"

Escape?

She searched his eyes, confirming he was serious. "Usually, the doors don't open until the hour stipulated."

"Oh." He looked genuinely disconcerted. "I assumed that was when the performance commenced."

She smiled and patted his arm. "In London, yes, but here"— with a small wave, she indicated the crowd—"people value the opportunity to meet as much as the music."

His expression grew faintly aggravated.

Then she realized what he'd said. "You secured a box? At such short notice?" Given this was the Council House hall, there were only a handful of boxes available.

He met her eyes and arched his brows. "Another of those things about being a nobleman—everyone wants to cultivate your patronage."

She couldn't miss the cynicism in his voice. "I suppose that's true," she murmured. "And here, there are far fewer nobles on the ground."

He grunted softly, then a stout gentleman and an overdressed lady sporting feathers in her hair and diamonds by the pound pushed out of the crowd before Kit and Sylvia.

"I say, Miss Buckleberry"—she recognized the gentleman as one of the city's aldermen—"pray do the honors and make m'wife and I known to your companion."

Sylvia had relaxed; now, she felt Kit stiffen beside her. But there was no help for it. "My lord, allow me to present Alderman Henshaw and Mrs. Henshaw." To the Henshaws, she said, "Lord Cavanaugh."

The alderman bowed low, and Mrs. Henshaw sank into a flamboyant curtsy.

A quick glance at Kit's face showed he'd adopted a carefully neutral expression. He bowed slightly—just enough not to give offence. "Alderman. Mrs. Henshaw."

Henshaw straightened and beamed. "I hope you enjoy your visit to our fair city, my lord."

Mrs. Henshaw hung on her husband's arm and all but gushed, "I'm one of the patronesses of the music society—it's an honor to have our gathering graced by your presence, my lord." Mrs. Henshaw's eyes brightened. "Do you plan to be in town for long?"

"As to that," Kit coolly replied, "I can't say."

The alderman made some comment about a recent council decision regarding the docks, one Sylvia as well as Kit took note of, but Kit responded to that and all other attempts to lure him into conversation with distinct coolness and an aloof, somewhat haughty mien.

His behavior in this company stood in stark contrast to the ease with others that Sylvia had seen him constantly display over the past weeks.

She wasn't surprised when, where the Henshaws had led, others quickly followed. She found herself called on to perform a stream of introductions for the luminaries of Bristol society. Only in a few cases did Kit unbend enough to freely engage with those wishful of making his acquaintance, and notably, those instances involved officials who connected in some way with his new business or, on two occasions, with the school.

For all the rest, Sylvia got the distinct impression that Kit bore with said luminaries on sufferance. To her, he appeared uncomfortable, almost defensive, which, given his background, seemed decidedly strange.

Then old Lady Creswick, resplendent in puce with the feathers from half an ostrich pinned about her person, stumped to a halt before them. She addressed Kit directly, claiming to have met him years before. "In London, although I daresay you won't remember. You were a dashing young scoundrel, turning ladies' heads right and left." Gripping his fingers in her claw-like hand, Lady Creswick grinned toothily into his face. "I knew your mother quite well."

Although Kit didn't move, with her hand still tucked against his side, Sylvia sensed him all but recoil. The smile he bestowed on her ladyship, while outwardly amenable, was distinctly brittle. "Indeed?" His tone couldn't have been more distant.

"Heard about her death," Lady Creswick continued. She cocked a brow at Kit. "Accident, was it?"

If he could have physically retreated, Sylvia sensed he would have. This time, his "Indeed" was cloaked in ice.

Lady Creswick noticed, but merely shrugged. "Happens to us all, one way or another."

A stir among the crowd had Kit looking over the heads. He'd expected to draw some attention, to meet a few people and chat, but he'd found the degree of interest well-nigh suffocating. How Ryder bore with it, he didn't know. Luckily, the doors to the hall proper were being opened, and the ropes cordoning off the stairs to the boxes had already been removed; he could see couples trailing up the red-carpeted stairs.

Closing his hand over Sylvia's where it lay on his sleeve, he smiled vaguely at Lady Creswick. "If you'll excuse us, ma'am, we should find our box."

Without waiting for any acknowledgment, he nodded to the old lady, and the instant Sylvia rose from her curtsy, he steered her toward the nearest staircase.

As they ascended and the noise and press of bodies decreased, he felt relief flow over him. When they found their box—the best in the house—and he followed her inside, that relief rose in a wave and swamped him, and the pressure about his lungs and chest fell away.

He seated Sylvia in one of the chairs at the front of the box, then sank into the chair alongside. He glanced out and down into the body of the hall, in which the serried rows of seats were slowly filling. Most of the orchestra were already on the stage, tuning their instruments.

After a moment staring at the sight, he drew in what felt like his first real breath since Alderman Henshaw had accosted them, then exhaling, he turned his head and looked at Sylvia.

With her hands lightly clasped in her lap, she was surveying the hall, her expression relaxed, her gaze interested. He could detect no remnant of the stiffness that had assailed her when they'd entered the foyer; that had faded away while they'd talked to all and sundry. Perhaps she'd simply been nervous.

"My apologies," he murmured. "I didn't anticipate…being quite such a cynosure of attention." As she turned to him, he met her eyes. "I hadn't realized the city's dignitaries would press you into service as they did—that certainly wasn't my intention in asking you to accompany me tonight."

Sylvia searched his face, his eyes, and found nothing but sincerity. *Well, that answers my question as to what moved him to invite me.*

And that meant he'd invited her…purely for the pleasure of her company.

She thrust the distracting thought aside; now was not the time to dwell on that. Smiling, she reached out, laid her hand on his arm, and lightly squeezed. "No matter." She paused, then added, "I was happy to help—because if you are to make a go of Cavanaugh Yachts and be sponsor of the school as well, then some of those who approached are people it will be useful to know."

He heaved a put-upon sigh. "I know." He gazed out at the murmuring crowd.

If he'd been a smaller man, she might have said he squirmed.

After a moment, grudgingly, he said, "I admit I don't like swimming in social waters. In some strange way, moments such as those in the foyer make my skin itch."

More specifically, they made him feel grubby, and Kit knew why. Whenever possible, his mother had ensured he attended her friends' social events—the ton crushes at which she'd delighted in showing him and his siblings off. She'd insisted on parading them before her peers with the expressed intention of trading their hands for the largest gain offered to her. Essentially, she'd intended to sell them to the highest bidder.

Unsurprisingly, Lavinia had concentrated her efforts on Rand, her eldest son and then-heir to the marquessate. Kit had done his best to avoid her notice and slide around her directives to attend this soirée, that ball, but he hadn't been able to avoid them all.

But that, thank God, was all in the past, and Sylvia was correct—he needed to gird his loins and seize the advantage his birth afforded him to further his business interests and those of the school, too.

The attendants were dimming the lamps in the hall below and an expectant hush washed over the audience.

Then the lead violinist swept onto the stage. After bowing to polite applause, with a flick of his coat tails, he took his seat, and the conductor appeared. After bowing deeply to the audience, the conductor strode to the lectern. He tapped the wooden frame with his baton, bringing the orchestra to attention, then with a majestic sweep of his arm, he led the assembled musicians into a pastoral air.

The music washed out and over the audience. Kit felt the knots of his earlier tension unravel. He enjoyed listening to such music—fanciful and imaginative and undemanding. He'd learned that it soothed in a way he couldn't describe.

At the conclusion of the introductory air, he shifted in the chair, angling his shoulders so he could glance at Sylvia's face without turning his head. Her expression was utterly serene, her eyes trained on the musicians; she was following the musicians' movements with the eye of one who truly appreciated their efforts.

His last remaining knot of concern dissolved. She was enjoying the performance, possibly even more than he. Quietly satisfied, he returned his attention fully to the music.

When the first sonata came to an end and the musicians paused to rearrange their music sheets and catch their collective breath, Sylvia turned to Kit. When he regarded her, a faint lift to his brows, she searched his face and found no hint of boredom. From the glimpses she'd stolen during the performance thus far, it seemed he genuinely enjoyed attending classical music concerts. "I confess I hadn't taken you to be an aficionado of classical music."

He tipped his head. "I wouldn't say I was any sort of aficionado, but..." His gaze drifted to the stage, and he shifted slightly in the chair. "Stacie—" His gaze swung back to Sylvia. "Eustacia, my sister. You met her at the wedding." When she nodded, he went on, "She loves classical music—adores it, more like. But our mother didn't approve of Stacie attending classical music concerts. To paraphrase Mama, she saw no benefit in Stacie attending such stuffy events. Much better that she spend every waking minute at balls and soirées and routs." He looked at the stage. "So whenever there was a concert Stacie especially wished to attend, she would claim to be ill, and Mama would leave her at home while she went gadding as she always did. Then Stacie would slip out of the house, and I would meet her in the garden and take her to the concert."

Smiling, Sylvia patted his arm. When he looked at her quizzically, she said, "What a very good big brother you were."

He chuckled and nodded. "I was. After those outings, my halo positively shone. But in the end, I benefited as much as Stacie. By having to sit through those concerts, I learned to love listening to such music, too."

The musicians were ready again. The conductor tapped his lectern, then led the orchestra into a piece by Haydn that was slated as one of the highlights of the concert.

Together with Kit, Sylvia gave her attention to the stage, but while the strains of the music wreathed through her brain, she found her thoughts dwelling on what he had revealed.

Stacie was a few years older than Sylvia and Felicia and, surprisingly for a highly attractive lady of her station, as yet unwed. Sylvia had spent only a day in Stacie's company and had liked as much of Stacie as she'd seen, but had found her a touch reserved.

Sylvia had gathered, more from what was not said than from any specific comment, that their mama—Rand, Kit, Stacie, and their younger brother, Godfrey's—had not been a model of maternal affection and support. Kit's tale of Stacie's concerts illustrated as much. Sylvia found such maternal deficiency difficult to imagine; in her case, although her mother had died when she was seventeen, her parents' love and support had been the foundation stones of her life.

No more than Lady Creswick did Sylvia know the tale of the late marchioness's demise, but like her ladyship, she suspected some story, possibly a grim one, was there.

What would it feel like to be the son of a lady who refused to allow her daughter to attend musical concerts purely because she saw no social gain in the exercise?

Sylvia pondered that as Haydn's music wrapped around her.

The end of the second movement brought an interval. The orchestra retreated from the stage, and Kit stirred and looked at her. "Shall we adjourn to the foyer for refreshments?"

She smiled and picked up her reticule. "There'll be refreshments served in the gallery on this level. We won't need to go down."

"Good," he muttered under his breath, and she laughed.

"You are not that cowardly," she chided.

"No," he admitted. "And despite being a provincial orchestra, the musicians have more than made up for the incidental drain on my patience."

She was still smiling broadly when he handed her down from the box, then wound her arm with his. Together, they strolled toward one of the booths set up to dispense lemonade, orgeat, and champagne.

While they stood in the short queue, she was conscious of attracting more than a few glances, all of which she pretended not to notice while inwardly admitting that never in her life had she felt so envied.

When they fronted the booth's counter, Kit requested two glasses of champagne. On receiving them, he turned and offered one to Sylvia—and froze. He raised his eyes to hers. "I'm sorry—I should have asked. Is champagne to your liking?"

She smiled laughingly and filched the glass from his fingers. "Yes—of course." She sipped. Over the rim of the glass, her teasing eyes met his. "My only complaint is that I don't get to drink it nearly enough."

He felt slightly silly over his discomfiture. "You are a clergyman's daughter, as you've reminded me often enough."

"Hmm." She appeared to be savoring the quite acceptable wine. "That doesn't mean I don't appreciate the finer things in life."

He watched her take another sip. Her lips—pale rose and delectably curved—glistened as she lowered the glass. He had a vague memory of her sipping the beverage at the wedding, so decided she wasn't simply trying to paper over his gaffe. He steered her away from the crowd now flocking to the booth toward a spot by the wall where the press of bodies was rather less.

Sylvia drank the champagne, enjoying the slight fizz on her tongue, and allowed her gaze to roam over those pouring into the gallery, many coming up from below. If they stood there much longer, they'd end besieged.

On the thought, Kit shifted—much as if he wished to, metaphorically at least, hide behind her skirts.

She cast him an amused glance. "I would have sworn that, in society, you would be much more at home than I."

His eyes were fixed on the shifting throng. "I seriously doubt that's true."

He really didn't like being there—being surreptitiously gawped at and ultimately targeted by the local hostesses and their husbands as well. While Sylvia felt vaguely tickled at being more assured in this sphere than he, she also felt an impossible-to-resist urge to ease his way. Glimpsing several ladies eyeing him from behind their fans, she drained her glass and handed it to him. He'd already finished his drink. He beckoned an attendant collecting glasses nearer and placed the empty glasses on the man's tray.

The instant Kit lowered his arms, Sylvia twined her arm with one of his. "If I might make a suggestion?"

His gaze, somewhat hunted, had returned to the shifting throng.

She leaned closer. "You can't hide, but there's no reason we can't go on the offensive, as it were, and choose with whom to engage—namely, those who might have relevance to the school or your business." When he blinked at her, she gently tugged and got him moving. "Just follow my lead, and rather than getting caught in conversations to no purpose, let's see if we can't put our time to better use."

He met her eyes, then acquiesced with a nod and faced forward. "All right. Wither away?"

She spied Councilor Peabody and his wife. "Why not start with Peabody? It won't hurt to connect with him again."

As he'd agreed, Kit followed her lead. Given he'd met Peabody before, their interaction with the councilor and his wife passed off reasonably easily, especially as Mrs. Peabody proved to be a gentle, motherly sort.

They departed the Peabodys' orbit and fetched up beside the mayor—a Mr. Forsythe—and his wife. Although Mrs. Forsythe's eyes lit, Forsythe himself was only too pleased to monopolize Kit's time, and Sylvia's, too, eulogizing over the establishment of Cavanaugh Yachts and all the great things Forsythe hoped would flow from that and also effusively commending the relocation of the school. Kit ended amused by Forsythe's earnestness and mentally labeled the mayor as a gentleman he could call on if Cavanaugh Yachts encountered any problem with the city council.

Sylvia accepted the mayor's accolades with what Kit sensed was a large dose of cynicism, yet she remained gracious throughout.

On quitting the Forsythes' circle—much to Mrs. Forsythe's ill-concealed dismay—they fetched up beside Mr. Hemmings, the chairman of the Dock Company, and a lady who proved to be his sister. Kit was glad of the chance to pick Hemmings's brain regarding the workings of the docks and the Floating Harbor, which Hemmings seemed only too happy to discuss. Miss Hemmings and Sylvia spoke of social matters, such as the school and several charities on the boards of which Miss Hemmings served.

Then two other couples arrived to join their circle. Kit thought the conversation would slide out of Sylvia's control, but after she deflected three probing comments directed at him with an artless ease he could only envy, in each instance firmly steering the conversation back to a discussion of some aspect of business, she tightened her hold on his arm, smiled at everyone, and made their excuses, then nudged him into walking on.

He was only too ready to do so.

While they continued to amble and stop here and there to chat with people she considered he should know, he realized that she'd been right. As long as they were moving with apparent purpose, no one was game enough to attempt to intercept them.

Increasingly, he relaxed and focused more definitely on using the opportunities Sylvia steered his way to further his knowledge of those who held power in Bristol's business world.

When, eventually, the bells rang and they returned to their box, he sighed and dropped into the chair beside Sylvia. Through the gathering dimness as the lamps were turned down, he met her eyes. "That was an entirely unlooked-for bonus to my evening." He dipped his head to her. "Thank you. I couldn't have managed that without you."

Sylvia's cheeks heated; she was glad of the deepening gloom. She glanced at the stage, but although the orchestra was in place, the conductor had yet to reappear. She hesitated, then ventured,

"From your questions to various gentlemen, I gather you're taking a long-term view regarding Bristol and your company."

Kit was now very much more relaxed, sitting in an elegant sprawl and looking at the stage. Lightly, he shrugged. "I intend Cavanaugh Yachts to continue in business for many long years. And I expect to remain at its helm, actively involved, for as long as I'm able." He turned his head and met her eyes, and his lips lightly curved. "You have a passion for teaching dockyard boys, while mine is building ocean-going yachts."

Even in the low light, she could see that truth in his face; he was committed to his business and to Bristol for life. He wasn't going to flit away; he was putting down roots there.

Her lips lightly curved, she inclined her head in acknowledgment of his comment, then the conductor walked out, and they both looked at the stage. Seconds later, the music swelled and, entirely at ease in each other's company, they lost themselves to Haydn's brilliance again.

★ ★ ★

At the end of the performance, Kit decided he'd done enough socializing for the evening. He called on skills honed in London to steer Sylvia down the stairs, reclaim her cloak, then guide her out onto the Council House steps ahead of the rush and before any others could bail them up.

Smiggs had the carriage waiting, as arranged to the right of the steps. Kit ushered Sylvia to the door that Ollie, bright and cheerful despite the hour, was holding open.

"Thank you, Ollie." Sylvia bestowed a warm smile on the erstwhile bootboy and allowed Kit to hand her into the carriage.

After a smiling nod to Ollie, Kit followed her inside. As he sat, Ollie closed the door, then the carriage dipped slightly as the lad scrambled up, and then they were away. Smiggs deftly steered the carriage into the still-reasonably-clear street and set off at a good clip, heading for Mrs. Macintyre's house.

The carriage rolled smoothly on, and the brighter lights of

the city's center and the bustle around the Council House fell behind. A companionable silence descended.

Kit glanced at Sylvia and, by the light of a passing streetlamp, saw the smile playing over her face. She looked as if she might be humming the final rousing passages of the symphony in her head.

He elected not to break the spell and, resting his head against the squabs, held his tongue.

In no time at all, Smiggs drew the carriage to a halt just past Mrs. Macintyre's gate.

Ollie was there all but instantly to swing open the door. Kit descended, then gave Sylvia his hand and steadied her down the carriage steps.

He looped her arm in his, drawing her closer, and they strolled the few paces back to the gate. To his mind, they'd grown significantly closer over the course of the evening and not just physically.

They reached the gate, and he held it for her, then stepped back to her side as they walked up the short path.

Their footsteps slowed—hers as much as his—as they approached the porch.

Kit sensed her nerves tightening—evidenced by the quick glance she threw him—then she looked down, raised her hems, and climbed the steps.

He followed and halted beside her—and realized that he, too, was experiencing that telltale tightening of nerves, the anticipatory tension he'd thought he'd left behind in his early twenties.

Apparently not.

When it came to Sylvia Buckleberry, it seemed he wasn't that far removed from a green youth fresh on the town.

She drew her arm from his and faced him.

Mrs. Macintyre's porch was inset beneath the upper floor of the house, and the small area was draped in shadows. Nevertheless, he could make out Sylvia's wide eyes as she held out her hand and, decidedly breathlessly, said, "Thank you for a wonderful evening, my lord."

He closed his hand about her fingers and arched a quizzical brow. "Am I really still 'my lord' to you?"

Although her eyes remained wide, she battled to suppress a spontaneous smile and, eventually, conceded with a tip of her head. "Kit, then." Her eyes had locked with his. "And I truly enjoyed the evening immensely."

Were he dealing with some London lady, he would have grinned and, using her hand, drawn her into his arms for a long, slow kiss.

But this was Sylvia Buckleberry, clergyman's daughter.

He shackled his impulses and gently squeezed her fingers. "Thank you for your company and your help in navigating the shoals of Bristol society. I definitely wouldn't have enjoyed the evening had you not been beside me."

She had to know that was the unvarnished truth.

Silence descended.

He didn't want to let go of her fingers—not until she drew them away.

She didn't. Instead, she looked up at him as if trying to read his eyes...

Impulse—instinct—slipped its leash. Slowly, Kit raised his free hand and gently—so gently—cupped her face. Then, slow and smooth, he tipped her face upward as—slowly, *slowly*—he bent his head.

He fully expected her to retreat—to pull away at the last second.

He held his breath and slowed even more. His gaze had fallen to her luscious lips; he flicked it up to her eyes.

And saw that she'd lowered her gaze to his lips. In reaction, they throbbed and hungered for hers.

Lowering his gaze to her lips again, he was just in time to see the tip of her tongue pass swiftly over her plump lower lip.

On a muted groan, he abandoned restraint and pressed his lips to hers.

Instantly, he sensed her uncertainty, like a bird fluttering anxiously, unsure what it wanted—to escape the net or not.

He kept the contact gentle, light, and made no move to draw her to him even though his entire body ached for the contact. Instead, he devoted himself and his considerable talents to worshipping her lips.

Reverently.

Until he sensed her following his lead, albeit tentatively. Not as if she was totally inexperienced; more as if she was stepping into the unknown, and she was wary.

Wise woman. There was a great deal more he wanted to do, so much more he wanted to explore, but tonight, he reined back his rakish impulses with an iron grip and settled to the challenge of luring her to him simply with the brush of his lips, the subtle sweep of his tongue over her lips, the pressure as he supped and discovered his first taste of her.

Innocence and boldness—a fascinating combination.

Yet he kept the caress simple, very much within bounds.

His reward came when her fingers lightly touched, then traced his cheek, then she kissed him back—no longer tentatively but firmly.

And he got his first sensual glimpse of that passionate, fiery female he knew dwelled inside her.

She was there, close, yet still so contained.

But now it was she who was exploring his lips, moving hers against them, taking her time experimenting...

He mentally gritted his teeth, fisted his hands, and held back from reacting.

As he would have with any other woman.

But not her. She was special, in a class of her own. A lady to be treated with the care lavished on the very finest crystal.

The kiss spun on, and he realized that, despite the fact they were barely touching, he was drowning in her.

In her elusive scent, in the lure of her lips, in the sensual warmth he sensed inside her.

It was he who had to draw back—it was that or go forward, and he was as certain as he could be that she wasn't yet ready for more.

Moving slowly, he drew his lips from hers, then raised his head. He hauled in a much-needed breath and looked down into her face as she slowly raised her lids and revealed eyes that were deep violet pools of wonder.

They'd eased closer during the exchange; there was barely an inch between his coat and her bodice.

Her cloak had fallen open, and above her neckline, her breasts rose and fell dramatically, the mounds pearlescent in the faint light. He couldn't help but notice, which didn't make it any easier to do what he knew he must.

He tensed to step back, but then, instead, asked, "Might I call on you on Sunday afternoon? We could go for a stroll if the weather remains fine."

Sylvia heard the gruff, gravelly words. Her head was spinning, her wits whirling. It took effort to find her voice and whisper, "Yes." Given what they'd just shared, that seemed insufficient, and she added, "I would enjoy that." At the last second, she managed to swallow the word "too."

If there was one fact of which she was sure, Kit Cavanaugh didn't need any encouragement in this sphere.

But oh, my, he most definitely knew how to kiss a wary woman.

Regardless of her wish to deny him any overt encouragement, judging by the rakish grin he flashed her as he—transparently reluctantly—stepped back, he'd caught the gist of her unvoiced revelation.

Experienced as he was, he definitely hadn't needed to hear the words said.

To her surprise, not even that mental reminder of his status as a rake of the ton—regardless of her past view of his character being inaccurate, that aspect of his reputation had never been in question—caused her appreciation of the past moments to dim. Not in the least. And he'd asked for the chance to create more such moments.

She couldn't resist returning his grin with a sincerely anticipatory smile. "Until Sunday, then."

He nodded as he stepped down to the path. "Sunday." He walked backward, his eyes on her. He tipped his head to the door. "Go in."

She laughed softly and turned to the door. She unlocked and opened it. As she stepped over the threshold, she heard him softly call, "Goodnight."

She paused and looked back and saw him waiting beyond the gate, his gaze still locked on her. Smiling softly, she called, "Goodnight," then slowly shut the door.

A second later, she heard his footsteps on the pavement as he strode to the carriage.

She turned and leaned back against the door, in her mind reliving that kiss as the sounds of the carriage and horses faded into the night.

Unbidden, memories of the evening scrolled through her mind.

Eventually, she recalled Mrs. Macintyre's questions and assumptions, right at the beginning of the magical time—assumptions she'd refuted.

So what is this, then?

She still didn't know, still couldn't be sure, but given that kiss—which incontestably bore little resemblance to the way he would have kissed countless ladies in the past—and given the way her heart was tripping, it was pointless to deny that she was starting to hope.

Just the thought made her mentally shy away; in all honesty, she could barely believe where she thought—hoped—she now stood.

Teetering on the cusp of falling into the arms of the riveting and until-recently believed to be utterly unsuitable lord of her dreams.

That said unsuitable lord had proved to be the man she'd come to know in much greater depth over the past weeks, with whom she'd just shared a truly pleasant evening even in the full glare of local society, was, to her mind, skating perilously close to a miracle.

She pushed away from the door and headed for the stairs. "Who knows?" she whispered into the darkness. "Perhaps even the most wayward dreams can rescript themselves into a reality that might—just might—come true."

Thirteen

At five o'clock on Saturday evening, Kit and Wayland locked the workshop and trudged around the corner to the tavern in Princes Street that Mulligan and the men had recommended.

Kit pushed through the tavern's heavy door. He halted and, with Wayland beside him, scanned the dimly lit, somewhat smoky space with its old and worn yet comfortable chairs, benches, and tables.

Kit continued to the bar-counter and leaned on it. Wayland did the same. After catching the barkeeper's eyes, ordering two pints of ale, and chatting for several minutes with the man, Kit mentioned their need of a spot to discuss business in which they wouldn't risk being overheard, and the barkeeper suggested they use the snug, located behind the bar.

After ordering their dinners, Kit picked up his pint and, with Wayland at his heels, ducked through the low door to the snug. Kit swiftly surveyed the small space, then slid onto the bench seat that ran along one side wall.

There were only two narrow tables in the snug, each running parallel to the side walls, but he and Wayland were currently the only occupants.

"This is cozy." Wayland settled on the bench opposite Kit and set his mug on the table. "I hope the food is as good as the men claim—I'm hungry enough to eat a horse."

Kit grunted. "You're always hungry enough to eat a horse."

Wayland saluted him with his mug and drank.

Kit stared into his ale. He and Wayland had kept watch in the warehouse throughout the previous night. Doing so had required a degree of preparation. As the only way into the warehouse had been via the doors—secured with chain and padlock—they'd had to quickly construct another entrance; if their would-be saboteur called again in the middle of the night and found the doors unsecured, he wouldn't venture inside to be caught.

In the end, after consulting with the men, they'd decided that having only one exit wasn't wise in any case and had opted to construct a proper escape hatch—a panel in the rear wall large enough for Mulligan to get through easily. Shaw and the carpenters had cunningly constructed the frame on the inside, and with the hinges and bolts securing the hatch also on the inside, nothing showed on the outside of the wall to draw attention to the existence of the hatch.

Last night, after the concert, Kit had gone home, changed into older clothes, then carrying a hammock rolled up in a blanket, he'd found a hackney to deliver him back to the Grove. Once the hackney had rattled off into the night, he'd slunk under the trees and made his way to the rear of the workshop. As arranged, Wayland had left the hatch unlocked; Kit had used a stick to pry it open. He'd ducked into the dark workshop, carefully closed the hatch, and slid the bolts into place. Then he'd paused, waiting for his eyes to adjust to the darkness.

From the gloom shrouding the design office, Wayland had mumbled, "Please tell me that's you."

"It's me," Kit had whispered. "Go back to sleep." Once he could see well enough, he'd crossed to the front office and found the hooks he'd had Shaw install in the beams. He'd slung his hammock between, then had rolled into it with his blanket. He'd settled and let his thoughts slide to Sylvia. His eyes had closed; he'd smiled and, to his surprise, had tumbled headlong into dreams.

Both he and Wayland were accustomed to sleeping on ships at

sea, in tight and cramped quarters and in circumstances where their assistance might be required at any instant. They both slept soundly yet lightly and would rouse at the slightest noise, ready to react, just as they would on board.

Of course, the night had passed without their would-be saboteur putting in an appearance.

Today being Saturday, the men had worked for half the day. They'd kept their eyes peeled, but no one had seen any man loitering or watching the workshop. Kit and Wayland had remained behind after the men had left, working on the design and drawings for their first yacht.

A maid finally arrived bearing two plates piled high with a rich mutton stew.

Kit and Wayland accepted the plates eagerly and set to. They hadn't bothered with luncheon, further exacerbating Wayland's ever-present hunger.

After clearing half his plate, Wayland grunted and reached for the platter of bread the maid had left. "I just hope that tonight, we have at least one visitor who walks on two legs rather than four. In fact, I could do without visitations from the four-legged variety entirely."

Kit chuckled. Last night, they'd discovered that, while the workshop was secure against human intrusion, rodents appeared to have ready access. "If Miss Petty can lay her hands on those mousers she has in mind, tonight and tomorrow night will be the rats' last chances."

When they'd mentioned the rats that morning, Miss Petty had overheard and promptly declared she knew from just where to get three good mousers. Apparently, her brother had a farm outside the city, and one of his barn cats had had a litter only a month or so ago.

Wayland gestured with his fork. "That woman's efficiency is frightening."

Kit grinned at his friend. "Meaning she's just what we need."

Wayland snorted, but didn't disagree.

Once they'd cleaned their plates, they pushed them aside and fell into a discussion of the subject that dominated both their minds—their plans for their first yacht and the next and the next. When it came to the future of Cavanaugh Yachts, their enthusiasm knew no bounds.

When the clock above the bar chimed seven times, Wayland grimaced. "I suppose we'd better get back."

Kit sighed, but nodded.

They left payment and a large tip on the table—the snug was the sort of place they would definitely use again—waved to the barkeeper as they went past, then walked out into the chilly darkness that had descended on the city.

Hands in their greatcoat pockets, they ambled toward the workshop. Both were alert and watchful, but saw no one acting suspiciously. Nevertheless, they took care to use the shadows to conceal their approach to the rear of the workshop, avoiding the front and the doors secured with the heavy chain.

After they'd let themselves inside, Kit quietly tested the front doors. "Still secure," he reported.

Straightening from setting the bolts on the hatch, Wayland gave a soft huff and went into his office.

Kit joined him there, finding Wayland perched on one of the pair of stools; Kit pulled up the other and sat.

With no light, they couldn't see the drawings well enough to work on them; they could barely see each other.

"I predict we're in for a long, boring night," Wayland murmured. After a moment, he said, "Do you think we're being paranoid imagining some blighter is going to break in and try to damage the keel again?"

Kit took a moment to consider the point, then replied, "No, I don't. I think he'll be back. He's already been back a second time and couldn't get in. There's nothing to stop him from returning with lock picks or even a sharp file and forcing the padlock."

"But…" Wayland raked a hand through his hair, the gesture only just detectable in the gloom. "Why?" He shook his head. "I just don't understand it—or him, whoever he is."

"No more do I," Kit said. "But the fact he came back a second time makes it clear he's not finished with us. And if you think about it, although he succeeded in damaging our work up to Monday, given we'd only just started, the impact wasn't all that severe—we got over it quickly, and we've forged on. That can't have been the result he hoped for."

As if feeling his way, Wayland said, "You think he wants to seriously damage our business? Not just cause damage for damage's sake but to actually bring us down?"

"We can't afford to take the chance." Kit paused, then went on, "He doesn't have to completely destroy the work to have a serious impact on the business. Just think how the men will feel if the new keel is wrecked again. We've inspired them to believe in their skills anew and to apply them in working on the keel—you know as well as I do that not only is the work advancing at a rapid pace but the quality's also exceptional. Which is just what we want to set Cavanaugh Yachts above all other yacht manufacturers.

"Yet despite all that, at this moment, our enterprise is young. We're in the process of building the reputation we want, but right now, we're vulnerable. We don't need any questions being raised about us having some ongoing feud with someone who is determined to wreck anything we build. You know how rumors fly around a waterfront. If our saboteur succeeds in damaging the keel again, the news will get out, and we'll find not just other people but even our men getting cold feet—just when we need their commitment the most."

Wayland huffed. "When you put it like that…" After a moment, he shrugged. "You're right, but I still predict he won't show—not tonight and not tomorrow night—simply because we're here, and Fate likes to play us mortals for fools."

Kit laughed and rose from the stool. "I was up late last night—I'm going to turn in."

Wayland grunted. "It's too dark even to play dice with myself." He rose and, turning to where his hammock was slung across the end of his office, waved Kit off. "Sleep tight."

Smiling, Kit ambled into the workshop. His eyes had adjusted and rendered the scene in shades of gray. The keel taking proud shape in the nearest of the three bays sat still and silent. Throughout the workspace, nothing moved, nothing stirred.

Satisfied, he went into the front office, picked up his blanket, and rolled himself into his hammock.

They'd checked and established that quiet sounds inside the workshop didn't carry outside. As Kit settled to stare up at the ceiling, he heard Wayland murmur, "I feel like we're boys again, out on some silly adventure-cum-lark."

Kit grinned. "I can't recall any of our larks involving sleeping in hammocks."

"Much less in a cold and drafty workshop. Even as boys, we had better sense."

Kit chuckled. As silence descended, he realized that, despite his earlier words, he wasn't sleepy. Although he hadn't said so, he felt that, as their would-be saboteur hadn't come last night, then it was more likely he would wait until Sunday night, when this area of the city was even quieter, even more certainly deserted. Faced with the prospect of a wasted evening and night, Kit decided he might as well use the time to think of other things.

Out of the darkness, Wayland murmured, "It occurs to me that, over the past weeks of non-stop discussions about what we want our business to be, the one topic we haven't touched on is how we see our wider lives developing once the business is established." He paused, then went on, "I suppose I mean what else we want in our lives besides the business."

As that was precisely the direction in which Kit's mind had gone, the subject he'd been wrestling with over the past week,

he bit the proverbial bullet and volunteered, "I've been thinking about that quite a bit in recent days."

"Have you? Do tell." Amusement rode beneath Wayland's
words.

Kit smiled into the dark. "You might have noticed that, over
the past weeks, I've had other calls on my time, namely the
school and the lady who manages it—a Miss Sylvia Buckleberry."

"I had noticed that," Wayland drily replied.

Kit went on, "I'd met Miss Buckleberry before—a month
or so ago. She was a bridesmaid at Rand and Felicia's wedding,
and being a groomsman, I was partnered with her throughout
the event."

"And?"

"She treated me as if I was…someone she definitely didn't
want to know." If he was brutally honest, he'd been fascinated
by her from the instant he'd laid eyes on her—as she'd walked
up the aisle ahead of Mary and Felicia. But that attraction had
been immediately quashed by the downright chilly way she'd
responded to him.

He'd written her off as a lost cause—as a spinster too strait-
laced to bother with. One he should forget as soon as he possibly could.

Instead, a bare month later, she'd stormed into his office and
shown him a completely different side of her—a vibrant, passionate lady—and his initial attraction had roared back to life,
stronger, more powerful. More insistent.

"What?" Pure puzzlement on Wayland's part.

"Indeed. To this day, I have no idea what caused her to be-
have as she did, but suffice it to say that, since we met again here
and have been working together to resolve various issues at the
school, she's altered her view of my poor self." Given their kiss
last night, he decided he could feel assured of that.

"Were you out with her somewhere last night?"

"Yes. She accompanied me to a concert at the Council House."

"Really?" Interest sparked in Wayland's voice. "You took a lady—an *unmarried* lady—out for an evening in the full glare of society?"

Kit's smile turned wry. "Indeed." Wayland knew all about Kit's late mother and her machinations and how that had affected Kit's attitudes toward ladies and marriage.

"Well, that *is* a development," Wayland said, amazement still flavoring his tone.

After a moment of staring into the dark, Kit said, "You know that, with my mother's example before me, I believed marriage was not for me—not for any of us. Not Rand, Stacie, or Godfrey, either. That none of us would ever be able to find our way to marriage, a family, and all the rest. When Ryder married so clearly for love, I could shrug that aside—he'd never been caught in Mama's coils and was our half brother to boot. But when Rand married Felicia… I was there and saw them, and as cynical as I am, not even I can deny they're in love."

He exhaled softly. "And that means I was wrong, and love is possible for us, if we look. If we find it—or it finds us. And especially after seeing Rand and Felicia more recently—seeing their relationship bloom, as it were—I found myself asking, if love could find a way past Rand's resistance, which was every bit as strong as mine, then why couldn't love come for me?"

He heard his question fall into the silence. Considered it again, then softly added, "If I look, if I find it—or it finds me."

Wayland didn't say anything, but Kit knew he was listening. Kit shifted in the hammock, then, as its swinging settled again, said, "In a nutshell, Rand marrying has had me rethinking my attitude to marriage—that perhaps Mama's influence is waning at last, and it's time I ought to actively think about finding a wife."

That brought a snort from Wayland. "You *are* thinking of a wife—specifically, Sylvia Buckleberry. You do realize that you've spent more time with her in recent days than you have with any other marriageable lady ever?"

Kit grunted. Wayland was right, but Kit had had enough of baring his soul. "So that's me—what about you? You've shown precious little interest in anything beyond yachts for years."

"I know. But it's only since returning here and feeling that, with Cavanaugh Yachts, I've finally got my feet planted solidly beneath me, that I've realized that the years are flitting past, and here I am, still a bachelor."

"You'll be an even more desirable parti in a year or so, once the business takes off."

"True. And unlike you, I have no excuse—nothing in my background to turn me against marriage. Admittedly, my parents' union isn't any great example, but at least, marriage-wise, I'm starting with a clean slate compared to you."

Wayland fell silent for a moment, then ventured, "I think it's been ambition that, until now, has consumed me. It was always my dream to be the designer of the world's best yachts. That was always going to be the way I made my mark in the world, and until I got there… Well, I literally didn't see anything beyond what I needed to advance toward that goal. As you know, ladies have barely impinged, and only when the itch got so distracting I had to attend to it—so that I could keep working as I wished to. My life over the last decade has been strictly defined by my one overriding goal."

In the dark, Kit nodded. "Single-minded focus. That is, indeed, your greatest asset and your besetting sin."

"Exactly." Wayland paused, then went on, "But now, being here with you and starting Cavanaugh Yachts, I can see the end in sight. And it suddenly occurred to me that achieving that goal is, in reality, only one step—one cornerstone, if you will—in building my life, the sort of life I want." Wayland sighed gustily. "So I started asking myself what else I wanted in my life, and I realized that to truly enjoy the fruits of my ambition, I need a wife and a family to share them with. I'm not explaining this well, but it seems to me that I need a wife and family in order to make sense of becoming the best yacht designer in the world."

After a moment, he continued, "I never before looked past achieving my ambition, but I suspect my wanting a wife and family has always been there, but with my focus locked on my central goal, I simply didn't notice. And now I have."

Knowing Wayland as he did, Kit could understand that. But there was something else in what Wayland had said... Kit murmured, "What did you mean by saying that a wife and family would make sense of your ultimate success?"

Wayland snorted softly. "I did say I'm not sure how to explain..." After several seconds had ticked past, he offered, "Think of it this way—seeing our first yacht on the water is going to be a great moment for us. Immensely satisfying. Seeing the first yacht we sell to someone else sailing away will be another instant of extreme satisfaction. But what happens when our twentieth hull slides into the water? Where will the satisfaction come from then?"

Kit let Wayland's words percolate through his brain. After some time, he ventured, "You mean that, in order to continue to give satisfaction, a successful business needs to enable something further—something beyond the walls of the business itself." As the words fell into the silence, he sensed he was on the right track. "A successful business needs to power some other, greater purpose."

He couldn't see Wayland, but suspected his friend was nodding as he replied, "I think that, for men like us, regardless of the details of our upbringings and younger leanings, a family is the one thing that will give us the greatest purpose in our lives."

Kit nodded, too. "A family will anchor us—be our port through any storm—and give us reason for continuing to strive to succeed."

Wayland sighed feelingly. "And with that, all should now be clear."

Kit smiled. As the night settled comfortably around them, cocooning them in dark and quiet, he let his and Wayland's words float through his mind, absorbed the thoughts those words conveyed, and let them sink in.

Of all their comments, his own about an anchor that held one in safety throughout any storm resonated most strongly—that, and Wayland's invoking the notion of cornerstones. Kit realized that he'd already started thinking of Sylvia as his…not cornerstone but lynchpin, the central anchor around which the family he wished to create would revolve.

For him, she was the key.

As for his mother's lingering if waning influence, he now saw that as a net constraining and restricting him—holding him back. Not being one of Lavinia's children, Ryder had never been trapped, but all three of Kit's other siblings and he had. Now Rand had broken free, and Kit felt as if he was on the cusp of doing the same. Stacie and Godfrey, being younger and more firmly under Lavinia's thrall, were, he suspected, still enmeshed, but for him, yes, it was time to snap the last strands and walk free.

It was time for him to seize the chance and take the risk of trying for love and happiness.

Those connected prizes were now his most fundamental desires.

In his mind's eye, he saw the look on Rand's face—the emotion he'd seen shining there when his brother had looked at Felicia. Kit could almost taste that emotion—one he'd never thought to feel himself—yet in his heart, he knew that was precisely the emotion that was growing inside him, focused on Sylvia. It was she—the fiery, passionate lady she truly was—who had given that emotion life and called it forth.

She'd rapidly become the personification of his future; in

her eyes, he saw the promise of a future wherein he would be free to love.

He dwelled on the prospect, and as sleep drew inexorably nearer, his mind skated back over all he'd assimilated in the past hour.

Quite aside from Sylvia being critical to his future, one idea rose above all others.

When it came to lasting achievements, while business was for now, family was forever.

★ ★ ★

Contrary to Wayland's prediction and Kit's expectation, their would-be saboteur arrived outside the workshop in the dead of night.

Kit woke to the sound of the heavy chain securing the door softly clinking as it was carefully pulled free of the heavy handles.

Instantly awake, he rolled out of his hammock and landed, light as a cat, on his feet. He didn't dare call to Wayland. He had to trust that his friend's senses were as acute as his own.

The doors slowly parted, drawn back to reveal a moon-washed scene inhabited by dark shadows—the trees of the Grove and, in the distance, the buildings on the other side of the Floating Harbor.

Then a large, dense shadow appeared around the edge of one door. Other than that the fellow was wearing a heavy coat and, beneath a wide-brimmed hat, appeared to have a muffler wound around his face, Kit couldn't tell more from the man's outline as he stepped into the workshop and tugged the doors closed.

Blinking furiously to readjust his sight, temporarily impaired by the moonlight, Kit held still and silent. A second later, he picked out the moving shadow as the man walked several paces into the workshop, then halted and fumbled with something.

Kit seized the moment of the intruder's distraction to steal closer to the open doorway of the office.

Then light flared. Kit swallowed a curse and dropped to a crouch—an instant before the beam of the lantern the man had lit swept through the windows on either side of the office door.

The beam swept through at chest height, showing the intruder nothing but empty space. The intruder swung the beam on, playing light through the open door of the design office, and the man paused.

For several seconds, he stood staring at whatever he could see. Given his lack of reaction, Kit surmised it wasn't Wayland who had caught the man's attention.

Then the fellow muttered, "Later," and swung around to train the lantern beam on the hull taking shape within its frame in the workshop's first bay.

In the backwash of light, Kit saw that, in addition to the lantern, the man was carrying a large sack. He set it down with a clink and a clunk.

The man straightened; he remained standing, playing the lantern beam over the hull—for all the world as if admiring its points.

Keeping low, Kit crept through the doorway, then edged sideways, along the office wall. He crouched and glanced to his right and saw Wayland inch out of his office. Wayland glanced his way, then tipped his head toward the man—who seemed engrossed in studying the keel.

Kit nodded and slowly rose.

The man crouched. Setting the lantern aside, his back to Kit and Wayland, the man opened the sack and started pulling out whatever was in there.

They couldn't hope for a better moment.

In a rush, Kit crossed the yards to the man, Wayland a heartbeat behind him.

The man sensed them coming and started to rise.

Kit lunged and, ducking his head, took the intruder down in a ferocious tackle.

The man's head hit the floor. "Ow!"

Kit rolled up and off the man and regained his feet as Wayland reached them.

The man was groaning and clutching his head between his hands; he remained flat on his back on the floor. Wayland bent and picked up the lantern. He fiddled until the flame flared strongly, casting a wide circle of light around all three of them, then set the lantern down to one side.

After a cursory glance at the man—his hat had fallen off, but his muffler was still in place, concealing his features—Wayland left Kit, the stronger and more physically powerful, to stand intimidatingly over their prisoner and crouched to see what the man had brought.

His gaze on the man, Kit heard Wayland's sharply in-drawn breath and glanced fleetingly his way.

From the sack, Wayland had pulled out a quantity of rags, a large glass jar of what looked like black oil or perhaps creosote, and a long length of fuse.

For a second, Wayland stared at the items, then his features hardened, and he rose to his feet. He looked at the unknown man with utter contempt. "Not content with simply damaging timbers, this time, you planned to burn us out."

Before Kit could react, Wayland strode to the man, reached down, tangled his long fingers in the knitted muffler, and violently wrenched it from the man's face. "You fiend!"

The jerk brought the man half upright, gasping like a landed fish; Kit had winded him, and he was still trying to catch his breath.

As the light washed over the intruder's face, he closed his eyes, groaned again, and slumped back on the floor.

To Kit's surprise, Wayland had frozen, the muffler dangling from his hand as he stared in shock at the man's face.

Then in a stunned tone, Wayland said, *"Hightham?"* His tone suggested he couldn't believe the evidence of his eyes.

Kit glanced sharply at the man—who continued to keep his eyes shut while he tried to get his lungs working again—then looked at Wayland. "You know him." It wasn't a question.

Passing a hand over his jaw, Wayland nodded. "His name's John Hightham. He was working as a junior designer at Debney's when I joined the firm."

Debney's was the Bermuda-based yacht workshop from which Kit had lured Wayland home.

"Hightham left shortly after I arrived, supposedly to return to England," Wayland added, which explained why Kit hadn't met the man.

Recovering from his shock, Wayland kicked one of Hightham's boots and growled, "What the devil's this about?"

Hightham—who Kit could now see was perhaps twenty-five years old at a pinch and thinner and lighter of frame than Wayland, much less Kit—scowled up at Wayland. "As if you don't know," Hightham spat.

Wayland sent Kit a befuddled look.

On seeing it, Hightham struggled half up and propped on one arm. "What did you expect," he said with an obvious attempt to sound scathing, "when you stole my design?"

Wayland looked, if possible, even more at sea.

Kit focused on Hightham. "Explain what you mean about Wayland stealing your design."

It was an invitation Hightham couldn't resist.

Kit stood and listened as the younger man poured out a tale, accusing Wayland of having stolen a certain keel design from him. Kit knew that whatever Hightham believed wouldn't be the truth; he'd known Wayland since Eton and knew his friend and partner through and through. Quite aside from the fact Wayland simply wouldn't stoop to stealing anyone else's design, there was the undeniable truth that he was a brilliant designer and had been recognized as such for nearly a decade—he didn't need to steal designs when his own were so relentlessly cutting edge.

When Hightham, now scowling even more blackly at Wayland, reached the end of his spiel, Kit glanced at his partner and saw comprehension dawning in his face. Hightham's details about keel designs hadn't meant anything to Kit, but obviously, Wayland had worked out the gist of the younger man's complaint.

His gaze resting on Hightham, Wayland asked, "That's what this has been about? Getting back at me because you imagined I'd stolen your design?"

"I didn't imagine anything," Hightham shot back. "You did!"

"When?" Wayland asked.

"It was in early thirty-eight. You came to visit Debney's. That was a couple of years before Debney persuaded you to join him."

Wayland nodded. "I remember. You'd just started in the design office."

"Yes, I had. And I was working on my own designs on the side." Hightham glared pugnaciously at Wayland. "You must have seen the plans when you came poking around the office. You have a faultless memory when it comes to designs, so one good look was all it took. Then you came back to England and started building yachts with my design. Don't bother trying to deny it—I've seen some of the yachts you've built, and they incorporate my keel!"

Hightham was still decidedly hot under the collar. He clearly believed Wayland at fault.

Unperturbed, Wayland shot Kit a glance, then held up a finger to Hightham. "One moment. Allow me to fetch a drawing that will, I trust, clarify this matter."

Kit watched Wayland go into his office, then swung his gaze back to Hightham, who was now sitting with his knees drawn up and his arms looped around them.

"I know he stole my design," Hightham muttered, jaw clenching tight. Now bathed in light, his face looked young, his expression more truculent than violent. "He's not going to make me believe otherwise."

Kit hid a smile at his tone and waited.

A few minutes ticked past, then Wayland exclaimed, "There you are!"

Seconds later, he emerged from the office carrying a large design sheet in his hands. Kit knew sheets that size were only used for final, formal designs.

Wayland halted beside Kit and held out the design for him to see. "Do you recognize this one—the yacht I designed and had built at the workshop in Southampton for the Earl of Sandwich?"

Scanning the design, Kit nodded. "Yes. I remember it—Sandwich was thrilled and took us out on it when it launched."

"Indeed." Wayland nodded. "As you say, you were there for the launch. Do you remember when that was?"

Kit thought back, seeking other dates around that time that he remembered more clearly. "It had to have been in thirty-seven—July, thirty-seven."

Wayland nodded. "According to the date written here"—he pointed to tiny figures written on the bottom right-hand corner of the design—"this yacht was launched on July twelfth, eighteen thirty-seven." He gazed at the design for a moment more, then turned it in his hands and offered it to Hightham.

Hightham's scowl had turned puzzled and wary. He stared at Wayland for a moment, then, almost reluctantly, reached out and took the drawing. His gaze fell to the lines, scanning the design...

Hightham paled. He stared at the drawing as if it were a snake, then he muttered a curse and shifted closer to the lantern, angling the sheet so he could study it more closely.

Sliding his hands into his pockets, Wayland waited.

Gradually, the angry tension in Hightham's body leached away. Eventually, he hauled in a breath that caught, then he looked up at Wayland, incomprehension and not a little despair etched across his face. "I...don't understand." He glanced at the design again. "This is my design...well, not absolutely exactly, but the critical design features of my keel are all here." He raised his gaze once more to Wayland's face. "But how?"

Standing at ease with his hands in his pockets, Wayland adopted what Kit mentally termed his friend's lecturing expression. "The thing you've forgotten—or perhaps never knew as you've patently never run across it before—is that great minds really do think alike. It's perfectly possible for two unconnected individuals to come up with the same, or at least very similar, design. Even identical designs—that's not unheard of."

Wayland tipped his head at the drawing Hightham still held. "That's what happened here. Unbeknown to you, a year before I met you and might have seen your design—I didn't, by the way, or I likely would have made some comment—I had already worked on and launched a design similar to the one you subsequently came up with. And apparently, my design incorporated the critical features you later re-created in your design." Wayland paused, then more gently said, "Sandwich's yacht wasn't the only yacht I built that year. I've evolved and refined that design in several ways over the years. Indeed, virtually every yacht I've built since then incorporates some variant of that particular keel design." Wayland glanced at the frame at Hightham's back. "Even the keel of the hull we're building now derives from it."

Hightham seemed to have nothing to say; he stared at the drawing, but Kit would have sworn he was no longer seeing it.

Wayland reached out and gently tugged the drawing from Hightham's grasp.

Letting the drawing slip from his fingers, the younger man sat unmoving. He looked shattered, his expression devastated. Then he licked his lips and, lowering his gaze to the floor, said, "So it wasn't you who stole my design—it was me who stole yours."

Wayland sighed and, in his lecturing voice, said, "You haven't been listening, John. We independently came up with a similar design. You hadn't seen my work any more than I'd seen yours—you couldn't have known. No stealing involved." Wayland shifted, his gaze on John's now-desolate face. "Don't berate yourself over it." Wayland managed to catch John's eye and fleetingly grinned. "As far as I can see, that you came up with a similar design just testifies to my brilliance."

Far from relaxing, Hightham looked even more shattered. "I've spent so much c-coming after you, seeking my revenge—time, money, and effort." He looked down and morosely shook his head. "And it was all over nothing."

Wayland looked at Kit. Kit arched his brows; he suspected they were both thinking of their earlier discussion about ultimate goals. The truth was, everyone needed a purpose in life, an ultimate goal to strive for. Apparently in recent times, Hightham's goal had been to wreak vengeance on Wayland. Now...

Hightham looked toward the door, where the open padlock dangled from the looped chain. He swallowed, then glanced at Kit and tonelessly said, "I expect you'll want to send for the constabulary."

His hopeless dejection made it plain he fully expected to be handed over to the authorities and charged.

Wayland looked meaningfully at Kit as he replied, "Given your talent, that would be a shame, not to mention a great waste."

Kit nodded in understanding. He and Wayland held a firm belief that gathering the best possible talent was the surest route to steering Cavanaugh Yachts to success.

Wayland tipped his head toward Hightham. "Do you think we can give him a chance?"

Hightham looked up, blinking as if he'd lost track of the conversation.

Kit studied the younger man's open face. He looked youthful, oddly innocent, yet Kit had seen the same passion Wayland possessed burning in Hightham's eyes earlier, when he'd spoken of his design. That glimpse of passion decided Kit. "Everyone deserves a second chance."

Puzzled, disbelieving—not yet willing to allow himself to believe—Hightham stared up at them, his gaze shifting between them. "You'd do that? But..." He twisted to look at the keel behind him. "I tried to destroy your work." Facing forward, he pointed at the jar and rags Wayland had found in his sack. "I was going to splash that under the keel and set it alight."

"Luckily for you," Kit drily said, "we decided to stay the night so we'd be here to welcome you."

"Don't worry," Wayland said. "We're not proposing to let you off lightly—not at all. We'll work you hard, and you'll pay your way by the sweat of your brow. You can work off your guilt while designing and overseeing the building of the very best ocean-going yachts the world has ever seen with me."

If they'd whacked Hightham over the head with one of the hull's massive ribs, he couldn't have looked more stunned. He blinked up at them, then a faint frown formed in his eyes. "This seems all wrong—that I came here to burn your work, and you offer me my dream job."

Kit rather thought Wayland was enjoying himself. Kit shifted and clapped a hand down on Hightham's shoulder. "You might think that now, but trust me, Wayland's a brutal taskmaster—he'll make you live up to his expectations, which are often beyond the scope of mortal man."

Wayland sent Kit a scoffing look, but then refocused on Hightham. "He thinks he's being droll, but he's not entirely wrong. We need a second draftsman now that construction is rolling along, and we could go faster—we could start a second hull in a week or two—but we're limited in that, at present, I'm the only one able to oversee the work and also draw out the designs." Wayland tipped his head toward his office. "You could take on the drawings while I continue designing and overseeing."

Hightham stared at Wayland, then slowly pushed to his feet, turning as he did to face the new hull. Almost reverently, Hightham put out a hand and ran it down one of the huge ribs. "Even after I damaged the first, you've replaced and got on so quickly and in such fine style... It's remarkable."

He glanced questioningly at Wayland, who nodded. "We opened our doors at just the right time. Many of the best craftsmen have been put out of work by the shift to iron ships and steam. We've been able to recruit some of the very best, and they're thrilled to work on projects such as ours. You can't beat enthusiasm for turning out quality work."

"I can see that." Hightham was now studying the rib joints.

Kit could envision Hightham and Wayland standing admiring the hull for hours. Kit shifted and, when Wayland glanced his way, said, "We've also had a healthy dose of luck."

Wayland read the question in Kit's eyes: Was he sure? Wayland nodded.

Kit looked at Hightham. "John, we can offer you probation for three months. You can start on Monday. Report first to my office in King Street and see my secretary, Miss Petty. She'll sign you on and sort out everything that needs sorting."

Hightham looked from Kit to Wayland, then back again. "I...can't thank you enough." He swallowed and left it at that.

Kit tipped his head. "Just don't let us down."

"I won't." The words were a vow, one Kit and Wayland both heard.

Satisfied, Kit glanced at Wayland, who yawned and said, "Now it's time for me to find my bed." Wayland glanced at Hightham. "Where are you staying?"

Hightham blushed and sheepishly admitted that he hadn't anywhere to spend the night. "I've a bag out on the cobbles, but... I was saving my funds for getting away quickly after I sent the keel alight."

Wayland snorted. "I suppose that demonstrates an ability to

plan ahead." He raked his gaze over Hightham. "It might not be the most comfortable bed, but you're welcome to the couch in my rooms for a few nights—until you can find a decent place to hang your hat."

Hightham was learning not to waste his breath protesting their decisions; he endeavored to accept Wayland's offer with as much humility as he could muster.

Kit left him to it and went into the office, unhooked his hammock, and rolled it up in the blanket. With the roll tucked under his arm, he walked out to join Wayland and Hightham in heading out of the doors.

Once all was shut and relocked, the three of them strode around the corner into Princes Street. Wayland's lodgings were halfway along. Kit saw a hackney idling a little farther on. He was about to hail it when he remembered a question he needed to ask. "Hightham?" When the younger man looked at him, Kit caught his eyes. "Have you, by any chance, been watching me as I've been going around town? For instance, when I've been squiring a lady about?"

Hightham looked thoroughly confused. "No." He added, "I've only been in Bristol since Sunday, and I've been keeping watch on the warehouse since then. I don't even know where in King Street your office is."

Every word rang true. Kit waved the odd question aside. "It was just a thought." He met Wayland's eyes. "I'll leave you both here—I'm for that hackney and my bed."

They exchanged quick farewells, and Kit strode for the hackney.

He slumped onto the seat, and the jarvey turned his horse and set out for Queen's Parade.

Kit felt tiredness dragging at his wits, but forced himself to review what he now knew about Sylvia's elusive watcher. Hightham had been totally at sea at Kit's mention of a lady. Ergo, his hadn't been the stare Sylvia had sensed.

No matter how Kit rearranged the facts, he kept coming up with the same highly disturbing result.

Someone else was watching Sylvia, and that someone was focused on her, not Kit.

A ridiculous compulsion to tell the jarvey to turn around and make for Mrs. Macintyre's house reared its head. Kit considered it for several minutes, but after spending two nights in the workshop, he needed at least a few hours' solid sleep.

"And she's a clergyman's daughter," he assured himself. "She'll go to church in the morning."

He'd already arranged to see her in the afternoon, and fortuitously, he hadn't stated a time.

"So I'll be unfashionably early."

Sylvia would be safe enough until then.

As the horse clopped on, its hooves ringing on the cobbles, his mind swung back to Hightham and the second chance he and Wayland had handed the younger man.

Second chances were all very well, but seizing a chance the first time around was infinitely wiser.

Kit wasn't going to let his chance to secure love and happiness with Sylvia Buckleberry slip through his fingers.

"Which means I definitely need some sleep."

He wanted to be at his best when next he saw her—the embodiment of his future happiness and, he hoped, his bride-to-be.

Fourteen

After church, the Dean of Christ Church drew Sylvia aside to inquire as to how the school was settling into its new premises. On being assured that all was well, he commended—again—Kit's offer to attach his name and title to the school. "Quite a coup, to get Cavanaugh's open support, and, indeed, it's heartening to see a scion of a noble house so willing to be involved in parish affairs. Mark my words, my dear, his lordship's declared support will mean more and more as his presence in the city becomes more widely known."

Sylvia smiled and agreed.

The Dean continued, "I was speaking with the mayor only yesterday—he has high hopes that his lordship's new enterprise will reinvigorate interest in ship building in the city." The Dean's eyes twinkled. "I understand you and Cavanaugh ran into the mayor at the concert on Friday evening."

Sylvia acquiesced with a murmur and endeavored not to blush.

She chatted with the Dean for several more minutes, then slipped away from the groups milling on the pavement, crossed the street, and set off down High Street. By the time she reached Mrs. Macintyre's door, her landlady would have a roast ready and waiting. Then after luncheon… Kit hadn't specified a time, but surely, with autumn deepening and daylight fading earlier each day, he would call before three o'clock. Possibly by two.

A smile of anticipation had taken up residence on her lips. All in all, she was exceedingly pleased with how the various aspects of her life were evolving; she couldn't think of anything she wished to change. Smiling to herself, she replayed the Dean's words in her mind; she was looking forward to reporting them to Kit and, most likely, watching him squirm. She'd noticed that he didn't like his good deeds being lauded; he certainly didn't crave the attention said deeds drew his way.

The image of Kit her thoughts had conjured remained front and center in her mind. After Friday night and their kiss on the porch, she was trying not to let her expectations race ahead... but that was proving difficult.

In just two short weeks, he'd resurrected the hopes and dreams she'd thought she'd left behind in moving to Bristol. More than being a declaration to others, she'd viewed her coming to the city and devoting herself to the school as a personal statement of intent. An unequivocal demonstration that she'd laid aside all hope of marriage and a family and had elected to devote her life to good works.

That was the decision she'd made then. It wasn't how she felt now.

Now...

Just thinking of what might be—what might evolve from what was already there between her and Kit—set butterflies flitting joyfully inside her and made her heart skip.

"Miss Buckleberry?"

Looking up and seeing an older gentleman hurrying toward her from the other side of the street, she halted. His tone had been urgent, and he appeared out of breath. She immediately thought of the school—the teachers or the boys. "Yes?"

The man reached the pavement and halted before her. "Oh, thank heavens I've found you!"

He appeared to be in his later middle years and was neatly dressed in a dark suit.

Before she could speak, the man gushed, "I'm Mr. Hillary, my dear. I've just called at your lodgings, and your good landlady told me you would be on your way home from church, and as time is of the essence, I put my faith in God and came on in the hope of reaching you as soon as may be." Hillary's face creased in concern. "There really isn't a moment to lose."

"Why?" Hillary's urgency was so compelling, Sylvia only just restrained herself from clutching his arm. "What's happened?"

There were others on the pavement. Noticing them, Hillary gently took her arm and solicitously steered her closer to the building, out of the flow of traffic. She didn't resist. In increasing alarm, she searched his face. "What is it? Please tell me."

His expression grave, Hillary met her gaze. "I'm afraid it's your father, my dear. He's very poorly and is asking for you. I drove as fast as I could from Saltford, hoping to fetch you to his side."

Sylvia's world spun; her stomach lurched and fell. She was glad Hillary had kept hold of her elbow, but then she pushed aside the faintness. "My father?" She heard the shock in her voice. "I hadn't thought..." She blinked. "He hasn't mentioned any illness in his letters."

She'd always seen her father as hale and hearty and had imagined he would continue in good health for many years yet.

Hillary looked at her with compassion. "I gather it came on very quickly. I'm afraid I have no details to share. I'm a visitor to the village—I've been staying with the Mathers, next door to the vicarage, for several weeks, and when Doctor Moreton asked if someone could drive to Bristol and fetch you home...well, I was there and had a fast horse and gig. Your father's housekeeper gave me your direction, and Moreton urged me to fetch you as soon as I might, so I leapt into my gig and came straightaway."

Sylvia was struggling to take it in. Her father! She hadn't expected any such disaster—not at all.

She felt Hillary's gaze on her face, then in a quieter tone, he said, "I regret to say, Miss Buckleberry, but I believe your father is only just clinging to life."

The words struck like an iced dagger to her heart. She nodded. "Yes. I understand." She blinked and refocused on Hillary. "If you're willing to drive me, I can come with you now."

Hillary smiled, but she saw the gesture through a film of tears. She blinked them away, and his earnest expression came into focus. He patted her arm. "Good. Good. We can be on our way in moments. My carriage is just this way."

"Thank you, Mr. Hillary." Sylvia heard the words, but distantly. She allowed Hillary to lead her down the street and around the first corner to where a gig waited in a side yard, the reins held by an urchin.

Hillary paid off the boy, then gave her his hand and helped her into the gig. She sat. She felt numb inside. Her mind wasn't functioning with its usual precision. An image of Mrs. Macintyre looking at her roast and waiting swam into her mind, but her landlady would understand. So would Kit—and she'd be able to send a message once she saw her father. Saltford was, after all, only ten miles away.

★ ★ ★

Kit strode along the pavement that bordered the small park, his gaze locked on Mrs. Macintyre's door at the far end of the street.

He'd arranged with Sylvia to call on her on Sunday afternoon, and it was after noon, even if a touch past one o'clock was rather early for a social call.

He just wanted to see her again—to prove to his inner self that she was perfectly all right. To put paid to the fanciful imaginings that had taken over his brain and hijacked all rationality.

After reaching home in the early hours, he'd fallen into bed, only to toss and turn, plagued by thoughts of the unknown person watching Sylvia and, even more worrisomely, their intentions. Now he knew that whoever it was had nothing to do with him or his business, he was running out of possible motives— he felt as if he didn't know which way to face to protect her.

He supposed it might still be something to do with the school, yet although it had been he who had saved the school, through-out, the watcher had focused on her.

No. It wasn't anything to do with the school. To his mind—churning with supposition and imaginings—that cast the continuing attentions of the watcher in a much more sinister light.

Yet it was difficult—well-nigh impossible—to imagine that Sylvia, a clergyman's daughter, had any enemies. As far as he knew, she'd lived a blameless life.

He couldn't see his way through the maze, and since he'd awoken, his inner self had been pacing relentlessly, pushing him to go and see her and assure himself that she was all right, that she was in no immediate danger.

He reached the end of the pavement, crossed the street, and made for Mrs. Macintyre's gate.

Jaw clenching, he opened the gate, strode up the path, and leapt up the steps. He grasped the brass knocker and beat briskly on the door.

Then he drew in a deep breath, stepped back, and told himself he would soon see with his own eyes that Sylvia was perfectly fine.

Mrs. Macintyre opened the door as if she'd snatched at it. Her face was creased in an anxious frown that took on over-tones of dismay as she looked at Kit. Then she bobbed and nodded. "My lord."

He managed to find his voice. "Miss Buckleberry?" He felt as if his heart was in his throat.

Mrs. Macintyre's anxiety deepened. "I'd hoped she was with you."

A chill clutched Kit's gut. "Where—when did you last see her?"

Mrs. Macintyre crossed her arms as if she was cold. "She went to church as she usually does every Sunday morning, right on a quarter to eleven o'clock. She's always back by half past twelve for luncheon, and she said she'd be here, only she hasn't come back." Mrs. Macintyre gripped her arms tightly. "She hasn't come in and gone out again—that I do know. I haven't seen hide nor hair of her since she left this morning."

Kit battled his rioting impulses, forcing them down enough to think. "No message or anything like that?"

Mrs. Macintyre shook her head. "And that's another thing—always very considerate, she is. It's not like her to just…not come home."

She'd been taken—seized. Kit knew it. That was what all the watching had been about. "I'll start at the church. I'll check that she attended"—she was well-known in the parish; there would be somebody there who could tell him—"and try to track where she went."

He needed to act—to do something, something to get her back. He seriously doubted she'd be at the church, but he had to start somewhere.

With an emotion perilously close to panic flaying him, he swung around and leapt to the path.

Just as a carriage came racing wildly down the street.

Kit recognized his horses. He ran out of the gate and reached the curb as Smiggs, on the box of Kit's curricle, drew the bays to a plunging halt. Kit put up a hand to calm the nearer horse as Ollie tumbled from his perch at the carriage's rear and came rushing up.

"Your lordship!" Ollie grabbed Kit's sleeve with both hands. "You've got to come quick! It's Miss Buckleberry, my lord—she's been 'napped!"

Ollie's face was full of urgent entreaty. Kit glanced at Smiggs, grimly managing the skittish horses. "Who? How?" Those seemed the most pertinent questions.

But Ollie mistook his meaning. "It was Jack the Lad, m'lord. He overheard you telling Mr. Cobworth as how someone was watching Miss Buckleberry nasty-like, and so we—Jack, Ned, and me—thought as perhaps we could help keep her safe by keeping an eye on her and spotting who was following her."

Kit freed his arm and grasped Ollie's, trying to keep the boy from jigging up and down. "Did you see who it was?"

"Aye—but we didn't think he was dangerous. Not then."

Kit held on to his patience. "He who?"

"The man with the boards front and back." Ollie stared into Kit's face, willing him to understand. "You know—one of those who paces back and forth on the Butts and the quays and blathers on about God and damnation and redeeming people if only they'll come to his chapel. Well, we thought he was a man of God, didn't we? That he was harmless, just a nuisance, only it turns out he's a blackguard, after all. We saw him take her!"

"This morning?" Kit was battling to piece events together.

Ollie nodded. "We was watching outside the church, all three of us, and she came out and talked with some church people, then she started off home, and we followed—hanging back a-ways so she wouldn't see us. That's when the man came up and stopped her. He was dressed better than usual, but we recognized him. Jack and I hung back, but Ned—he's the sneakiest of us—he sidled really close, and he heard the man say as he'd been staying next door to Miss Buckleberry's father and that her father's doing poorly and the doctor had sent him to fetch her home straightaway." Ollie added, "The man wasn't wearing his boards, but it seemed Miss Buckleberry knew him…or at least, she believed him, 'cause she went off with him."

"To where?" Kit realized he was holding his breath and forced air into his lungs.

"He led her around the corner into St. Maryport Street. He had a gig waiting in a yard along there." Ollie rushed on, "Well, we didn't know what to do, did we? We didn't want to let Miss Buckleberry go off with the man because we thought he might be a bad'un. We knew he hadn't been staying near some vicarage—his room is off the Butts—and if he'd lied about that, perhaps all the rest was made up, too. But with the man right there, we didn't think we could explain and talk her out of going—not when she thought her father was dying. So Jack waited until the man handed Miss Buckleberry into the gig to dart up behind it, then when the man—he was holding the reins by then—went around to climb in himself, Jack slipped into the gig's boot. Because the man was rocking the gig himself, he didn't notice."

"You sure of that?" Smiggs rumbled.

Ollie nodded earnestly. "And they didn't see me and Ned, either."

"Mercy me!" Mrs. Macintyre had come to the gate and had been listening to Ollie's outpourings.

Kit knew just how she felt. He was still floundering, trying to make sense of it all. "So Jack's gone with them to wherever the man is taking Miss Buckleberry."

"And me and Ned followed the gig to see which road the man took. It wasn't so hard in the city, what with all the other carriages. We ran behind all the way across the bridge, down St. Thomas Street, and into Portwall Lane. We saw the man turn the gig onto the Bath Road. Ned's faster'n me, so I came running back to fetch you while Ned followed the gig to see which way the man went—to Bath or to Wells." Ollie caught Kit's coat and tugged. "We've got to go and help. Ned'll be waiting at the junction to tell us which way to go."

Kit was astounded and also trying to think ahead.

Ollie tugged again. "So can we go? I had to run all the way to Queen's Parade, and Mr. Smiggs has brought your carriage with the fast horses. Ned'll be wondering what's become of us by now, and then there's Jack and Miss Buckleberry, driving on with that man…"

"Yes." Kit met Ollie's eyes, then gripped the boy's shoulder, glanced at Mrs. Macintyre, and nodded. "Let's go and get Jack and Miss Buckleberry back."

Mrs. Macintyre gripped her gate. "You'll bring her home safe and sound?"

Kit's jaw clenched as he marched Ollie to the rear of the curricle. "Count on it," he replied.

He tossed Ollie up to his perch, then climbed to the box, exchanged a swift glance with Smiggs, and sat.

Then Kit took up the reins and, ignoring all other traffic, drove hell for leather for the Bath Road.

Fifteen

Kit drove like a madman through the city streets and out onto the highway.

Eventually, Smiggs, white-faced, begged him to slow down. "Won't do your Miss Buckleberry any good if you wreck this rig."

Kit could see Durley Hill rising ahead. He grunted and consented to ease the pace, knowing that, regardless, he had to save his horses for the long climb into Keynsham, or they'd be blown when they reached the town.

They'd found Ned at the junction where the road to Wells peeled off to the south. Ned had scrambled up beside Ollie and confirmed that the gig had gone on toward Bath. The boy had run like a Spartan and had managed to keep the gig in sight until then.

Kit sent up a prayer of gratitude for the boys' efforts. If they hadn't acted as they had… He thrust the thought away. What was before him was bad enough; his imaginings were no longer relevant.

While managing his horses and avoiding catastrophe, he'd dredged his memory, going over his conversations with Sylvia as well as the snippets he'd heard of her background and home at the wedding.

As the increasing grade slowed the horses even more, Kit raised his voice so the boys could hear. "It's possible the man is taking Miss Buckleberry to her father. This road goes through the village of Saltford, where Reverend Buckleberry has the living."

After a moment, Ned called, "Does that mean her father preaches in the church and lives at the vicarage?"

Despite all, Kit's lips twitched. "Yes—that's exactly what 'having the living' means."

But given that was the case...

After several minutes of wrestling with the issue, Kit said, "Boys, I want you to think very carefully over all you heard the man say. As he is driving Miss Buckleberry toward her home, is there any chance at all that he might actually be doing what he said and fetching Miss Buckleberry to her dying father's side?"

He glanced over his shoulder to see the boys exchanging a long glance. Kit faced forward and waited.

Eventually, Ollie said, "The man said as he'd been staying next door to the vicarage, but we know he's been living in the city and his rooming house is off the Butts. We saw him yesterday, parading around with his boards, so how could he have been staying at this village?"

"And that's not all he lied about," Ned piped up. "He told Miss Buckleberry his name was Mr. Hillary—I heard her call him that. But when we were following him to learn where he lived, we heard other people call him Nunsworth. So he lied about that, too. Why would he do that if he wasn't up to no good?"

"And," Ollie said, in the tone of one sealing an argument with irrefutable logic, "why's he been watching Miss Buckleberry, all secret-like, for the past week?"

Kit stared ahead, digesting all that.

From beside him, Smiggs growled, "Those are three good questions, and it doesn't sound as if this Hillary bloke would have any good answers."

"No," Kit conceded. To the boys, he called, "You're right. Hillary or Nunsworth or whoever he is has to be a villain."

And the situation was shaping up to be as bad as Kit's instincts were insisting.

Given the boys' information, he couldn't see how the man could be genuine, but at this point, he really didn't care. It was more important that Sylvia and Jack came out of the incident safely; if it turned out Kit and the boys had made fools of themselves over nothing, so be it.

Kit chafed as the horses plodded up the long incline; he knew both incline and pace would only get worse closer to the top of the hill and resigned himself to frustration. They were roughly halfway to Saltford; he didn't dare push his horses too hard.

The thought drew his attention to the relative speeds of a gig pulled by a single horse versus a well-sprung curricle with two top-notch carriage horses in the traces. Estimating the difference distracted him as they toiled up Durley Hill.

Even with the additional weight of Smiggs, given the quality of Kit's horses and curricle, they would be faster over any distance than Hillary's gig could possibly be.

Despite this interminably slow stage, the distance between them and the gig had to be closing.

They could—and would—reach Sylvia and Jack in time.

★ ★ ★

Sylvia was clutching the side of Hillary's gig with a white-knuckled grip when the first roofs of Saltford came into view. She felt rattled to her back teeth, but as she'd urged Hillary to get her to her father's side as fast as he could, she could hardly fault him for taking her at her word.

Although she'd questioned him further, he'd sworn he didn't know anything more to tell her. She'd spent the drive imagining the worst.

But she would know all soon.

Scanning ahead, she knew just where to look to spot the top of the church tower, away to the left of the main road. Seeing it made her stomach clench even tighter. Her father *couldn't* be dying—her mind simply refused to accept that.

Hillary had to slow his horse as they approached the village proper, but instead of turning left along the lane that led to the church, he drove straight on.

Surprised, Sylvia stared back at the lane, then rounded on Hillary. "You've missed the turn!"

"Ah, sorry." Hillary didn't lift his gaze from his horse nor did he slow the beast. "I should have said. There's been subsidence after the recent rains—a huge pothole opened up in the lane. I have to go around via the Shallows."

Sylvia sank back against the seat. "Oh." She knew the alternative route he spoke of; the lane known as the Shallows started just beyond the other side of the village and looped back along the banks of the river, ultimately connecting with the end of the lane that led to the church.

Inwardly grimacing, she told herself that going via the Shallows wouldn't be that much longer—especially if the pothole was close to the highway and she had to walk most of the length of the lane.

As Hillary's gig rattled along what had become the village street, she sat woodenly beside him, feeling hollow inside as she waited to learn the terrible truth in a way that would force her to believe it.

Doctor Moreton would be at the vicarage. He was an old friend of her father's and could be counted on to tell her as much as he knew without any roundaboutation. How could her father, who had seemed in his usual robust health only three weeks ago, have faded so quickly?

She saw several villagers who, recognizing her, waved and smiled…

Presumably, they hadn't yet heard. She forced herself to raise a hand in return, but she couldn't manage a smile.

Gripping her hands in her lap, she mentally urged Hillary to go faster. She needed to see her father, needed to hold his big hand.

Finally, they were through the village, and Hillary slowed for the turn into the Shallows. Seconds later, they were bowling along, with the river—the Avon—murmuring darkly beside the road.

She raised her head. Through a break in the trees, she glimpsed the church tower again. Nearly there—

Hillary swung the gig sharply to the right—so abruptly Sylvia nearly lost her grip and went flying. She half smothered a shriek as the gig shuddered and plunged at breakneck speed down a short track and into the clearing before the brass mill.

At the last second, Hillary hauled on the reins, and the carriage slewed, throwing Sylvia against his shoulder.

It was a shock to come to a halt.

Before she could even drag in a breath, Hillary seized her hands, first one, then the other, wrapping a fine cord around her wrists and cinching the cord tight.

Sylvia stared at her now-bound hands, then she jerked her head up and looked daggers at Hillary. "What on earth— *What?*" She gasped as Hillary tore off her bonnet and looped a scarf about her face, tugging the scarf tight and knotting it into an effective gag.

Her heart was racing. She fought to catch her breath. What on earth was going on?

Hillary spared not so much as a glance for her as he leapt to the ground, rushed around the horse to reach her side, then he hauled her down and half dragged half carried her toward the mill, until he could shove her to sit on a bench set against the mill's front wall.

Sylvia landed hard. Before she could blink, Hillary had crouched and wound another strand of cord around her ankles, hobbling her. Stunned, she fell back against the wall.

From inside the mill, she heard slow, heavy footsteps heading for the mill door farther along the wall.

The mill was never locked as the fires to melt the metal were kept constantly stoked, and a watchman was always on duty.

She looked at Hillary, who had stalked back to the gig, and horror crept up her spine as she saw him draw a heavy iron bar from the gig's footwell. He strode to the mill door. Holding the bar down beside his leg, he hauled the door open and walked inside.

Sylvia sucked in a breath—as much as she could—but she couldn't push any real sound past the gag. Desperate to warn the unsuspecting watchman, she drummed her feet on the ground, but this close to the river, moss covered any available soil; her soles raised nothing more than soft pats.

She heard cheery voices—Hillary's and the watchman's—then a heavy thud reached her. The watchman had hit the ground.

She slumped against the mill wall as panic stole through her.

She glanced at the gig—then sat up as she saw the lid of the boot slowly rise.

A tow-headed lad peered out. He saw her, and his eyes flew wide. Quick as an eel, he slipped to the ground.

He started toward her—just as she heard Hillary's heavy steps returning.

Violently, she shook her head at the lad. *No!* With her eyes, she signaled to the door, willing him to understand.

The lad's eyes swung to the door, and he halted. Then he turned tail and whisked around the gig, freezing where Hillary wouldn't see him.

Sylvia sagged with relief. Then Hillary reappeared in the doorway, and panic surged once more.

She kept her eyes locked on Hillary and prayed he wouldn't spot the lad. If the boy could get away, he could summon help…

But the lad was likely from Bristol. He wouldn't know where

they were or which way to go to summon help quickly, and there were no houses along that stretch of the river.

She didn't have time to think further. Hillary strode out and halted before her.

She kept her gaze apparently lowered, but watched him from beneath her lashes. With his Good Samaritan mask long gone, he was surveying her coldly through narrowed, piggy eyes.

Then a chilly smile curved his lips. He reached down, seized her arm, hauled her up, and propelled her before him into the mill.

★ ★ ★

Kit drove the curricle into the outskirts of Saltford without having sighted the gig. From the position of the church tower well away to the left, he surmised the vicarage, no doubt close to the church, lay some distance off the Bath Road, closer to the river.

Kit eyed the tower.

Hillary had said he would drive Sylvia to the vicarage, but Hillary had lied about multiple things. What if he'd lied about that?

If Kit drove to the vicarage and Sylvia wasn't there, he would lose precious time—time she and Jack might not have.

Kit swiftly weighed his choices; as they reached the village proper, he drew on the reins. As soon as the horses had halted, he handed the reins to Smiggs. "Follow along behind us." Kit swiveled on the seat and looked at Ned and Ollie. "Boys, we need to ask everyone who might have seen it if the gig passed this way. We need to be sure which way it went."

The boys nodded and scrambled down to the road.

They joined Kit in ranging along the road, asking anyone they saw if they'd spotted a man and a lady driving past in a gig.

Soon, Kit came upon an old lady, a basket on her arm.

When he asked his question, she blinked at him "By lady, do you mean Miss Buckleberry, dear?"

"Yes." Kit managed to keep his voice even. "We're trying to work out which way she went."

The old lady pointed down the street. "On along the Bath Road."

"Thank you." He wanted to rush on, but paused to ask, "How long ago was that?"

"Oh, not much more than five or so minutes," the old lady said. "I was just on my way into the shop, and I didn't spend that long in there." She paused, then added, "I did wave, but dear Sylvia seemed a tad distracted."

Kit flashed the old lady a smile. "Again, thank you. I'll mention that when next I see her." Quickly sobering, he moved on.

He called the boys to him and told them what he'd learned—that as he'd feared, Hillary hadn't driven Sylvia to the vicarage. "We need to keep going as fast as we can and see if he continued on toward Bath."

Letting the boys go ahead, Kit dropped back to tell Smiggs the news.

Smiggs frowned. "He must've spun her some tale about where her father is, else she'd have kicked up a fuss when he didn't head to the vicarage."

Grimly, Kit nodded. Smiggs was right. But their only option was to follow the gig's trail, such as it was.

Ollie found an older man seated outside a cottage, watching the passing traffic. The man remembered the gig and Sylvia; Kit came up in time to hear him say, "Aye. 'Bout five minutes ago, it were. Odd, I thought, seeing our Sylvia up beside that ramshackle fella."

Ollie turned wide eyes Kit's way.

Kit halted beside Ollie, dropped a hand on the lad's shoulder, and nodded to the man. "Why ramshackle?"

"Well, it was that Nunsworth fella." The man gestured with his pipe. "He was run out of the village years ago. Claimed to be a churchman, but all he was interested in was stealing from those silly enough to listen to him." The man paused, then looked struck. "Mind, that was a good long time ago. Sylvia was just a child then—she might not know."

Kit's heart sank. He gripped Ollie's shoulder and dipped his head to the man. "Thank you."

He and Ollie swung around and hurried on down the road.

They went as fast as they dared, but there were several lanes leading into the countryside; they had to be sure the gig hadn't taken one of them.

Urgency rode Kit's shoulders, gaining weight with every passing minute.

They reached the other end of the village proper; ahead, the road continued on through fields dotted with the occasional farmhouse or cottage.

A farmer driving a yoke of oxen pulling a heavily laden cart was toiling up the slight rise.

Kit hailed the man and asked if a gig carrying a man and a lady had passed him.

The farmer studied Kit for an instant, then said, "Not passed, no." When Kit blinked, the farmer turned and pointed. "I saw them head down the lane there."

The entrance to the lane lay ahead on Kit's left. His heart thudded. "How long ago?"

"Not that long—say ten minutes. Might be less." The farmer gestured down the rise. "Me and the beasts were just rounding the corner down there when I looked up and saw them." Kit opened his mouth to thank the man when the farmer went on, "Odd, really, to go that way." The farmer glanced at Kit. "It's called the Shallows on account of following the river along." The man shrugged. "Scenic, I suppose."

Reining in his impatience, Kit thanked the man. Smiggs drew up the curricle. Kit leapt to the box seat; while the boys scrambled up behind, Kit stood and peered down the lower-lying lane. All he could see were the tops of trees.

He turned and called to the farmer, "What lies that way?"

The farmer looked back. "It'll eventually land you near the church, but along the way, there's just the brass mill. Not much else."

Kit saluted the farmer, then, grim-faced, sat, picked up the reins, sent his horses pacing forward, then swung them in a tight arc and plunged down the narrow lane.

Sixteen

Sylvia struggled to make sense of what was happening. Hillary had all but flung her to the ground so she was sitting with her back to the side of the huge stone platform on which the brass was pounded into sheets. He'd squinted at her for a moment, then gone off muttering, apparently searching for something.

She tugged and twisted, trying to free her hands. The lad, at least, knew she was there. She had no notion who he was, but he'd known her; perhaps he was a friend of one of the schoolboys. Regardless, she had to believe that he would find and tell someone eventually.

She wondered whether she could get her feet under her and, hobbled though she was, make a dash for the door, but Hillary loomed out of the shadows to her left, clutching several lengths of rope.

He came to stand over her, his boots thudding down on the floorboards, one on either side of her knees.

She glared up at him, but he appeared oblivious. Indeed, he seemed to be smiling to himself.

"This will do nicely," he muttered, then he reached down, seized her bound hands, and hauled them high.

Sylvia gasped as her arms were wrenched.

Hillary didn't seem to hear. He drew a small knife from his pocket and, with a quick flick, sliced through the cord binding her wrists. With one big hand, he held both her wrists while he maneuvered to wind separate lengths of the heavier rope around each of her gloved hands, the ropes passing over her palms.

Then he released her left hand, leaned to her right, and secured her right hand to the base of the railing of the stone platform, tying the rope securely so her arm was stretched wide.

Confused, she stared, then Hillary stepped to her left and secured her left hand in a similar position on her other side.

Hillary drew back and surveyed his handiwork. There was nothing in his gaze as it passed over her to suggest he saw her as anything more than an inanimate object—a prop for some scene he was constructing.

Her gaze on Hillary's face, Sylvia felt cold dread run icy fingers down her spine.

What in all the heavens is he planning?

★ ★ ★

"I can see a roof on the right," Ned reported in a hushed whisper. "'Bout a hundred yards on."

Kit slowed his horses to a walk and looked. An old, lichen-covered roof loomed beyond a stand of trees; it appeared to cover one large building, with an add-on to the rear. Several tall stone chimneys pierced the roof, also toward the rear of the building.

"Presumably that's the brass mill," Smiggs murmured.

Kit nodded. *Has Hillary stopped there or has he gone on?*

Kit was debating his options when the bushes lining the lane ahead rustled, then a figure burst through, yanking his jacket free and stumbling into the lane.

"Jack!" Kit managed to keep his voice muted.

Jack caught his balance, swung around, and saw them, and the relief that washed over the boy's face told its own story.

Then Jack started running toward the curricle, waving at them to stop.

Kit drew on the reins and halted the bays.

Jack raced to the curricle's side and, as Kit stepped to the ground, looked at him imploringly. "That blackguard who's call-

ing himself Hillary took Miss B into that old building there."
Jack pointed at the brass mill. "He tied her hands and gagged
and hobbled her, and I couldn't rescue her in time."

Smiggs, Ned, and Ollie had leapt down; they gathered around.

Kit dropped a hand on Jack's shoulder and gripped reassuringly. "You've rescued her now." He glanced toward the mill,
then looked at Jack. "Where should we leave the curricle?"

Jack scratched his ear. "Best leave it here, I'd say—otherwise,
he'll hear, and God alone knows what he'll do."

The curricle would block the lane, but that couldn't be helped,
and it seemed a rarely used route, at least on a Sunday. Kit nodded and handed the reins to Smiggs.

While Smiggs secured the horses, Kit focused on Jack. "Right,
then. Tell us what happened from the moment Hillary reached
here."

That didn't take long.

All but jigging with impatience, Jack tugged Kit's sleeve.
"We've got to go and save Miss B. Best go through the trees,
just in case he looks out."

Accepting that Jack had superior knowledge of the terrain,
Kit urged him to lead the way. The boy wriggled through the
bushes; Kit followed, with the other two boys on his heels and
Smiggs bringing up the rear.

Jack paused at the edge of the cleared space that stretched
along the front of the mill. When Kit halted beside him, Jack
pointed to a gig, the horse standing with head hanging, then to
the closed door of the mill, toward the other end of the building from where they stood.

Kit nodded. Judging by the brightly painted sign above the
door, the neatly trimmed clearing, and the thin stream of smoke
that curled lazily upward from the chimneys, the mill was a
going concern. He considered the closed door for several seconds, but given the size of the building, depending on where
Hillary and Sylvia were inside it, a frontal assault would al-

most certainly give Hillary time to seize Sylvia and use her as a hostage.

Kit glanced at the others and signaled that they should circle toward the rear of the mill. He took the lead, pleased that the others remained silent as they crept in his wake. Impatience had dug its spurs deep, but the overriding need to ensure Sylvia's safety gave him the strength to resist all unwise compulsions.

He was banking on there being more than one reason the mill was built so close to the river's edge.

Sure enough, in the rear section that had been enclosed as an add-on to the main building, he found not just the two waterwheels that must at one time have powered the now almost-certainly steam-driven mill but also a hatch for loading barges to be sent downriver.

The hatch was cut in the side wall of the rear section; it was low and wide and secured with a simple hooked latch on the inside.

Kit crouched by the hatch and tipped his head. He could hear the rumble of a male voice from inside. He signaled to the others, and they obediently froze as he drew out his penknife. After opening the knife, he inserted the blade through the gap at the edge of the hatch and carefully eased the hook up, then slowly let it down...

The hatch eased open a crack.

And the voice inside reached him clearly.

Along with the others, who edged nearer, Kit paused to listen.

★ ★ ★

Sylvia had managed to make a few questioning noises around the gag, and that was all it had taken to prompt Hillary into loquaciousness.

He'd rambled for several minutes about how long it had taken him to find his way after being so badly done by—how he'd been forced to take himself to Bristol and tout his brilliance as a preacher on the docks. His lip had curled contemptuously. "Parading up and down with boards exhorting sinners to pray and pay for their repentance!"

Yet according to him, despite his brilliance, he'd been reduced to a hand-to-mouth existence, one entirely inappropriate for a man of his stamp.

At least she now knew it was he who'd been watching her.

While he ranted on, Sylvia surreptitiously tested the ropes anchoring her hands. There was only a little—insufficient—give. However, Hillary had wound the ropes over her gloves. If she could manage to slide her hands free of the leather...

With an expansive gesture, Hillary concluded, "Indeed, my dear Sylvia, I cannot tell you how very pleased I am to have finally found the perfect revenge."

He smiled at her in an unctuous way that reminded her forcibly of his recent occupation; his eyes seemed to shine with what, in other circumstances, might be taken for evangelical zeal. There was also something strange about his familiarity toward her; he seemed to know her, while she couldn't place him.

She still had no idea what he was talking about—why he'd kidnapped her for his revenge—but she had a bad feeling about the way he'd tied her, almost in a position of a sitting crucifixion.

Her only chance lay in keeping him talking and praying the boy found someone to help. *"Why revenge on me?"* She tried to enunciate clearly through the gag and adopted a mystified expression to boot.

Hillary studied her for a second, putting sounds together with her look, then he understood, and that smile she'd rather not see wreathed his face again. "Ah, no, my dear Sylvia—this isn't about revenge against you. No, no—you, it must be said, are merely an innocent pawn to be sacrificed in a deeper game." His smile took on an ecstatic aura. "It's your father, the good Reverend Buckleberry, whom I intend to strike and hurt—to flay with a flail that will cut deeply into body and soul."

Horrified, Sylvia stared at Hillary while her mind raced, assembling the critical thrust of his plot—his revenge. He was correct in thinking that if she was killed—sacrificed in some brutal fashion—less than a mile from her father's door, and he learned it was because of him...

She *still* couldn't make sense of this. *"Why?"*

Hillary blinked at her. "Why?" He paused, head tilting as he considered her, then said, "I suppose it's been to my advantage that you haven't recognized me. As you were only a child at the time, I daresay you don't remember, but my name, my dear, is Hillary Nunsworth, and at one time—a sadly short time—I was deacon of this parish. Your father's parish. Unfortunately, your sanctimonious father took a dim view of the monies I was collecting—in my opinion, nothing more than my due—from the parishioners and reported me to the bishop. Thanks to your father, I was defrocked and denied the vocation I had trained for—along with my ability to make an easy living as a suitably respected member of society."

His voice took on a darker, distinctly ugly tone. "Rather than being looked up to, rather than having people curry my favor, I was shown the vicarage door, and the village turned against me. I was hounded out!" His eyes flared, and he trained his feverish gaze on Sylvia. "And it was all your father's fault! Because of him, I've been forced to eke out a living exhorting money from the gullible in Bristol." His eyes narrowed to burning shards, and he lowered his voice to a grating growl. "And day by day, week by week, month after long month for a good decade and more, I've nurtured and nursed my hatred for your father."

As Nunsworth glowered darkly at her, Sylvia swallowed. Her heart was thudding in a panicky tattoo.

Then even more disturbingly, Nunsworth's expression lightened and cleared. "And then, my dear Sylvia, a few weeks ago, I saw you in the city." In conversational vein, he went on, "At first, I wasn't sure it was you, so I asked around." His gaze resting on her face, his expression one of pleased anticipation, he said,

"When I learned that you were, indeed, Sylvia Buckleberry—well." His lips drew back in a gloating smile. "I knew the time for my revenge had come."

★ ★ ★

Kit didn't wait to hear more. He'd already peeked around the hatch and found that, as he'd hoped, it opened into a deeply shadowed area of the mill's rear section, out of direct sight of where Hillary's—no, Nunsworth's—voice placed him, which was somewhere in the middle of the main building.

There on the riverbank, daylight was starting to fade, cut off by higher land to the west. That would work to Kit's and his helpers' advantage; with any luck, when Kit went through the hatch, no sudden shaft of bright light would give him away.

He swiveled on his heel and pointed to Smiggs, then, with his hands, mimed that Smiggs should go around to the mill's front door, wait until he heard Kit pounce, then come storming in to assist.

Smiggs gave a curt nod and, moving silently, vanished into the bushes.

Kit fixed the three boys with a stern look and mouthed, "Stay here." He knew it was futile, but felt compelled to try to protect them.

All three looked at him with innocent eyes and said nothing.

Resisting the urge to roll his own eyes, Kit turned and, opening the hatch as little as possible, slipped through. He didn't have time to argue with the boys, not with Sylvia facing a madman.

He found himself beside the old waterwheels. The entire area was shrouded in deep shadow and a low wall—about chest high—cut the area off from the main floor of the mill.

He carefully rose and spotted Nunsworth standing on the far side of a raised stone platform. He was looking down as he continued to talk, suggesting that Sylvia was sitting on the floor with her back to the platform.

Kit crouched and quickly made his way to the edge of the

partition. He glanced around it, but Nunsworth's gaze remained lowered, his attention fixed on Sylvia.

There was a large skylight in the ceiling above and behind where Nunsworth stood, and the soft, late-afternoon light illuminated a square of floor between Nunsworth and the main door. Kit glimpsed a figure sprawled, unmoving, on the ground not far from the door. A watchman? From the look of the man, he wasn't going to be able to help.

Kit refocused on Nunsworth. The light from above made the shadows wreathing the rest of the mill floor appear darker and gloomier. Clinging to those shadows, placing his feet with care and keeping to a crouch, Kit ghosted forward using benches and tool racks for cover, eventually fetching up at the rear of the stone platform. He paused, but Nunsworth continued talking, enumerating and railing against all the supposed slights visited on him by the villagers.

The stone slab was roughly twelve feet by twelve feet in area, about waist high, and had rails running along three sides. As he'd neared the slab, Kit had seen that Nunsworth had tied Sylvia's hands, arms spread wide, to the railing on the opposite side.

Kit glanced up and saw the huge iron plate suspended above the slab. Presumably when the mill was operating, the plate would pound down on crude brass sheet spread on the slab, flattening it to the desired thickness.

Given the way Nunsworth had positioned Sylvia, he didn't plan on using the iron plate to enact his revenge; Kit took some small comfort from that.

Dismissing the gruesome thought, he crept to the corner of the slab and eased his way around it.

A whisper of sound from the depths of the mill told him that, as he'd expected, the boys had followed him inside. He had to trust that their sneaking skills were at least as good as his; he couldn't afford to shift his attention from Sylvia and Nunsworth to check.

Nunsworth was a larger man than Kit had anticipated; he was as tall as Kit, of heavier build, and powerful with it.

Kit needed some weapon to tip the scales and bring this situation to a safe end—safe for Sylvia as well as the others. Inch by inch, Kit crept toward the next corner, scanning the benches and tool racks nearby for some implement he could use.

★ ★ ★

Sylvia had nearly eased her left hand from her glove. One tug, and that hand would be free.

She'd also managed to stretch the gag somewhat, enough that, when Nunsworth's tirade against the villagers of Saltford ran down, she managed to mumble reasonably clearly, "It was you who I sensed watching me."

She was perfectly certain she needed to keep him talking as long as she could. She hadn't yet worked out how to free her feet.

His hands in his pockets, Nunsworth blinked at her. "Was I the one watching you?" When she nodded, he smiled, transparently pleased by what he saw as his own cleverness. "Yes, indeed. I made sure I knew all about you before I acted. I required the better part of a day to enact the scenario I've devised as most likely to cause your father the maximum excruciating pain."

He paused, looking over her head as if relishing the thought of her father's agony, then lowered his gaze to her face and smiled smugly. "I needed a day during which no one was likely to realize you were missing. Well, other than your landlady, the estimable Mrs. Macintyre, but I believe I can rely on her to dither. She won't want to go to the authorities in case she's acting precipitously and ends somehow sullying your reputation. I know how those like her—like the villagers here—think. No. Mrs. Macintyre will wait to see if you return, and by the time she realizes you aren't going to, it'll be far too late."

Nunsworth's smile of anticipation grew. "Far, far too late for anyone to save you." He studied her for a moment, then went on, "Sunday, of course, was the obvious day. As a clergyman's daughter, your movements on Sunday are entirely predictable—you go to church in the morning and return to your lodgings to take luncheon with your landlady, and she is the only one to see you through the rest of the day. The Sabbath, our day of rest."

Except, Sylvia thought, Kit had been coming to walk out with her. She glanced upward, at the softening sky visible through the skylight. She didn't know what time it was, but surely Kit would have called long since. He would guess that something had befallen her...

Was it possible he might realize what had happened and be driving to her rescue?

She couldn't see how. Surreptitiously wriggling her still-anchored right hand, she decided she couldn't hope for rescue; she would have to save herself.

In gloating vein, Nunsworth continued, "Indeed, Sunday is the *perfect* day—the day of the week on which your father is at his most righteous." Nunsworth all but preened. "I've laid my plans quite brilliantly, if I do say so myself." He looked down at her, yet didn't seem to actually see her, and purred, "This is going to be so very satisfying."

She got the distinct impression that, in looking at her, he was seeing not her but some vision that pleased him to no end; her skin crawled.

But she almost had both her hands loose. Desperate to keep him dwelling on his plan rather than acting it out, she mumbled, "But why here?"

Refocusing on her, he tipped his head, then ventured, "Why bring you here?"

She nodded, trying to let nothing more than sincere interest show in her eyes.

He arched his brows in a superior way. "I would have thought that obvious, my dear. I want your father to see your body, and that sooner rather than later, so he can appreciate it in all its gory glory. As close as we are to the vicarage, I think that's guaranteed. I want him to see what his piety has bought him." Nunsworth's features contorted, viciousness overtaking his expression as he raised his head. "I want to watch and see his shock. I want to watch him grieve! And ultimately, when he reads my note, I want to see guilt swamp him and bring him to his knees!"

The last was said like a clarion call—a summons to battle.

Abruptly, Nunsworth looked down and pinned Sylvia with his gaze. All humanity had leached from his face. "I want," he stated, "your father to understand that your death and the manner of it is a judgment I've passed on him. He took from me the life I should have had. In return, I'll take a life from him."

Kit was crouching by the corner of the slab, a mere two yards from Sylvia. His blood ran cold at Nunsworth's words. The man might be insane, but he was also deadly serious, driven by compulsive intent and a hatred fueled by obsession.

A rack of tools off to Kit's right offered a pair of long, heavy iron tongs, the most useful implement Kit had spotted. But in going for the tongs, he would immediately be seen by Nunsworth.

The man was droning on, "I admit that I will regret marring such loveliness, but sadly for you, my dear, you are your father's only child. So I fear it's you who must pay." Nunsworth bent, reaching for something on the floor.

Kit couldn't see what Nunsworth was about to pick up, then his gaze was caught by movement on the floor behind Nunsworth. The watchman was starting to stir.

An in-drawn breath close behind Kit had him nearly jumping from his skin. He glanced back and saw Ollie just behind him, peering over the top of the slab, his eyes widening and a horrified look breaking across his face.

Kit snapped his gaze back to Nunsworth.

Just as Nunsworth said, "And now, it's time for my revenge."

His face alight with unholy fervor, in a two-handed grip,

Nunsworth hefted a heavy iron bar, swung it high, and brought it down with maximum force.

Sylvia screamed.

Kit's heart stopped. He died—or so it felt.

But at the last second, Sylvia tugged one hand free and flung herself to the right—toward Kit.

The bar hit the edge of the stone slab, and shards flew.

Kit leapt to his feet and raced for the tongs.

Momentarily surprised, then realizing he'd been thwarted, Nunsworth bellowed with rage.

Kit grabbed the tongs and spun as Nunsworth raised the bar again—this time angling to where Sylvia cowered, her other hand still tied to the railing despite her frantic tugging.

His features contorted with black fury, Nunsworth started a vicious downward swing—aiming at the back of Sylvia's head.

Kit lunged between Sylvia and Nunsworth.

With the tongs gripped between his hands, Kit caught the iron bar on the tongs's long handles.

The force behind the blow drove him down to one knee, but he gritted his teeth, straightened his arms and braced them, then surged upward, to his feet, flinging Nunsworth back.

Nunsworth staggered, but didn't fall. He shrieked in frustration and, this time swinging the bar from the side, eyes slitted in fury, came for Kit.

Again, Kit caught the bar on the tongs, the force jarring through his arms and shoulders.

Nunsworth shrieked like a banshee and fell into a frenzy, hammering down blows so quickly it was all Kit could do to meet them.

He couldn't turn the tide. In strength, he and Nunsworth were evenly matched, at least with Nunsworth in a destructive fury. All Kit could do was grit his teeth and pray the man's energy flagged soon.

Where was Smiggs?

Through the all-but-continuous clangs as Kit fended off Nunsworth's assaults, Kit heard banging—on the front door.

Nunsworth had barred it; Smiggs couldn't get through.

Then Nunsworth jerked and staggered forward half a step.

Sylvia was still frantically trying to get her right hand free. From her position behind Kit, with her gaze trained on the battle and a prayer on her lips that the demented beast that was Nunsworth wouldn't break through Kit's dogged guard, she caught sudden movement in the shadows. On a blink of disbelief, she saw the lad from earlier wielding a metal pole; he'd whacked Nunsworth across the back of his legs with it.

But Nunsworth regained his footing. Now even closer to Kit, Nunsworth clenched his teeth in a rictus grin and brought the iron bar down with punishing force.

Kit got the tongs up just in time, catching the bar on the long iron handles with a deafening clang.

Then the muscles in Kit's arms bunched, and once again, he flung Nunsworth back.

Before Nunsworth could recover, Ollie—*Ollie!*—rushed past Kit. Arms extended, with all his boy's might, Ollie shoved Nunsworth in the chest.

Just as the lad swung his pole, this time, catching Nunsworth squarely across the backs of his knees.

Nunsworth teetered, but still didn't fall.

Sylvia saw her chance; she could just reach. She slid down and lashed out with her bound feet, sweeping Nunsworth's boots from beneath him.

His expression dissolving into one of shock, Nunsworth toppled backward. Arms flailing, the iron bar flying from his grasp, he lost his balance and fell heavily on his back.

Before anyone else could move, another slight figure darted in, and Ned upended a metal pail of ashes, pail and all, over Nunsworth's head.

Coughing and spluttering, Nunsworth collapsed on the floor.

Ned had shoved the pail down hard, and it appeared to be stuck on Nunsworth's head. The pail thudded on the floor as Kit's groom rushed up.

Kit glanced back at Sylvia. Her gaze was locked on Nunsworth. She was—thank God—unhurt.

He looked at Smiggs, who had run around and entered via the rear hatch, then at the three boys—all standing around their fallen foe as if daring him to try to get up.

Nunsworth obliged and tried to struggle up—and Jack thumped the pail hard with his rod. Nunsworth yelped and fell back, and all three boys smiled grimly.

Kit felt the tension of battle leaching from him. He lowered the tongs. "Well done, boys! Keep an eye on him."

Their gazes ferociously intent, they did; not one of the three even glanced at Kit to acknowledge the order.

Kit met Smiggs's relieved gaze and tipped his head toward the downed watchman, who chose that moment to groan. Kit didn't want to think of what the man's fate would have been had he and the others not arrived in time.

In time to stop Nunsworth bludgeoning Sylvia to death.

The ice that had flooded Kit on realizing what Nunsworth had planned still chilled him.

He spun and went down on one knee beside the lady who now held his heart.

She was tugging at her still-bound right hand; she flicked him a frowning glance. "I thought I had it, but no." She tugged at the knotted rope. "Blast it!"

Relief that she was safe—and well enough to frown at him and grumble—swamped him, only to rise in the next breath in a wave so intense and immense it threatened to choke him. He reached for her bound hand and managed to gruffly say, "Here—let me."

She sniffed and desisted and let him have at the knot.

He worked swiftly, loosening the knot—wrenched tight by

her panicked tugging—then unravelling it and unwinding the rope lashing her hand to the rails.

When her hand, still in its glove, was finally free, she drew it close, massaging her no doubt bruised flesh. Kit helped her to sit upright, tugged her other glove free of the rope and handed it to her, then swung around and sat beside her.

When, still rubbing her abused hand, she leaned lightly against him, something deep inside him settled and subsided. After a second, he raised his arm, draped it around her shoulders, and drew her closer—and she came.

That entity inside him who viewed her as his calmed a little more.

Together, they watched Smiggs, who had unbarred and opened the main door, help the watchman outside.

Ned and Ollie had armed themselves with identical metal poles to the one Jack wielded. Any attempt by Nunsworth to so much as lift his head was met by a hail of sharp raps on the pail; he'd learned to lie still.

"You came for me." Sylvia's ungloved fingers slipped into Kit's hand where it rested on his thigh.

Kit gripped—harder than he'd intended. Gentling his hold, his gaze still on the boys, he softly snorted at the silliness of her words. "I will always come for you no matter what monster tries to steal you away."

He turned his head enough to meet her gaze as, with an un-voiced question in her eyes, she looked at him. He read that question and replied, "I'm not about to let anyone steal my future."

Lost in the warm caramel of his eyes, Sylvia felt her heart, which had slowed, start to beat faster. She arched her brows. "Your future?"

His lips eased. His gaze still locked with hers, he raised her hand to his lips and brushed a kiss across her knuckles. "You," he whispered. "You are my future, and I'm not of a mind to allow anyone to steal the years I hope you'll agree to share with me."

Her heart leapt, then raced. She studied his eyes. "Is that an offer, my lord?"

He tipped his head, his lips curving. "Not as such, but it's the promise of one." His expression remained relaxed, but there was seriousness behind his next words. "You're a clergyman's daughter—I plan to do everything by the book in wooing you."

She felt her heart soften and shift, and in that instant, she knew to her soul that her heart was already his.

That she'd succumbed to this nobleman reputed to be a rakehell, who was, in fact, so much more.

Certainty filled her; she let it show in her eyes, let the radiance of it fill her smile.

"M'lord, what do you want us to do with this blighter?"

Ollie's question broke the moment. Together with Kit, Sylvia looked to where the three boys still had their attention focused on the fallen Nunsworth.

"He's getting squirrelly," the lad, who Sylvia had realized from the boys' exchanges was none other than Jack the Lad, reported.

And, indeed, Nunsworth appeared to be trying to surreptitiously shift into a position from which he could swing away from the boys.

Not that they would let him escape.

Smiggs lumbered up, a length of heavy rope in his hands. "The watchman told me where to find this. He's—pardon the pun—ropeable about letting Nunsworth down him."

To the boys, Smiggs said, "Keep those poles handy. Whack him if he gives me any trouble."

The boys shuffled and circled as, none too gently, Smiggs rolled Nunsworth over, hauled his hands behind his back, and secured them with the rope. Then Smiggs reached down and bent Nunsworth's legs at the knees, looping the rope around his ankles and cinching it tight. "See?" Smiggs said to the boys.

"This is how you hog-tie a man. It'll keep him right where he is until we decide different."

While the boys, curious, inspected Smiggs's handiwork, Kit rose, crouched by Sylvia's feet, and untied the hobble Nunsworth had fashioned. Then Kit straightened, reached down and gave her his hand and, when she put her fingers in his, drew her upright.

She swayed, and he caught her around the waist. She leaned into his support as the boys turned their way. "Thank you, boys, for coming to save me. I don't know how you realized that I was in danger before I did, but I thank you from the bottom of my heart."

All three boys blushed and looked bashful.

"Tweren't nothing but what you deserve, miss," Ollie said, "for all your hard work at the school an' all."

The other two nodded earnestly. Then Jack's eyes lit, and he added, "And it was fun!"

Kit chuckled, and she smiled. Then he urged her to the door.

They left Nunsworth, trussed and mumbling curses muted by the metal pail, on the mill floor and walked out into the gathering dusk. Kit led her to the bench against the wall and gently—as if she was porcelain—eased her down to sit.

She shot him a grateful smile; she could do with a moment to gather her wits and simply breathe.

With a last glance to reassure himself that she was as well as she could be, Kit walked to the other end of the bench to speak with the watchman.

Smiggs headed for the lane, calling, "I'll fetch the curricle."

The boys, Sylvia was touched to note, hovered protectively beside her; if she wasn't much mistaken, the Cavanaugh effect was rubbing off on them. She summoned a smile and focused it on Jack. "Jack, isn't it?"

He blushed and essayed an awkward bow. "Pleased to meet you, miss."

She smiled more broadly. "Not half as pleased as I am to meet you." She included Ollie and Ned with a glance. "All I know is that Jack somehow ended up in the boot of Nunsworth's gig." She arched her brows at the three. "How did that happen? How is it that all three of you are here?"

They told her, with a great deal of color and explanation thrown in.

By the time they'd finished recounting it all, and she'd commented appropriately along the way, they were quite puffed up with pride—in her opinion, entirely justifiably—and, with the usual resilience of youth, had already forgotten the tenser moments of the drama and were inclined to cast the whole as a magnificent adventure.

She envied them that ability. It would be a long time before she forgot Nunsworth and his terrible plan.

Smiggs drove Kit's curricle into the clearing and drew up before the open mill door.

Along with Smiggs, the three boys, and even the watchman, Sylvia looked at Kit.

Kit read the question writ large in all the faces turned his way. *What now?*

He glanced through the open mill door, beyond which Nunsworth remained securely hog-tied, then looked at Sylvia. "I believe it's time we called on your father."

Seventeen

The watchman—Gibson—agreed to remain at the mill and watch over their captive; Sylvia assured him they would send relief as soon as they could, then Kit handed her up into the curricle, climbed up, and accepted the reins from Smiggs. Kit waited while Smiggs and the boys crammed in behind, then, with a flick of the reins, sent the bays in a wide turn and set them pacing back toward the lane.

Sylvia pointed to their right. "It's faster to continue along the river."

Kit turned the horses that way. Once they were bowling along, he glanced at Sylvia, his gaze lingering for a long moment on her face before he was forced to look to his horses. Under the cover of the noise of the rattling wheels, he murmured, "Are you truly all right?"

He felt her gaze, soft and warm, trace his cheek. "Yes, I am." After a second, she went on, "We reached the mill before I had the slightest inkling that I had anything to fear. Prior to that, I was consumed by anxiety over my father." She lightly touched his thigh. "Did you hear about that—the story Nunsworth used to get me to go with him?"

He nodded. "The boys overheard and told me."

From the corner of his eye, he caught her swift smile. "They really are amazing. I had no idea they'd got so close."

"Apparently, they've been following you on and off for days, seeking to keep you safe from whoever was watching you. It was Ned who got close enough to you and Nunsworth to hear what was said. Evidently, Ned is the sneakiest of the three—or so I've been told."

She laughed—and the sound teased apart the remaining knot of his own anxiety.

After a moment, she went on, "I saw Jack slip out of the boot before Nunsworth dragged me into the mill, so despite not knowing who Jack was, I realized someone had gone to fetch help, yet not knowing you were already on the way, I truly didn't think anyone would reach the mill in time." She paused, then said, "I suspect I should have been much more frightened than I was. Instead, I was trying to keep Nunsworth occupied with telling me how clever he'd been until I could get free of his bindings."

"Thank God you did." The desolation that had threatened in the instant he'd thought she would die would stay with him for the rest of his life—an evocatively effective reminder of just how much she mattered to him.

"Looking back," she said, her tone considering, "I was only truly terrified in that moment after I'd avoided his first blow, but thought I had no chance of escaping the second."

Kit felt his jaw clench and fixed his gaze on the narrow lane ahead.

Then he felt her gaze on his face again, a softly radiant touch tracing his profile.

"But then you were there, between me and him. And I wasn't afraid for myself anymore—I was afraid for you. That Nunsworth would somehow overwhelm you—he was so violent and ferocious."

Kit admitted, "I'm not entirely sure he was sane—not in those moments after I intervened."

She went on, "But then the boys were there, and… I have to say I'm finding it hard to be afraid of a man with a pail on his head."

Kit felt his lips lift in what was assuredly his first smile in hours. "They did lighten the drama somewhat."

From the corner of his eye, he saw she was smiling.

"I honestly don't think I'll be having any nightmares about Nunsworth."

Kit let his gaze linger on her face, on her increasingly serene expression. For himself, he wasn't so sure.

"Around to the left," Sylvia said as they approached the village's High Street. "Then take the first turn to the right, and the vicarage is the first house along."

She accepted that the tale Nunsworth had spun about her father being at death's door was all lies. Nevertheless, she wanted to see her father with her own eyes. Only then would she be completely cured of the anxiety Nunsworth had provoked.

Kit turned into the vicarage drive as the last of the light faded from the sky. Looking ahead, Sylvia saw lamplight filling her father's study, the welcoming glow spilling through the mullioned windows onto the neat path that circled the house.

Kit drew the horses to a stamping halt level with the front steps. Ollie dropped to the ground and raced to hold the horses' heads, crooning to quiet them.

Smiggs descended more slowly, joining Kit on the gravel as he stepped down. Accepting the reins Kit held out to him, Smiggs glanced at Sylvia. "Is there a stable out back?" He tipped his head at the horses. "After the afternoon they've had, I really should rub them down and give them some feed."

Taking the hand Kit offered, Sylvia climbed down and smiled at Smiggs. "If you walk them around to the back of the house, you'll find the stable. The stableman, Egbert, will probably be there—he's a curmudgeonly old soul, but he'll love to help with horses such as these."

Smiggs grinned. "I know the sort—I'll be like him one day. We'll get along." To Kit, he said, "I'll take the lads with me. They can help."

Kit nodded. "Settle the horses and leave them in the stable until we know what we're going to do next."

Sylvia met his eyes and realized what he meant. This would be the first time he would meet her father, who Kit hoped would eventually be his father-in-law. She let her smile deepen and looped her arm through Kit's. He set his hand over hers where it rested on his sleeve, and together they walked toward the door while Smiggs and the boys led the horses and curricle away.

As, beside Kit, Sylvia climbed the shallow steps to the porch, she glimpsed movement through the nearer window of her father's study. She didn't try to suppress her smile; she wasn't sure she could have. She'd caught sight of two faces as their owners—her father and his close friend Deacon Harris—had stood at the window and, with open, not to say avid, curiosity, watched the action in the forecourt, and now, both men were making for the front hall.

Kit halted before the door and reached for the bellpull.

"Don't bother." Sylvia smiled at him, grasped the doorknob, and opened the door. "It's never locked."

That was one of her father's dictums—that he was always available to his flock.

"Trusting," Kit murmured, as he pushed the door fully open and ushered her in, "but admirable in a vicar."

Sylvia thought so—and then she saw her father standing in the middle of the hall with Deacon Harris beside him. With one swift glance, she confirmed that Nunsworth's tale had been a complete fabrication; her father's lean figure appeared as sprightly as ever, with the soft tufts of his white hair framing his face, and his blue eyes alight with the curiosity concerning all God's creatures and their doings that had marked him throughout her life.

Her smile deepening—indeed, wreathing her face—she went quickly forward, hands outstretched. "Papa!"

He opened his arms, and she went into them, and they closed, enveloping her in warmth and the faint scent of tobacco—his secret vice.

She hugged him back, ineluctably relieved to feel muscle and bone so strong beneath her palms.

Clearly recognizing the unusual intensity of her greeting, he eased his hold, then patted her shoulder. "My darling Sylvia, is everything all right?"

She uttered a short laugh and drew back from his embrace. "It is now." She went up on her toes and pressed a kiss to his cheek, then turned to Deacon Harris—who looked every bit as curious as her father. She put out a hand. "Uncle William—it's lovely to see you as well."

William took her hand and patted it. "It always does my old heart good to see you, my dear."

Smiling still—she couldn't seem to stop—she squeezed the deacon's fingers, then drew her hand from his clasp.

With a swish of her skirts, she half turned and held out her hand to Kit; he'd remained just inside the front door, which he'd closed. "Papa—allow me to present Lord Christopher Cavanaugh."

Kit came forward and offered his hand. "Reverend Buckleberry."

Kit had an easy smile on his lips and a relaxed expression on his face, but Sylvia was now sufficiently attuned to the nuances of his behavior; he was just a tad nervous over meeting her father—and that lurking vulnerability only made her love him all the more.

Beaming, she watched as her father welcomed Kit "to his humble abode," then introduced William Harris.

As Kit and William shook hands, Sylvia's father looked her way, brows arching in interested query.

Kit saw Sylvia hesitate, but this was not a subject on which to spare her father distress; he would be more distressed if she didn't tell him of Nunsworth's motives. "There's been an incident," Kit said, catching Sylvia's eyes as she looked at him, "and although we would have been heading this way shortly, that incident is why we're here today." Succinctly, he related the facts of Nunsworth's actions, concluding with, "We left him trussed inside the mill. The foreman—Gibson—is watching over him until we can return with the authorities."

"Great heavens!" Although understandably deeply shocked, with the evidence of his daughter's continued good health before his eyes, Reverend Buckleberry quickly came about. He looked at Harris. "We'll need Quigley and Jenkins." To Kit, the reverend explained, "Our local magistrate and sergeant. Both live just along High Street."

Harris filled his lungs, then grimly nodded. "I'll go." He started for the door, then turned and asked, "Shall I bring them here?"

Reverend Buckleberry thought, then shook his head. "No. We'll meet you at the mill."

What followed was far more fuss than Kit had anticipated. For a start, the vicarage butler, Henley, had been standing in the shadows of the front hall and had heard their story; he, in turn, informed his wife, the housekeeper, who came sailing into the hall to reassure herself that all her charges—in which category she plainly included Sylvia—were coping with the shock and, Kit suspected, to cast her eyes over the gentleman-lord her chick had brought home.

From Mrs. Henley's slowly evolving but ultimately approving smile, Kit surmised he'd passed inspection, but reassuring the redoubtable housekeeper that Reverend Buckleberry and his daughter were truly bearing up required the good reverend's focused attention.

Sylvia tugged Kit's sleeve. As he moved with her down the hall, she called to her father, "We'll harness the gig and wait for you in the stable."

They reached the stable to find that a similar chaos had taken hold there, courtesy of the boys' colorful retelling of their tale. Apparently, several ostlers from the local inn had been visiting the old stableman, and they were all avidly drinking in the drama. Thinking of poor Gibson waiting alone in the gathering dark—and who knew what reaction Nunsworth might provoke from a man he'd left nursing an aching head—Kit quickly put the ostlers to good use, setting them to help Smiggs reharness the bays to the curricle and Egbert to put a neat chestnut between the shafts of the reverend's gig.

Kit hadn't intended for the boys to return to the mill, but they rebelled and insisted, and Sylvia pointed out that it would be better for them to tell of their parts in her rescue—and the facts about Nunsworth that they had ferreted out—to the magistrate and sergeant now, rather than having to remain in Saltford overnight.

She glanced at Jack and Ned. "Your mother," she said, looking at Jack, "and your aunt and father," she said to Ned, "will be wondering where you are."

Kit saw both boys' faces fill with sudden consternation and not a little guilt and took pity on them. "After we return from the mill, Smiggs can drive the three of you home in the curricle." Smiggs could return with the carriage for Kit and Sylvia tomorrow. Given they were at the vicarage, given the events of the past hours and their outcome—the impact of Nunsworth's scheme on Sylvia and him—Kit saw no reason not to take advantage of where Fate had landed them.

Then Reverend Buckleberry came hurrying from the house, and they sorted themselves into the two carriages. Jack and Ned squeezed in beside Sylvia's father, and with the others following in the curricle, the reverend led the way back to the mill.

They drew up in the clearing outside the mill, with the magistrate and the sergeant in the magistrate's gig on their heels. After securing the horses and exchanging greetings and introductions, they walked in a group to the mill's open door.

Gibson, the foreman, had lit several lanterns inside the mill. They entered to find Nunsworth exactly where they'd left him, the pail still on his head; at the sound of footsteps, he started to thrash and call for help.

Seated on a narrow bench along the inside wall, Gibson had recovered some of his color. He snorted. "He's been silent until now. Not a peep, even when I asked him what he'd planned for me."

When Reverend Buckleberry inquired as to Gibson's state, Gibson gave a gap-toothed grin. "I'm on the mend. Can't wait to tell the wife that there's benefits to having the hard head she's always bemoaning."

The reverend smiled and patted Gibson's shoulder, then turned to where the magistrate and sergeant had halted on either side of Nunsworth. Reverend Buckleberry sobered.

Nunsworth, accepting that whoever had come in was not going to help him, had fallen silent, although his arms still tensed and shifted as he strained at his bonds.

The following minutes were an exercise in futility. At a sign from Quigley, the magistrate, the sergeant cut the rope connecting Nunsworth's bound hands to his feet, then hauled the miscreant up to sit, at the last, removing the pail from his head.

The boys, peering around Kit, Sylvia, and Smiggs, sniggered at the sight of Nunsworth, with his expression enraged, his color high, and ashes in his hair and in streaks down his face and dusting his shoulders and chest.

The boyish sound drew Nunsworth's attention. He glared at the boys, then noticed Smiggs. Nunsworth looked at the magistrate. "I want to lay charges against those boys and, I believe, that man there." He nodded toward Smiggs. "They attacked me and tied me up and subjected me to a humiliating experience. I'm a man of the cloth!"

Quigley, an older gentleman Kit judged to be the sort frequently referred to as the backbone of a county, studied Nunsworth, then succinctly replied, "No, you're not. If you recall, it was I who allowed myself to be persuaded by the good reverend here and his bishop to allow you to be defrocked and run out of the parish rather than send you for deportation as your stealing from our villagers warranted. It seems I have lived to regret that decision."

With his hands still tied behind him and his feet, also tied, before him, Nunsworth scowled, uttered a sound very like "Pshaw!" then stared straight ahead at the floor.

After regarding him for several seconds, Quigley raised his gaze and surveyed those gathered inside the door. "Very well. Now, which of you would like to start telling me what this is all about? Just the facts, if you please."

"It started," Kit said, "when Miss Buckleberry sensed that someone was watching her."

Quigley took the cue and looked inquiringly at Sylvia. In a clear, steady voice, she recounted the various incidents and what she'd thought at the time—that the person was watching her with malevolent intent.

"But you never saw who the watcher was?" Quigley asked.

"No," Sylvia admitted.

Kit then explained that he'd mentioned those incidents to his business partner, and that Jack had overheard. He glanced at the boys. "That led to Jack, Ned, and Ollie deciding to spend their spare time trailing after Sylvia, trying to spot who it was that was watching and unnerving her."

Quigley demonstrated his sound sense in the way he drew the boys' information from them. In short order and with surprisingly little extraneous detail, they'd related all they'd learned about the man others living near his lodgings knew as Nunsworth—the same man who had accosted Sylvia, calling himself Mr. Hillary.

The magistrate paused and looked at Nunsworth. "Well, Hillary Nunsworth, do you deny anything these boys have said?"

Nunsworth didn't look up. "It's all lies—every last word," he spat. "I deny everything!"

Quigley was unimpressed. He moved on, drawing out all that Smiggs, Kit, and Sylvia had to report.

Nunsworth's only contribution was to loudly and frequently proclaim his innocence, insisting that he knew nothing of the events the others described.

Several times, Sergeant Jenkins was moved to cuff Nunsworth over the head to silence him.

Kit, Sylvia, Smiggs, and the boys told all to the point of them tying up Nunsworth.

Quigley nodded sagely, then asked, "Does anyone have anything more to add?"

To everyone's surprise, Gibson called, "Aye—I have."

They all turned to where the watchman still sat on the bench along the wall.

"Seems to me that having a local's word on it won't hurt. That blackguard"—Gibson nodded at Nunsworth—"knocked me out when he arrived, right enough, but like I said, I've a hard head. I came to m'senses—enough to hear and see—as he finished tying Miss Buckleberry to the railings. I couldn't lift me head to save meself, mind, but I heard and saw everything that followed, and it was exactly like these people have told you." Gibson's gaze rested heavily on Nunsworth, who made no attempt to meet it. "If it hadn't been for Miss Buckleberry getting one hand free, enough to avoid Nunsworth's first blow, and if the gentleman hadn't arrived and flung himself in front of her... Well, Nunsworth would have had his way and left nothing but tragedy behind."

That, Kit felt, was an excellent summation and final word.

Quigley seemed to think so, too. He nodded to the watchman. "Thank you, Jake."

Then Quigley looked down on Nunsworth—at the top of his head as Nunsworth was still belligerently staring at the floor.

"Hillary Nunsworth, currently of Bristol, I'm binding you over to the next assizes, where, without a shadow of a doubt, you will be judged guilty of kidnapping and attempted murder." Quigley paused, then gestured to Sergeant Jenkins to haul up his prisoner. "Take him to the cells. We can keep him there until the judges arrive—the assizes is only a few weeks away."

The sergeant bent and cut the rope tying Nunsworth's feet.

Quigley waved the others to precede him back into the open air. Gibson waited until the sergeant passed, dragging his uncooperative prisoner along by main force. Then Gibson doused the lanterns, pulled the door closed, and joined the small crowd outside.

Reverend Buckleberry had arranged for Jack and Ned to squeeze into Kit's curricle; he turned as Gibson came up. "Come along, Jake—I'll drive you home. Your wife will be glad to see you."

Gibson grinned. He directed a bow at Sylvia, Kit, and the others, then addressed the reverend. "Aye, I'm thinking to make the most of the lump on me head. Just as well if you come along and vouch for how I got it."

With smiles and chuckles, everyone dispersed. While Jack and Ollie squeezed onto the box seat with Smiggs, Sylvia shooed Ned into the curricle. Then Kit helped her up and, reins in hand, followed.

He was about to give his horses the office when, through the encroaching darkness, they heard Quigley, who was standing studying Nunsworth as the sergeant lashed his prisoner to the rear of the magistrate's gig, say, "It occurs to me, Nunsworth, that while I may regret not sending you for transportation all those years ago, you now have cause to regret that even more. While the punishment for thieving is a sojourn in the colonies, the punishment for kidnapping and attempted murder is the noose. You might want to dwell on that while sitting in your cell."

Kit flicked the reins and turned his horses. There was just

enough light left to see the way. At a neat clip, he drove back to the vicarage.

He'd barely drawn rein before the porch when Mrs. Henley appeared and declared that Smiggs and the boys were going nowhere without filling their bellies with the supper she and the cook had prepared.

Having descended from the curricle, Smiggs and the boys looked at Kit.

He refrained from rolling his eyes and nodded. "We wouldn't want any of you fainting with hunger on the drive home."

That earned him four grins and another of Mrs. Henley's approving nods before she spread her arms like a mother hen and chivvied Smiggs and the boys into the house ahead of her.

With a resigned sigh, Kit descended and handed the reins to the groom who'd come running. "Walk 'em. They won't be that long."

He handed Sylvia down.

Smiling, she linked her arm with his and led him inside.

His prediction of how long it would take the boys and Smiggs to sate their appetites proved accurate. Less than half an hour later, having entrusted Smiggs with a message for Mrs. Macintyre that Sylvia was safe and well and would return on the morrow, Kit and Sylvia stood on the front porch and waved the foursome away. Unsurprisingly, the boys were grinning, and even the normally dour Smiggs was smiling.

The curricle passed the reverend's gig on the drive.

Sylvia and Kit waited for her father to join them, then together, they went inside. She'd expected that having Kit in her childhood home, under her father's roof, would feel a touch awkward. Instead, he and her father seemed to get on famously. They settled comfortably in her father's study. On learning that Kit's new business was building ocean-going yachts, her father revealed a hitherto unknown-to-her passion for sailing.

"Oh, yes. Quite a feature of my youth," he assured her, then proceeded to engage Kit in a discussion of the various novel features he and Wayland intended incorporating into Cavanaugh yachts.

Eventually, Henley arrived to announce that dinner was served, and the three of them adjourned to the dining room.

Sylvia ate and watched the two most important men in her life as they animatedly described masts and sails, hull designs, and rudder conformations.

Only after the meal, when they returned to his study, did her father notice her relative silence. "My dear, his lordship and I have been quite remiss—we've been chatting non-stop and must have bored you to tears."

She laughed and sat on the small chaise. "No, I assure you— it's been quite a revelation." She smiled at Kit as he sank down beside her.

From the armchair opposite, her father looked on; when she glanced his way, she saw a glimmer of understanding and expectation in his eyes.

"But tell me," he said, looking from her to Kit, "how did you become acquainted? Bristol is a large city, after all."

Kit directed a laughing glance at Sylvia. "Actually, we first met at my brother's wedding in August."

"Ah—of course!" Reverend Buckleberry nodded. "I remember now—the other Lord Cavanaugh who married Felicia."

"Indeed," Kit returned. "Your daughter and I were partners in the bridal party. Sadly, Sylvia seemed entirely unimpressed by my beaux yeux."

He heard the soft snort Sylvia tried to suppress before she hurried to say, "Be that as it may, when the Dock Company withdrew their support from the school, saying we had to vacate their warehouse on the Grove in just days, I sought out the owner of the business displacing us to appeal for help in finding new premises, and lo and behold, the owner was Kit."

Kit shifted on the chaise so he could watch her face. So he

could drink in the liveliness and underlying happiness that glowed in her features as she told her father of all the recent changes in her school for dockyard boys.

"And," she concluded, "we'll shortly have a sign hanging above the door proclaiming that we're now 'Lord Cavanaugh's School.'" She glanced at Kit, and he saw the affection in her eyes.

One day, he was going to have to ask her why she'd so taken against him at the wedding; having come to know her so much better, he couldn't believe it had been solely due to his reputation. But now, pride and warmth in her voice, she went on, "I suspect that will deter any future naysayers."

He stirred. "And if it doesn't, I will."

That declaration prompted a meandering conversation that touched on many political and social issues, drawing Kit and Sylvia both into airing their opinions, which, to Kit's relief, seemed perfectly aligned.

Reverend Buckleberry was no more of a fool than his daughter. Once they'd covered a broad scope of subjects, proving just how alike their thinking and how compatible their life-visions, Sylvia's father fell silent, and when they did as well, he looked from Sylvia to Kit and back again and arched his brows.

Kit shared a quick glance with Sylvia, then reached across and took her hand.

He looked at her father and simply said, "With your permission, sir, I would like to ask for your daughter's hand in marriage."

Reverend Buckleberry studied him for one more second, then smiled delightedly. Then he hesitated, looked at Sylvia, then returned his gaze to Kit. "To be frank, my lord, my daughter has been so remarkably reluctant to view any gentleman in a matrimonial light that I had quite despaired of hearing those words." His smile grew teasing as he switched his gaze to Sylvia. "That said, my dear, the decision remains yours. Do you wish to take Lord Kit Cavanaugh for your husband?"

The gaze Sylvia turned on Kit held a radiance he'd never before seen. "Yes, I do." For a second, she held his gaze, letting him see to her soul, then she looked at her father. "But it's important to me—and to Kit—that we have your blessing."

Her father studied her face for a second, then beamed upon them both. "You have my blessing and my very best wishes. I am delighted and, indeed, expect to be eternally grateful that you have chosen to marry such an eminently worthy man."

Kit felt his heart swell, not with pride but with gratitude. With a warmth and a burgeoning joy he couldn't—and didn't wish to—deny.

Love—it had to be love.

Sylvia looked at him. He captured her gaze, raised her hand to his lips, and gently pressed a kiss to her knuckles. "Thank you," he said and meant every syllable. He might have had the capacity to be the worthy man her father now saw, but only through the challenge of wooing her had he looked for what lay inside him—those qualities he knew she would admire—and brought them to the fore. In many ways, the man he now was—the man he would henceforth be—was the product of his pursuit of her, of his love for her and hers for him.

His voice lower, he said, "I vow to you now, here, tonight, that I will make it my life's overriding mission to ensure that you never regret that decision, as long as we both shall live."

Sylvia gripped his hand and fell into the love filling his caramel eyes.

★ ★ ★

Later that night, before they retired to their separate bedrooms, Sylvia walked with Kit in the cool of the vicarage garden.

"I smell roses," Kit murmured.

"My mother's rose garden." Sylvia led him to the entrance. "There's a bench at the end of the path."

They stepped down to the flagstone path that bisected the garden and walked between mature bushes to the stone bench that stood in a shell-like alcove. They turned and sat, settling comfortably side by side. The last flush of roses bobbed in the moonlight, wreathing them in delicate scent.

Kit retained his hold on her hand. "When did your mother die?"

"When I was seventeen." She paused, then lightly squeezed his hand. "The household here was long established. Papa had the Henleys, Egbert, and our cook, and Deacon Harris, and all the parishioners—let alone the bishop and Papa's other friends in the church. Once our sorrow had passed, Papa didn't need me to keep house for him or entertain him—he still had his life." She tipped her head, as if viewing something only she could see. "Eventually, I realized that I needed to make a life of my own, and that led me to start on the journey that, ultimately, led to me founding the school."

Kit suspected there had been more to her life than that, but learning of her past could wait; he was more concerned with her future. He raised her hand and dropped a kiss on her knuckles. "How soon can we wed?"

She glanced at him sidelong, a smile curving her lips. "Impatient?"

"Very." Now he'd got past the proposal and her father's agreement, he wanted nothing more than to formally claim her as his and install her in his home.

"Banns, I fear, are a necessity in this case."

He'd expected that. He nodded. "So three weeks clear, then the wedding?"

"And today's the first of October and a Sunday, too," she said, "so late this month or early the next." She arched a brow at him. "Will that suit, my lord?"

With his free hand, he sketched a flourishing bow. "It will." It would have to; he could only hope the time flew. But the weeks between would give her time to prepare, to arrange a wedding gown and her attendants and all the other things females so delighted in when it came to weddings. Felicia, Stacie, and Mary would, undoubtedly, throw themselves into assisting, and Kit realized he wanted that period of building anticipation and joy for Sylvia.

He liked to plan ahead, and so did she. "Once we're wed, I take it you won't be averse to living in the city?"

She turned her head to study him. "You have a house, don't you? I assumed we'd live there."

He inclined his head. "That would be my preference, but if you wished to reside somewhere outside the city itself…"

"No." She tilted her head, her gaze on his face. "Is your house big enough? You mentioned it's in Queen's Parade—that's a very acceptable neighborhood."

"It's definitely big enough. I have the beginnings of a staff—a majordomo, an excellent cook, Smiggs, and, of course, a footman-in-training. I daresay you'll wish to—indeed, will need to—add to them."

She smiled. "I imagine hiring a housekeeper and maids would be wise."

"I'll leave that to you and Gordon—my majordomo. He's young and learning the ropes, so he'll be grateful for your guidance. He was a footman at Raventhorne Abbey—I stole him away from Mary, but as they have a surfeit of footmen, she didn't really mind."

"I'm glad you warned me." Consternation seeped into her expression, then she gripped his hand a little tighter. "I just realized I've agreed to marry into the nobility. I'll have to entertain lords and ladies and, possibly, even duchesses." Her tone had turned faintly aghast.

Smiling, he squeezed her hand reassuringly. "Behind the titles, we're all just people. Wealthier, perhaps, but you can't take even that for granted. And you've met Mary and Stacie and several others of the family already, at Rand's wedding. And if Felicia, of all ladies, can cope with the challenge of us without turning a hair, then I'm more than confident that you will, too."

She tipped her head consideringly. "There is that. Felicia is more...unworldly than I am."

"Buried at Throgmorton Hall as she was, she unquestionably had much less experience of the wider world than you. You've been dealing with the directors of the Dock Company, the Dean, and the luminaries of Bristol society for years. Handling a few members of the haut ton won't even count as a challenge."

He shifted on the bench, half facing her and drawing her hand to where he could enclose it between both of his. "But enough of others. What of us?"

Turning slightly, she met his gaze. "What about us?" Before he could reply, she went on, "I assume you'll spend your days working on building your yachts, while I continue to manage the school..." Her eyes widened. "You didn't think I would give up my position with the school?"

"No." Disgruntled that she'd even thought of it, he frowned. "Of course not. I assumed you would continue to manage all— perhaps that I would see you to your office every morning before going on to mine, then meet you at the school in the afternoon, before we head home." Together in all things was his vision.

"Then...what?" She looked at him encouragingly.

He narrowed his eyes at her. "I was trying to be delicate. So—children?"

She blinked. "Oh." Faint color touched her cheeks. "I assumed...well, that if they came, they did." Her gaze grew dreamy. "But..."

He watched her face, her eyes, as, clearly, she examined the prospect. "But...? Would you like children? My children? To have children—perhaps even a whole tribe—with me?"

Her lips curving, Sylvia refocused on Kit's eyes. "Can I just say yes and leave it at that?" She couldn't describe the feelings that had surged to life inside her simply at the thought of holding a tiny Kit in her arms. And later, overseeing a brood of adventurous children—one challenge she would embrace with her whole heart.

He held her gaze for a long instant, as if reading her emotions in her eyes, then, his voice lowering, said, "Yes is acceptable. Entirely acceptable." His gaze fell to her lips, and the rhythm of her breathing fractured.

Slowly, he leaned closer—as if he, too, was as mesmerized as she.

She lifted her face, her lids lowering.

His lips brushed hers. Warm, inviting. Then they settled, and she gave herself up to the moment—to his kiss.

To a caress that consumed her and sparked passion in her soul.

She'd known many passions—enthusiasms, desires—but nothing to compare to the surge of feeling he and his kiss evoked.

Emotions she'd only recently come to know stirred and rose, and compulsions she'd yet to come to grips with flared.

Physical desire was new to her, but she could taste it now—a need on her tongue and in her veins.

He shifted closer, and she leaned into him. His arms slid around her, gathering her into a possessive embrace, as under the skillful pressure of his lips and the artful stroking of his tongue along her lips, she parted them and welcomed him in.

His tongue stroked, then languidly probed, and she relished the sensation, so much so she felt compelled to return the pleasure. Soon, they were engaged in a duel of sorts, of tangling tongues and hungry lips and a quest to lavish as much pleasure on the other as they could.

So this is what passion is all about.

On the thought, she lifted her hands and framed his face the better to kiss him more deeply.

In response, he hauled her even closer, crushing her breasts against the hard planes of his chest—making her aware of how much her breasts ached.

His kiss had turned dominant, subtly aggressive—possessive—but she discovered she could meet him and match him even there, provoking and inciting and even daring to challenge him.

In this, in their wanting, they were evenly matched. Despite her lack of experience, in this arena their desires clashed and merged, neither overpowering the other, yet overwhelming in their combined force.

The kiss had turned desperately hungry and needy—transforming into a ravenous exchange she previously would have labeled wanton.

But now, she understood. Now, she felt the rabid hunger, the driving need, and the clawing desperation that rose and claimed her.

She didn't know what came next but was certain he did. Through the melding of their mouths, she urged him on.

Then he shifted, his head angling over hers as his tongue stroked hers in heated temptation. Between them, his hand rose, and he cupped her breast, then closed his strong fingers about the aching mound.

Her senses leapt, then his fingers kneaded, and a soft, yearning sound purled in her throat.

Heat welled and washed through her while lightning danced down her nerves, flashing and sparking.

Never had her body felt like this—as if her senses had risen and claimed it as their territory. Never had her nerves felt so alive, awake to every nuance of the shifting caresses he pressed on her. Her breasts seemed to have swollen and now felt too constrained behind her light stays. She wanted...

She wanted...

Tightening her grip on his face, holding him in place, she poured all that wild, undirected wanting into their kiss.

For a split second, she sensed she'd surprised him, then his response roared through her—in the fire of his scorching kiss, in the possessive pressure of his hand at her breast, and in the steely clamp of his arm about her waist.

But then, just as suddenly as his heated desire had risen to her siren call and swamped her, he reined it in. Pulled it and himself back.

On a gasp, Kit broke the kiss. With a mental wrench, he forced his lips from hers and hauled desperately hard on his— on their—reins. He hadn't expected her to filch them.

Breathing far too rapidly, he rested his forehead against hers and tried to remind himself of what was right. Of what, in this instance, had to be.

Her hands about his face gentled. One fell away, while she trailed the fingers of her other hand lightly down his cheek.

He raised his heavy lids as she shifted her head back, just enough to look at and study his face. He barely needed the moonlight to read the question in her eyes—one that compelled him to find his voice, gravelly and gruff as it was, and declare, "I want you—never doubt that for even an instant—but if we don't stop now…"

Hoping she wouldn't ask for further clarification, he shifted awkwardly on the bench, fleetingly wincing as restraint cut where he would much rather it didn't.

Sylvia blinked, then the reason for his shift and wince and what else he'd said and implied impinged.

Heat claimed her cheeks, but perversely, an inner confidence— her sensual confidence—welled. No—she couldn't doubt that he wanted her.

Trying to suppress or at least mute a rather smug smile, she turned to sit more properly on the bench.

He shifted again, rearranging his long limbs, then settled beside her.

She seized the moment to ask, "I know I should thank you for your restraint—and I do—but can I ask why?"

He softly grunted. "You're a clergyman's daughter." He paused as if collecting his thoughts, then offered, "Being that is an intrinsic part of you. I expect you have beliefs about indulging before our wedding, and in the same way that I respect you, I feel I should respect and honor any deep beliefs you hold."

Without looking at him, she reached for his hand and lightly squeezed. "Thank you. And yes, I do hold those beliefs and sincerely thank you for calling a halt."

If he hadn't, she was perfectly certain she wouldn't have, although she might well have regretted that later.

She felt him lightly shrug.

"We can wait until after the ceremony to go any further."

She noted that declaration didn't preclude them continuing to indulge at least as far as they had. Was it possible to go further without quite tipping over that forbidden edge? It was, she suspected, a point to ponder—and, possibly, explore.

Somewhat to his surprise, Kit didn't feel as grumpy over the situation as he'd expected. Sylvia's confirmation that she adhered to a more strait-laced code than ladies of his class generally favored made him feel vindicated in taking what was, for a gentleman of his ilk, a definitely unusual stance.

The knowledge that, in four weeks' time, she would be his, declared before God and man as such, was all the assurance his inner self needed to be patient. And while he'd said his decision had been taken to honor her beliefs—and it had—and, indeed, having met her father, Kit felt compelled to honor the reverend's expectations as well, his principal motivation had been even simpler. He would always do whatever it took to make her happy.

That had already become his touchstone—his guiding principle with respect to her.

Weighed in that scale, waiting until the wedding to have her in his bed was a minor price to pay.

His heart was still thudding a little too heavily, but it was calming and soothing sitting in the softly scented moonlight beside his soon-to-be wife.

He freed his hand from hers, raised that arm, draped it over her shoulders, and urged her closer.

She accepted the unvoiced invitation and snuggled nearer, then leaned her head on his chest.

"I never did tell you why I behaved as I did to you at Felicia and Rand's wedding."

Cautiously, not wanting to sound demanding, he admitted, "No, you didn't."

Sylvia sighed. "You're not allowed to laugh." But as a reward for honoring her wishes and exercising restraint for them both, he deserved to know her old secret.

"I promise I won't."

She drew breath and said, "You never knew, but during the Season I spent in London, going about with Felicia among the ton, supposedly to find suitable husbands, I saw you—as they say, across a crowded ballroom. Not once, but many times at various events. Yet from my very first sighting of you, you captured my attention. You became a lodestone of sorts—if you were in the same ballroom, no matter how much of a crush the event was, my eyes would find you, even when I was trying my damnedest not to encourage my obsession."

"Your *obsession*?"

Clearly, she'd piqued his interest.

Lips firming, she nodded. "Yes, my obsession with you. That's really the only word for it. You became my fantasy gentleman— the gentleman who inhabited my dreams. Or more correctly, who I constructed dreams around." A quick upward glance showed him looking faintly stunned. "You can imagine what sort of dreams those were. But it wasn't hard to learn of your reputation."

That jolted him to focused attention. "I feel compelled to point out that, although supported by a scant framework of truth, my reputation within the ton at that time was a carefully fabricated façade designed to render me persona non grata with every matchmaking mama in town."

So she'd come to suspect, but hearing the confirmation from his lips was nevertheless reassuring. She pressed her head against his chest in wordless acceptance. "I understand that now, but I had no way of knowing it then, so your reputation ensured that I steered well clear of you." She paused, then forced herself to admit, "However, far from dousing my obsession, learning the length and breadth of your reputation—based on your reputed deeds—only made my obsessive fascination with you all the more intense."

She could almost hear him thinking, remembering things she'd said before she'd come to know him better.

"That's why," he eventually said, dawning understanding in his voice, "you behaved so repellingly at the wedding."

"Until I arrived at Throgmorton Hall on the day before the wedding, I had no idea I would be partnered with you in the bridal party." She softly snorted. "You can imagine my dismay. Which, I might add, only grew when I discovered—as I walked down the aisle, no less—that my obsession with you hadn't faded over the years, but instead, had become even more intense. That my senses were even more fixated on you—my forbidden fantasy lord."

He made a sound halfway between a laugh and a scoff. "You hid it well."

"I had to." She raised her head and looked into his eyes. "I was terrified the whole time. Terrified I would do or say something hideously embarrassing that would give me away...and then you claimed me for that waltz!"

He didn't look repentant in the least. "It was my waltz to claim. Others would have noticed if I hadn't led you out."

She jabbed a fingertip into his chest. "Yes, but you enjoyed it."

His wicked smile bloomed. "I did. And I didn't."

Kit looked into her eyes, then softly said, "I was attracted to you, too. I tracked you through the crowd, chose my moment, and pounced. But I couldn't work out what you were about—what game you were playing. It wasn't one I recognized, much less understood. You kept your shields up, and I couldn't get past them. With me, you were a cold and disdainful lady, yet I saw you laughing and smiling with others…and I wanted your smiles, even then."

She arched her brows. "Really? I thought I'd succeeded in putting you off."

He nodded. "You had. I drove away thinking I would never see you again, so attraction aside, I should just put you down as a peculiar and unattainable lady, forget you, and be done with it."

"I watched you drive away and thought the same—that I'd survived the encounter, and I wouldn't see you again."

His lips curved, and he smiled into her eyes. "Luckily for us, Fate had other plans. The instant you stormed into my office and started berating me over the school, I knew my view of you was grossly in error. After that, of course, I was never going to rest until I learned all your secrets."

He paused, looking into her eyes and reveling in the wordless connection, then he bent his head and brushed a kiss to her forehead. "Thank you for telling me. Our past now makes sense, and I don't have to worry that you'll suddenly revert to ice-maiden again."

She laughed. "I can promise you that." After a moment, she added, "You might have had a false façade, but I had one, too."

"Mind you," he mused, "I doubt any man can live up to a lady's forbidden fantasy, even if that fantasy is about him."

Her chuckle turned innocently sultry, a contradiction that tightened his groin. "In that, my lord, you're once again in error." Her teasing eyes suggested she was enjoying setting him straight. Her gaze lowered to his lips. "I decided some days ago that, on closer acquaintance, the real you possessed the abilities to significantly trump every fantasy I've ever fashioned."

She had to mean the kiss they'd shared on Mrs. Macintyre's porch. He widened his eyes at her, but her gaze remained on his lips. They curved as, unable to resist, he inquired, "Really?"

"Definitely." Siren-like, she turned in his arms and lifted her face to kiss him—but then she paused and, at tantalizingly close quarters, met his eyes and breathed, "Of course, that means you've already set a high standard, one you'll have to strive to live up to for the rest of our lives."

Kit smiled wolfishly, then lowered his head, closing the last half inch to murmur against her lips, "My darling wife-to-be, you perceive me ready, willing, and very able to take up that challenge." He touched his lips to hers in the lightest, most delicate of kisses, before adding, "Now and forever."

Then he kissed her, and she kissed him, and he let her lead him as she would, into the future they both desired with every iota of their beings and with all their hearts.

Epilogue

Lord Christopher Cavanaugh and Miss Sylvia Buckle-berry were married on the fourth of November in Christ Church in Bristol. The bride wore white satin lightly ornamented with pearl-encrusted lace, with a glorious trailing veil fashioned from the same lace anchored in her golden-blond hair by a fabulous pearl-and-diamond band—a wedding gift from the proud bridegroom. Everyone in attendance agreed that no happier, more serene bride had ever been walked down an aisle. There was an air of confidence in Sylvia's step that was echoed in her bridegroom's eyes, signaling that here were two people who knew what they wanted from life and were acting determinedly to secure it.

Indeed, Kit looked like a man eager to plunge into matrimony. His responses to the Bishop of Bath and Wells—a friend of the bride's family who had volunteered to officiate—were uttered in a voice that rang with commitment.

Although in terms of ton invitees, the guest list had been restricted to close family, when the couple were duly proclaimed man and wife and, after sharing a chaste kiss, turned to the body of the nave, there was a horde of well-wishers filling the space between the newlyweds and the church door.

As had been the case at the previous weddings of her older brothers, Lady Eustacia Cavanaugh had acted as one of three bridesmaids. Together with Mary and Felicia, Stacie stood on the altar steps and, smiling, watched as the crowd closed around Kit and Sylvia, people pressing in from all sides to shake Kit's hand or thump his back and to press kisses to Sylvia's gloved hands.

Kit had lived in Bristol for only a few short months, yet, as usual, he'd fallen on his feet. And judging by the way the on-lookers were greeting her, Sylvia plainly belonged. As well as those Stacie had expected to see—Wayland Cobworth and several of Kit's other gentlemen friends plus local adults from Bristol and Saltford, Sylvia's home village—a gaggle of schoolboys were eagerly pushing close to shake Kit's and Sylvia's hands, and behind the boys came a troop of smiling laborers and tradesmen, all decked out in their Sunday best.

Two older ladies seemed to have taken charge; one flanking Kit and the other by Sylvia's side, the pair appeared to be imposing some degree of order on the milling throng.

Standing beside Stacie, Felicia sighed. "I'd almost given up hope of seeing Sylvia wed, but to have her marry Kit and become my sister-in-law is beyond even my most inventive dreams."

Stacie glanced at Felicia, then returned her gaze to Sylvia. "It must be nice to be able to have a childhood friendship transform into a long-term familial one."

"Indeed." Mary stepped closer on Felicia's other side; Stacie saw her sometimes scarifying sister-in-law understandingly squeeze Felicia's arm. "Ryder and I couldn't be happier over this union. While some might say Kit could have done better, I strongly suspect he never would have—that if he hadn't found Sylvia, he wouldn't have married at all. He certainly had no thoughts of marriage when he left the Abbey for Bristol." After a second of observing the happy couple, Mary added, "Ryder says Sylvia brings out the best in Kit, not by pushing but simply by giving him the opportunity to be all he can be."

Felicia nodded. "I agree. Sylvia has no concept of how to manage a man—she never has had. Instead, she'll simply assume Kit will step up to the mark—"

"And," Stacie concluded, "because he's besotted and is happy to do whatever she wants, he will."

Mary chuckled. "The power of positive expectations. Hmm." Her gaze cut to her husband, standing to one side talking to Kit's other groomsmen, Rand and Godfrey, then to her three children, who had acted as pageboys and flower girl and who were presently standing opposite their father and, uncharacteristically quietly, watching the newlyweds. After a second of observing her children, Mary rather distractedly said, "I really must see if I can use the same tactic—and now might be an excellent time to attempt it. If you'll excuse me, I suspect I have mayhem to avert."

Stacie and Felicia chuckled as Mary stepped down and headed to where her children stood.

Shortly afterward, Kit and Sylvia were ushered by the crowd to the church doors. Along with the rest of the bridal party, Stacie followed and, from the porch, watched as the newlyweds descended the church steps to the pavement, showered with rice all the way. Laughing, arm in arm, the pair turned at the curb, waved, then made for the hall of the Council House on the other side of the street, where the wedding breakfast was to be held.

Those invited to partake—family and close friends—waited on the church steps while the rest of the crowd, smiling and laughing, dispersed in groups of twos and threes, heads together, excitedly reviewing all they'd seen and heard. Once the crowd had gone, the invited guests strolled after Kit and Sylvia.

Stacie had attended so many wedding breakfasts over her twenty-six years that, once the speeches started, she tended to stop listening. In this case, however, she found her attention transfixed, not so much by the words uttered as by the sight of Kit and Sylvia and the emotion that glowed all but tangibly between them. It was there in their faces whenever their gazes met. Visibly there even when one merely looked upon the other.

Of her mother's four children, Stacie would have marked Kit as the least likely to put his faith in love. To take the risk and give his heart to any lady, yet plainly, he had.

It wasn't that she couldn't see the attraction—the lure of a home, a welcoming hearth, and a loving and supportive family. With Ryder and Mary, and Rand and Felicia, and now Kit and Sylvia all marrying for love, Stacie couldn't pretend not to understand the benefits and joys of giving one's heart into the keeping of another.

Another person one trusted to that depth, to that extent.

Trusted to the point of placing one's most precious and vital inner secrets into that person's hands.

It was that critical issue of trust that had long ago convinced her that love and marriage could never be hers—that she should never aspire to such a union.

She let her gaze travel over her older siblings—her half brother, Ryder, and her brothers Rand and Kit. Despite the misgivings she imagined all three must have harbored courtesy of Lavinia, the late marchioness, all three had had the courage to willingly trust another. She knew they wouldn't have done so lightly, and, indeed, she felt certain all three had made the right decision.

Mary could and did manipulate with the best of them, but in that she merely matched Ryder, and Mary would never, ever, harm Ryder, much less her children. If any dared threaten her family, Mary transformed into a tigress—not a being wise people crossed.

As for Felicia, she, too, knew how to manipulate, but her love for Rand meant she rarely attempted to manipulate him. She and Rand shared a passion for logic and order and, from all Stacie had seen and heard, discussions between them tended to occur on a very rational and direct level.

And as Felicia had earlier said, Sylvia didn't seem to know how to manipulate at all, which was just as well; Stacie didn't think that, after being caught too often in their mother's coils, Kit would ever respond well to being manipulated, even for his own good.

Of the five children of the late Marquess of Raventhorne, only Stacie and Godfrey remained unwed, and as Godfrey was only twenty-five and, in Stacie's opinion, almost as unlikely to marry as she was, the present celebration seemed set to be the last Cavanaugh wedding for some years. Possibly for decades.

Kit's was the last of the speeches. When he concluded and invited all to charge their glasses, Stacie lifted hers and, with a smile as bright as anyone's, toasted first the bridal party, then Sylvia.

After that, everyone rose from the tables and mingled.

Stacie made a point of stopping beside the few Cavanaugh connections who were present and dutifully passing the time of day. As usual, several of the ladies inquired in an arch tone as to her own matrimonial intentions, but she'd long ago learned how to turn such queries aside without giving offense and also without revealing any of her thoughts.

If they only knew...

But no one knew as much about what Lavinia, the late marchioness and Stacie's mother, had done than Stacie. No one else knew the full extent of the scandalous behavior in which Lavinia had indulged. As a child, then a young girl growing up in her mother's shadow, always in her mother's household and held very close under her mother's not-so-loving wing, Stacie had seen far too much to ever trust herself.

To ever allow another to trust her with their heart.

She was her mother's daughter. As many had reminded her even today, she was the spitting image of Lavinia in her heyday. Before the lines and wrinkles of dissipation had started to show.

And the similarity extended beneath the skin; manipulation was a skill that came far too readily to Stacie's mind.

Sometimes, it was almost second nature.

A nature she'd sworn to resist.

She had no ambition whatsoever to follow in her mother's footsteps. That, in fact, was her one ambition—to never become another Lavinia.

Which meant that she could never marry.

She would not risk it. Even marriages of convenience had been known to end in mutual affection—and even that was a temptation to manipulation she might not be able to resist, not if the lure was constantly before her.

She'd been there, in her parents' household; she'd seen what manipulation had done to their marriage—how deeply the slow death of her father's trust in his wife had hurt him.

The payments Stacie received from the marquessate as stipulated by her father's will were generous; she didn't need to marry to keep a suitable roof over her head or pay an appropriate staff. And as Lady Eustacia Cavanaugh, with her connection through Mary to the powerful Cynster family, she didn't need a husband's title to give her standing in the ton.

The tables had been removed and chairs set in the corners for those who needed to sit. Now the musicians started up, and Stacie joined the other guests in watching Kit and Sylvia circle the floor in their first waltz as a married couple. As was expected, she and her partner—Godfrey—joined the other couples of the bridal party in the second revolution. Then the rest of the guests joined in, and laughter and merriment bubbled all around.

Subsequently, she danced with Wayland Cobworth, Kit's longtime friend and business partner, and learned how their new enterprise, Cavanaugh Yachts, was faring.

Then exhibiting not the slightest preference, she danced with the others who admiringly solicited her hand.

She was a past master at slipping from their side with a smile at the end of each measure.

Finally, the musicians put up their bows, and she was free to wander the hall. She'd noticed Godfrey circling the walls, pausing before each portrait that adorned the paneling. She caught up with him, sliding her arm through his and looking up at the portrait he was presently studying.

He glanced at her, then returned his gaze to the picture—of a man in robes with a chain of gold discs hanging halfway down his chest. A past mayor, she supposed. "What are you doing?"

"Hmm? Oh, examining these. Some are really quite good. I wonder if the council knows the value of what they have hanging in this hall."

She peered more closely at the painting, trying to find a signature. "Are they really that valuable?"

Godfrey sent her a sidelong glance. "Enough to warrant stealing. Not that I'm about to embark on a life of crime."

"Good to know."

The exchange reminded her of something that had struck her the day before, when the bridal party had gathered at Kit's house and everyone had been sitting around catching up with each other's news.

Everyone else had had something to say; she'd been the only one with no actual purpose to her life and, consequently, nothing in terms of goals achieved to report.

Mary had her children, her household to run, and she was also working to establish schools and other improvements for the workers on the marquessate's far-flung estates.

Felicia worked hand in glove with her brother, William, on steam-powered inventions and also with Rand in evaluating the inventions of others; the pair were planning a trip to Paris to investigate some new type of pen, of all things.

And Sylvia was neck-deep in running her school—a school she'd more or less single-handedly founded.

Her brothers all had occupations—Ryder managing the marquessate's estates, Rand and his investment syndicates, Kit with his yachts, and even Godfrey was tiptoeing toward some sort of position in the art world.

Only she was utterly without purpose.

As on Godfrey's arm, she moved around the room, pretending to study the paintings, she decided that, as she wasn't going to marry, her lack of occupation needed to be rectified.

She'd noted that all the others had found their purpose in their strongest passion—Godfrey and his obsession with art being a perfect example.

Her only true passion was music. Sadly, among the ton, a liking for music was hardly unique, but for her, the fascination went much deeper. So what life-purpose could she create for herself based on music?

She continued to cling to Godfrey's arm and the relative privacy that bought her. Ignoring the dry judgments he passed on each painting, she set her mind to the task of devising some position for herself—some absorbing career to which she could devote herself.

One that wouldn't harm anyone else but, instead, would help others.

Eyes narrowing in concentration, she told herself that there had to be something she could do.

She was still trying to imagine what that something might be when a stir ran through the guests and calls went up for all the unmarried young ladies present to gather in the center of the hall.

Stifling a sigh, Stacie drew her arm from Godfrey's, pulled a hideous face that only he could see, then left him chuckling and dutifully joined the small group of ladies smiling and jockeying for position before the chair onto which Kit had lifted Sylvia to stand. From long experience, Stacie knew that arguing that she was beyond marriageable age—that, indeed, she was old enough that in earlier times, she would have been termed an ape-leader—would get her nowhere, especially not with those around her being mostly family, connections, or Kit's friends.

Smiling wryly to herself, she joined the very back of the small pack.

She was shorter than most of those in front of her—no real risk of Sylvia's bouquet reaching her.

She'd reckoned without Sylvia, who turned to face away from the group. On a count of three, to cheers and whoops, Stacie's new sister-in-law slung her neat bouquet in an energetic fashion sideways around her shoulder.

Instead of flying high and landing among the shifting ladies, the bouquet whizzed toward them just above head height, causing some to instinctively shriek and duck, while others belatedly raised their hands toward the prize—bobbling the small bouquet and sending it tumbling and skipping across their reaching fingers.

Until it was flying toward Stacie.

Instinct took over. It was catch the thing or have it smash into her face.

She caught it, then, horrified, realized what she'd done.

She promptly told herself she didn't believe in such silly superstitions.

Others gathered around her, congratulations and arch speculations on their lips.

Stacie barely heard them.

As she stared at the delicate bouquet resting in her hands, her only thought was that Fate, in her infinite wisdom, had made a truly stupid mistake.

★ ★ ★

It was evening when Kit and Sylvia slipped away from the continuing family celebration, which had moved to Ryder and Mary's suite in the city's best hotel.

When Kit led Sylvia up the steps of the house they would

make their home, she felt as if she stood on the cusp of entering a new world—and indeed, she did.

Kit unlocked the door and ushered her into the front hall—a light, airy space that, during the day, was lit by a circular skylight high above. Sylvia glanced up and saw stars twinkling, diamonds in the black velvet of the sky.

After closing the door on the night, Kit came to lift her cloak from her shoulders. She'd changed out of her wedding gown and left it and the glorious veil in Mary's keeping; the gown Sylvia now wore was a simpler style in blue satin the same color as her eyes.

She'd kept her new diamond-and-pearl band anchored across her hair; just looking at it still thrilled her, purely because it had come from Kit with a simple message penned in his masculine scrawl: *For now and forever.*

She registered the quietness that pervaded the house—and the absence of Gordon and, indeed, all the staff.

Kit noticed her glancing at the door at the rear of the hall. When she looked at him questioningly, he smiled. "They're being discreet."

"Ah." Her own lips curving, she nodded. "I see." She ignored the butterflies that had started to dance in her stomach. In search of distraction, she directed her mind toward those who, henceforth, would be her staff.

She'd met his people often over recent weeks when, at Kit's invitation, she'd used the period of their engagement to take up the reins of the household. Together with Gordon, she'd hired a housekeeper, a Mrs. Sutchley, who had already proved to be a godsend. The good lady had coped with the influx of Kit's family, including the three boisterous imps who were Ryder and Mary's children, without batting an eye.

In addition, she and Gordon had settled on a footman, a parlor maid, a kitchen maid, a scullery maid, and a lady's maid. Never

having had a personal maid in her life, Sylvia had been doubt-
ful about the need for one, but Gordon had assured her that she
would find the assistance invaluable, and so it had proved. Now
that she was Lord Kit Cavanaugh's wife, she'd rocketed to the
top of every Bristol hostess's guest list; there was a small pile of
invitations already on the mantel in the drawing room, and that
was for just the next few weeks. Her wardrobe had needed to
expand dramatically to support her sudden prominence, and for
that alone, Polly was already indispensable. The girl also had a
deft touch with arranging hair in the latest fashion.

Kit closed his warm hand around one of hers, and side by
side, they started up the stairs.

The gallery at the top lay wreathed in silent shadows.

The master bedroom was situated in one rear corner of the
house, overlooking a walled garden that Sylvia hoped to fill with
roses. It was a large, south-facing room; when Kit opened the
door and ushered her inside, her gaze went to the wide bank of
windows to find them screened by the heavy velvet curtains in
forest green, several shades darker than the walls. During the
day, with the skirting boards, paneling, and cornices picked out
in ivory, the room's atmosphere was that of a soothing wooded
glade, while at night, with the lamps casting pools of warm
golden light, the space felt like a roomy, luxurious cave.

One with a very large, richly appointed bed.

A bathing room was attached, and doors in one wall led to separate dressing rooms. Sylvia had already explored everywhere—
and knowing Polly's delight over having her mistress finally
residing under this roof, Sylvia's gowns would already be hanging in the lady's dressing room, and her brushes would be laid
out neatly on the dressing table in there.

Several interesting paintings graced the walls, and two arm-
chairs stood angled before the window.

But it was the huge tester bed with its plump ivory pillows, silk sheets, and forest-green-and-gold coverlet that dominated the room, at least in Sylvia's eyes.

She halted beside it and turned as she heard the door click shut.

Kit stood with his hand still on the knob and his eyes locked on her. His gaze was weighty, intense, and seemed to grow more acute with every passing second.

Then he released the doorknob and prowled toward her.

Her breathing suspended as he halted before her. The look in his melted caramel eyes was hot enough to scorch.

Slowly, he raised both hands and cupped them about her face, gently tipping it up to his.

Instinctively, she raised her hands and wrapped her fingers about his wrists, lightly gripping as she studied his eyes. The potent mix of hunger, desire, and raw passion she saw—that he let her see—swirling in the depths left her utterly breathless.

Very nearly witless.

She—her mind—couldn't think beyond this moment; she had no experience upon which to draw. Here, tonight, she had to place herself wholly in his hands and trust him—put her trust in him—in this most intimate arena.

Luckily, she had complete and unshakeable faith in him—in his honor and in his need to protect and care for her. On that, she would stake her life.

And while he wanted her, she wanted him...

She sensed his hesitation, but to her mind, they'd waited long enough.

She pushed up on her toes and kissed him. They'd shared many kisses in recent weeks, and caresses, too, but into this kiss—their first private kiss as a married couple—she poured everything she'd held bottled up inside her.

She opened her heart, found the fire within, and set it free.

It was past time for caution, past time for restraint.

With her lips and tongue, she painted a picture of her need, her wanting—and made it as vibrant, as compelling, as she could.

His hands slid from her face, and she raised hers to clasp his head and hold him—hold them steady to the kiss as her hunger stoked his, as her passion swirled, flamed, and ignited his.

A low growl sounded in his throat, then his arms came up and locked about her.

Kit felt giddy, spun around by passion in a way he'd never felt before. Desire was a thunder in his blood, but it was her fire, her passion, that had swept him from his moorings.

All he could think about was having her beneath him. His only driving need was to claim her.

Her mouth was open to him, surrendered, a gift beyond price. He'd instinctively reacted and staked his claim, and her response only ratcheted the tension that drove him higher.

Only made him harder, the thud in his blood more insistent.

He angled his head and plunged deeper. Found her tongue with his, stroked, then plundered.

And she followed his lead, enticing, inciting, every single step of the way.

He'd needed her—to have her and hold her—for weeks, and tonight, his dreams would transform into reality, and the gnawing hunger in his soul would finally be sated.

With that aim in mind, he backed her toward the bed.

Sylvia felt her legs hit the side of the bed, but before she could rejoice that they were finally moving on, she sensed Kit hesitating. Almost dithering.

She was already too heated, with a slowly building urgency coursing through her veins, to countenance any unnecessary delay.

Closing her fists in his lapels, she stretched up on her toes and kissed him with all the passionate hunger in her soul—and tipped backward.

She landed on the silk coverlet and, to her delight, succeeded in toppling him with her.

But he broke the kiss and twisted to land on his shoulder by her side, rather than atop her as she'd hoped.

No matter. Using her grip on his lapels, she used his weight as an anchor, swung to her side, and pressed her body flush against his.

For just one second, he froze. She seized the moment, clasped his face, and pressed a fevered kiss to his lips.

Then she sent her hands wandering—a desire of hers that, until now, he'd severely curtailed.

Tonight, the bonds of marriage had set her free, and she was determined to make the most of it.

To experience and savor her first foray into conjugal bliss to the hilt.

She felt sure it would be bliss. With a husband like him, it simply wouldn't be anything else—he would never allow it.

But she wanted—*needed*—to get to the blissful point sooner rather than later.

Dispensing with his cravat took several minutes—minutes during which she strove to keep him engaged through the increasingly ravenous kiss so that he didn't focus on her busy hands.

The instant she'd unraveled the silk folds, she left the cravat lying about his neck and fell upon the buttons of his waistcoat, then his shirt.

Over the past weeks, in preparation for tonight, she'd assiduously practiced kissing him. She'd learned the art of give and take, of aggressor and appeaser, of conqueror and conquered. It took all of her accumulated skill to keep him engrossed in the kiss...

Until finally, the last button slipped free, and she slid her greedy palms across the hot skin stretched over the heavy muscles banding his chest.

So firm and hard; on a soft gasp, she broke from the kiss and opened her eyes. Taut skin sheathing hard muscle met her wondering gaze. Delight swelled inside her, and she swept her hands wide, pushing him onto his back and parting the shirt so she could savor the width, the solidity, the sheer overwhelming masculinity of the lightly tanned expanse laced with crinkly brown hair that curled about her slender fingers.

His muscles tensed and shifted beneath her questing hands. Delighted anew, she stroked, then sank her fingertips into the resilient, steely strength.

Hers. All hers.

She sent her fingers tripping down, over the ridges of his abdomen, feeling the muscles twitch under the light caress. A trail of crisp brown hair bisected his torso, circling his navel before extending farther down...

As her eyes and her trailing fingers followed the line, he sucked in a short breath. Then he caught her hands, one in each of his, and hauled her hands above his shoulders so that she fell full length atop him. Releasing her hands, he locked one arm about her—pressing her aching breasts flush against that glorious chest—while his other hand cupped her head, and he hauled her into a ravaging kiss.

One that temporarily distracted her.

But as the heat from his body sank through her skin, she was suddenly certain she had on far too many clothes.

Luckily, her hands and arms were free. Too caught by the fire in the kiss to draw back, she wriggled and squirmed while she released the tiny buttons and the hooks and eyes that ran down her side.

Then she planted her palms on his chest and, reluctantly pulling her lips from his, panting, flushed, and very ready to get on, she pushed back and sat up, straddling his hips, and tugged and pulled and hauled her gown and petticoats off over her head.

She flung the yards of fabric away, hearing them fall with a sibilant *swoosh* to the floor.

But her gaze had fixed on Kit's face. On all she could see washing behind his wide eyes, coloring his faintly stunned expression. Hunger, need, and yearning. She could see those and more in his caramel eyes.

Holding his gaze, she set her quick fingers to the front closure of her light corset. Within seconds, his gaze had fallen to her digits. With precise movements, she slid the hooks free. The corset gaped, then released; she caught it and flung it after her gown as every muscle in the large body beneath her locked tight.

She was still sheathed in her fine silk chemise, the translucent fabric a subtle screen against which her breasts proudly jutted, nipples peaked and rosy. His hot, hungry gaze raced over her, yet his jaw clenched tightly, and from the corner of her eye, she saw his hands, which had fallen to his sides, fist.

Playing to the molten passion she could sense rising in him, barely held back by his will, reaching for the passionate tide she wanted nothing more than to call forth and bathe in, she raised the fingers of one hand to the ribbon closing the neckline of her chemise. His eyes locked on her fingers; she played with the ends of the ribbon for an instant, then gripped and tugged—and the bow unraveled.

He swallowed, his throat working.

She smiled, grasped the chemise's gathered neck in both hands, with a swift jerk, widened the neckline, then drew the whisper-soft garment off over her head.

He uttered another growly sound as she sent the chemise to join her corset.

Abruptly, he sat up, simultaneously gripping her hips between his large hands and shifting her back so she ended straddling his hard thighs.

Then his head swooped, and his lips crushed hers, and his hands were on her.

Hard, hot palms stroking and caressing.

Long artful fingers tracing, then possessing.

She lost her breath to him, to the kiss, to the fire he laced over her skin.

Her world spun, and she tipped her head back on a gasp as, with his clever fingers and his even cleverer lips and tongue, he paid homage to her breasts—until they ached almost painfully and molten heat pooled low in her belly.

Suddenly, she needed to feel him against her; nothing else would assuage the maddening ache that seemed to rise from her bones.

She caught his coat and tugged. When he didn't immediately respond, she found his lips with hers again, then nipped the lower. When he pulled back, blinking, their eyes mere inches apart, she panted, "Coat, waistcoat, shirt—get them off!"

He blinked again, but she was already wrestling with his coat. As if dazed, he complied, shrugging the garment off and tossing it to the floor. By then, she'd dispensed with his cravat and was pushing his waistcoat and bundled-up shirt off his shoulders.

He made a frustrated sound and complied, dragging his arms from the sleeves, then having to pause and open the cuffs before flinging both shirt and waistcoat away.

Then he spread his arms wide. "There. Satisfied?"

She smiled delightedly, flung herself against him, certain he would catch her, and hauled his lips to hers as she exulted, "Yes, yes, yes!"

His arms wrapping around her, he fell back beneath her onslaught.

Hostage to impulses and a driving need she'd never before known, she plundered his mouth, then turned her attention to the long, strong column of his throat, nipping and tasting as she worked her way down, sensing from the way his hands stroked over the skin of her naked back that he rather liked her attentions.

She smiled against his skin and took her kisses lower. To the wide muscles banding his chest, to the discs of his nipples that hid beneath the crisply curling hair.

His hands were busy, stroking over her back, learning the planes and contours. She had to pause, shuddering, when his thumbs cruised the sensitive sides of her breasts, and he chuckled deep and low.

The sound skittered over her nerves; anticipation lit and smoldered, even as she lowered her lips once more to his skin.

They fed each other a banquet of caresses, lavish and enticing, yet ultimately unsatisfying. The activity only tightened their nerves more and drove them harder.

She could sense the coiling tension in him, in the contraction of his muscles, in the increasing pressure of his hands.

Emboldened, she reached for the waistband of his trousers and deftly flicked the buttons there free. Then she slid her hand beneath the opened flap and closed her fingers about his hard length.

He uttered a choked protest, but she doubted she was causing him any true pain as she stroked the steely rod encased in fine velvety skin.

Then she closed her fingers around the girth and gently squeezed.

Every muscle in his body tensed—as if to some breaking point.

On a muttered curse, he caught her wrist and hauled her hand away. Capturing her other hand as well, he came up in a roll.

Intrigued, she let him roll her to her back. As he settled over her, she wriggled and shifted until his hips lay between her spread thighs. Expectantly, she smiled up at him.

Only to realize he was almost glaring at her. "We're supposed to be taking this slowly!"

She blinked and stared up at him. "Why?"

Through gritted teeth, he muttered, "In case it's escaped your notice, you're a virgin."

"Yes, I know." And she wasn't of a mind to waste time discussing it. "It's an issue I anticipate rectifying in short order."

To underscore that intention, she slipped one hand free, caught his head, and hauled his lips back to hers, then seizing the moment, she undulated beneath him, using her breasts, her hips—as much of her as she could—to caress his hard body and urge him on.

He'd been patient, kind—generous. Tonight, she was his reward—and what a thought that was. She wrapped it around her like a safety net and plunged into the moment.

Into the unknown.

Into passion. His and hers.

She poured all her longing, all her passion and desires, into her kiss, let need and that hungry, now-ravenous wanting flare and invest her movements as, with wanton deliberation, she used her body to tempt him to sate them both.

Kit gave up—surrendered. What else could he do? He hadn't allowed himself to think too much about this night, yet he'd had a vague notion of having to go step by slow step, gently easing her—a virgin—along the path to intimacy.

Instead, he had a commanding, demanding, fiery and passionate female in his arms.

He suddenly realized his error—the stupidity of his assumption. This was *her*—the real her he'd glimpsed for the first time when she'd stormed into his office weeks ago. The lady he'd been dealing with ever since—strong, confident, fiercely passionate. A lady who knew her own mind.

This was *his* Sylvia without any guise—exactly as he always wanted her to be when with him.

And she wanted him, valued him, and matched him in this arena as in all others.

He'd thought to claim her, and she patently intended to claim him.

He was already hers.

Releasing the reins he'd tried valiantly yet vainly to hold on to, he let her have her way.

And when her knowledge ran out and her certainty faded, he took over—and as she blatantly wished, he surrendered without reservation to the drumbeat in his veins and in hers, to the heat of the passion-filled flames that threatened to consume them.

Their skins were alive with need, their bodies beyond ready when he settled more deeply between her widespread thighs. The head of his erection sank into the scalding slickness of her entrance. His jaw clenched, his eyes closed as he battled his instincts, he forced himself to grind out, "This might hurt." She was so tight, and he was distinctly well-endowed. He gritted his teeth and managed, "No, strike that. This *will* hurt."

He felt her, hot and heated and panting beneath him, draw breath.

"I don't care!" The words were almost a wail. "Just do it!"

He did. With one powerful thrust, he sheathed himself in the fiery embrace of her body. He froze, battling to give her a few moments at least to adjust, desperately reining in the instincts that urged him to plunder.

Then he heard a soft "Oh." A sound of wonder.

Beneath him, she softened, the flaring tension the spike of pain had caused melting away.

Then she raised one arm, looped it about his neck, and drew his head to hers. She captured his lips in an open-mouthed kiss, then drew back just enough to whisper, "Now show me."

Needing no further invitation, the man inside him leapt to comply.

He showed her how this oldest of dances went—the movements, the rhythm.

She was a quick study. Soon, she was meeting and matching him, fully linked with him as, their desires one, their passions fused, they strove to gain the beckoning pinnacle.

They reached it and flew as ecstasy gripped them.

As their senses overloaded, then shattered in a mind-blinding starburst that sent shards of brilliance lancing down their nerves and white fire scorching through their veins.

In that primal moment cut off from the world, they clung to each other and, exulting, held on, held tight.

Slowly, the glory faded and released its hold on their minds. They returned to earth, to the here and now of the rumpled chaos of the bed.

Uncounted minutes later, still wrapped in the aftermath, still rejoicing in the glory, Sylvia heard Kit utter a soft grunt, then he gently disengaged from her and fell to the bed beside her.

Breathing seemed to be something they both needed to remember how to do.

The night air was cool against their dewed skins. He tugged the coverlet and sheets from beneath them and drew the covers over them. Then he found her hand and raised it to brush a kiss over her fingers. "Thank you, my wife. Not just for this, but for linking your life with mine."

She turned toward him, and he raised his arm and urged her closer. Settling against him, she smiled into his eyes. "Thank you, husband. Not just for the last hours, but for all you've given me and for the promise of a life with you by my side."

His eyes held hers. "Always by your side, forever and ever."

He kissed her fingers again, then flattened her hand beneath his on his chest.

She pillowed her head on his shoulder and heard him whisper, "Now sleep."

Smiling to herself, she did.

★ ★ ★

She woke hours later, in the depths of the night, and discovered that she and Kit had shifted in their sleep. She still lay on her side, but her head rested on the pillow. He'd turned onto his stomach. One heavy arm lay draped over her waist, and his face, half buried in the pillow, was turned her way.

She drank in the sight of him sleeping. Let her eyes trace the features she could see. And felt her heart swell with the emotion that had been growing inside her ever since she'd started interacting with him—the businessman rather than the ton lord.

They were one and the same—she understood that now; both were facets of this man who had stolen her heart when she'd thought that organ forever unassailable.

Ironic that he—the rakehell she'd long ago fallen in lust with from a distance, and against whose allure she'd built walls of cold stone to protect herself and her heart—had proved to be the right man to take her hand and make her life complete.

Just as, in the months and years and decades to come, she would work to make his life complete.

Her eyes dwelled lovingly on his face as she savored the sense of closeness, born of their recent activities, that hadn't faded entirely but persisted, real and almost tangible, a golden thread linking them—one that, she suspected, would only grow stronger with the years.

He made a soft sound. His lashes lifted just enough for him to squint at her. "You're thinking awfully hard. What about?"

She smiled, reached out, and brushed a heavy lock of hair off his forehead. Pleasure was still a faint thrum in her veins, a lingering warmth beneath her skin. "If you must know, I was thinking that, in my opinion at least, every second of the experience was worth the wait."

Kit searched her eyes, confirming her smug delight, then grunted and turned over. "I would have to agree." Who could have guessed that enforced abstention would result in such an earthshaking result?

Then again, this was her—his Sylvia—and she was very definitely in a different, more meaningful category than all who had gone before.

Staring at the canopy, he looked inside. In gifting him with her body and linking her life to his, she'd given him more than he'd ever dreamt he might have. He found her hand, drew it to his lips, and gently bussed her knuckles. "Thank you." He let the murmured words fall into the warm dimness. "For giving me something I thought I would never have—the chance of a real marriage blessed with true and abiding love."

There was no doubt in his heart that love of that caliber had grown between them.

She turned toward him; he felt her puzzled gaze trace his profile. "Why had you thought such a thing was not for you?"

She'd given him her secrets. It was time for him to give her his.

He drew in a deeper breath, then haltingly picked his way through a condensed version of his mother's life, omitting nothing, yet not dwelling overlong on the more shocking aspects. "My father...tried. Although theirs was a marriage of convenience, he was prepared to accord her all due respect, to give her his trust and even his affection. But she..." He shook his head. "That wasn't what she wanted—that wasn't why she'd accepted him." He paused, then more quietly admitted, "Given all I saw of her actions, her self-serving manipulations and machinations, I really didn't think I would ever overcome my consequent distrust of ladies. To give my heart to one, I would have to trust her implicitly, and I truly doubted I could ever do that."

He turned his head and met her eyes. "Until I met you at the wedding, and you and your attitude got under my skin like a burr. Then you—the real you—erupted into my life here in Bristol, and"—his lips twisted wryly—"I couldn't look away, much less stay away." He turned toward her and cupped her face in his palm. "You drew me from the first, as if, even then, I recognized that you could be my salvation." Holding her gaze, he smiled into her eyes and said, "And so you've proved to be. By marrying me, you've saved me from a lonely fate, from hiding away from love forever, deeming it too dangerous to risk.

"You convinced me loving you was worth any risk. You, Sylvia Amelia Cavanaugh, have opened my eyes to all the joys and benefits of sharing a life, and you are now the central and most vital element in mine. Without you, I would have drifted through life, restless and unsatisfied. Now you're here by my side, I can look forward to a long and happy life loving you and basking in the warmth of your love for me."

He smiled. "From where I lie, our shared future looks well-nigh perfect."

Sylvia finally understood what had been behind the occasional hesitations she'd sensed in his early dealings with her.

Unbeknown to her, he'd been battling demons she hadn't known existed. Yet with quiet courage, he'd trusted in her and stepped over his inner hurdle and offered her his heart.

She'd understood that she could trust him within days of meeting the real him. Until now, she hadn't appreciated how very much he had trusted her.

Although he hadn't asked for it or for any other reassurance, she held his gaze and stated, "I don't have any of the…inclinations it seems your mother had."

"I know." His lips twisted in a fleeting grimace. "I suspect that, in reality, few women truly do. Thank heaven."

He continued to hold her gaze, then said, "I feel as if in loving you and marrying you, I've passed out of the shadow my mother cast and shed her malignant influence once and for all."

"Good. Because I'm not of a mind to share my influence over you with anyone."

That elicited a deep chuckle, and Sylvia smiled. She raised one hand and ran her fingers through the tousled locks of his hair, then she met his eyes and confessed, "For me, the single greatest discovery in falling in love with and marrying you is that, in confirmation of my recent assessments, it is, indeed, possible for a forbidden fantasy lord to live up to expectations—indeed, even to exceed them."

Lord Kit Cavanaugh—her husband—laughed and reached for her. "And I plan to devote myself to exceeding your expectations"—he smiled into her eyes—"for as long as we both shall live."

★ ★ ★ ★ ★